Robert Thomas Wilson, Herbert Randolph

Life of General Sir Robert Wilson

Vol. 1

Robert Thomas Wilson, Herbert Randolph

Life of General Sir Robert Wilson
Vol. 1

ISBN/EAN: 9783337414658

Printed in Europe, USA, Canada, Australia, Japan

Cover: Foto ©Raphael Reischuk / pixelio.de

More available books at **www.hansebooks.com**

LIFE

OF

GENERAL SIR ROBERT WILSON,

COMMANDER OF THE IMPERIAL MILITARY ORDERS OF MARIA THERESA OF AUSTRIA,
AND ST. GEORGE OF RUSSIA ;
KNIGHT GRAND CROSS OF THE ORDER OF THE RED EAGLE OF PRUSSIA,
AND OF THE MILITARY ORDER OF ST. ANNE OF RUSSIA ;
KNIGHT COMMANDER OF THE ROYAL PORTUGUESE MILITARY ORDER OF THE TOWER AND SWORD,
OF THE TURKISH CRESCENT,
AND OF THE ORDER OF MERIT OF SAXONY ;
COUNT OF THE HOLY ROMAN EMPIRE ;
ETC., ETC., ETC.

FROM AUTOBIOGRAPHICAL MEMOIRS, JOURNALS, NARRATIVES,
CORRESPONDENCE, &c.

EDITED BY HIS NEPHEW AND SON-IN-LAW,

THE REV. HERBERT RANDOLPH, M.A. Oxon.

WITH PORTRAIT.

VOL. I.

LONDON:
JOHN MURRAY, ALBEMARLE STREET.
1862.

INTRODUCTION.

This is the last will and testament of me, Robert Thomas Wilson, General in the British Army, Colonel of the 15th King's Hussars, and for the time being Governor of Gibraltar, Commander-in-Chief, &c. &c., Knight Grand Cross and Commander of various Orders won in the fields of battle.

*   *   *   *   *   *

I give, devise, and bequeath to my son Belford Hinton Wilson, Chargé d'Affaires and Consul-General in her Majesty's service, as heir-looms, all my military decorations and insignia, including the Commander's Cross of Saint George of Russia given me by the Emperor Alexander on the field of battle at the head of the Imperial Guards, after having had it first put round his own neck and then having with his own hands placed it round mine. Also Rembrandt's picture as copied by my father, and the manuscript of his life written by himself. And do further recommend that he and his son living, Robert Belford Wallis, should be considered the representative successors to such memorials, records, and property as may be conducive

VOL. I.   *b*

to family distinction and correspondingly meritorious exertions.

I give, devise, and bequeath, &c. &c. &c. all my manuscripts, letters, journals, &c. &c. &c. But direct that none shall be published without the most complete revision and judicious opinion as to the utility or innocuous consequences of such proceeding. Also my narrative of the Russian Campaign, the publication of which will require the sanction of the Foreign Secretary of State, as I was serving under the orders of the Foreign Department. And I also recommend a previous communication to the Russian Sovereign; and that the same measures should be adopted before the publication of the remainder of the work, should I live to finish it, up to the conclusion of the war in Italy. The publication of the private letters, many of which are of great interest, must likewise undergo similar careful revision and decorous observance of social propriety, &c. &c. &c.

Witnessed and signed, August 17, 1847.

CROSSING the line of "threescore years and ten," with a steady gaze on death as now certain by God's ordinance within a fast-closing boundary of time—death so often fearlessly confronted in his violent assault in the prime of manhood—Sir Robert Wilson deliberately and religiously set his hand to his last will and testament on the seventieth anniversary of his birth.

His vast intercourse with men during the momentous events of his day in war and politics, and the part that he had borne amidst those passions of contending nations and parties, imposed upon him special duties of public and social relation. These would not die with him ; for the written records of the facts, like the facts themselves, would continue in being: and therefore by the solemnity of his " will" he handed down his view of these obligations and his charge to fulfil them, to those to whom he was now constrained by the law of mortality to entrust their execution. That charge, to those who loved him in life and who honour his memory in death, is sacred and inviolable.

The " Narrative of the French Invasion of Russia " in 1812, was the only finished work among the masses of MSS. devised by his will ; consisting of journals, narratives, note and anecdote books, letters from and to persons of both sexes, of all ranks and degrees, and of many nations—English, French, Russians, Germans, Poles, Italians, Spaniards, Portuguese, Spanish Americans, Greeks, Turks, Egyptians, &c. &c.

In compliance with this solemn charge, before the publication of the " Russian Campaign " the sanction of her Majesty's Secretary of State for Foreign Affairs was asked and obtained. A copy was transmitted through the Russian Ambassador to S. Petersburg ; the wishes of the Emperor were ascertained and as far as possible complied with ; and the work was published in the spring of 1860. It was received with universal favour. In the words of one of its critics, " it at once placed Sir Robert Wilson in the first rank of military writers."

The intention expressed in his will to carry on the work, if his life were spared, to the conclusion of the war in Italy ; and the existence of all the materials from which, aided by his memory, he would have drawn that history, in the shape of a journal kept with singular regularity and care during his employment in negotiations and with the armies, and of letters and despatches through that time, seemed to render the publication of his "Private Diary" next in order both fit and natural.

There was a further family reason for this course of publication. In the title-page of the "Russian Campaign," the Orders of Knighthood which he had received for meritorious service from Foreign Sovereigns were as usual inserted after his name. This marked the absence of British honours. It was due therefore to Sir Robert Wilson's memory to bring forward at once the proofs, gathered to a point in those closing efforts of the struggling nations, that, while the Sovereigns of Continental Europe who personally witnessed his prowess and his loyalty emulously decorated him with the ensigns of their chivalry, he had deserved as well of his own King and country.

The "Private Diary," with its appendices, was accordingly published in January, 1861.

The proof thus furnished was received without a challenge and with general recognition. It was confessed to be unimpeachable and perfect in the following words, by one* whose own name will deservedly command attention and respect :—

"In these volumes Mr. Randolph redeems his promise,† and lays before us the evidence upon which Sir Robert Wilson must be acquitted or condemned, and by which we must judge whether he really won the title to that favour which his sovereign withheld from him, and which we are told he 'proudly claimed.'

* Mr. Russell—at that time Editor of the "Army and Navy Gazette"— the distinguished Correspondent of "The Times" during the Crimean War.—Ed.

† See Introduction to the "Narrative of the French Invasion of Russia."—Ed.

Let us say at once that never was vindication more complete and conclusive. It is a vindication resting upon no whimsical theories, nor laboriously drawn out by subtle reasoning; it rests upon a much broader and more solid foundation—a foundation of facts—a very concrete of brilliant services, performed in the light of day, and before the eyes of Europe and its allied kings and statesmen, acknowledged by all but the nation whose duty it was to cherish those services, and render in return the meed of gratitude and honour which was their due. What these services were is related in these volumes. We have now abundant proof that the exception, so galling to a loyal and patriotic man, by which Sir Robert Wilson, *decoré* on all hands, remained unrewarded by his own sovereign, was due to no misconduct or shortcomings on his part, but to the jealousy, or worse, of others. * * * We may remark, at the same time, that the testimony to Sir Robert Wilson's eminent services which is collected in these volumes, is of the highest order, consisting, as it does, not merely of the detailed narrative which is found in Sir Robert's own journal—a journal, the value and interest of which may be judged of from the fact that throughout the stirring scenes in which the author was an actor, under all circumstances and difficulties, he kept it up with the greatest care and minuteness—but of a number of despatches and letters, by which the journal itself is supplemented and confirmed."

The "proofs" then of high desert from his Sovereign and his country may be regarded as so far established. But more is required: and more shall be done.

Evidence shall be produced in the proper place and time that Sir Robert Wilson's exclusion from the customary rewards of conspicuous merit was the determined and systematic injury of successive *Governments* on party grounds.

It shall be shown in one instance that the man who resented it with vehement indignation, and denounced it with impassioned eloquence when it was the act of political adversaries against a political and personal friend, inflicted the same injury when those relations were altered in after years, and when he had himself succeeded to ministerial power.

The two volumes of Biography now published bring down Sir Robert Wilson's personal history to the peace of Tilsit.

The third volume will follow as speedily as time and circumstances permit: containing a narrative of his services in the formation and command of the Lusitanian Legion in the Peninsular war in 1808-9. A short abstract of the "Private Diary," which is a full autobiographical record during the years 1812-13-14, will be necessary to render the "Biography" complete; and the "Life" will thus be brought down to the conclusion of his military and diplomatic employment under the authority of the British Government. The same volume will fitly commence the history of ministerial wrong in the distribution of the rewards of service.

Sir R. Wilson's "defence of the claim of Marshal Ney to the benefit of the capitulation of Paris," which, in his own words, "brought down upon him" [for the time]* "the implacable resentment of the Duke of Wellington;" his share in the escape of Lavalette;

---

* "For the time" only. In after years, as will be seen, when the cause of this temporary irritation had ceased to operate, Sir Robert Wilson enjoyed the warm and appreciating friendship of the Duke of Wellington.—Ed.

the part which he took at the funeral of Queen Caroline, not yet fully known to the public because, in deference to the interests of others, he abstained from giving all the details even in his masterly defence in the House of Commons;* his volunteer service in Spain in 1823 ; his career in Parliament as member for the borough of Southwark ; his private life from 1832 to 1842 ; and finally his conduct as Governor and Commander-in-Chief of Gibraltar, from whence he only returned home to die;—will be the subjects of the following volumes.

It will be seen in them whether his dignity as a man and his merit as a citizen were equal to his renown as a soldier.

One episode there is of extraordinary interest. A carefully detailed account of the negotiations on the side of the Whigs, in 1827 for the formation of Mr. Canning's Ministry, in which he took a principal part. This will be published in its place.

Sir Robert Wilson "proudly claimed" the honours which he had "nobly won." Vain men only will call his estimate and his vindication "vanity." Wise men know, and just men and *men capable of equal merit* will feel, that it was true "*greatness of spirit.*"† He pressed his claims through many years upon many persons successively holding high offices in the State. All acknowledged his rights, none conceded or effectually vindicated them.‡ Not one was found of the

---

* The publication of the letter of Mr. Joseph Hume on this subject by Lord Dundonald in his " Autobiography "—a worthy act of sympathising justice—is an authoritative correction of the chief errors and misrepresentations of the day.—ED.

† " Μεγαλόψυχος. ὁ μεγάλων αὐτὸν ἀξιῶν, ἄξιος ὤν,"—"The magnanimous man is one who judges himself deserving of great things, being truly deserving."—Aristotle, Nicomachean Ethics, Lib. 4.

‡ Not till Dec. 1835 did he even obtain the Colonelcy of a regiment.—ED.

noblest in *rank,* noble enough in *nature,* in his "*inbred dignity,*" to rise above the pettiest jealousies of party. Not one in his high station remembered that place and authority, regarded as God's gifts are for the exhibition of the godlike attribute of justice, regarded as held by the will of their fellow-men are a trust for the public weal.

Near relationship in one who undertakes to write or to edit the biography of a famous man has one great advantage. As a general principle, such a one, presuming him to be endowed with competent powers by the gift of nature, brings a sympathetic intelligence to bear upon actions and motives; and honesty only is wanted in addition to give the highest value to his work. But it has one disadvantage. A prejudiced suspicion almost invariably arises, and may always be appealed to by men whose instinct it is to disparage those who transcend their own powers, that kindred affection closes the eyes to faults and disposes to exaggerate virtues.

For this reason among others the "Private Diary" was published without excision and with (almost literally) no correction; and the "life" of Sir Robert Wilson shall be recorded throughout as nearly as possible in his own words.

It is no part of the design of these volumes—it would be most discordant from the intention of Sir Robert Wilson's "will," and a violation of the sacredness of friendship and confidential correspondence—to publish anything to the injury of private character. But the conduct of public men, as it affects public interests and the rights of others, must be dealt with according to a different rule. Posthumous exposure, as a certain penalty of unjust oppression, is almost the only check upon the unscrupulous abuse of power.

"The Lives of Lord Castlereagh and Sir Charles Stewart" have been recently published. In this work there is in general a sound estimate of Sir Robert Wilson's character and actions: and his own relation of one of his most prominent * deeds of valour is honestly given in a note in full: so that careful readers who know that *small type* may carry great truth, can compare it with the dislocating narrative in the more conspicuous type of the text. But occasionally a fact is misstated, a questionable opinion expressed, or a faulty conclusion drawn, in a manner that does him less than justice: these shall be controverted in the volumes to be published hereafter.† The grave maxim of Quintilian should be in

* In the great redoubt of Dresden.

† In the mean time it is necessary to meet some of the more prominent errors to which circulation has thus been given.

In vol. ii., page 180, Lord Castlereagh's words are quoted from the "Private Diary"—without Sir R. Wilson's comment upon them—in justification of his transfer to the army of Italy in 1814. "If Sir R. Wilson has the confidence of all other Governments, he wants that of his own." There is a fallacy here. "Governments," in reference to Sir R. Wilson's estimation in Europe, signify sovereigns with their ministers, the commanders of their forces, their armies, and their people. "Government," in reference to his estimation in England, signifies Lord Castlereagh and *one other.* Who that other was shall be shown when the next error receives its authoritative contradiction.

In vol. iii., page 298, a correspondence is reprinted from "The Times" of May, 1853, in which the late Lord Londonderry, noticing a conversation published by Lord John (Earl) Russell in his "Life of T. Moore," respecting Sir R. Wilson, denounces the facts stated as "invention from the beginning," "a mare's nest," &c., "without a shadow of foundation." Lord Londonderry's memory failed him. The facts were, as they probably would be from hearsay, inaccurately stated *in details:* but they were no "invention," no "mare's nest;" they had much more than a "shadow;" they had a *solid substance* of "foundation" *in the main particulars;* and of this evidence shall be produced in its place.

In vol. iii., page 161, the author writes, after giving a very superficial

the minds of writers of all times : * "Modeste et cir-
cumspecto judicio de tantis viris pronuntiandum est,
ne, quod plerisque accidit, damnent quæ non intel-
ligunt."

P.S. The thanks of the Editor are due and are
gratefully tendered to Lord Donoughmore for his
voluntary offer and courteous transfer of valuable
MSS., letters, and despatches addressed by Sir R.
Wilson to Lord Hutchinson, several of which are
published in these volumes.—Ed.

London, November 25, 1862.

---

and unsatisfactory account of the proceedings at Cumberland Gate on the
14th of August, 1821, "It was a melancholy day for Sir Charles Stewart
and the British army, when one of its brightest ornaments, *and the man
who had stood by his side on the summit of the great redoubt at Dresden,*
ceased to dignify its ranks!" The only man who *stood by Sir Robert
Wilson's side* when *he* first scaled the redoubt, surmounted the crest, and
waved his cap in triumph on its summit, was Captain *Charles,* his own
faithful and gallant aide-de-camp. No sufficient evidence has been given that
Sir Charles Stewart was on the summit at all. Sir Robert Wilson's statement is inconsistent with the supposition, and this note is an open challenge
to produce trustworthy witness of the fact.—Ed.

* "Modesty and a circumspect judgment should be used in pronouncing
upon the characters of men so great ; in order that we may not, *as very
many do*, condemn what we do not understand."—Quint. Ius. xl., § 26.

CONTENTS OF VOL. I.

APPENDIX.

LIFE

GENERAL SIR ROBERT WILSON.

CHAPTER I.

Birth and early career of Sir Robert Wilson—His father's biography—
Family long settled in Leeds—Introduction to Hogarth, &c.—Syste-
matic course of study—Philosophical researches and experiments—Sir
William Young's presents—Rembrandt's etching—A visit to France—
Introduction to the Duke of York—Management of a theatre—the
Speaker's wig—Married to Miss Hetherington—Lightning conductors—
Belshazzar's Feast—Portrait of Erasmus—Compliment from Reynolds
—Visit from the King and Queen—Becomes Fellow of the Royal
Academy—Paper presented to the King — Garrick's funeral—Figure
of Queen Elizabeth—The Royal Family—Death and character of Sir
Robert's father.

SIR ROBERT WILSON was born in London on the
17th of August, 1777. His childhood was passed in
the calm of a philosopher's home during the comparative tranquillity of Europe. In 1788 his father died.
Soon after the political scene was changed, and the
sense of intolerable oppression in 1789 burst forth
in the desperate madness of the French revolution.
The circumstances of young Wilson's life and the
events of the day, acting upon a nature of extraordinary energy, urged him on at that early age when
for the most part a boy is ruled by the hand of others
to assume the responsibility of self-direction. At the

age of sixteen he stepped out upon the arena of life—in bearing a man and in spirit a hero.

In 1794 he entered the army ; and his military career traversed the twenty years of war that followed, to the peace of Paris in 1814.

Although in the course of these years he was once only invested with a separate command, and that over a foreign auxiliary corps, yet in every service and in various employments he found or made opportunities of beneficial activity ; formed close and lasting friendships with all the most worthy men of every rank and in the most exalted and important offices in every nation ; upheld the character of his country ; and moved among soldiers a knight and among citizens a patriot—loyal and true-hearted—the never-failing advocate of humanity, and the champion of freedom.

The tragical grandeur of war, its vast stage gorgeous scenery and majestic action, its horrors and its woes, excite the strongest emotions of admiration, pity and terror ; its issues determine the place of nations in the history of the world ; and men read in the records of its defeats and triumphs the political destinies of their race in coming time. The life of a soldier, therefore, who has won his way to fame by conspicuous service during these great struggles for national existence or for empire possesses an enduring interest.

It is natural to inquire under what circumstances of birth and social station the character was formed, which has thus left a lasting name, and its impress upon a generation. So long as no authentic memorial exists room is open for imagination : random conjectures take a shape and are committed to writing by careless authors, and at last from frequent repetition obtain a credit which belongs only of right to the substance of truth.*

Benjamin Wilson, the father of Sir Robert, was born at Leeds in 1721. He left to his children for their example and instruction a manuscript history of his remarkable and eventful life, but added a strict injunction that it should never be published. This injunction has been obeyed: but it was obeyed with great regret by Sir Robert Wilson. He saw in this biography that which, in addition to various incident and amusing anecdote, renders such narratives of the highest value—the true relation by a perfectly honest man of his own arduous and successful efforts in the conscientious use of his natural gifts, to place himself

---

* This has been singularly exemplified in the instance of Sir Robert Wilson. In his place in Parliament on one occasion in a debate on the Mutiny Bill, he stated in substance that no man had had more opportunity than himself of acquaintance with *all classes in the army*. This was commented upon in the Clubs, and it was concluded that the words could only mean that he had *served in the ranks*. A general officer who heard them spoken, and had joined in this conversation and conclusion, some years after, in a letter to an intending author who asked him to give any particulars with which he was acquainted of Sir Robert Wilson's early military career, wrote, You may "safely assume that he *first carried his Brown Bess* as a volunteer. *From this position you cannot be driven.*" Upon such *authority* the name of Sir Robert Wilson appeared in a small volume entitled "Risen from the Ranks;" in which there is also much of faulty inference, and much of pure invention.

The truth is that from the moment of his entrance into the army Sir Robert Wilson made the living human material with which he was to work the subject of his nearest interest and most immediate study. He felt that nothing was beneath him as a man which brought him into unity with the mind and the feelings of his soldiers. And this was the secret of his popularity: it was the vast moral power of sympathy. One as he was in heart with the worthy and the brave, but showing himself considerate of weakness, hopeful of reformation, temperate in punishment while scrupulously just, all felt that in their commanding officer they had a comrade and a friend, true as he was gallant, who would never fail to lead them along the paths of duty to the heights of honour.—ED.

worthily among his fellow-men. The record must still
be held sacred; but it is considered that there will be
no violation of the spirit of the injunction if, in order
to correct the erroneous impressions that have arisen
from entire silence hitherto on the part of the family,
an outline of Benjamin Wilson's life is extracted and
made public: more especially as many of the facts of
his life are already recorded in the "Philosophical
Transactions of the Royal Society," and elsewhere.

The father of Benjamin Wilson, whose Christian
name was Major, was born at Leeds in 1674. He
married there in 1697 Miss Elizabeth Yates, of whose
family nothing is recorded in the manuscript. Fourteen children were the issue of this marriage, of whom
Benjamin, therefore so named, was the youngest.

The family appear to have been long settled in Leeds.
Richard, a near relative of Major, was recorder of the
town. He left at his death 150,000*l.*; and upon his
authority Benjamin Wilson states that his father
" was the most considerable merchant in Leeds." Of
his wealth, influence, and popularity among his fellow-
townsmen, some remarkable instances are given. But
the misfortunes incident to great commercial prosperity
and extended speculation befel him about the time
that his youngest son was born.

At an early age the boy was sent to the great
school at Leeds: in consequence of a difference
with the master he was taken from it and sent to
another school; there he remained until he was head
of it, when just as he had begun Greek he was
finally removed. This " cost him many tears," for
the spirit of emulation had been awakened in him, and
he felt a " strong desire " to " improve himself," and

to " excel others," and an " ardent ambition to be a scholar."

But his natural genius had received an earlier direction. His father, in the time of his prosperity, had employed Parmentier,* a French artist of note, for three years in decorating the walls and ceilings of his house on Mill Hill with historical paintings in fresco the subjects of which were chiefly scriptural. When the work was finished "people flocked to see it." The beauty of these paintings moved the admiration of the child, and his inborn faculty of imitation soon shewed itself. " I never," he writes, " was so happy as when I made something like them." These copies were commended and purchased "for pence and halfpence" by his schoolfellows, and by this means his natural power was stimulated to greater exertions. During this time he taught himself writing, and had advanced so far as to "attempt an imitation of a very fine specimen by Mr. Allen, a famous writing-master in Leeds," before either his schoolmaster or his parents knew that he had touched a pen.

The check upon his industry and ambition by his removal from school was a cruel grievance, but after some time of comparative idleness " Providence began to hold out a hand for his deliverance."

Monsieur Longueville, a painter employed by Mr. Liston, Member of Parliament, of Gisborne Park in Craven, in painting historical pictures in three colours, having obtained possession of some of his drawings, became interested in his welfare and offered to instruct

---

* Parmentier painted the altar-piece in St. Peter's Church at Leeds—Moses receiving the Law. He also painted the staircase at Worksop Manor, the seat of the Duke of Newcastle: this is considered his best work.—Ed.

him in the art. With him he remained nearly twelve months; when by the advice of a friend, a merchant in Leeds, he determined to go to London. He travelled by waggon and walked, and upon his arrival was furnished by a relation with complete new clothing and two guineas: this was the whole of his worldly substance for his start in life. He found a lodging for the first year in the house of a person who was under some obligation to his family. The wife of this man washed for him without charge; and thus, during this time, his only expense was for meat and drink. He "lived upon bread and milk," and employed himself in painting, writing, and reading. *The whole cost of his living during these twelve months did not exceed his two guineas.*

At the end of this year he obtained a clerkship at the Registry of the Prerogative Court in Doctors' Commons, where he received a salary of three half-crowns a week. Out of this he saved "five shillings a week and lived as well as an emperor."

He had always "*an ambition to keep better company than himself:*" and as long as his means did not permit this, he was "content," he says, "to stay at home and pass his time in self-improvement." Patiently and hopefully he worked on, until he was master of 50*l.* He then thought himself entitled to improve his manner of living; and in a short time having obtained a recommendation to the Registrar of the Charter-house he became his clerk, at an enlarged salary amounting with fees to 15*s.* a week.

Improved means, and less laborious duties, enabled him now to follow the bent of his genius, and more freely indulge his taste in painting. He soon suc-

ceeded so well as to attract the attention and secure
the friendly offices of Hogarth, Hudson, Lambert,
Gravelot, Hayman, and others more or less eminent
in their art; and was recommended by them to make
painting his profession. His young ambition, however,
would acknowledge no such bounds; for already had
the accidental touch of another chord roused new sym-
pathies and awakened the consciousness of new powers.

Feeling a "desire to render himself agreeable in all
societies," and "determined that none should reproach
him with ignorance," he formed a resolution to "know
something of everything," and therefore set himself the
task to make some specific addition to his knowledge
every day for a year; regularly recording his progress
and acquisitions in a note-book.   ·

He began this systematic course with the periodicals
of the time—"Spectators," "Tatlers," and "Guardians;" then "Gil Blas," "Don Quixote," and other
popular books. Next he read the "History of England," "Rollin's Ancient History," "Cæsar's Commen-
taries," and "The Life of Charles XII. of Sweden."
Then the poets—"Shakespeare," "Dryden," "Pope,"
"Prior," "Pope's Homer," "Virgil," "Milton" and
"Swift." After these he laboured long, and at first un-
successfully, with "Locke," but mastered him at length.
Then "Euclid," "Helsham's Lectures," "Desaguliers,"
"Bacon," "Boyle," and "Newton's Principia and
Optics."

His study of these latter subjects excited a taste for
experimental philosophy, and this taste introduced
him to the acquaintance of Mr. Watson then an
apothecary and afterwards a doctor of medicine.
Mr. Watson was fond of experiments in electricity,

at that time a novel science. In exhibiting the velocity of the fluid he caused it to pass through the length of a lark-spit: this seemed to young Wilson a childish mode of proving so important a fact, and he suggested the employment of a piece of wire several hundred feet in length.

Among other friends whom he had made was Mr. John Smeaton the celebrated engineer. To him he communicated his project, and Smeaton undertook to prepare an apparatus for him at his house in the country: but in the meanwhile Wilson proceeded with experiments in his own rooms at the Charter-house.

Mr. Watson had been accustomed to use a glass tube to excite the electricity, but Wilson " employed a globe which he turned with a coach-wheel ;" and excited the fluid by friction with the hand. Watson seeing his success tried three globes, "but the effect was not proportionate."

These pursuits introduced him to a very large circle of acquaintance, from among whom he chose as intimate friends only those of the most prominent intelligence and of the highest worth ; and his time being almost at his own command he continued his studies of painting, mathematics, and philosophy with vigour, and soon forced himself into wider notice.

From observation of the facts of electricity, especially of the effect of isolation, he suspected that the fluid was not resident or engendered in vitreous and resinous substances only, but that it was merely collected in them and proceeded in reality from the earth itself. This idea he communicated to Mr. Wollaston, Mr. Hyde, Martin Ffolkes the President of the Royal Society, and to *Mr. Watson.*

Mr. Ffolkes urged him to prepare experiments for the proof of his theory and gave him the further advice, that as he meant to keep up his original study of painting he should go to Ireland for two years for that purpose; saying, in explanation of the reason of his advice, that early works painted there would not appear against him in this country, and that so he would start here with fuller mastery of his pencil and better chances of success.

Wilson saw the prudence of this advice and determined to adopt it, but chose first to pay a short visit to Dublin to prepare the way for a longer residence. He started on this first expedition with a friend on the day on which Balmerino and Kilmarnock were beheaded; stopping on the way at Chester where his friend was to join him. There he was entertaining some of his acquaintance with electrical experiments, when an idea suddenly struck him of a mode by which he might positively determine his theory; but being pressed by his friend to proceed on their journey without delay, he wrote to Mr. Elliot in London and desired him to make the trial for him. This letter he sent through the hands of Mr. Watson.

A letter of introduction which he took with him to the Surgeon-general of Ireland procured him admission to his friendship, and at his house he became acquainted with Dr. Bryan Robinson, author of a treatise on the Æther of Sir Isaac Newton. Through him he had access to all the learned men of the University. Dr. Cartwright, Professor of Experimental Philosophy, gave him the use of the experiment-room at the College, and there he made trial of the idea suggested to his mind at Chester. He succeeded per-

fectly, and wrote at once an account of his "*discovery*"
to Martin Ffolkes, Mr. Wheeler, Mr. Smeaton, and
others. After remaining about three weeks in Dublin
he returned with his friend to England. The vessel
in which they sailed struck upon a sand-bank near the
bar at Park Gate. Wilson overheard a whisper of
the mate to the captain, that she " would be lost."
The captain, with an oath, bid him " hold his tongue."
This alarmed Wilson and he communicated what he
had heard to his friend and some of the passengers.
Soon after the captain ordered his boat out under
pretence of fathoming; but the passengers in consequence of this suspicious whisper rose and declared
that they would kill the first man who endeavoured
to leave the ship. The captain gave up the point, all
hands were employed to remove the cargo abaft, and
with the help of the flowing tide the vessel was got
safe off.

Wilson upon his landing was anxious to arrive in
London in time for a meeting of the Royal Society, at
which the letter written from Ireland on the subject of
his "discovery" was to be read: he therefore rode
on post-horses a hundred and eighty-eight miles in
twenty-three hours, and accomplished his object. Soon
after this in the same year, 1746, he published his
" discovery " in a paper entitled " An Essay towards
an Explication of the Phænomena of Electricity
deduced from the Æther of Sir Isaac Newton." It
attracted notice, and procured him many friends;
among whom was Mr., afterwards Sir William, Young.
This acquaintance proved of mutual interest and advantage. Wilson introduced Sir William to several
philosophical friends of his own who entertained him

with various experiments in different sciences, and
Sir William invited him to his house in Kent, presented him with a valuable reflecting telescope, and
wished to give him a *" library of philosophical books."*
Wilson thinking this a disproportionate generosity
declined the gift; but as Sir William Young persisted he at last was induced to " accept the works
of Bacon." At this house also he painted several
pictures for his host and his friends, and here he
enlarged his acquaintance considerably.

Soon after this he paid a visit to Cambridge and
there, through the introduction of Mr. Mason the
author of " Elfrida," and Mr. Edward Delaval the
author of several learned publications, became acquainted with Gray the poet, Mr. Mitchell, and others.

In 1747 Dr. Franklin published his discovery of
the identity of lightning with electricity. Wilson's
attention was immediately awakened. On the occurrence of the first succeeding thunderstorm he happened
to be at the house of a friend near Chelmsford, and at
the moment was acting with others one of Shakespeare's plays. He was playing the part of Henry IV.
when the storm came on, and running out in his royal
robes he extemporised an apparatus to test the discovery—a curtain-rod inserted in a clean, dry quart
bottle, with a pin (or needle) fastened to it at the
other end. The bottle he held in his hand as he stood
upon the bowling-green, and the fluid was collected in
the rod so that sparks were drawn from it by himself
and all the rest. On the same day the same effects
were observed by Mr. Canton in London, and this
storm was the first occasion of the experiment being
tried in England.

In the same work, addressed to his friend Collinson, Franklin suggested the idea of protecting buildings from the effects of lightning by means of conductors, and particularly recommended that their ends should be *pointed*. Wilson at once saw the value of the invention; but he dissented from the form recommended by Franklin and published a paper in the "Transactions" in which he recommended that the ends should be *rounded*; giving it as his reason that the *pointed* form was likely to "invite" or "solicit" the lightning.*

A warm controversy arose upon this question. It was purely, however, a question of philosophical principle.

In the spring of 1748 he set out once more for Ireland to spend two years there, in compliance with the advice of the President of the Royal Society. During this visit he spent his time in painting, philosophical experiments, and writing his treatise on electricity which was published soon after his return in 1750. Among other advantages derived from this visit was the friendship of the Earl of Orrery.

On his return to England he took the house in Great Queen Street, Lincoln's Inn Fields, previously occupied by Sir Godfrey Kneller.

The first portraits painted after his return were those of Martin Ffolkes, Lord Orrery, Lord Chesterfield, David Garrick, and Mr. Foote. Here too he painted Garrick as Romeo and Miss Bellamy as Juliet in the tomb scene. From this picture an engraving was taken which sold freely.

As an illustration of his talents for imitation, a cir-

* Franklin appears to have accepted this as a premiss but to have questioned the inference.—Ed.

cumstance may be related which amused the artist world at the time. Wilson was an enthusiastic admirer of Rembrandt's works and a successful student of his style and manner. At a public sale of pictures a very fine drawing by that master was to be sold, and he was anxious to possess it. He accordingly attended the sale, and bid for it as far as 10*l.* against Hudson the painter. Hudson obtained it at last but was very angry at being obliged to give more than he intended, and expressed himself *very uncourteously.* Wilson restrained his resentment, but determined on taking a pleasant revenge.

There was a very rare etching of Rembrandt's, called the "Companion to the Coach." He obtained a sight of this, observed it closely, and made a drawing and then an etching of it from memory One great difficulty was to obtain the sort of India paper which Rembrandt used, but Wilson's resources did not fail him : he suspected the cause of the greater thickness of the paper to be that more sheets than one were pasted together and pressed. In order to test this he obtained a portion of Rembrandt's paper and soaked it in hot water, when it separated at once into four or five leaves. Having thus obtained the means of carrying out his plan he struck off a print from his etching, wrote in Dutch upon it " The Companion to the Coach," and sent it in a portfolio with a number of genuine Rembrandts, by a Dutchman, to Mr. Hudson for sale. Mr. Hudson immediately purchased it for 6*s.* and told Mr. Herring, nephew to the Archbishop of Canterbury, and others, that it was " the *best piece of perspective,*" and " the *finest light and shade that he had ever seen by Rembrandt.*"

c 2

Wilson communicated the success of his scheme to his friend Hogarth, " who," he says, "loves a little mischief." Hogarth persuaded him to repeat the experiment and try its effect with Harding the famous printseller, who had the reputation of being a first-rate connoisseur. He accordingly etched an old man's head, and sent it by the same Dutchman to Harding. Harding desired time to examine it by candlelight. The next evening he gave the two guineas demanded and a bottle of wine into the bargain; at the same time desiring the Dutchman, if he met with any more such prints, to let him have the first sight of them. After this Sir Edward Dering, to whom Wilson mentioned his arti- fice, asked his permission to take in Lord Duncannon afterwards Lord Bessborough. In this he completely succeeded. Mr. Pond the artist, and Dr. Chauncey fell into the same snare—all supposed connoisseurs of Rembrandt's works.

Wilson now determined to spend the money ob- tained by his humorous fraud in a supper. Accord- ingly he invited twenty-three artists to an " English roast." Hogarth sat on his right, Hudson on his left. The chief dish at table was a large sirloin of beef; " decorated," he says, " not with greens or with horse- radish, but covered all over with the same kind of prints" which he had sold. Mr. Hudson would not at first believe that he had been taken in ; but " Hogarth stuck his fork into one of the engravings, and handed it to him." Wilson also produced his portfolio full of the engravings in various stages of progress. All expected that Hudson would have joined in the general laugh ; but he took serious offence, and again ex- pressed himself *uncourteously*. Wilson then told him that from that moment he determined to publish both the prints, and to make known the fact of their sale to him and to Mr. Harding. The landscape sold for six-pence and the head for a shilling; and so great was the demand that both plates were almost entirely worn away by frequent printing.

Among his acquaintance formed at this period were Mr. Anthony Champion, Sir Thomas Robinson, and the Marquis of Rockingham. Lord Rockingham bestowed on him many singular marks of favour and attachment, and at his house he stayed many months in the first year of that nobleman's marriage, painting portraits for him.

In 1756 he became a Fellow of the Royal Society.

His most successful portraits so far were those of Lord Rockingham, Lord Harcourt, Lord Camden, and Sir George Savile.

We have now brought down the personal history of Benjamin Wilson to the time when his paintings were bringing him in 1,500l. a year. His philosophical experiments and researches, however, were not inter-rupted. In this year he published, in conjunction with Dr. Hoadley, the son of the Bishop of Winchester, who had sought his acquaintance for that purpose, a work entitled "Experiments and Observations upon Electricity." A second edition was published in 1759.

Having heard that the Duke of Orleans had in his gallery at Paris the picture by Rembrandt of which the drawing purchased by Hudson at Richardson's sale was the first sketch, he determined upon visiting France. His friends Mr. Champion and Mr. Alston

accompanied him on this expedition. By the favour
of the Abbé Mazeas, librarian to the Duke de Noailles,
an old correspondent on scientific subjects, he obtained
permission from the Duke of Orleans to copy this
original. By the study of this picture he greatly advanced his knowledge of the art, and valued his copy
proportionately, specifically "desiring that it should
never be parted with."*

In order to convince the French philosophers, and
among others Dr. Le Monnier, of the truth of his
theory respecting the origination of electricity, he
repeated his experiments at St. Germain-en-Laye, and
communicated the results to the Royal Society.

Soon after this French expedition Æpinus, a celebrated philosopher at S. Petersburg, published some
curious experiments upon the tourmalin. They attracted the notice of Wilson and he repeated them
upon two very large specimens of that gem given him
by Dr. Heberden and Dr. Moreton. He improved
upon the discoveries of Æpinus and received in acknowledgment the gold medal of the Royal Society.
This he bequeaths by this MS. to his family,† but in
case of failure of succession orders it to be given to
the British Museum. His experiments are published
in the "Transactions" and in a separate treatise. This
publication called forth a rejoinder from Æpinus, to
which he replied and explained that the difference
depended upon the size of the tourmalins upon which
experiments were made.

His labours of various kinds now required larger

---

* It is now the property of Robert B. W. Wilson, his great-grandson—
a minor.—ED.

† Also the property of Robert B. W. Wilson.—ED.

space and he took the house adjoining his own dwelling—also the property of the heirs of Sir Godfrey
Kneller—formerly tenanted by the celebrated Dr. Rad-
cliffe and afterwards used as Queen Anne's wardrobe.
Here he received for the exhibition of his experiments
most of the foreign ministers and many philosophers,
among whom he mentions Clairaut, Condamine, and
De Lalande.

At this time Reynolds was rising into celebrity; and
Hogarth, who had not equal success in portrait painting, proposed to Wilson to join him in this branch of
the art in order to secure what he considered a just
proportion of the public favour. Hogarth was so
anxious for this partnership that he applied to Garrick,
with whom both on account of his dramatic excellence
and his high qualities Wilson had formed a close intimacy, to persuade him to accept the proposal: for
good reasons, however, Wilson declined it.

Governor Watts, who had made a large fortune in
India with Lord Clive, employed him liberally in his
art and treated him with warm and generous friendship. Among other acts of kindness he ordered two
very large pictures. One was the ceremony of Meer
Jaffier, Surajah Dowlah's general, taking the oath by
having the Koran placed on his head in the presence
of his son and the governor, on account of a treaty
made with Meer Jaffier in favour of the East India
Company before the battle of Plassey. The other
represented Lord Clive placing Meer Jaffier on the
Musnud. In this picture also Governor Watts was
introduced, in company with two famous jugga-Zeats or
black merchants—said to be worth twenty millions
sterling each—who had assisted the governor with

large loans in order to enable him to keep his engagements with the Company. Watts died before this
second picture was finished, and Wilson sold it some
years after to Dr. Hird of Leeds for an annuity of
31*l.* 10*s.* for his life.

Lord Mexborough, his sister Lady Stanhope, and
Sir Francis Delaval—all introduced to him by his
friend Mr. Edward Delaval—also showed him many
marks of special favour, and he painted several pictures for them. But the most important kindness for
which he was indebted to Lord Mexborough was an
introduction to the Duke of York. As this was of
great consequence to him he relates the circumstances
very minutely.

On one occasion, at Lord Mexborough's table, Sir
Francis Delaval took an opportunity of mentioning to
the duke that Wilson was intimately acquainted with
Mr. Garrick. The duke upon this hinted that he was
somewhat displeased with Garrick for refusing to perform the " Fair Penitent " at his request. Wilson conveyed the information to Garrick the same evening,
and was desired by him upon the first opportunity to
tell the duke that he was ready at all times to perform that or any other play at the wish of his royal
highness. The duke was well pleased and appointed
a time ; and by this means the matter was adjusted
to the satisfaction of all parties.

Soon afterwards the duke told Wilson that he was
going to rehearse the play of the " Fair Penitent," in
order to perform it with Lord Mexborough's family ;
and asked him to attend and give his opinion of the
performance, " especially with respect to himself."
Wilson felt a little alarm at the delicacy of the posi-

tion, but resolved at all hazard to speak his honest sentiments. After the duke had gone through one remarkable speech in the character of "Lothario," he appealed to Wilson for his opinion. "Sir," he answered, "it is a new idea entirely;"—(the exhibition of the character)—"and I think if there was a little more spirit introduced into the character it would heighten it extremely." The duke was pleased, in a little time after appointed him manager of his intended theatre, and from this time appealed to him in all his rehearsals and would never rest till he had satisfied his judgment both in speech and action.

Many efforts were made to dislodge Wilson from this place and favour; but none succeeded and he continued a trusted friend and a frequent guest at the duke's table, dining with him "three or four times every week at York House." The duke also mentioned him with commendation to the King; and told him of it, as a satisfaction to his own conscience for some trifling haste which he felt to have been unreasonable.

The whole fitting up and preparation of the theatre in James Street Westminster, the painting of the scenes, &c., was intrusted to Wilson; and the entire expenses under his management "did not exceed 600l. from first to last." This, he says, "as it was the entertainment of a prince to some of the first people in the land, did me no discredit." The duke was well satisfied with the effect and with his frugality.

This theatre was by order constructed only for fifty persons. Much opposition was made to his arrangements, but the duke supported him in everything and the theatre was, for its size, the most com-

plete that had yet been seen in England. The
duke's habits were very exact and orderly, and
everything was conducted with the most perfect
regularity, silence, and propriety. The company also
was most exclusively select: Mr. and Mrs. Garrick
were indeed admitted to one rehearsal and two plays,
but this was a great favour. The duke generally
gave twenty tickets to Lord Mexborough and Lady
Stanhope for their "disposal to such persons *as were
agreeable to him*," but reserved the remaining thirty
to himself. The company used to assemble in an
elegant drawing-room, and the signal for their entrance into the theatre was Wilson's appearance in
the room. This was by the duke's special order.

Political party ran high at this time, and the duke
being in opposition resolved upon getting up the play
of "Jane Shore," as there were some words in it very
applicable to the times which he was desirous of
speaking. He insisted that Wilson should play the
Chancellor. Wilson earnestly declined it: but the duke
would take no excuse and even "held him while the
robes were put upon him." "The wig of the then
Speaker of the House of Commons was upon his head:"
and, as he had warned the duke, the consciousness of
his ridiculous figure threw him into uncontrollable
laughter. This was increased by the purposed gri-
maces of Mr. afterwards Sir John, Wrottesley equerry
to the duke—who played the part of Shore—behind
the side scenes. Wilson as Chancellor had to sit
by the duke, who often whispered to him to "blow
his nose:" but all to no purpose; his mirth continued, and infected the audience who could not refrain from laughing also. This "disconcerted the

duke a little," and after the play was over he told
Wilson that " he should never be his Chancellor
again."

Soon after this the Duke of York was suddenly
obliged to leave the kingdom *for political reasons.* He
told Wilson that he would give all his money to stay
in England a *fortnight longer*   In *about a fortnight* the
ministry was changed, and the duke's friends, the
Bedford and Grenville party, came into office.   On
the morning of his leaving Wilson breakfasted with
him at York House, and wrote several letters at his
dictation.   The duke took his leave of him with many
expressions of kind feeling; thanking him for his
conduct and the economy of his management of the
theatre, and desiring him to communicate to him
through Mr. Wrottesley all public news.

In the course of this intimacy the duke, in a
serious mood, told Wilson that he purposed soon to
change his manner of life.   Wilson had often observed that the excitement of hurry and late hours
was injurious to him, " his pulse at such times beating seldom less than eighty-six in a minute ;" and as
the duke permitted him always to speak freely, he
told him he feared that " this continual fever would
become very serious to him."   This fear soon proved
to have had too good foundation, for the duke died
abroad three or four months afterwards.

Shortly before the duke went abroad, Wilson, in
order to please Lord Rockingham who was then
prime minister and who had promised to "take care
of him," published a print called the " Tombstone."
It represented the tomb of the Duke of Cumberland,
then recently deceased; near it were Lords Bute,

Gower, Grenville, and the Duke of Bedford dancing the Haze. Many more lords and others were introduced. The print was very successful in its object; and Mr. Edmund Burke, Grey Cowper, and others, pressed him much to try another political print. An opportunity soon offered in the proposed repeal of the Stamp Act in America. He called his second print the "Repeal, or the Funeral of Miss Amy Stamp." The Honourable George Grenville who strongly opposed the Bill was represented as the bearer of Miss Amy in a little coffin. Lord Bute was chief mourner: the Duke of Bedford, Lord Sandwich, Lord Halifax, Lord Temple, and others, made up the train: Sir Fletcher Norton and Mr. Wedderburn were standard-bearers: the funeral service was performed by Anti-Sejanus (Mr. Scot, of Leeds). Near the open vault were skulls like those on Temple Bar, on one of which was the inscription "Rebellion, 1714;" on the other, "Rebellion, 1745." In the distance was the Thames with its wharves, where goods for America were loading. In compliment to Mr. Pitt a large box was being carried on board a vessel with the inscription "Statue of Mr. Pitt;" and further off, on the river, were three ships of war, named, in compliment to the ministry, the "Rockingham," the "Grafton," and the "Conway." This print he published within ten minutes after the Act was repealed. In four days he sold above 2,000, at a shilling each. On the fifth day two pirated copies came out at half the price, and he was informed by credible persons that above 16,000 of these were sold.

Soon after this publication, while he was in favour with the Duke of York, Mr. Worsdale, painter to the

Board of Ordnance, died. Lady Stanhope and other persons of influence interested themselves in Wilson's favour for the place; and Lady Stanhope, as she was walking with the duke in the park, persuaded him to send Colonel Morrison one of his aides-de-camp then with him, to Lord Granby the Master of the Ordnance, to ask for it. The answer was, that the place was given away to a friend of the Duke of Gloucester. Soon after, however, as he was dining at Lord Mexborough's where a large company were assembled, a letter was brought to him from Colonel Morrison with the information that Lord Granby had given him the place. He immediately rose and presented the letter to the Duke of York, who was at table and who received it with expressions of great satisfaction. The success was owing to the duke's personal application to the Duke of Gloucester to abandon his claim for his friend in Wilson's favour. He told Wilson that "his brother had done this in the most obliging manner:" he then desired him to waive his thanks to himself and to "wait upon the Duke of Gloucester the following morning to thank him for the honour he had done him; and after that to wait upon Lord Granby."

Having now, at the age of fifty, a permanent position and fixed income he determined to marry. He might often, he says, have "married before ladies of good fortune," but he could not endure a "gay, dressy, dissipated turn, and flaunting disposition." Soon after his appointment he became acquainted with Miss Hetherington, a lady of good birth, but with no dowry except her rare beauty and her many virtues. He speaks with admiration of the first and with warm affection of the last, and adds, "Something further I have to say in her favour—that I saved more money from the time I first knew her than I had ever done in the same space of time." They were married in 1771. By her he had seven children: 1. Frances, married first to Col. Bosville, and secondly to General Lewis Bayly Wallis. 2. Major Gilfrid, who died in infancy. 3. Major William. 4. ROBERT THOMAS, born Aug. 17, 1777. 5. Jane Maria, who died in infancy. 6. Edward Lumley. 7. Jane, married to the Rev. Herbert Randolph.

The application of lightning conductors to buildings was now becoming frequent and exciting much public interest. Mr. Daines Barrington, brother of Lord Barrington, after consultations with Wilson who still after his marriage carried on his philosophical pursuits in the leisure of his employment for the Board of Ordnance, recommended the Dean and Chapter of St. Paul's to secure their church by this means. Acting upon this suggestion the Dean and Chapter addressed a letter to the Royal Society, and a committee of electricians was nominated to carry the recommendation into effect. The members were Mr. Cavendish, Dr. Watson, Mr. Canton, Mr. Delaval, Dr. Franklin, and Mr. Wilson. Wilson strenuously urged that the iron rods for so lofty a building should be much thicker than those in general use: and although he could not prevail to the full extent of his wishes and suggestions, after much deliberation a partial concession was made; and it was determined that they should be one inch and a half in diameter.

Some time after this he was commissioned by the Board of Ordnance to inspect the gunpowder magazines at Purfleet with a view to their protection by the means of conductors, and to send in a report. Upon the production of this report he was ordered to carry it into effect: but delays and obstructions arose, and the matter was eventually intrusted to the same committee of members of the Royal Society that had acted in the former instance.   In this committee Dr. Franklin contended, against the recommendation of the report, for pointed conductors and it was carried in opposition to Wilson.   He, however, defended his views, and gave further reasons for preference of the rounded form in a paper printed in the " Transactions."   It was said that Franklin would answer this but he never did so.

Wilson's naturally candid and truthful character sometimes made him enemies.   On one occasion a noble lord, a member of the Royal Society, was entertaining a company of his friends when experiment was made of an alleged invention of the host.   Wilson observed that this very experiment was to be found in Newton's " Optics;" and notwithstanding the hints of his friends he maintained his ground.   His lordship at last said, with some warmth, " *Are you sure of that?*"   Wilson answered, " Yes."   And upon being asked further, " *Can you show it me?*" again answered in the affirmative.   The book was brought, and he immediately turned to the passage and presented it to his lordship, who was much disconcerted and declared that he had " never seen," or " did not remember it."   He treated Wilson very civilly for the rest of the evening, but never forgave him.   On another occasion a " diploma " was designed and executed on copper to be printed on vellum, for presentation to foreigners who were to be admitted members of the

Society. "Such a design," Wilson says, "with regard to taste was never seen. On the top of it were the sun, moon, planets, stars, comets, meteors, lightning, rainbow, &c., &c. Down each side were suspended mathematical apparatus, and other things that were supposed to be the inventions of members. Not only was the perspective of these instruments false, but the design was so badly executed that it looked like a show-board of a mathematical instrument maker. At the bottom of this grand composition was the Giants' Causeway, with a view of the sea. On the shore were corals and several shells. The shells appeared as large as haystacks, and one of the corals was taken for an old oak-tree by Lord Moreton." As it was thought by the council of the Society that some part of the design required alteration, they requested Wilson to undertake it. This he declined by letter, and told them generally that the "design was bad, and the perspective false;" adding that "as perspective was a branch of geometry it would disgrace the Society" to have such a thing exhibited abroad. One of the designers threatened to have him censured for this letter; but some of his friends told him that if he attempted it they would move the Society to return their thanks to Wilson, and so the matter dropped. The diploma was rejected by a vote of the council.

In the autumn of the same year he visited Yorkshire; and at the houses of Sir George Savile, Lord Mexborough, Lord Scarborough, Lord Irwin and others, painted as many portraits as produced him 600*l.*

He had been at work at intervals for fourteen years upon a large picture of Belshazzar's Feast.

This he now determined to finish. He did so and it was sold for 460*l*. His own criticism of this picture is, that it had "many faults but was not without considerable merit; particularly in the light and shade, the disposition of the figures, and the richness of the colouring." It was painted entirely from imagination.

He painted also the whole-length portrait of Shakspeare for the Town Hall of Stratford on the occasion of the Jubilee in 1769, at Garrick's expense; and was present and assisted much in the celebration. It was at his suggestion, as they were returning to London in Garrick's coach, that the Ode and Jubilee were brought upon the stage. This representation was very lucrative.

In 1776 he published a work on phosphori, and sent an account of his discoveries respecting the properties of light as they are exhibited by the effect of the coloured rays upon these substances, to most of the learned societies in Europe.

The celebrated Professor Euler, of S. Petersburg, wrote a "Memoir" upon this paper, which was read to the Imperial Academy. He transmitted a copy of it to Wilson, who at the same time received notice that he was elected a member of the Academy. Flattering letters were also written to him from the Royal Academy at Berlin, the Academy of Sciences at Paris, and the Academy of Institutes at Bologna; with warm congratulations from many learned persons at home and abroad, and especially from the President of the Royal Society.

His friend, Dr. Heberden, wishing much for a copy by Wilson of the celebrated portrait of Erasmus by

Hans Holbein, in Windsor Castle, procured a warrant for his admission for this purpose from the lord chamberlain. During the progress of this work, as Wilson was breakfasting one morning with Mr. Ramus the favourite page of the King and an old friend of his own, his Majesty entered the apartment, and seeing a stranger retired immediately taking Mr. Ramus with him. The purpose of this was to inquire who he was: upon the information being given he asked very particularly whether he was the *landscape* or the *portrait* painter. Hearing that he was the portrait painter, the King returned to the room and commenced a conversation on the subject of the " Erasmus " and other matters. Wilson finding his Majesty very gracious, took occasion to mention his picture of " Belshazzar " and asked permission to show it; giving an account of its progress and execution which so interested and pleased the King that he easily gave the leave. Wilson then showed his copy of the " Erasmus " with which his Majesty was much satisfied, and "carried it himself to show it to the Queen."

Upon his return to London he sent the " Belshazzar " to the Queen's house, and on the 22nd of August, 1776, it was placed by himself in a good light ready for her Majesty's inspection. About a week afterwards he attended there ; but the King not having yet come from the levée, Reynolds the page in waiting went with him into the room where he had disposed the picture. Upon entering, Reynolds suddenly cried out, " Zounds ! this is a fine thing indeed !" " An involuntary compliment," Wilson says, " which pleased me not a little, as it reminded me of Molière's old woman."

Upon the return of the King and Queen from St. James's, they both saw the picture and expressed their approbation in flattering terms, the King asking many pertinent questions. "He did not appear," however, "to know the history of Belshazzar so well as the Queen, for her Majesty explained a great part of it to the King so readily," that Wilson suspected her of having read it up very lately. The King inquired whether the characters of the handwriting were legible. He answered that "they were not; for that the soothsayers were not able to read them." Their Majesties both remarked that the picture was very rich without being gaudy, and that it had a magnificent effect. At this interview the King made many inquiries respecting Wilson's early life, habits of study, pursuits, &c.; and specially asked whether at that time he had painted any other historical pictures. He mentioned that he was then engaged in painting one by request for the hospital at Leeds his native town, the subject he had chosen being the Raising of Jairus's Daughter : that he had made this choice because it gave a good opportunity of contrast in light and shade; a manner which, as he was a great admirer and student of Rembrandt, was favourite with him.

He added, that as he conceived it difficult to give the face of Christ a proper expression on that occasion he had shown only the back of the head, which gave him an opportunity of heightening the dignity of the figure by representing the whole light illuminating the chamber as proceeding from the face of Christ only; and that by this means the imagination of the spectator was left free to conceive what expression he pleased.   Their Majesties were much struck with this idea, and inquired closely into the proposed mode of treatment, &c.   The King observed that he "supposed Mr. Wilson was a long time in settling the design and making alterations before he began to finish off a picture."   To this he replied, that he "never made sketches or drawings for his pictures, but painted them on the canvas at once : that before he attempted anything he settled the plan and conduct of the whole in his mind as to composition, light, shade, &c.; and when this was done, sat down to sketch it with his pencil in colours, and finished it off at leisure."

In the course of this conversation Wilson's candour placed him in an embarrassing predicament.   The King in speaking of Hogarth, concerning whom he made many inquiries as he was aware of Wilson's intimate acquaintance, observed that he was highly commendable for his "knowledge of light and shade." Wilson replied that he "*did not think Hogarth excelled in that particular branch of his art so much as he did in others.*"   The Queen gracefully and amiably interposed an observation which enabled him to recede so far as to allow that his Majesty was partly right, for that he "remembered some instances in which Mr. Hogarth had managed that branch of the art to great advantage."

Referring to the picture of "Erasmus," the King asked how long he had been engaged upon it, and whether in copying it he had attended more to the drawing or the pencilling.   He replied that he attended to both equally, but in the execution having first settled the drawing, after the dead colour was laid on he endeavoured to imitate the pencilling; and that he was eight or ten days about it: adding, that although there was a circumstance connected with it, which he explained, that threw some doubt upon its genuineness, he himself was persuaded that it was an original and considered it one of the finest Holbeins he had ever seen.

In this conversation the King made repeated inquiries respecting the personal history of Hogarth, and his paintings of which he was a great admirer. As his Majesty spoke of the "Marriage à la Mode" with high commendation, Wilson mentioned that Hogarth had begun a subject which he called "The Happy Marriage" but had never finished it. Upon more particular inquiry he informed their Majesties further, that it was only one picture, and that not half finished; that it was of the same size with the "Marriage à la Mode;" that "the subject was the ceremony of breaking the cake over the heads of the bride and bridegroom, which was an old English custom; and that he had *made the bride very handsome.*" The Queen asked particularly whether this was so. He repeated the assertion, and added that "the father of the bride, old Sir Roger de Coverley, was introduced with a glass of wine in his hand and as a very happy man; and that in a corner of the room—a true old English hall— were nine musicians playing upon various instruments but in a whimsical way and with droll expressions, as if they were intended to ridicule the nine Muses." The King and Queen laughed heartily and inquired where the picture was. Wilson did not know with certainty at the time, but afterwards found that it was in the possession of Garrick. Upon this discovery he asked

Garrick to lend it to him which he readily did. Wilson had it conveyed to the Queen's house, and placed it by permission on a chair in the room where their Majesties dined. In the middle of dinner the King sent to inquire *who painted the picture :* he sent back word that it was painted by Hogarth ; and suspects that the reason of the inquiry was that the bride was a *handsome likeness* of the Queen, and that it looked as if it had been *newly painted.* He adds, " It was the best coloured and most beautiful head I had ever seen Hogarth paint." After dinner the King sent for Wilson and made many inquiries about the picture. In the course of conversation he observed that he supposed that Hogarth told a story very well. Wilson answered, " Pretty well, but he is apt sometimes to tell the *wrong story.*" " How is that ?" said the King. " Sir," he answered, " Mr. Hogarth was one day dining with Sir George Hay, Mr. Garrick and others, when he said he had an excellent story to tell which would make them all laugh. Everybody being so prepared he told his story, but instead of laughing all looked grave, and Hogarth himself seemed a little uncomfortable. After a short time, however, he struck his hand very suddenly upon the table and said that he had told the wrong story. This caused no small amusement, and when he told the right one at last it was so good in its way that all the company laughed exceedingly." The King inquired some more particulars of " The Happy Marriage," and Wilson told him that Hogarth had drawn the ornaments of the chimney-piece in that picture from some old carvings in a room in the Charterhouse, which he had shown him when he was a clerk

there. " What!" said the King, hastily, " did he paint
that picture so long ago?" " Yes," said Wilson,
" except the head of the bride which was painted
only ten or twelve years ago."

After a lengthened conversation their Majesties
retired, both expressing their thanks very graciously
for the view of the picture. From this time Wilson
was often at court, and was always received with
flattering marks of favour.

On one occasion, having spoken of his philosophical
occupations, he thought it a fit opportunity to present
his work on phosphori to the King. This he did
through Mr. Ramus; who afterwards told him that the
King had expressed himself much pleased, and had
spoken of it as " extremely clever."

To Mr. West the King's painter his Majesty spoke
in terms of high praise of the copy of the " Erasmus,"
and at the same interview inquired whether he had
seen the " Belshazzar." He answered that he had seen
it and that he admired it greatly : upon which the
King said that he entirely agreed with him, and spoke
particularly of the management of the light and shade.
Mr. West explained that Wilson excelled greatly in
these effects from his philosophical knowledge. He
told the story of the roast beef decorated with the
offending imitations of Rembrandt, at which " his
Majesty laughed excessively;" and then communicated the facts of the controversy with Franklin. The
King inquired minutely into this, and was " much
struck with Wilson's views and reasons."

These conversations Mr. West himself repeated to
Wilson; but they were fully confirmed to him by
Mr. Ramus, who was present, and who added, that

Mr. West spoke of him in a very friendly manner, and " very like a gentleman."

In the month of June, 1777, the board house belonging to the powder-magazines at Purfleet, to which pointed conductors had been attached by recommendation of the committee of 1772, was struck by lightning. In consequence of this accident the controversy with Dr. Franklin and his supporters was revived in full activity; but as the series of papers on this and one or two other similar occasions are published in the " Transactions " it is unnecessary to relate particulars. Wilson was not treated handsomely by the Society in general, for a spirit of party mischievous to the interests of true philosophy had been engendered: yet he had many friends and warm defenders in it; among whom Dr. Musgrave deserves particular mention.

Notwithstanding the opposition which by force of numbers bore down his views in the meetings and excited some warmth, he persevered in maintaining them with calm dignity, and proceeded to establish his principles by the evidence of experiment.

He addressed a paper to the Society in answer to the report of a committee appointed to examine the facts; and a letter to the King expressive of his anxiety for the safety of the royal residences, which had been fitted with pointed conductors in the same manner as the magazines at Purfleet. This letter he presented himself to the King at Kew. On the same day he received a letter from Signor Zanotti, President of the Academy of Institutes at Bologna, announcing his election as a Fellow of the Society. Wilson was the only Englishman who had yet received that honour ; and this was the fourth European academy of which he was now a member.

The King had suggested to him to prepare an apparatus upon a large scale for testing his opinions on the subject of blunt conductors. He determined, however, first to finish his picture of "Jairus's Daughter," in order that he might have full leisure to devote to the subject. He did so accordingly; and exhibited it to their Majesties at the Queen's house on the 17th of July in the same summer. An engraving was taken from this picture.

He now commenced his preparations. The King took great interest in the proposal, and at Wilson's request, in order that the experiments might be conducted on a sufficient scale, promised the use of his riding-house for their exhibition. This, however, was rendered unnecessary by the offer of his friend Mr. Wyat, the surgeon, of the use of the Pantheon in Oxford Street for the purpose.

With the King's approbation he applied to the Board of Ordnance for the means of carrying out his project. Lord Amherst was at the board when he explained his views. Having acquainted the members with his Majesty's pleasure they at once made an order for him to have everything he wanted from the Tower, and undertook to pay all his other expenses. From the Tower he ordered 24 drums to form his cylinder, 2,800 yards of wire, and 600 yards of tin-foil. All other requisite articles not in store he provided, as authorized, at the cost of the board.

In about three weeks all was ready, and he proceeded to test the apparatus. As it was found to succeed according to his expectations he made the result known to the King. In a few days he was sent for to the Queen's house, when the King told him that he, with the Queen, the Prince of Wales, the Bishop of Osnaburg, the Princess Royal, and two others of the royal family, would be with him on the following morning at the Pantheon to see the experiments.

They arrived accordingly, and stayed three hours. All succeeded to Wilson's perfect satisfaction; and when the exhibition was ended the King said, that "if the Royal Society would not now be convinced the apple-women from the street should be called in; for *they* certainly would be." He afterwards told many of his nobles, and particularly Lord Suffolk one of the secretaries of state, that they were "all wrong about points; for he had seen the experiments at the Pantheon and was perfectly convinced by them."

Two days afterwards they were shown to the Board of Ordnance, and then to the Royal Society for six days together. After further exhibition to the public at the request of the proprietors of the Pantheon, the apparatus was sent to the Tower by order of the Board of Ordnance.

On the 13th of November he presented to the King a paper which he had drawn up on the subject of these experiments. It was afterwards presented to the board and then to the Royal Society, and a committee was appointed to examine the facts.

Soon after the appointment of this committee Wilson waited upon the King with his paper, and was asked by him, " Whether he intended to publish it, whether the Royal Society did so or not?" He answered that

"he did intend it, and proposed asking the Board of
Ordnance to be at the expense of engraving the plates,
as he thought they ought to do so." The King said
that he thought so too; and added, that "*If they
would not he knew where to go.*"

Up to this time, in consequence of a private arrangement of the late painter to the Board of Ordnance
before his death by which a natural son had been
taken into partnership with him, Wilson had only
received half the emoluments of the office. In this
year this Mr. Worsdale died; and upon Wilson's own
application, seconded by a strong appeal from the
board to the Master-General, the full appointment
was conferred upon him by Lord Townshend.

Dr. Demainbray the King's astronomer at Richmond, to whom he paid a visit in the course of the
summer, showed him the observatory then perhaps
the best in Europe, and told him that "the King had
made the best observation on the transit of Venus,
it being within 2″, whereas that at Greenwich was
32″."

In September he printed his paper on the experiments at the Pantheon. He presented a copy in
person to the King, who received it very graciously
and entered into conversation upon it. He also sent
copies to the Empress of Russia and the King of
Prussia by their respective ambassadors. This paper
was published in January, 1779.

On the 20th of January in this year Garrick died
and his funeral was celebrated with great magnificence in Westminster Abbey. Wilson followed the
remains of his friend to the grave; and the King afterwards told a friend of his that "Dr. Samuel Johnson

and Wilson were the only two persons who shed tears"
on that occasion.   Garrick had been a pupil of Johnson's in his early years.

Among some remarks on the characters of his
children at this time, he observes, "As to *Robert*,*
although he is but one year and a half old, he seems
to be more lively than his brother and likely to turn
out a cleverer fellow."

Professor Allamand, of Leyden, with whom he had
a correspondence on the subject of phosphori, wrote
to him in reply to his communications that, in his own
opinion and that of others, he had "proved by his
experiments that rounded conductors were better and
less dangerous than pointed ones."   In the course of
this correspondence an idea suddenly struck him,
which promised to account for some strange phosphoric
appearances which he had observed and published in
the second edition of his book on that subject; and as
Professor Euler had noticed this publication and
attempted to account for these appearances upon a
theory of his own, he wrote a letter to him on the
25th of May, 1779, pointing out an error in his data
and giving his own solution in correspondence with
the philosophy of Newton.   This paper he presented
to the Royal Society.

A Mr. Berkenholt, the son of a merchant in Leeds
and an acquaintance of Wilson's, had been twenty years
in the King's service without advancement, when a
common dyer in the town discovered a method of
dyeing cotton scarlet.   This suggested to Wilson a

* It is singular that the mother of Lady Wilson, when her daughter
was a few months old, makes a similar observation.   "I never had so
sprightly and forward a child."—*Journal of Mrs. Belford.*

means of helping his friend and he advised him to apply himself to this invention; telling him that "industry and attention, with patience, produce astonishing results in any study." At the same time he pointed out to him what authors he should read, made some chemical experiments for him, and explained the philosophy on which they seemed to depend, and the reason why animal substances were more apt to receive the scarlet dye than vegetable substances; the object being to discover some means of giving to these latter the same repulsive property. Mr. Berkenholt soon made great advances in this direction and succeeded in making a better scarlet than that of the Leeds inventor: besides improving several other colours. Wilson, through the instrumentality of Sir George Savile and others of his friends, assisted him in an application to Parliament for a reward for his discoveries. They were tested before the Lords of the Treasury, Lord North being present: and upon the report five thousand pounds were awarded to him.

On the breaking out of the Spanish war in the summer of 1779 it was suggested to the Board of Ordnance, that as there was no figure of Queen Elizabeth among the mounted sovereigns in the horse armoury in the Tower, although the armour worn when she reviewed her troops at Purfleet on the invasion of the Spanish armada was kept there, it was desirable that this defect should be supplied. Upon this suggestion it was determined that a figure of the queen properly accoutred and attended by a page should be placed among the rest, and the execution of the design was intrusted to Wilson. He gave great attention to this work and finished it in a manner very superior to that in which the other figures were done : it was resolved, therefore, that the group should be placed in the *Spanish armoury* where the arms and implements taken from the armada were deposited. From the richness of the ornaments and trappings and the striking effect produced, it was supposed that Wilson had "put the board to a very large expense for this magnificent group." The total cost, however, was only one hundred and forty-nine pounds.

In 1780 he published a small popular treatise entitled " A Short View of Electricity."

On the 12th of August in this year he set out for Windsor with his family : Sir Grey Cowper having lent him his apartments in the Castle. As he was passing the Queen's lodge on the following day, the King called him by name from the window ; and after inquiring whether the children were his, and "*praising Robert who would not pull his hat off*," he "called to the Queen who was dressing, *to see Bob.*" On the 14th, Wilson presented his book to the King, the Queen, the Prince of Wales, and the Bishop of Osnaburg. The whole royal family, and the Queen especially, were "exceeding gracious ;" and one day on the terrace " the King took hold of Bob and introduced him to those who were in attendance as an *exceeding fine boy.*"

Frequently during this visit he was admitted to familiar intercourse " with the King and several of the Princes," who all treated him with marked attention and kindness. Prince Adolphus once, " when walking hand in hand with Major," said, " he supposed that Robert was a very funny boy." " The next year," his father writes, " Prince Octavius wanted to take Bob's hand, but he refused by taking away his hand." These are small incidents of childhood, but they indicate the early bent of character.

The condescension and kindness of the King and the royal family continued to the time of Wilson's death, June 6th, 1788, but the manuscript ends abruptly with the year 1783.

Of mild philosophy and courteous manners, faithful to duty in all the relations of life, beloved by his family, valued by his friends, sufficiently prosperous in the world, and useful in his generation, he left to his children and his children's children a legacy of honest fame ; and one more example, brought home to their own bosoms, of the power of the human will to accomplish all that it proposes for human happiness in accordance with God's will and under His blessing.

After the brief references to his favourite son's early character quoted above, no further mention is made of him in the manuscript; but one traditional fact may be added, illustrating the spirit and principles which through life animated Sir Robert Wilson as a soldier and dignified him as a man. When he was first sent to Westminster he found his elder brother subject to the capricious tyranny too often exercised by the stronger over the weaker in a public school. He at once resented the wrong, and "fought thirty boys, one after another, in his brother's defence."*

* This was related to me *in these words* by Edward Lumley Wilson his younger brother, in May, 1849, as we were following the remains of our relative to his grave in Westminster Abbey. The occasion was a remark of mine, that I had never seen in death a form of such magnificent proportions, or of more athletic power. My uncle spoke at the same time with great impression of his brother's uncommon beauty of countenance in his boyhood.

I had no idea at the time that the family papers would ever come into my hands for publication, and therefore made no minute inquiry : but the exact words remain in my memory.—Ed.

The generation of brothers, sisters, and intimate early friends has passed away, and beyond these slight notices, all that can now be known of the boyhood of Sir Robert Wilson is contained in the fragment of direct autobiography in the next chapter.

EXTRACTS FROM A JOURNAL KEPT DURING A TOUR OF VISITS, COMMENCING AUG. 16, 1825, AND ENDING JAN. 4, 1826.

Dec. 4, 1825.—To Grove Hall, the seat of Mr. Lee, a connection by marriage. Mr. Lee's father, aged eighty-five, told me that he remembered my grandfather, his uncommon stature, and remarkable beard, very well. That he remembered also Mill Hill House, which was sold to the Recorder when my uncle, who was the first English merchant settled in Russia, and whom Peter the Great used familiarly to call "his English Jack," was shipwrecked. In the wreck of this vessel property of my grandfather's to a great amount was lost; and this first caused the misfortunes of the family.

The lands then sold are now in the possession of Mr. C. Wilson of Lidstone : the son of the Bishop of Bristol, and grandson of the Recorder. Mr. Fountain Wilson is also a grandson of the Recorder by another son; and has, it is said, property to the value of 40,000*l.* per annum. My grandfather was reported to be the richest merchant in Leeds of his time; and, Mr. Lee says, was greatly esteemed by high and low. He lived till he was 110 years of age.

Dec. 5.—Went to Leeds and saw the Mill Hill property, now worth, as I am informed, 100,000*l.*

The best hotel in the town is built on the site of Mill Hill House.

Went to the infirmary : to which my father gave his picture of the Raising of Jairus' Daughter.

The "Daughter" in this picture was painted to represent my mother in her youth. She was only forty-five when she died. On looking at the picture I was instantly and forcibly struck by the likeness to my own eldest daughter. It is still a family portrait.

The place of painter to the Board of Ordnance, procured for my father by the Duke of York, was worth, it is said, 7000*l.* per annum in time of war, and 4000*l.* in time of peace. My father was the first Englishman ever made a member of the University of Upsal. The gold medal, and the diploma of Russia *signed by the Empress Catherine*, are in my possession.—R. W.

CHAPTER II.

My dear Children,

THE example of my father has determined me to write a narrative of the principal transactions of my own life. The relation merits attention and will, I hope, contribute to your welfare.

There is always much to learn from private history, when there is not only a record of actions, but when the motives which determined and guided them are unbosomed; and you may rely on candour as well as truth pervading the whole of my statements.

Guile has never been any part of my character. What I have thought right I have always avowed and done, to the great prejudice of my fortune but not to the reproach of my name: I have no reason, therefore, to shrink from any exposition of the circumstances or feelings by which my conduct was governed.

I might and must have been much richer and more prosperous if I had regulated this innate contempt of worldly prudence by considerations of self-interest : but perhaps under their influence I should have relaxed those energies which obtained for me the regard which I possess; and, notwithstanding titles and wealth, I might have sunk into insignificance, rendered intolerably painful by loss of self-respect.

I have taken as large a part as any man in the affairs of the world in my time : I have seen more of it, been more acquainted with its rulers and distinguished and remarkable men, had more opportunity of being intimate with every class of society from the highest to the lowest, than perhaps has ever fallen to the lot of any other individual : and at this eleventh hour I can indulge the proud reflection that I have maintained the post of honour in general esteem to which all my aspirations were directed, in subordination to the higher claims of duty. Offended power has in vain attempted to wrest from me the "golden opinions of mankind" as well as of my own country, and the lightnings which it hurled have only provided illumination for the more conspicuous display of universal kind feeling and support.

Whether I am entitled to this "favour among men" you shall now determine ; and a plain, unvarnished, ingenuous tale shall be presented and submitted for your judgment.

Your grandfather's memoir unfortunately ceases at the end of the year 1783, when I was only six years old. He lived till the year 1788, but no papers have

come into my possession which supply me with sufficient means to execute what he left unfinished.

I can only generally state that the same upright
conduct, the same spirit of philosophy, the same domestic virtues which are registered so modestly yet in
such palpable characters in the pages traced by his
own hand, continued to grace the last years of his life.

Although the interests of his family had been para-
mount over every consideration of self-indulgence,
although for their benefit his life had been one of
much sacrifice as to worldly enjoyments, still his high
spirit of independence and sense of right determined
him, some years before his death, to resign the place
he held in the Ordnance when the Duke of Richmond
required that one of his political dependants should be
admitted as a rider upon the income.   This act was
indeed censured by some, but it obtained the approbation of his most valued friends; and even the King
himself took the first opportunity my father offered
his Majesty at Buckingham House—where he always
went on the birthday—to commend a proceeding which
exemplified so much disinterestedness and character.

My father continued to pass the latter days of his
life tranquilly in the bosom of his family, until a year
or two before his death when he was seized with a
paralytic affection : from this and from a second he
recovered, but was carried off by a third attack, after
several days' illness and at the age of sixty-seven.

I was then a Westminster boy, but had been
brought home and was sleeping in his apartment
when I awoke with a feverish dream—occasioned, no
doubt, by an expectation of the event and a half-
consciousness of what was passing.   I fancied I saw

him open my bed-curtains and heard him call me: I sprang to his bedside and reached it almost the instant after the spirit had departed.

My father was buried in St. George the Martyr's burial-ground, then in the fields but now surrounded by the noblest squares and streets of the metropolis. I attended the funeral with my elder brother Major, and shed tears of unfeigned sorrow. No father had ever more tenderly loved a child: none was ever more entitled to filial affection. I was indeed cherished by him with a fondness which made him frequently converse with me on serious subjects: as if he had found reason in infancy, and as if he might with safety repose confidence in its discretion.

On one occasion, however, I violated the secrecy he had imposed without impairing his good will. After his first paralytic attack he communicated to me, as we were walking to dine with Mr. Delaval, that, "it being his conviction that I might, if I would, cultivate natural talents and rise to eminence honourable to myself and beneficial to my family, he had in his will left me 1000l. more than he had left any of my brothers and sisters; to be applied to payment of the expenses of my education without prejudice to the principal of my fortune." I was gratified by this expression of my father's opinion and proof of his love: but I had no desire to benefit by the hold I had acquired upon his affections to the mortification and prejudice of my brothers and sisters. I therefore told my mother what had passed, who very soon challenged his partiality and persuaded him to cancel the bequest.

My father, on the same occasion, had earnestly advised me not to go into the army, and not to marry before I was thirty-five ; to make the law my profession, and Parliament the object of a patriotic ambition.

It was my lot to disobey three of these injunctions ; given indeed with too little attention to the peculiarities of my disposition, but certainly not at variance with the true interests of most young men gifted with promising abilities, and assisted by a fortune sufficient to secure them due means of development.

I also, from a searching spirit and eagerness for information rather than from mere passing curiosity, had become acquainted, even at an earlier period, with my father's ideas on the general nature of religious systems and on some of the most prominent doctrines of the Christian Church. While he respected too much the divinity of truth to mystify the acute perceptions of a dawning reason, and to endeavour to darken the light which poured in upon a young intelligence from the Source of all light, he always earnestly directed me to the duty of contemplating God through His works, and to the great practical rule of Christian morality, " Do to others as you would have them do to you:" teaching me that it is our wisdom thus to qualify ourselves to meet death, and what may be, in God's will and providence, the destination after death of that spirit which in this world animated the mortal body.

My father was particularly fond of reading Shakespeare to us all on winter evenings; and I well remember his devotional fervour in giving effect to those passages which expressed his feelings on the subject of the Creator and the mysteries of mortality.   His philosophy taught him to revere the Almighty Architect of the universe, and his practical wisdom was to make the social virtues the incense of his adoration.

My mother and guardians, soon after my father's death imagined that my education would proceed with less interruption to study and less anxiety to themselves in the country than in London, and therefore removed me to Winchester, where I was placed under the care of Dr. Joseph Warton; a master whose name must be dear to every one who cherishes the memory of benevolence adorned with learning and high intellectual gifts.

My mother—who, gifted as she was with the imperishable charms of grace, had preserved her remarkable beauty in her advancing years—had long been in a declining state of health, and my father had predicted that she would not survive him two years. This prediction made a deep impression on her mind. An abscess soon after his decease formed in her side; and a constitution always delicate sunk under the disease within the prescribed time.

I was at Winchester when the danger was pronounced to be imminent, and an express was sent for me to return home. On receiving the letter I carried it to Dr. Warton who gave me instant permission to set off for London. But as it was the eve of a contested election between Sir William Heathcote and Mr. Chute, no post-horses could be procured. Dr. Warton no sooner learnt my new distress than he ordered out his own carriage, drawn by a pair of pampered blacks seldom working, and directed his coachman to " proceed with me until I could hire a conveyance, even if to London."

It was not till the second stage that I could procure

a post-chaise. I arrived too late. My mother had expired the preceding day: often before her death calling me by name to receive her blessing.

She was buried by the side of my father, whose coffin I again looked upon with unaffected pain, although the sorrow of youth is not of a permanent character.

The day on which I received the news of my mother's danger was that on which I first knew also of her serious illness: but the morning of that day had dawned with an incident which, in spite of my understanding and in the absence of any superstitious tendencies, had made a sinister impression; this, as it were admonished me and made me certain that I should not pass the day without some tidings of calamity. Many years have rolled away: my common sense revolts at and mocks the folly of the omen: but I see now, as it were, before my eyes that omen, and feel now again the heart-sinking sensation that I felt then and at that moment when I was awakened by a flight of crows hovering about my window. One advanced, and cawed repeatedly, Woe!—woe!—woe! I got up, tried to shake off the load on my thoughts, but the foreboding was immoveable; and the more I tried to treat it as a dream of the fancy, the more I combated it as one of the follies which I had so often been astonished at and ridiculed as a superstition of the ancient world, the more I was persuaded it was a messenger of some adversity if not of death. Such is the infirmity of our nature that no man, I believe, has ever existed who has not discredited his mental powers by some such weaknesses, and made himself the sport of shadows probably created by traditional recitals and practices.

I returned to Winchester, but only for a short time. However, before I left I got, as it is termed, "best command" by a powerful exertion of memory at that time unprecedented in the school ; having repeated at standing out * no less than 11,500 lines out of Homer's Iliad and Odyssey, Virgil, Horace, and Sallust. It was an effort of ambition which I think rather pre-judiced than strengthened the faculties : I had been obliged during the preceding four or five months to deprive myself of the greater part of the allotted time for rest ; since for this exhibition no respite was allowed from the ordinary daily business of the school.

I by no means pretend to have been a distinguished classical scholar. I never drank deep enough of that stream to root myself as an academician ; but I had a great aptitude for learning and could master all I undertook in the way of translation, was a ready Latin versifier generally aiding all the boys of my form who wanted help, and so far advanced in Eng-lish literature and in composition that soon after my father's death I had written a tragedy regularly traced, and with so much general skill and merit as at least greatly to surprise. My brothers and sisters acted the play, and your aunt† Jane was a principal per-former. The play was called "Alonzo," whom I first made a tyrant, and afterwards had the pleasure of slaying as such. My plot was founded on the passage in Cicero which I had read as a quotation, "How

* Seven days prior to Midsummer vacation : others have since done more than I did.— R. W.

† Married March 27, 1806, to the Rev. Herbert Randolph, Rector of Let-combe Bassett, Berks, and Vicar of Chute, Wilts ; the father of the Editor.

beautiful! how lovely! it is to slay a tyrant"—
"Tyrannum occidere."

On removal from Winchester, after passing some
little time in the house of a very respectable old lady
—a Mrs. Thompson—where I stayed during the course
of a dispute which I had with my guardian about
money allowances, I became the pupil of the Rev.
Mr. Thompson the clergyman of Tottenham Court
Chapel. My guardian was a very worthy man, but
so adverse to the general usages of public seminaries
that he sternly withheld those pecuniary supplies
which custom rendered indispensable. The contrac-
tion of small debts, which caused me vexation, was
a source of continual misunderstanding between my
guardian and myself, and was the consequence of his
unreasonable resistance to the habits of the time ; but
the spirit of opposition which it also generated in me
accelerated the hour of my emancipation, and hurried
on that awful moment of independence when all the
interests of life hang on the selection of an honourable
path.

During the time that I was under Mr. Thompson's
care I frequently officiated as his clerk in the desk
and at funeral services in the burial-ground ; but I
never ventured to attempt any of the musical duties
of the office. There never, perhaps, was a family less
gifted with musical capabilities than ours in my generation; but the incompetency has happily not descended. It was here also that I became acquainted
with a person of some subsequent notoriety and fame,
—Mr. Gale Jones, then apothecary and surgeon to
Mr. Thompson's establishment. He afforded me the
opportunity of witnessing several dissections, dis-

coursed metaphysics with me so as really to enlarge
the powers of my mind, and would have persuaded
me to qualify myself for public speaking, by learning
to repeat the orations of the day and then extracting
and putting together the passages calculated to illus-
trate given subjects of argument.   I promised to be a
fellow-student but relaxed.   He steadily and inde-
fatigably proceeded ; and by a fund or stock of this *rôle*
eloquence attained much distinction at the spouting
clubs, at this time beginning to attract great public
attention, as avenues for the expression of public feeling then highly excited by the agitators on the other
side of the water.

In the house of Mr. Thompson an accident occurred
to me which happily was confined to the ludicrous,
when a few moments more might have converted it into
the fatally serious.   Having got into bed, I perceived
what I thought was a flame on the wall of the room.
I jumped up to examine it ; and as it seemed to recede
nearer the window as I approached I threw the window
open, thinking it might be the reflection from some
house on fire in the neighbourhood if not from our
own.   I could perceive no burning source of light out
of or in the room itself; still, wherever I placed myself, an increasing reflection of flame danced along
with me.   At last, much alarmed, I opened the door and
called out, *Fire!* Mr. Thompson rushed up-stairs, made
a spring at me as he approached, and plucked off my
nightcap which was burning nearly to my brow without my having been conscious of the danger.   The
nightcap being of woollen, the flame had fortunately
only crept ; except when, upon my opening the window,
it had been fanned into a momentary flare by the

current of air. It was still a mercy that the bed had not caught fire when I lay down.

Displeased by the rebuke I received—though it was most justly merited for the negligence by which the accident must have been occasioned—I soon after quitted Mr. Thompson, returned to Mrs. Thompson always my friend in the hour of tribulation, and determined to be subject to no further pedagogue government.

My sister Fanny had in the year 1793 married Colonel Bosville of the Coldstream Guards, brother of Mr. Bosville of Thorpe Hall and of Lady Macdonald and Lady Dudley and Ward. On account of that marriage he was deprived by his uncle Sir William Blacket, of the immense estate subsequently left to Mrs. Beaumont, whom he had required Colonel Bosville to marry when she was yet Miss Blacket. Obliged a week after he had married my sister to embark with his regiment for Holland, he was soon afterwards killed in the action of Lincelles, where the Guards acquired great credit. No officer in the corps was more esteemed; and though 6 feet 4 inches in height,* he was, from his corresponding symmetry of form, considered one of the handsomest men in Europe.

On hearing the intelligence my sister, then at Stamford, miscarried of a male child: so that even the brother's estate was thus lost to the family, and my sister left with but the remnant of her own fortune; part having been already applied to discharge Colonel Bosville's debts, which she herself most generously undertook to settle.

---

* His height occasioned his death, for a musket-ball struck him in the head.—R. W.

Before Colonel Bosville went abroad and when he was abroad I was strongly advised by him to be guided by my father's counsel and not to enter the army, which he described as a bad profession for profit, unfavourable for intellect, and destructive of an independent spirit. But such is the contradiction of youth in general to the dictates of experience that few listen to its teaching when offered as a gift: almost all like to buy their wisdom at great cost; and I was of such a temper of mind that the more I was enjoined not to pursue a military career the more I was desirous of doing so. My brother-in-law's death, together with the honours paid to his memory, instead of enfeebling did but strengthen that inclination. This feeling was at last kindled into an enthusiastic passion for the profession, when I heard the cheers of the multitude saluting a reinforcement going out to the Guards as it was embarking at Greenwich. I said to Mr. Bosville, with whom I had gone down to witness the embarkation, that from that moment he might consider me as one of those glory-hunters who, he used to say, were "the derision of philosophy and the plague of humanity."

Being a ward of Chancery I found that much time must be consumed in getting an order for the purchase-money of a commission. I therefore obtained a letter of introduction from General Morrison—an old friend of Colonel Bosville's—to Lord Amherst then acting Commander-in-chief and to him I presented myself with a request that he would give me a commission in one of the regiments in Flanders. Lord Amherst received me very kindly, expressed himself anxious to gratify a wish formed in so good a spirit, said that the

Duke of York had all the commissions in his gift, but advised me to present a memorial to the King at Windsor and ask for a commission in one of the regiments of Guards.   I immediately drew up myself a memorial recalling to the King's recollection my father's enjoyment of his most gracious favour, my sister's marriage and loss : and I concluded with the expression of a hope that I might obtain the opportunity of proving my attachment to his Majesty.

General Gwynn, then equerry, approved; and gave me an opportunity of presenting the memorial to the King in person at Windsor.   The King took it as he was going into chapel : and on coming out, seeing me again, made several very encouraging remarks, asked me many questions to no one of which did he give me time to answer, and left me with the impression that I had gained my cause.

The next day General Gwynn sent for me, and told me by the King's command, that he would recommend my going out to Flanders to the Duke of York "who would provide for me."   "Tell him," were the words, "Frederick will take care of him."   My friends in general were not disposed to "put much confidence in princes," and did all in their power to dissuade me from an enterprise which had no other guarantee of success than a verbal communication.   I however was firmly persuaded that their doubts were not warranted ; and therefore I prevailed on my sister Fanny to let me have the money I wanted for equipment—about 60*l.*: and 100*l.* for my expenses, which I was sure would be ample—till I could get a commission and an authority from the Court of Chancery to receive my allowance, 180*l.* per annum, if my guardian persisted in his opposition to apply it as I required, and rendered an application to the court necessary. I took out with me also a beautiful English mare—the pride of her race and sex for she was as good as she was fair—a very serviceable horse, and a groom of the name of George, who was a civil brave fellow but with a head too weak for his love of strong liquor. The mare and horse I bought on credit of a liveryman of the name of Bath, whose horses I had often ridden at the expense of Mr. Bosville ; and George who was the ostler of the yard took pleasure in following my fortunes "for better or for worse." Two very clever Scotch terriers, ugly to an exquisite degree of beauty and well known in London, completed my family.

Thus fitted out, with a red coat on my back something like a surgeon's, I bade farewell to my many friends in London ; from whom, in consequence of the ease and indulgence in which I had been long living with them, it was certainly an effort and a pain to withdraw myself.

I have before spoken of my very early introduction by my father into the world's affairs, and his direction of my mind to subjects very seldom brought under youthful notice. But by Mr. Bosville's adoption of me into his house and society, with whom my intimacy commenced soon after I left Winchester, I was made acquainted with men, manners, and politics, to a degree of information that qualified me peculiarly for intercourse with the circle in which I was living. Mr. Bosville was himself very well informed, full of anecdote, a *philosophe* and zealous politician of the Cromwell school purified of its cant and hypocrisy.

He had served in the American war, and quitted the army because he would not act any longer against the cause of American independence. He had travelled the grand tour, lived much in France, had made acquaintance with the most remarkable men of Europe, and expended a great portion of a large fortune in the practice of an unbounded hospitality that attracted to his board the most agreeable and eminent persons of all countries, classes, and opinions. For many years his table was open to them at the Piazza Coffee-house, where he established it to avoid trouble: and here Fox, Grey, Sheridan, Erskine, Fitzpatrick, Sir Francis Burdett, Horne Tooke, Paine, Parson East (the most instructive and wit-exciting companion I ever knew), Sir John Sinclair, Lord Moira, and all their friends and friends' friends, associated on terms of perfect ease and freedom, so that we frequently sat down to dine two dozen when only half a dozen were expected. The only rule of the ménage was that no one should come in after the clock had struck *five*, at which moment dinner was announced. If any one entered afterwards it discomposed Mr. Bosville; and to mark it he desired every one to rise and make all possible noise and confusion with chairs, plates, knives and forks, &c., as if the arrival occasioned a general derangement.

This rule, and the penalty of its infraction, continued till Mr. Bosville's last illness, not many years after he had established his table-d'hôte in his own house in Welbeck Street: so that very few persons indeed ever ventured to present themselves after the clock in the hall had finished its fatal stroke. Sir Francis Burdett, who always wished to be yet notwithstanding never could be, punctual, was a gentle

exception; but he frequently went away, rather than
expose himself to the frown or the clatter.

Toast-drinking after dinner was here, I believe, first
abolished; and health-drinking at dinner was not encouraged. Ladies at that time were also not admitted.
It was only after I had married that your mother had
the privilege of a carte d'entrée without ceremony.

It was impossible, in a circle so gifted with intelligence and intellectually communicative, not to acquire
knowledge, habits of thinking, and manly tendencies.
It was a hot-bed for a young mind: and the passing
events of the day were impressed on my attention, as
I was appointed by the social meeting reader of the
evening paper—"The Courier"—which, during the
first period of the Revolution, teemed daily with important news of what was passing in Paris, bulletins
from the armies, &c.

My sister Fanny accompanied me to Dover, where I
embarked in an Ostend packet. Colonel Burton of the
Guards, and Colonel Milman, were fellow-passengers,
and it was settled that I should accompany them to the
Duke's head-quarters. Our passage was so good a one
that we arrived in ten hours after we left the pier—of
which I slept nine, not having been able to enjoy my
rest for a long time before from apprehension of some
untoward accident occurring to disappoint my hopes
or delay my departure. For several hours, however,
after landing I had a complete vertigo in my head,
and was obliged to go to bed. I have never forgotten
the seeming swimming of the room.

Having dined with the Governor we departed next
day for Courtray where we arrived without any accident. Colonel Edward Morrison, of the Coldstream

Guards, received me at Courtray with the most cordial
and flattering welcome, obtained my admission to the
Coldstream Guards' mess as an honorary member, and
undertook to present me to the Duke of York. The
Duke in the kindest manner addressed me, and after
some general conversation asked me whether I preferred a cornetcy of cavalry, or an ensigncy in the
Guards; and, if I liked cavalry, whether I had any
choice of regiment. I had already made acquaintance
at the Guards' mess with Colonel Churchill of the 15th
Light Dragoons; and the fame of Elliott's Light Horse,
added to his engaging manners and gallant character,
determined me to select this corps. Colonel Childers
of the 11th, aide-de-camp to the Duke, would have
persuaded me to join him; but Colonel Churchill urged
his claim of preference to the Duke, who rallied them
at the competition being so vehemently pressed and
acquiesced with my wish. I was immediately put in
orders as a Cornet; and with no small degree of pride,
and feeling that I had shown a more correct discern-
ment than they, despatched the news to my friends in
England.

As the army was to move shortly it was thought
most eligible for me that I should not join the regiment
until the march commenced. In the interim I passed
my time very agreeably, and experienced general attention. Drinking and gaming were then very general
habits; but I always considered the first vice as the
indulgence of a beast, and the latter as too replete
with peril, misery, and shame to afford any gratification. Once in my life I did indeed suffer myself to
play whist two nights successively for high stakes,
and lost two hundred and fifty pounds: but I was

impelled by *peculiar circumstances* from which I could not well disengage myself and not by any of a gamester's passion. It was my first and last offence. The money I could ill afford; but the self-reproach for such an act of criminal folly was the severest punishment.

The army broke up its cantonments about the beginning of April; and I fell into the ranks of the troop to which I belonged as it filed through Courtray. A further acquaintance with the corps of officers made me feel still more pleased that I had become a member; and indeed the men themselves took an interest on all occasions in my welfare.

The corps of officers consisted of Colonel Churchill; Major Aylett; Captains Pocklington and Ryan; Lieutenants Granby Calcraft, Blount, and Keir;* Cornets Butler and myself. Mr. Beaver was chaplain. A Captain Dare, of the York Chasseurs, was for the first few weeks a volunteer. After the storming of one of the hornworks at Valenciennes he had jumped on the parapet, and, after several bravadoes, turned round and presented his *seat* to the enemy who saluted it with a shower of grape, several of which entered and avenged the indignity offered to the Republicans.

Although I was naturally cheerful and good-tempered, I was occasionally self-willed, and deservedly checked in consequence. My chief resistance to discipline was at mess, where I could not brook the duties of *Boots*; but various heavy fines at last brought me to my senses.

On passing to our first encampment we traversed

---

* Afterwards Sir William Keir Grant.—Ed.

the ground near Câteau where General Mack had obtained an advantage over the enemy a short time previously.   About five hundred Frenchmen had been killed, and the hands and feet were still protruding from the graves.

On the 16th of April the allied army, nominally one hundred and twenty thousand but not more than ninety thousand effective, assembled on the heights above Câteau on a table-land to be reviewed by the Emperor.   It was a spring day of the *old seasons*, and a magnificent spectacle was presented to the eye. Philosophers would perhaps have contemplated it with other feelings, but none could have been present. I thought, however, that a beautiful girl* of the 14th regiment of foot dressed with English cottage simplicity, engaged more the attention of majesty, royalty, and high authority than the lines of warriors and the parade of war.   Certainly she arrested the career of the Court and Staff, and fixed their gaze for several minutes.

The next morning, as soon as the fog cleared the different columns were seen moving in their prescribed directions : and ideas connected with the object of their operations first caused some serious thoughts ; but they were quickly dispelled by the animation of the scene.

The army had been divided into eight principal columns, commanded by Prince Christian of Denmark ; Lieutenant-General Alvinzi ; the Emperor, with the Prince of Coburg as Commander-in-Chief ; the Duke

---

* Her name was Sally—she served in all the actions, and united courage and generosity with her beauty.   It will be seen how we met afterwards in Asia Minor and Egypt.—R. W.

of York, with General Otto as his lieutenant; Sir William Erskine; Major-General Count Hadig; the Hereditary Prince of Orange; and Major-General Grosau. The points of attack were: Mazingenet, Oisy, and the Forest of Nouvion; Ribeauville, Wassigny, and Genappe; Vaux and the Bois de Bohain; Maretz and Prêmont; Crèvecœur and passage of the Scheldt; St. Hilaire.

The 15th was attached to the column of Sir William Erskine, and in General Harcourt's brigade. On arriving at Prêmont we found that the enemy were disadvantageously posted as to natural position, the village being in a hollow, but strongly entrenched. The regiment of Kaunitz was ordered to deploy, descend the height, and storm the village in front. During the execution of the manœuvre the enemy opened some guns, and a ball killed Captain Carleton, aide-de-camp to General Vyse and uncle of your cousin Dorchester. Whilst the Austrian infantry was advancing to the attack, which was gallantly made and afforded a brilliant spectacle, the 15th and the Cuirassiers of Zetchwitz moved against the right of the village; to dislodge some French cavalry formed in front of a wood to the right of Prêmont, and gain the rear of Prêmont so as to intercept the retreat of the infantry.

Too much time was lost in making the disposition; and when the French cavalry, who showed good countenance to the last, retired, there was an apprehension that the wood was ambuscaded: so that the operation was not accomplished before the French flying from Prêmont had crossed the plain which separated them from the next village, where they had a reserve strongly posted. They lost, however, some cannon and baggage. The other columns also succeeded, and the enemy were driven back from all their advanced works, leaving behind above thirty pieces of cannon and about fifteen hundred killed, wounded, and prisoners.

The night was a memorable one, and I have never forgotten the awful and meditative sight of thirteen villages in flames. The horizon seemed to be indeed on fire; and, inexperienced as I then was in the horrors of war, nature and education combined to make me feel unhappy at so much calamity.

The distress of the poor children, amidst the tears of their parents and their burning homes, the carnage roar of cannon confusion and violence, particularly moved my pity. I commiserated the sufferers on the field of battle; but, as they had reason to anticipate their lot I have ever thought them less objects of compassion than the inhabitants; who, in all the campaigns I have since witnessed, were made the prey of friends as well as foes.

Prémont having been carried by assault, I was told that the lives of the survivors, the persons of the women, and the property of every one, became the lawful spoil of the conqueror; but I found that this right was also extended to all villages and hamlets peaceably as well as forcibly occupied. Indeed, how could it be otherwise, since the example was given by battalions of barbarians in the Austrian service, privileged to plunder and serving on the engagement of maintaining themselves by rapine?

The next morning I went forward to observe the work of devastation, and before I reached the large

village in front of our post, which the enemy
had evacuated during the night, we met hundreds
of soldiers returning with booty of all descriptions.
Some, indeed, had covered themselves with the silk
gowns, caps, &c., of the matrons; others had put on
the Sunday garments of the peasants; and every one
seemed anxious to play a part in the masquerade.
Those who knew *old France* may best imagine to
themselves the ludicrous character of a scene which
metamorphosed Pandours and Croats into *les gens de
la campagne* of Picardy.

The houses had escaped conflagration at this hour,[*]
but the most virulent spirit of mischief had completed
the destruction of everything within them. The inhabitants had all fled or been murdered: but here and
there a cat was seen on the roofs, squatting in fearful
contemplation.

While I was roaming about, satisfying a melancholy
curiosity, a shot was fired at the extremity of the
village, and I then had an opportunity of seeing that
guilty employment made men very cowardly; for the
streets were filled with marauders pouring out of
every house, and flying as if their lives depended upon
the speed of their heels. Several, having quilted
petticoats on, fell; but their comrades were too
frightened to laugh. The alarm having subsided the
fugitives returned, and their pillage system continued
during the whole day: every man and woman carrying
away something as a relic if not as a prize.

I have given this picture of first impressions. Continual repetitions never effaced them, but I shall only
notice in future extraordinary enormities. Do you,

---

[*] They were fired during the night on which we retired.—R. W.

however, recollect that what I have described is the daily occurrence of war.

The Prince of Orange, who had been charged with the investment and siege of Landrécies, having opened his trenches, the army reunited near Câteau on the 20th. I was very glad to see a movement in progress: as I conceived that, whether we went to right or left, forwards or even backwards, we were sure of accomplishing the capture of Paris in time. But occasionally this confidence was staggered by the bold attitude of the enemy and the skilful points of defence he had chosen wherever we presented ourselves.

On the 21st Bellegarde's corps was attacked at Nouvion, but he repulsed the assailants: and about the same time we received accounts that the Hessians had maintained their ground near Denain.

On the 23rd the 15th had taken the advanced posts at Fontaine Antique with two squadrons of Leopold Hussars, to observe the enemy who were stated to have collected a large force in the Camp of Cæsar, near Cambray. We made a strong patrol in the evening, and found the enemy so numerous that General Otto who commanded on this flank of the army, sent to the Duke of York for reinforcements. Two squadrons of Zetchwitz Cuirassiers, an English heavy brigade, and the 11th Light Dragoons under General Mansell, were ordered to support us; and they arrived the same night.

On the ensuing morning, the 24th of April, we mounted and marched to attack and dislodge the enemy from Villiers en Couché. The 15th and the two squadrons of Leopold preceded ; and, as all supposed, were closely followed by the heavy cavalry though the

undulating character of the ground kept them from
view. This error continued until the 15th and
Leopold were within half cannon-shot of the enemy's
position: yet, although every head was constantly
turned round with anxious look, especially as we
approached the French line, we were unable to perceive a vestige of them.

At this period General Otto who had moved on
with the advance, received advice that the Emperor
who was on his road to Câteau, was intercepted by
the enemy in our front and must infallibly be taken
unless they were obliged to throw back their left.
Otto immediately halted our advancing line: and,
calling together the commanders told them the perilous
situation of his Sovereign, and the desperate position
in which the corps they commanded were placed by
the unexecuted orders given to General Mansell, and
the necessity of perishing sword in hand as assailants
rather than attempt an impracticable retreat, and by
it assure a dishonourable death. He then added,
"Gentlemen! remember, your numbers do not permit
prisoners."

This speech, repeated to officers and men, was
received with enthusiastic cheers: and several non-
commanding officers of the English and Austrian
squadrons dashed forward and grasped each others'
hands to pledge mutual support; while others mingled
their sabres and pointed to the sky, as if appealing
to Heaven as witness of their plighted faith.

The French cavalry appeared to be in one line, supported by a wood on the left and the village of Villiers
en Couché on the right. No infantry or cannon were
visible. On the word "March" being again given,

although we could ill spare the detachment a small body of Hussars was ordered to move on the wood, as Otto suspected that there was a corps of the enemy concealed in it: his suspicion was quickly verified by two squadrons of cavalry withdrawing from it so soon as the Austrian Hussars had fired with their skirmishers a few *feeling* shot.

The enemy immediately sent forward from their apparent main line a swarm of Chasseurs à Cheval, who fired at a few paces from us,* as we were too small a body to allow of being weakened by skirmishing parties of sufficient strength to protect our advance, and too well instructed and too resolved to answer the fire from our squadrons.

When we began to trot the French cavalry made a movement to right and left from the centre, dashed in a gallop towards wood and village, and at the same moment we saw in lieu of them, as if created by magic, an equal line of infantry with a considerable artillery in advance, which opened a furious cannonade with grape while the musketry poured its volleys. The surprise was great and the moment most critical; but happily the heads kept their direction and the heels were duly applied to the "charge," which order was hailed with repeated huzzas.

The guns were quickly taken; but we then found that the chaussée which ran through a hollow with steep banks lay between them and the infantry. There was, however, no hesitation: every horse was true to his master, and the chaussée was passed

---

* A Black Hussar fired at me as I was riding on the left flank of the whole, and the ball grazed along my helmet just above the ear, striking off the silver edging.—R. W.

in uninterrupted impetuous career.   It was then as we
gained the crest that the infantry poured its volley—
but in vain.   In vain also the first ranks *kneeled and
presented a steady line of bayonets.*   The impulse was
too rapid and the body attacking too solid for any
infantry power formed in line to oppose, although the
ranks were three deep.   Even the horses struck mortally at the brow of the bank had sufficient momentum
to plunge upon the enemy in their fall and assist the
destruction of his defence.

The French cavalry, having gained the flanks of
their infantry, endeavoured to take up a position in its
rear.   Our squadrons still on the gallop closed to fill
up the apertures which the French fire and bayonets
had occasioned, and proceeded to the attack on the
French cavalry, which, though it had suffered from the
fire of part of its own infantry, seemed resolved to
await the onset; but their discipline or their courage
failed, and our horses' heads drove on them just as
they were on the half turn to retire.

A dreadful massacre followed in a chase of four
miles.   Twelve hundred horsemen were cut down,
of which about five hundred were Black Hussars.
One farrier of the 15th alone killed twenty-two men.
The French were so panic-struck that they scarcely
made any resistance, notwithstanding that our numbers
were so few in comparison with the party engaged that
every individual pursuer found himself in the midst of
a flock of foes.

For a moment I was quite lost, having pursued a
well-mounted non-commanding officer and granted his
life after inflicting a *severe wound in his sword arm* as
he threw back his sabre at my face.   While I was in

doubt what course to take that I might save the
prisoner by consigning him to some special care,* he
assured me that a squadron to which he pointed was a
British squadron, and implored me to deliver him up
to it as he had no other chance of being preserved. I
began to move in the direction, when Quartermaster
Stewart, afterwards made an officer, rode up, and
without paying any attention to my words shot the
Frenchman through the head and then bade me follow
him " at speed."   It was high time I did it, for at the
same instant the horsemen whom I had conceived to
be friends proved to be enemies and in their turn
pursued us : but I was well mounted and soon rejoined
the troops.   I then learnt that Stewart† had watched
my course and guessed the perfidy of my captive.   We
did not stop our foaming horses until we received a
salute from the guns of Bouchain.   We then sounded
trumpet of recall, and the dispersed victors collected to
retire, but in very reduced numbers; particularly the
Austrians, as their horses had been unable to keep up
with us: indeed, at the original charge, notwithstanding the equal zeal of the riders, we certainly gained
three yards in ten.   This retreat was not less formidable than the attack ; for we had only perforated not
dislodged the enemy, who, incredible as it may be
thought, had positively *twelve thousand men* with fifty
pieces of cannon in his position when we attacked and

---

* The preservation of a prisoner was in fact a disobedience of orders ;
but I could not resist his appeals ; and I knew that if I left him he would
be overtaken by some of our men and killed.—R. W.

† I met this brave fellow afterwards in Devonshire, where he was
serving with a corps of Yeomanry.—R. W. A memorable presence of mind
in the man, and a noble watchfulness of guardian courage over a boy soldier
in his first trial of battle. The Providence must be confessed : it was the
first among many instances.—ED.

penetrated, and through the survivors of whom we had to make our way back by force or stealth. We did, however, retrace our steps in a good trot without interruption, although squadrons and battalions were formed on both flanks on the plain over which we returned. Some might have been astounded, but I believe most of the enemy thought we were a fresh succour from Bouchain; and indeed one officer came so near on that supposition that he paid with his life for his mistake.

When we arrived at the ravine we found it full of retreating French baggage-waggons, artillery, &c., and the village of Villiers en Couché, also choked with the fugitive columns; but we did not venture to stop and secure any part of the prize. With difficulty, on account of the steepness of the declivity, we descended the very bank up which we had mounted in a gallop. On the other side we found the guns we had captured and they finally remained in our possession, for the heavy brigade with failing hearts and humbled looks soon afterwards made their appearance and enabled us to recover the field of battle; the enemy's intact columns filing on Bouchain and Cambray.

General Otto was the first person who received us on our return, but he had already sent word to the Duke of York that we were lost by our excess of ardour in the pursuit after an achievement which rivalled any in military story. And reflecting on it at this distant date, I do think it the most daring in conception, the most resolute in execution, and the most unaccountable in its success, that ever fell under my notice: for the troops, particularly the infantry, were the best regiments in the French service, and not a man quitted his ranks until they were pierced by our charge.

Our Commander, Sir William Aylett, was pierced through and through the body with a bayonet at the charge, and every man and horse was killed or touched more or less severely by shot or steel.

General Otto, as I said, was the first to hail our return: and his expressions were accompanied by the most frantic gestures, especially when he heard that no prisoners were taken by the enemy. Throwing up his hussar cap in the air, he exclaimed, " C'est la fête de St. George! Huzza! huzza! huzza!" He was a Hungarian, and at this time was above seventy years of age. I heard him say he should die happy if he could once more hear the trumpet sound a charge against the Prussians. I thought him a savage; but nevertheless I was flattered when I afterwards found his moustaches pressed to my cheek, in the customary foreign manner of expressing cordiality and friendship.

We were sitting eating some refreshment on the field when General Mansell was announced; but Otto immediately turned his back upon him, and said to us, that " he never wished to see an Englishman who was not brave although the sight was so rare." This was a very unjust censure: for General Mansell's conduct was entirely owing to a misconception of the order brought to him by the aide-de-camp of General Otto when on march, in consequence of which he carried his brigade too far to our right. When he heard the guns and volley he then discovered the mistake, but too late to correct it. Otto, however, would not receive him or hear his explanations, but desired that they might be made to the Duke of York.

On the 25th I went on picket and was obliged to withdraw from my post five times during the night, as the enemy, who had reassembled in our front, endeavoured to surprise or cut us off. An old Hungarian Hussar had been sent with me to conduct my operations, and I owe to his lessons on that occasion a tact for that species of service in which I will venture to say no British officer at a later period ever excelled me.

At daybreak on the 26th I was attacked, but although obliged to retire no prisoners fell into the enemy's hands. At the same time the French army under General Chapuis, fifty thousand strong, having changed their plan of operations in consequence of the defeat at Villiers en Couché, filed through Cambray and made, under cover of a favouring fog, an assault on all the positions of the allied army : but the cavalry of the Allies rushing forward broke through their three lines, overthrew the whole, and took the commander-in-chief, sixty pieces of cannon, &c. Never was a victory obtained more rapidly or more completely, the troops being surprised who calculated on surprise.

In this action General Mansell fell, being determined on death. His command had been taken from him, but restored on the morning of the 26th at the entreaties of General Ralph Dundas who had been appointed to supersede him. The Duke of York in passing his line before the charge had also said, "Gentlemen, you must repair the disgrace of the 24th." Mansell had, however, before resolved on paying with his life for a mistake which subjected his character to reproof and ineffaceable injury. As the brigade was advancing

he ordered his son and brigade-major to different points
of the line; and, commanding his orderly dragoon not
to follow him, he darted on the enemy and met an
inevitable death. His body was found after the action,
and the Duke of York and others attended the inter-
ment. As far as I could judge from the countenances
of these personages, they seemed to feel that a brave
man had been untowardly sacrificed.

The next day the Duke of York invited me to dine
with him, presented me to the Austrian general, &c.,
and said many generous things. On the third day,
going over the field, we saw many wounded who had
neither eaten nor drunk nor had their wounds
dressed since the action.

On the 30th Landrécies surrendered, but the joy was
damped by news of the defeat of Clairfait at Mouscron,
where he had assembled some Austrians and Hanoverians to attempt the relief of Menin.

As the communication between Tournay and Courtray was menaced the allied army was obliged to
move to support Clairfait, and we marched on the
night of the 31st in one of the darkest and severest
storms I ever remember. It caused the greatest confusion, since deep ditches flanked the roads when they
were not traversing forests; and horsemen and guns,
baggage-waggons, &c., were constantly plunging in the
water. The lightning was so vivid that objects during
the flash could be perceived as in broad day; while the
eye was so affected by the glare that man and beast
staggered as if struck with blindness. On arrival at
Tournay we learnt that Courtray and Menin had both
been taken, but that general Hammerslein had cut
his way through the enemy with several battalions of

Hanoverians, and four companies of loyal emigrants—
for whose sake this bold enterprise was indeed undertaken, since all emigrants found in arms were immediately shot by the Republicans. The loss had been
very severe but the action extorted the enemy's
admiration.

The allied army took post in front of Tournay, and
we were sent forward with the Hussars and remaining
light cavalry to the heights above Baisieux, &c. Our
outpost duty was severe from continued skirmishing
in the morning which occasionally engaged several
thousand men, and picket-service on which from the
scarcity of subalterns I was employed four nights out
of five. But then we had our agrémens : for by preserving good discipline in our camp the peasant girls
from far and near flocked daily into it, bringing in
baskets of butter, cream, fruit, eggs, flowers, &c. : and
to this time I never saw so much youth, beauty, and
fascination combined in any society.

An hour before daybreak we were always on horseback : but so soon as it was seen that we had dismounted, there being no attack, the field was covered
with Atalantas rushing to the goal where profit first
invited them, but where more generous sentiments
soon were kindled and glowed not merely to passion
but to the most ardent affections. In a climate like
that of England where the sun's ardour is so faint, this
picture may appear too highly coloured : but the description is one of memory not of imagination. Behind us
also lay a town full of every luxury ; and every evening
there was horse-racing in the grand camp, at which all
the princes, generals, &c., regularly assisted.

While we were keeping, night after night, our watch

with our horses in hand, or patrolling from post to
post that no enemy might glide between, the officers
of the line were there enjoying uninterrupted repose or
carousing without any anxiety.   But I preferred the
animation of our life, arduous as its continuance was
made, and I would not have exchanged my bivouac
for the Duke of York's quarters.

At that time it was the fashion to drink as drunk-
ards daily, and the drink was strong port wine instead
of the pure vintage of France.   The vice, however,
did not prevail so much among the light troops,
though far too much, and I never was once inebriated
during the whole campaign.   I had the good fortune to have an example of sobriety set by Colonel
Churchill and several other officers.   What shocked
me most was to see courts-martial adjudging men to
be punished for an offence of which the members themselves had often been guilty at the same time, and
from which they had frequently not recovered when
passing sentence.   I hope the day will come*—and it
seems to be advancing—when such a statement will
be deemed the assertion of an impossibility, or, in
plain English, an outrage against truth and the
honour of the army.

On the morning of the 10th (May) the enemy,
thirty thousand strong, attacked us and made an
impression on the left of our advanced line.   But the
Kaunitz regiment, getting up to the retiring troops
before they were driven out of an extensive wood,
repelled the assailants.   A considerable effort was then
made against our centre, and we were sent down with
sixteen squadrons of British and two of Austrian Hus-

* It is almost come : October 14, 1824.—R.W.

sars, to attack the enemy in flank as he attempted to cross the plain with the design of storming our position. So soon as he perceived our intention he formed a corps into squares and opened upon us a severe fire of shot and shells: he persisted in an advance, and as there seemed to be only level ground between us, a charge was ordered and the order obeyed; but before we could reach the enemy who had partly deployed, to our great surprise, as we advanced, we found ourselves in a range of rape-fields; and in a few seconds two-thirds of the horses were prostrate under a volley of musketry and grape which if well directed must have annihilated the whole. At this instant fortunately the Hungarian Grenadiers, for whose simultaneous operation we ought to have waited, were seen ascending the heights to storm the squares. This obliged the enemy to withdraw and take up a new position nearer his reserves and enclosed country, or a few men detached from the ranks would have put to death those who had escaped the fire.

I was mounted on my English mare who extricated herself by extraordinary activity; but she carried me to the enemy, and I should infallibly have been taken if a soldier had not made a blow at her head with the butt-end of his musket: this frightened her so much that she turned like a hare and ran obliquely along the line until I could find a clear piece of ground, when I succeeded in giving her a new direction. I suppose upwards of a hundred shots were fired at us, of which only one struck her in the neck.

As soon as the squadrons could be reassembled another charge was ordered on the retiring squares; it failed; a third also was repulsed, although some

of the angles were pierced.   At length, the squares
having nearly passed the plain in retreat, all hope of
making any impression was abandoned.   The enemy
observed this, and imprudently changed their formation into columns of march without taking any precaution to line the extreme of the wood into which they
were entering.   This negligence afforded the opportunity for a sudden attack which succeeded.   Fifteen
pieces of cannon were taken and several hundred men
massacred, for quarter was implored in vain.   A more
cold-blooded butchery was never perpetrated, since the
execution lasted near half an hour.   During this transaction five French gendarmes who had been on a
patrol, finding themselves cut off and seeing the fate
of their comrades, boldly determined to cut their way
through or die in the attempt, and at all events
make their attempt memorable.   A shout from behind announced that they had already pierced through
to the Blues, and I saw them keeping on a steady
course, pursued by hundreds but dealing death to
all who approached.   The boldest withdrew as they
thundered down towards them ; and some felt so much
admiration for their desperate courage as to wish that
they might escape, and therefore would not oppose
their progress; but just as they were gaining the
wood one fell and was shot immediately.   Three
others almost instantly dropped quite colandered with
balls ; and the fifth, being dismounted by his horse receiving a leg wound, stood like Mars, bidding defiance
to the crowds which assailed him and refusing to yield
his sword.   At length a trumpeter took deliberate
aim ; and the hero sank to the earth with a wave of
his sword-hand as if he were exulting in his doom.

To the honour of the French of those days, I must say
I never witnessed more devoted courage than they
showed generally; and "Vive la République!" seemed
to be the consolation of every misfortune. Most of
the soldiers who were killed as described shouted during the slaughter, "Vive la République!" Even when
the sword was about to fall on their heads I have
heard them continually make that exclamation, which
in most instances more envenomed their enemies.

Such is man! or rather, such is mercenary man!
that a Republic founded on the principles of liberty
and equality excited the individual passions of the
rest of mankind against it, as if it had been an establishment incompatible with their happiness and one
which placed its members without the pale of humanity.
I know that at that time Robespierre and his associates
had outraged humanity by their cruelties, and that
afterwards a decree to give no quarter had in some measure justified severity; (although it is due to the French
soldiers to state that they expressed the greatest indignation when it was promulgated): but I am sure that
neither the crimes of the Revolutionary Tribunal nor
any of their sanguinary edicts were the real sins
which confederated the governments of Europe against
France, though they enabled them to create that exas-
peration in the minds of their people which prevailed
generally. Their hatred and machinations were
directed against that cry of liberty, which honest and
amiable and humane men in the first instance raised
to check the tyrannising abuse of power, and to provide security of law for person and property. It is
my conviction that the same atrocities which were
perpetrated in France under the provocation of foreign

powers and by the secret influence of the Emigrant
Councils at Coblentz would have passed in those days
unpunished and even without remonstrance, had they
been committed by kings in possession of arbitrary
authority.   It is universally known that Louis XVIII.
and the French princes had a secret and most authoritative influence over many of the revolutionary chiefs
in France; and it was stated in my presence, and not
denied, at a trial before one of the tribunals of
Paris after the Restoration, that Louis XVIII. pen-
sioned the sister of Robespierre.   The assertion was
made by one of the counsel, who offered proof.

It was the object of all the then existing governments in Europe—even our own—to keep France in
the shackles of slavery and " wooden shoes," from the
fear of her reforms becoming the desiderata of all
nations, and of her resources and prosperity being de-
veloped by them.   It was the erroneous and illiberal
principle of the statesmen of that day that the improving condition and increasing wealth of one country
must be accompanied by the corresponding impoverish-
ment of its neighbours.   It is useless to dilate upon
the motives of the crowned heads.   They have always
held in abhorrence the advocates of popular rights, and
placed every impediment in their power in the way of
progressive freedom.   At the same time it would be
unjust to attach to their race exclusively these antipa-
thies to free institutions and their champions.   They
are but the creatures of the system in which they have
been educated, and their views have been formed by
the regulators of their instruction generally : these are
almost without exception men taken from a class who
consider the influence and property of their body to

be placed in jeopardy when monarchy is not revered as an institution of divine right, and when encroachments are making on its absolute and irresponsible jurisdiction.

The King of France was an amiable man, but weak and false; the Queen a beautiful woman accustomed to the homage of mankind from her first appearance in the court, but she had been reared in the doctrine that the interests of courts alone constitute the welfare of nations. Abuses had driven the French people to the adoption of measures which circumscribed the pretensions of the Throne, and set up the public happiness as the just end of government. Every engine was assiduously employed to oppose and prevent the tranquil settlement of the legislative struggle, and the Court party succeeded but too well in infuriating the passions of the multitude.

The detected treachery of the King (the Queen never played a deceptive part) and the invasion of the French territory kindled a vindictive rage that made humanity shudder; and Robespierre, who had proposed in a speech on record to abolish the punishment of death altogether, became the director of the bloody revels which followed.

Perhaps it may be said that I am framing a charge against myself for engaging in a service which aimed at the re-establishment of an unlimited monarchy, for though so young I was fully master of the subject in all its bearings: but my sense of the injustice of reimposing such a government on France was not so strong as to control my martial inclinations; and it may also be considered that until I came into contact with the French themselves I did not and could not know their

devotion to the cause they had espoused, and the
genuine patriotism by which they were animated.

To return, however, from this digression. After a
pursuit of about a league, in which some baggage was
taken but in which a part of our cavalry suffered by
too eager an advance in a close country, the army
returned to its position, and we regained our encampment where we found our fair friends collected to welcome the survivors and weep over the fallen. I was
however commanded off on picket the same night
and for the first time marched like a conscript, or, as a
Frenchman had that same day described himself to
me, a "volontaire forcé."

The enemy had the same day attacked the Hanoverian corps which was posted on the right of the Duke's
army, and had also been repulsed; but on the Sunday
following, instead of going to church, they made a
vigorous attack on General Clairfait who had crossed
the river Deule, and were at first unsuccessful; but
the Austrians not being able to take possession of
Courtray where the enemy had rallied, Clairfait
was in his turn obliged to retire and was pursued to
Thielt, suffering very considerably. This advantage
was, however, counterbalanced on the 14th by their
defeat in an action with General Kaunitz posted near
Mons, who cut through several thousand men and
some pieces of cannon.

Mons being thus secured, the Austrian army, commanded by the Emperor and the Archduke Charles,
marched to unite itself with the Duke of York's army,
that an offensive movement might be made which with
a co-operation of General Clairfait should throw the
enemy back upon their own frontier line of defence.

The junction having been effected at Orchies, the army marched in five columns. The 15th marched in the Duke's column, composed of six squadrons British (15th and 7th Light Dragoons), four of Hussars, seven battalions British, five Austrian, and two of Hessians; while the two columns on our left proceeded to force the passages of the Marque. This they did eventually, but not in time to do any good. As they were moreover too much fatigued when they had succeeded to proceed further, we moved on through Templeuve, then a large rich and happy village, to Lannoy where the enemy were posted. They evacuated it, however, after a cannonade which on their part seemed to be intended as a signal communication rather than as a resisting fire; though one of the shots killed a very brave officer of our artillery of the name of Wright, who had shown me great attention and whose loss was generally much regretted.

From Lannoy, after leaving the two Hessian battalions there, we advanced to Roubaix where the enemy were strongly posted. The action was very obstinate though short, as they found themselves likely to be turned and therefore retired. After taking Roubaix there was some doubt whether the Duke's column should advance further, as no advice had then been received of the columns ordered to force the Marque or of the two columns on our left. One of these was commanded by General Burke, who, as it appeared afterwards, instead of taking Mourons had found it prudent from the very superior force opposed to him to regain his original position at Tourcoing; the other was commanded by the brave Otto who had forced his way through Lens and Waterloo to Tourcoing.

The Emperor, however, being apprehensive that General Clairfait relying upon our advance to Mouveaux might be compromised by a corresponding movement when we were not at the presumed station, expressed so earnestly his desire that this point should be gained that the column proceeded.

The flank battalion of Guards, supported by the battalion of the 1st regiment of Guards, led the way through a very close country. On arriving in front of Mouveaux it was found strongly entrenched and palisaded. About fifteen hundred men defended the place with several pieces of cannon. The British guns having opened a practicable entrance, the Guards stormed while the cavalry were ordered to proceed at a gallop round the work and get in the rear and cut off the flying enemy. When we moved the Guards had not got into the place. The enemy were still firing their cannon charged with grape down the road lined with an avenue of trees, and had set on fire a house on the roadside. By the scorching flames of this we were obliged to pass, as a deep ditch and fences rendered it impossible for us to break off the road till we got close to the walls. The rattling of the shot through the trees, the falling branches, the burning house, the huzzas of the infantry, and shouts of " *Go it, Young Eyes!*" (the name by which the Guards always designated the 15th, who in turn called them " Old Eyes"), and the roar and smoke of the guns, with all the confusion of an assault, was a sublime spectacle for me and excited all to the highest degree of animation. The French kept their ground manfully until they saw us in spite of their fire wheeling round the very edge of their entrenchments, when they deserted them and fled. We took three guns and a number of prisoners on the other side of the town, but the greater part of the garrison escaped by favour of the wooded environs and approaching night.

The infantry on entering the town had set it on fire, and the church catching the flames a column of light gave fatal intelligence to the distant enemy of our success and position. Some of the French soldiers in the place were bayoneted, and the usual licence of war could not be restrained in the village ; but several women, concealing themselves at the first rush and subsequently, as night darkened, escaping out, found refuge and protection in our posts.

After we had given up the pursuit and had fallen back on Mouveaux, we did what we could to discover the wounded among the bodies scattered around. Having accomplished this duty as well as we could, the officers—holding their horses' reins in their hands —as well as the men, sat down on the ground until it came to their turn to remount and patrol : this was done very anxiously and carefully in every direction, for every one had a misgiving from a variety of incidents and observations.

While we were so sitting an artillery waggon came towards us, and we directed the drivers to go off more to our left that we might not have to move. In taking that new direction we saw the wheels lifted as they passed within six yards. I got up to examine the cause of the impediment in the way of the gun, and found it to be the body of a French soldier—one of the little fellows who wear casques, and whom we used to call " Crapauds." Of course I conceived that it was a corpse, and was going back to my post when

I thought I would look again to observe what wound
had caused his death.   On leaning down I heard a
stifled respiration.   I immediately addressed the poor
wretch in French, and in the kindest tones that I
could command for I was not then much of a French
scholar.   He was at first quite silent, but on my calling
for some one to aid me in helping him he spoke and
asked for mercy.   His confidence was soon restored
by our attentions, when he told us that he had only
received a wound in the leg which prevented him
from getting off with his comrades; that hearing us
coming back as he was creeping on he had lain down
in the grass, and to his terror had seen the gun
taking its direction over him; but the fear of being
put to death if he discovered himself had induced him
to prefer the chance of escape from the gun, which,
however, had gone over his thighs and broken one in
two places.   We ministered all the relief in our power,
and our surgeon, after examination of the fracture
and setting it as well as circumstances permitted, did
not despair of his life being saved without amputation
—a hope cruelly disappointed next day.

While we were uneasy from our ignorance of what
had occurred at other points, the Duke of York was
rendered no less uncomfortable by his knowledge of
what had passed; but, as the best disposition for the
night he directed General Abercromby to remain
with the Guards and 15th at Mouveaux.   Four Austrian battalions were ordered to cover Roubaix, and
the "little brigade" composed of the 14th, 52nd, and
37th, under General Fox, was marched to secure the
left by taking post in the road between Lille and
Roubaix; while our right was put in communication

with the posts of General Otto, who had possessed himself of Tourcoing and Waterloo, as before stated.

Morning had scarcely streaked the sky when a rattling of musketry was heard on our right, and we thought at first that it was the blowing up of some musketry ammunition-waggons; but we soon perceived, by its continuance and the firing of cannon and small arms which immediately followed in all directions, that we were environed and attacked by the French army. Some prisoners made by our patrols confirmed this very unsatisfactory suspicion, and informed us that on seeing Mouveaux church in flames orders had been given by General Pichegru for the immediate march of thirty thousand men, who had been in movement all night, to intercept our communications. Thus this unjustifiable conflagration, acting as a telegraph, called down upon us a prompt chastisement.

Tourcoing was the first point attacked. Two battalions of Austrians were sent by the Duke of York to make a diversion in its favour; but unfortunately they pushed on to Tourcoing instead of combining with their attack the protection of our right. The enemy poured in his tirailleurs through the opening, which they immediately discovered for they were as sharpsighted as ferrets and as active as squirrels. The only battalion of reserve was thrown forward to check them but it was quickly driven out of its position. While a corps which had forced its way through General Otto's post at Waterloo attacked the rear of our columns, the main body of the enemy, twenty-five thousand strong, moved upon us at Mouveaux past Lille. At the same time and almost before we could commence our retreat, Roubaix was taken from the

four battalions of Austrians; and the Hessians after a
very gallant defence had been driven out of Lannoy.
Of the " little brigade " under General Fox, which
had been posted to assist in covering Roubaix and our
left, we knew nothing but by a tremendous firing of
great guns and small arms in the direction of its
station, every discharge of which seemed sufficient to
sweep this, even then in fame immortal, band of heroes
from the face of the earth.

To add to our embarrassments and anxieties, it
was reported, as we proceeded towards Roubaix—our
only line of retreat—that the Duke of York was cut
off; which was really the case. With great difficulty,
and attended only by a few dragoons, he was fortunate
enough to reach General Otto's column.

I had the command of the rearguard, which was
constantly under fire from behind and from both
flanks after we quitted Mouveaux and moved on the
Roubaix road; but Colonel Blunt, afterwards Sir
Charles, very generously kept with me and gave me
most useful advice and aid. By steady march and
charging occasionally back we left our pursuers behind and prevented a rush upon us, which would have
been fatal not only to the rearguard but to the column
obliged by flanking ditches to keep the road. Bag-
gage-carts, and carts with the wounded enemy taken
the night before, were of course soon abandoned and
formed useful barricades; but I wish I could pass
over the disgusting and sorrowful scene which the
slaughter of the prisoners and even of the wounded
amongst them exhibited. Nothing could exceed the
ferocity which thus revenged itself on the helpless,

and of all the events of the day the most horrible was the sight of this ungenerous execution.

The supplications of the victims and the fatal shots which answered their prayers rang for many days in my ears. It was a butchery, though not so extensive as that which occurred on the 10th of May yet still more piteous; for it was if possible more cold-blooded.

As we approached the entrance of Roubaix we heard firing in the village, and several abandoned ammunition-waggons of the Guards assured us that the disorder of retreat had commenced.

Roubaix had a long street at the end of which one road ran on continuing in a straight line; another road *pavé* turned immediately to the right at the termination of the main street. Hedges lined each side of the straight road; ditches very deep—one, indeed, a rivulet—flanked the other. Before the head of the retiring column could gain the village the enemy had made a lodgment, but were driven out. Part took post behind the hedges which lined the straight road and commanded the town into and up the pavé road; and part, on retiring along the straight road, faced about at a little distance to fire into the street and on the troops sallying out to gain the pavé road. Here also they stationed a piece of cannon which was actively discharged. The infantry, however, and cannon—fifty-six pieces—with the greater part of the tumbrils, &c., had cleared the village when the cavalry entered; but there was then a very long halt in the street, and from the volleys of musketry heard just out of the village on the pavé road the cause of the delay was evident. While the cavalry was so pent up, the enemy from their elevation on the straight road kept firing their cannon and small arms into the village.

The enemy's advance coming from Mouveaux, eager to cut me off with the rearguard before I got into Roubaix, had pressed me so sharply that I had been obliged to close upon the main body, and on reaching the houses dismount some men to act as tirailleurs and check their progress, which experiment succeeded. I was therefore in the street itself when the first cannon-ball flew through it with a dreadful whirr. There was no escape apparent from those which would follow. The second struck off the heads of two of the Austrian hussars.* The Austrians could endure the coop no longer, but, dismounting, broke through the houses on the right, and leading their horses scrambled through the gardens, ditches, fences, &c.; some of them being killed by the sharpshooters already lodged in them, others succeeding in getting through all difficulties and dangers, and many being obliged to return into the street. The fifth or sixth shot rendered the stay of the cavalry no longer practicable. The cry of " Charge to the right ! " ran down the column, and in the same moment we were all at full speed. The enemy redoubled his efforts, and struck at us with his bayonets fixed at the end of his muskets as we wheeled round the dreaded and dreadful corner, already almost choked with the fallen horses and men which had perished in the attempt to pass. My little mare received here a bayonet-wound in the croup and a musket-ball through the crest of her neck. Two balls

* The Barco Hussars.—R. W.

lodged in my cloak-case behind the saddle, and another carried away part of my sash. Our surgeon and his horse were killed close at my side, and above a dozen of my detachment fell at that spot under the enemy. We still urged on, *ventre à terre*, pursued by bullets. I had got about two hundred horses' lengths distance from the town when, before the least notice could be given, the whole column of cavalry was arrested in its career, and at the same moment of course recoiled several yards. The confusion, the conflict for preservation, the destruction which ensued, baffles all description. Three-fourths of the horses, at one and the same moment were thrown down with their riders under them or entangled by the bodies of others. The battling of the horses to recover themselves, the exclamations of all sorts which resounded through the air, accompanied by the volleys of the triumphing enemy, presented a picture "*d'enfer*" which, as one of the French then firing upon us and afterwards taken told me, even made his own and his comrades' hair stand on end ; and, according to him, we were indebted to the magnitude of our distress for a moment or two's relaxation of the fire. I was up and down several times ; but my dear little mare, as white as a sheet with foam where not discoloured by her blood, and *snorting* as if she raged in spirit, always regained her feet, and kept under them whatever struggled to rise and dislodge her. At length I saw an opening to the right, and at the other side of the ditch some of the Guards endeavouring to form. I immediately directed my mare to the part of the bank which I thought most favourable, and commending myself to my fortunes applied the spur that was to excite the needed energy.

My noble *Snorter*—for so I called her from that moment—bounded over like a deer and brought me to
my friends.   The first person I saw was Major Pocklington, dismounted.   I procured him a horse that
was running loose without saddle, on which after some
persuasion he mounted; for he was so bad a horseman that whenever he took the least leap the men
used to cry, "Two to one!" "Three to one!" and
so on—"the Major is off!" and sure enough, after
several bounds and rebounds he always fell.   It was
not till I got over the ditch that I saw the cause of
our calamity.   Fifty-six pieces of cannon, with their
tumbrils, &c., stood immoveable in the road; the
drivers having cut away the traces and escaped with
the horses when they found the enemy's fire surrounding them.   Such was the consequence of sending out as
drivers the refuse of our gaols—for that was the practice at that day.   It was there also that I saw a soldier's
wife take a baby from her breast and giving it a kiss
fling it into the stream or ditch, when she frantically
rushed forward, and before she had got ten yards was
rent in pieces by a discharge of grape that entered
her back, sounding like a sack of coals being emptied.

More fortunate was pretty Sally, the pride of the
British fair; for when I was assisting in rallying the
fugitives that we might at least show some countenance
and thus obtain the only chance of safety, she came
up to me and gallantly promised to give me one of her
best kisses for my exertions.   She showed me how
three shot had already perforated her petticoats.   I
soon afterwards procured her a seat upon the limber
of a gun, for which she was always most grateful.   In
my zeal, however, to form something like a rearguard,

I very nearly had a serious quarrel; for I addressed myself in a strong German term of reproof to an Austrian officer passing me at full speed, mistaking him for a private galloping away from the post of duty and danger. Our swords clashed, when an old Austrian sergeant who had been several times on outpost service with me passed his sword between ours and explained to the officer that I did not understand German enough to know the force of certain expressions; saying that I was far from being likely to offend intentionally, as I was "a very good-natured boy." The officer then addressed me in French and we came to an immediate good understanding; he explaining to me that it was not a proper place to form the cavalry; that the infantry should cover the retreat through the enclosed grounds; and that he was going to endeavour to re-assemble the Hussars on the other side where there was offered more open ground.

I felt properly humbled for having been so ignorant and accompanied him to the spot where the surviving cavalry reunited and formed into squadrons: the far greater part of them were in a wounded state, and the escapes had been remarkable. One man had received twelve shots in his cloak, and the saddle-bags of many were riddled with bullets numbers of which were found lodged in them.

The enemy kept moving on the higher land that commanded the road, and with their cannon played on our retiring troops no longer moving in any order. A vigorous charge of cavalry would have annihilated all the remains.

General Abercromby, who came up to us and praised the steadiness with which we were now moving, desired me to try to " get but one company formed to assist us ;" but it was impossible, and he was obliged to move on in despair and leave us to do the best we could for the protection of the flank of the line of retreat.

We had hoped to have fallen in with the " little brigade," but it had been obliged to retire after a very severe action and, as the enemy had driven the Hessians out of Lannoy, to proceed to Lens where it had received protection from General Otto's column.

The enemy's occupation of Lannoy greatly added to our peril, and it would not have been possible to save any part of our column if it had not been for the extreme vigour with which General Otto attacked the enemy to make a diversion in our favour. His guns kept up the sharpest cannonade for their number I have almost ever heard, and the spirit of the attack revived the drooping courage of our men almost exhausted by heat, dust, fatigue, and thirst. The enemy, however, kept Lannoy and also maintained a very heavy artillery fire against our column as we rounded the town. At length we reached Templeuve where fresh troops were stationed, and reposed in safety. The Duke of York, who had found refuge with General Otto, joined us soon afterwards and was very cordially received.

I have dwelt much on the details of this affair, as it was one of extraordinary and happily rare occurrence. Never could a column be more completely surrounded, and by five times its numbers—never did a body of men so circumstanced escape with such comparatively small loss, exclusive of that of the artillery which all fell into the enemy's hands.

The Austrians said that the British were surprised

and the Emperor was obliged to give a denial to that imputation in the general orders—a most just denial, for the charge had not the slightest foundation in fact. We owed our misfortunes, first, to the telegraphic communication made by the flames of the church at Mouveaux; and, secondly, to our position being quite *en l'air* from the columns on the right and left not having taken their assigned posts. We owed our preservation to the want of energy on the part of the enemy: and I have my suspicions that General Pichegru did not even then wish our destruction; though being under the surveillance of the Commissioners of the Convention, he could not help profiting in some measure by the opportunities the Allies afforded for their own disasters.

From Templeuve we marched to re-establish ourselves in our original posts; discomfited but not dismayed.

The arrival of the Austrian army restored confidence completely, and made us all eager to resume the offensive.

It was on the morning of the 22nd of May, as day dawned, that the first popping shots were heard at the outposts in front of Templeuve. The discharge of a piece of artillery from the Austrian works thrown up round the village assured us that the attack was serious. The possession of Templeuve at first seemed to be the enemy's object, and in this he succeeded after an obstinate defence: but between eight and nine o'clock the firing commenced on the right of Tournay, and it was manifest that the enemy proposed to pass the Scheldt and by investing Tournay cut off our communications.

The allied army was about eighty thousand strong; the French one hundred and ten thousand.

The battle raged unremittingly, except during one shower of rain, for twelve hours, and was undeniably the greatest musketry battle of the whole war; though the artillery fire, however heavy and destructive, was in no proportion to that of many others.

The Austrians had resolutely defended themselves till four o'clock in the afternoon, but became then much exhausted. As Templeuve, after having been taken and retaken five times and cruelly sacked, remained in the possession of the Austrian grenadiers and all firing had ceased in front of our posts, the Duke of York detached from his army—the left—seven Austrian battalions, and the "little brigade" which had been so severely handled on the 18th of May, but which had acquired great distinction with the enemy for the valour which it had displayed.

Granby Calcraft with myself had been sent to report to the Duke what was passing on one side, and the Duke at the desire of the Emperor ordered us to go to the Archduke Charles and state that the reinforcements were marching down to his succour.

It was a very interesting and inspiriting sight to witness the wounded Austrians, many of them Hungarian grenadiers, while they were being removed from the field of battle in carts to the hospital at Tournay singing the national war song. The musketry was pouring furiously and the cannonade was heavy. The Austrian front lines were lying on the ground, having been ordered to do so that they might be less exposed. The reinforcement having arrived, the " little brigade," undaunted by its loss on the 18th, proceeded immediately to the attack of the village of Pontachin where the enemy was strongly posted. Nothing could exceed the pride of that moment for an Englishman. The Austrians it is true were but obeying orders after the long, exhausting, and sanguinary combat when they crouched to conceal their lines ; but it was nevertheless a gallant sight—and the Austrians themselves by their cheers acknowledged it—to view this handful of brave men step through them into the rain of fire that poured as they appeared, and with .inflexible intrepidity press to the charge. The enemy panic-struck fled and column tumbling back upon column the retreat became general, but it was ten at night before the last cannon was discharged.

Pichegru and his Staff were dining at the moment the "little brigade" made its attack. The increased firing engaged attention, according to the evidence of an Austrian taken prisoner and afterwards retaken and who was under examination at the moment before the General. An officer arriving at full speed announced that an assault of the Austrians was being repulsed. In a minute or two afterwards an estafette cried out, "Les Anglais!" "Les habits rouges!" The scramble was universal and some of the officers got out of the window in order to gain their horses sooner. The dinner was found by "les Anglais" and was a good prize, but the plate also left was a more valuable one. Seven pieces of cannon and several hundred prisoners were taken, and the total loss of the enemy was admitted by themselves to be fourteen thousand ; the Allies did not lose less than eight thousand.

The next morning I rode over the field of battle, beginning at Templeuve which had been taken and

retaken five times during the day as already stated,
and which presented a tragic spectacle, all the horrors
of assault having been perpetrated.   One very old
man with silver locks was seated at the door of a house
weeping bitterly.   On my asking the particular nature
of his calamity, he pointed to the upper apartment.
There we saw the body of a beautiful girl of about
sixteen who had too evidently died under violence,
and an infant sister and brother bayoneted by her
side, as if they had been struck in the act of giving
her help.   About three miles on the right we witnessed
another terrible spectacle, but of a different character.
A column of eighteen hundred French had endeavoured to force its way through some orchards.   When
the mass was wedged in one of them which had a very
small outlet, the Austrians had opened a battery of
twelve guns—12-pounders—upon it, and with such
remarkable razing precision and effect that I myself
counted two hundred and eighty headless bodies.
The trees and branches were all indented or covered
with the smashed bones and brains.   Such a beheading
carnage was perhaps never paralleled.

The Emperor was so pleased with the intrepid gallantry of the British " little brigade " which had returned to the charge with colours flying and music
playing, that he gave an order for the Austrian battalions always to move to the attack in the same
manner ; but this order was not one of long duration.

I have often thought that this " little brigade "
afforded the most exemplary proof of national courage ;
for the greater part of the men were recruits from the
gaols, sent out in such a state of equipment as to excite
shame and derision.   Even the recruits sent to the

Light Dragoons came out in many instances with un-dress jackets and without boots, those who sent them presuming that they might be fitted out from the dead men's kits, as if the effects of the slain were regularly collected and stored.

At the same time that these men and the British soldiers in general were maintaining with such devoted fortitude the glory of England, their camps daily pre-sented the most disgusting and painful scenes of punishments. The halberds were regularly erected along the lines every morning; and the shrieks of the sufferers made a pandemonium, from which the foreigner fled with terror and with astonishment at the severity of our military code.

Drunkenness was the vice of officers and men, but the men paid the penalty; and the officers who sat in judgment in the morning were too often scarcely sober from the past night's debauch.

The highest in rank and station were often on the evening parade or on the race-ground, for races were established in the camp, in a state of flagrant inebriety; and of course, "like master like man" held good in all the gradations of rank, though with many most creditable exceptions.

The light cavalry, being kept at the outposts to watch over the safety of all, were not allowed these bacchanalian orgies; and the 15th in Colonel Churchill had happily a commander who not only discounte-nanced drinking by his practice, but who never per-mitted the cat-o'-nine-tails for mere venial offences to degrade one of his companions—for so he always esteemed those whose valour guarded his reputation. These facts will perhaps be disbelieved when hereafter

they come before the public eye, as they may do ; and
it is desirable that they should be considered as errors
of the historian.   It will be a consummation of one of
my most anxious wishes, grounded upon my memory
of these early scenes of abuse of power and often expressed in publications and in Parliament, when the
system of punishment, such as I have described it,*
shall be referred to only as a traditional exaggeration.

———————————

[With this expression of his eager hope for the
soldiers, whom, from the first hour of his entrance into
the army he regarded as companions, friends, and
fellows in the service of his king and country, Sir
Robert Wilson closes this brief commencement of a
regular autobiography.   How faithfully and well he
pleaded the cause of humanity and policy for the
gallant men who won England's battles and supported
her renown will appear hereafter.

He has left no account of his reason for so soon
abandoning a design deliberately formed; but the
fact that he did abandon it is much to be lamented.
If it had been carried out into full execution it would
no doubt have been the duty of his editor to present
to the public a far more valuable work than he can
promise now : an authentic narrative by a perfectly
competent witness of some of the most important
military and political events, and of the most ener-
getic action on the grandest stage and scale in the
drama of the world's history.   In the course of such a
work Sir Robert Wilson would have carefully reviewed the journals written currently, while the events
were passing, for the pleasure and information of his

* See " Inquiry " published in 1804.—Ed.

family; they would have recalled to his singularly accurate and retentive memory many circumstances which diplomatic prudence and the sense of official responsibility compelled him to pass by in silence then, but which might now be revealed to the public advantage. At the same time he would have brought to bear upon the record the light of a high intelligence fully matured by experience: and he would have corrected, disentangled, arranged, and combined the voluminous materials at his command as no other man could do.

The memoir addressed to his children brings down the history of the campaign of 1794 only to the action of the 22nd of May, when the 15th again occupied its position in front of Tournay; but in the summary of Sir Robert Wilson's military career, published in the introduction to his posthumous work "The French Invasion of Russia in 1812," it is stated that he was " present in all the battles, combats, and operations in the campaigns of Flanders and Holland, the 15th being always engaged." A very short statement of these operations is extracted from the "History of the Regiment," published by authority in 1847.

On the 5th of July Sir Robert Wilson was with his corps when " they engaged a column of the enemy moving along the road from Malines to Duffel, and in conjunction with the 8th and 16th Light Dragoons drove them back with great loss.

" On the 22nd of July the army was again in retreat; a succession of retrograde movements brought it to the vicinity of Bois-le-Duc, and while at this station a squadron of the 15th and some dragoons of Hesse Darmstadt were directed to patrol towards Boxtel, on the Dommel. The French army, under

General Pichegru, was advancing in three columns ; but the patrol, nevertheless, penetrated by by-routes to the head-quarters, found the general's cooks preparing dinner against his arrival, made prisoners an aide-de-camp of General Vandamme's and two gendarmes, mounted them on the general's horses, and, notwithstanding that a regiment of red hussars and a regiment of dragoons pursued for six miles on separate roads to cut off the detachment, it effected its retreat with the three captives ; and on the same evening falling in with a party of French infantry cut it to pieces."*

" From Bois-le-Duc the enemy retired and took post beyond the Waal, leaving a body of troops at Nimeguen." On the 4th of November, Sir R. Wilson was engaged with his corps, which formed part of the garrison, in the sortie ordered against the investing enemy. " The success was complete ;" Nimeguen was afterwards evacuated, and the 15th, with " much difficulty, danger, and loss," rejoined the main army.

" The British troops defended the passage of the Waal until January, 1795, when a severe frost enabled the French to pass on the ice. The 15th were engaged at Guelder Malsen on the 5th of January, supported the 82nd Regiment and the 7th Light Dragoons, and afterwards charged a body of French hussars with great spirit, pursuing them on the ice-bed of the river ; they were also very instrumental in the recovery of the guns attached to the light brigade."

Circumstances rendering it " impossible to preserve

* This was the " famous Peloton." See Sir R. Wilson's " Russian Campaign : Introduction, page 17, note.'

" Captain Calcraft and Lieut. Wilson were the officers engaged in this service."—*History of the 15th Regiment.*

Holland the British forces marched for Germany.
The 15th were attached to the troops under Lord
Cathcart; they furnished outposts, covered the rear,
had occasional encounters with the enemy, and performed much harassing duty."

The enterprise being abandoned "the infantry
returned to England in the spring, but the cavalry
remained and during the summer were encamped
near Bremen. The 15th embarked in the winter,
landed, and joined the depôt at Croydon in February,
1796." Before this period Sir Robert Wilson had
purchased his lieutenancy, and soon after his return he
purchased a troop.

" In the summer of 1796 and 1797, the regiment
was encamped with other corps near Weymouth, at
that time the favourite resort of the king; and the
troops were reviewed by his Majesty."

Here Sir Robert Wilson first met Jemima Belford.
The acquaintance soon led to an engagement, but no
narrative relating to this period has been found among
the papers in his handwriting. The feelings of the
husband and wife are sacred: and the history of
their courtship and their faithful affection through
their married life is only preserved by memory in the
enduring love and grateful reverence of their children.

Jemima Belford was the daughter of Colonel William
Belford, eldest son of General Belford of the artillery,
of Hall Place, Harbledown, near Canterbury; by Mary
his wife second daughter of Thomas Jones, Esq. of
East Wickham in the county of Kent, and his wife
Martha only child and heiress of Charles Pelham, Esq.
of the family of the Dukes of Newcastle. The other
children of Thomas and Martha Jones were Ann (the

eldest), married to Colonel, afterwards Sir Adam, Williamson, of Avebury, Wilts; Mildred, married to Richard Warner, Esq.; Colonel Richard Jones—father of Richard Jones, Esq., now of East Wickham, Kent, and of Avebury, Wilts—and Lieut.-Colonel John Jones, both of the 1st Regiment of Guards.

The issue of the marriage of Colonel William Belford and Mary Jones was one son who was accidentally killed, being at the time a colonel in the army and unmarried, and two daughters: Priscilla, married in 1798 to Christopher Carleton* eldest son of the first Lord Dorchester; and Jemima—Lady Wilson. The two sisters were coheiresses of Sir Adam Williamson.

Sir Robert Wilson and Jemima Belford were wards

---

* She was drowned on the 29th of October, 1815. The event is thus related in a letter to Sir Robert Wilson from a friend at Ostend. " The vessel that was conveying Mrs. Carleton and her daughter from Ramsgate to Ostend was wrecked last night in attempting to enter this harbour in a violent gale of wind, and Mrs. Carleton, her daughter, and servant, were all drowned." A remarkable circumstance occurred. An intimate friend of Mrs. Carleton dreamt the night before she was to sail that she saw her friend, and her son and daughter, drowning. The impression upon her mind was so vivid and powerful that she immediately followed her to Ramsgate, and with extreme urgency endeavoured to persuade her to give up the voyage. Preparation, however, had gone too far, and she could not prevail; but she succeeded in inducing Mrs. Carleton to leave her son, Lord Dorchester, behind in her care. It is singular that the baggage was all embarked in an English cutter bound to Ostend, but in consequence of some difficulty respecting the passage, it was transhipped to another vessel, the *Sir William Curtis*, on board of which Mrs. Carleton and her daughter, a very beautiful girl of seventeen, ultimately embarked, and both perished as described. After the ship struck one of the passengers, confident in his power of swimming, offered to save one or the other. The mother immediately commended her child to him, but the daughter, equal in the strength of her heroic love, refused and implored him to save her mother. In this touching contention which should die to save the other's life, the time of possible preservation for either passed away, and both were lost. The passenger saved himself alone.—Ed.

in Chancery, and under age. This created a difficulty in the way of their immediate marriage which, however, had the full consent of their guardians and friends: and all parties were anxious for it on account of the probability of Sir Robert Wilson's employment on foreign service. It was therefore arranged that they should be married according to the law of Scotland, and the facts of the time are thus recorded in a memorandum in the handwriting of Lady Wilson.

"Robert Thomas Wilson was married to Jemima Belford at Gretna Green,* July 7th, 1797. We set off from my uncle's, Sir Adam Williamson's, house in Dover Street, with his and my mother's consent; as we could not have been married for some time if we had not gone there, being both under age. We were afterwards married in St. George's church."†

* The Scotch certificate is preserved with this memorandum. It is in the following printed form :—

"These are to certify to all person or persons whom it may concern that Robert Thomas Wilson, of the county of Middlesex, and Jemima Belford, of the same county, came before me, and both declaring themselves single persons, were married by the way of the Church of England, and agreeable to the law of the Kirk of Scotland.

"Given under my hand at Gretna Green this seventh day of July, 1797.
                          " JOSEPH PASLEY.
                          " ROBERT THOMAS WILSON.
" Witness, ANN SAUL."   " JEMIMA BELFORD.

† " PARISH OF ST. GEORGE, HANOVER SQUARE.
" *Marriages in March*, 1798.
" 170.   ROBERT WILSON and JEMIMA BELFORD,
both of this Parish, were married in this Church by Banns this tenth day of March, in the year 1798, by me, THOS. ASH, Curate.

" This marriage was solemnised between us—
                          " ROBERT WILSON.
                          " JEMIMA BELFORD.

" In the presence of CHRISTOPHER CARLETON,
" MARY CHEVELEY."

" Wilson left me on the 4th of May, 1798, to go with General St. John to Ireland."

" Charlotte Frederica Mary,* born August 12th, 1798, the Prince of Wales's birthday, at Windsor."

On the day of the marriage at St. George's crowds assembled in the church and in the street as to a spectacle. The fame of the young soldier, who, in mere boyhood, had sounded his knightly challenge in the lists of honour and had thus borne away one of its noblest prizes, and the reputation of the beauty of the lady† among the first in the ranks of courtly fashion, had kindled a popular enthusiasm. It would be scarcely possible to avoid the appearance of romantic exaggeration in any attempt to give the family traditions of the marriage, or to describe the impression made by the presence and bearing of the bridegroom and the transcendent loveliness of the bride. One record alone of that impression shall be given in a letter written many years afterwards, when Sir Robert Wilson in his canvass for Southwark solicited the writer's vote.

---

* So named from her godmothers, the Queen and the Princess Mary, and from her godfather, the Duke of York.

† A lady of the highest rank, herself distinguished for her beauty, told Sir R. Wilson's daughters that it had been the " height of her girlish ambition to be as beautiful and as fashionable as Jemima Belford." A bust by Camolli, and a painting in crayons, beautifully copied in miniature on ivory by the first wife of the late Lord Essex, in the possession of the family, preserve in some measure the singular graces of her figure and countenance. The miniature more especially exhibits the delicate tints of complexion, while the bust shows a line of the face which Sir Robert Wilson always said he had never seen in any other living person or in any statue: it is the line of the cheek at the three-quarter view, the blending of curve with curve by almost imperceptible degrees as you move slightly round, which strikes the eye with an indefinable sense of a hidden but perfect beauty.—ED.

"W. PENN TO SIR ROBERT WILSON.

"22, Lambeth Road,
June 2, 1826.

"MY DEAR SIR,

"ALTHOUGH I am here an actual housekeeper, the tenure under which I hold will prevent my attending you to the hustings, from there voting for you and my old friend Calvert, and even from following you in your calls in my neighbourhood. Our very early acquaintance, however, authorises me to assure you how eagerly and how warmly I wish you success in the impending poll for Southwark. At your last election, party politics were predominant; and however natural I might conceive to be a brave man's enthusiasm towards one whom he thought an injured woman, still a difference of opinion on that specific point, and a strong wish on my part that our dear native land might not be convulsed, induced me *then* to differ most widely with you in politics. The politics of that day have passed away as a dream, although to me an earlier dream remains of the day when the 'bravest of the brave' won the 'fairest of the fair.' On the present occasion, I should disgrace the name I bear, the blood running in my veins would turn, and the engraved features of my ancestor over my humble chimney-piece would frown upon me did I not loudly hail the warm and able champion of religious toleration. During your canvass, pray bestow a friendly call on one who will duly appreciate it. Remaining your very sincere friend and well-wisher,

"W. PENN."

" In the year 1797, it is stated, in the memoranda

cited above in the preface to the Russian Campaign,
that " Sir Robert Wilson was allowed to quit his corps
to go on Major-General St. John's staff to Ireland,
where he served as brigade-major and afterwards as
aide-de-camp during the rebellion." It appears by
Lady Wilson's memoir that he did not actually leave
her until the month of May, 1798. It is probable,
therefore, that the appointment was made and the permission given in the close of 1797, but that all was
not ready for his departure until the time stated by
Lady Wilson, and that they passed the intermediate
months together in their home at Windsor. "During
my service in Ireland," he writes, "I opposed myself
to the tyranny and tortures of the high sheriff of Tip-
perary, and rescued several victims, among whom was
Fox, the miller, from his flagellation horrors. For
this I was reported by the high sheriff as a protector
of rebels."*

" In 1799, on hearing that there was about to be
an expedition on the Continent, he rejoined his regiment and proceeded to the Helder with his troop."
He embarked in the month of September, and landed
on the 25th on the Dutch coast.

In the affair of Egmont-op-Zee, on the 2nd of October, the 15th were actively engaged ; and acquired so
much distinction against an enemy vastly superior in
numbers that they received the authority of the king †
to " bear the word *Egmont-op-Zee* on their guidons and
appointments."

On the 4th, 5th, and 6th of October, they acquired

* Extract from Note-book of Sir R. W.
† History of the Regiment.

additional honour, and on the 10th they "charged and took the two guns that swept the beach."*

Sir Robert Wilson was "engaged in all the affairs," but he has left no other memorial of his personal services; and when the Duke of York withdrew his army, "on the convention being signed, he returned with his corps to England."]†

* Introduction to Russian Campaign—Note.

† "Before the end of November the regiment was assembled in Canterbury Barracks."—*History of the Regiment.*

CHAPTER III.

[IN the short campaign of the Helder Sir Ralph Abercromby was at the head of the first division that landed in Holland. Under him, at Egmont-op-Zee, the 15th acquired their honours; the cavalry being under the command of Lord Paget, afterwards Marquis of Anglesea: and here first Sir Robert Wilson learnt to estimate the military qualities of the chief whose heroic services and glorious death he so soon afterwards witnessed and recorded.[*]

Inaction was little suited to his fiery spirit: no sooner was one avenue to the glory which was the object of his ambition closed than he sought new opportunity of service in other fields. " Being

---

[*] " History of the British Expedition to Egypt." By Robert Thomas Wilson. London: 1802.

I 2

desirous," he writes, in the memoir already quoted, " of joining the British army in the Mediterranean under Sir Ralph Abercromby, he bought the majority of Hompesch's Hussars. His Majesty's Government then despatched him to Lord Minto, at Vienna, by whom he was sent to the Austrian army in Italy." At this point commences the autobiography of his journals.]

On the 21st of September, 1800, I set sail from Yarmouth in the *Captain Hearne* with a heavy heart, having left my wife expecting her confinement very shortly: grateful, however, for a very happy additional day with her and my little Charlotte who happened to be more amusing than I had ever seen her, as if she were to leave a compensatory impression on my mind. I was indebted for this day to the accident of my having left my portefeuille behind—a lesson to me not too rashly to pronounce any event a misfortune.

We arrived at Cuxhaven on the 23rd. I determined on proceeding the same night, and did so in a Blan-kenese boat in which I embarked with the same persons with whom I came over—the Portuguese Chargé d'Affaires to Sweden, a Hamburgh bookseller, a Frenchman, a Bohemian, and two or three others of no note. The Chargé told us he was a captain of horse, and "the greatest poet and tragedian since the time of Shakespeare, as he had written more than eighty plays," of which he specially named " Pizarro," and " far better than Mr. Sheridan." This man's life had been saved by a singular event. He had overheard the poor Bohemian lamenting on the pier at Yarmouth that he had not sixpence to pay the boat

to take him off to the packet; at the same time he
tendered fourpence—his all—but it was refused.   The
Portuguese instantly advanced the money, and the
man entered the boat.   As there was a heavy swell
it was difficult to ascend the side of the packet.   I
passed up in safety: the Chargé attempted to follow,
but the boat heaved from the vessel and he remained
suspended in a most dangerous position.   Another
moment and he must have fallen into the sea; but the
grateful Bohemian, who had mounted before, sprang
forward and with violent exertion drew him upright
and enabled him to ascend.

Mr. Camperz, the Hamburgh bookseller, is a young
man of excellent abilities—a good heart, generous, and
honest.   He proved a great friend in aiding me to make
all my arrangements, and spared no trouble or fatigue.
I obtained his gratitude by an act of common civility
and confidence.   He had expended all his money at
Yarmouth, having been obliged to travel in post-chaises
to overtake the mail: and having, when he left his
friends at Edinburgh, only brought such a sum as he
calculated would be just sufficient to pay all demands
to the coast, in order that he might not infringe the
law against carrying out money from England.   The
Commissioner, however, did not like to let him go on
the promise of paying his passage to the captain at
Cuxhaven (for by a regulation the captain of the next
packet was to receive all money, as he had arrived at
Yarmouth some hours later than the time to which the
Captain Hearne was limited).   I immediately offered
him my purse and lent him five guineas, which he
afterwards repaid me.

The Frenchman was wretchedly poor but always

gay, even when vomiting—laughing most when most frightened.

We reached Hamburgh the next day about two o'clock; having been detained two hours at Stadt, where each vessel since the Danish quarrel is obliged to go and pay tribute as an acknowledgment of the right of the Elector of Hanover to search all vessels.

I went to the " King of England," a good clean hotel. Prince Adolphus's son came to call on me, and chatted for an hour: he is an excellent well-meaning young man. He gave me Buonaparte's map of Italy. Late at night I had the pleasure of seeing Mr. Este * enter my room as gay as ever. He introduced me every-where. On the 26th I left Hamburgh in my barouche, and felt as if parting with a parent when I took leave of Mr. Este. His superior knowledge, his manner, kindness, advice, and friendship, must ever command my sincerest attachment.

The works of Hamburgh are immense, and had it a sufficient garrison would be excessively strong. The outworks extend so far as to protect the shipping and town from the reach of shells.

I soon found that it requires a very strong carriage to travel in Germany. I shall not record every occasion of breaking down: it would tire in words—how much more in fact! Suffice it to say that this accident happened to me seventeen times between Hamburgh and Trieste.

On the 29th I arrived at Berlin: a handsome city; fine buildings; but thinly inhabited and very gloomy. Having seen Lord Carysfort I hastened on to Dresden. Here I saw Mr. Elliott who informed me that the

* The Danish Ambassador.

armistice was agreed to by England.   Two stages from
Dresden is the Austrian frontier, where unless you
are a courier or pay bribe-money they search your
baggage most strictly.   I did not choose to be taxed
or rifled and therefore, as courier, claimed the right
of having my trunks sealed only.   This being done
I told the officer that I wore the British uniform, consequently that I was no contraband merchant; that I
had submitted to my trunks being sealed, in order that
they might not be censured ; but that now I should break
the seals off—which I did to their great surprise.

At the beginning of the Bohemian States are the
worst roads in the world, for two posts left pur-
posely so as a fortress frontier.   Prague is a very fine
city.   Here I went to pay my respects to the Archduke, who received me most graciously and paid high
compliments to the British cavalry.   I afterwards went
and called upon Mr. Windham whom I found in company with Dr. Maclise.   I liked my reception much :
though he has since told me that I was much indebted
to my countenance and address for it ; since before he
saw me he had formed an idea that I was either
" Major Simple " or an " adventurer."   He gave me
much information.   In his company I travelled on to
Vienna, having prevailed on him to journey all night.
We reached Vienna about 4 P.M. on the 5th of October,
and I passed the gates without the trouble which I
had anticipated from breaking the seals.   At Wolfe's
Hotel we got excellent roast beef, introduced by Lord
Nelson who resided there.   I slept very soundly the
first night ; having been eleven nights in my barouche,
during which, from the badness of the roads, repose
was impossible.

The next day I went to Lord Minto,* who received me very kindly and warmly promised his support in the business of my mission. In the evening I saw Baron Thugut, who was equally kind; he referred me to his secretary to arrange with him my memorial. When I saw the secretary, Mr. Pillau, he informed me that Baron Thugut had desired him to say that I must not think of accepting anything but the cross, pension, privileges,† &c. Thus I saw my hopes realized ; indeed I had now the prospect of obtaining more than I had ever hoped for. Without any memorial from me Baron Thugut recommended our claim to the Emperor, who instantly accorded it. This transaction was very flattering also, from the interest which Lord Minto took in it and the reception I met with from Count Cobenzal, Prince Colloredo, &c.

On my being introduced to the Emperor he behaved most graciously, and I had the singular good fortune to hear him talk about and defend the convention of Hohenlinden, which he did most ably. The Empress was very civil. I like the manner in which ladies go to court here, without hoops : the effect is very elegant. Only on very great occasions is the circle formed : on common days each person is introduced singly into an apartment, where the Empress, attended

---

* See "Historical Record of the 15th, or King's Regiment of Light Dragoons," &c., &c., &c.

† " By the Statutes of the Order of Maria Theresa all knights are created barons of the Holy Roman Empire. In commemoration of the affair of Villiers en Couché the Emperor Francis I. granted the British knights, as supporters, an Austrian Hussar of Leopold and a soldier of the 15th Light Dragoons."—R. W.

When Sir Robert Wilson, in 1814, received the additional honour of the Commander's Cross of the Order, he became entitled by virtue of it to the dignity of a Count : but he never took out the patent of the higher rank of nobility. By the original patent the title is hereditary in his family.—Ed.

by one of her ladies, receives them. The Emperor's levee is conducted nearly in the same manner.

One day in the week a custom introduced by Joseph II., which does him much honour, is still adhered to. The poorest individual of the State has a right to speak in private with the Emperor. This right is constantly asserted. Every Friday the ante-chamber is filled with ambassadors, princes, nobles, statesmen, washerwomen, soldiers' wives, &c. &c.

I had learnt on my arrival that Sir Ralph Aber-cromby had suddenly—though expected in Italy where all the arrangements for his landing had been made—sailed for Gibraltar. This has disturbed my plan of operations, and I am advised by Lord Minto to wait for further intelligence. The unfortunate precipitancy of the Emperor had annihilated the accepted armistice. Mr. Windham, who was anxious to get to Tuscany, set off four days after his arrival at Vienna for Trieste. In a day or two afterwards the account arrived of the French having entered Tuscany, which rendered my idea of proceeding at all events to Leghorn abortive. As I was confident that I should by remaining at Vienna sooner get all the intelligence which I was desirous of obtaining, I determined to wait and push on the business of the crosses, which though accorded were not given. Lord F. Bentinck had arrived to join our party and I passed my time agreeably enough. Captains Loftus and Duff, Sir Francis Vincent, Captain Morgan, a Mrs. Phillips, and Mr. Foresti—son of the Consul at Corfu, were the English who lived with us. Lord Minto's house was always open, but it was distant. Lord M. is a man who thinks everything beneath him but his diplomatic duties and all that advances the

interest of his country; he is absent in the extreme in
society his head being full of political thoughts; but
his conduct in private life is excellent, and his attentions and kindness to all around him are fascinating
and endearing. His public conduct is such as in the
important crisis through which he has acted at Vienna
to have considerably exalted our national character
even in the opinion of his greatest enemies.

By means of Mr. Este's introduction I became
acquainted with a most valuable friend, Abbé O'Reilly
the great favourite of Maria Theresa and Joseph II.
He lives in the monastery of the Franciscans. I used
almost daily to breakfast with him, and was delighted
with his society, and flattered by his particular esteem.
Among the Germans, through Mr. Este, I became
an inmate of Baron Arnstein's house; one of the
worthiest families I ever met with; his daughter the
most accomplished girl in all Germany, with a fortune
of at least 300,000*l.* Truth, and not vanity, makes
me mention that Miss Arnstein heard with no small
regret that I was a married man. Lord F. Bentinck
had been commissioned by me very early to make
this known, but he forgot it. My great pride at
Vienna was to hear it circulated, as I did everywhere,
that I was married to one of the most beautiful
women in England.*

There were many other houses open in the evening.
Among the most pleasing persons was the Countess
Daghburgh, the well-known friend of every English-

---

* Sir Robert himself came in for his share of admiration. His youth,
and the honours he had obtained, the rank he held in the army, and his
uniform the magnificence of which was much suited to the taste of
foreigners, were the theme continually of conversation at Vienna and
everywhere. – ED.

man. Indeed, an Englishman found universal admittance and respect. Our character stands highest in the estimation of the Germans, although the ladies find more amusement in the society of other foreigners, from their greater freedom of conversation and ease of manners.

From day to day I had been expecting news from Sir Ralph, and my crosses. At length Colonel Hope received a letter from England, informing him that the expedition was about to return to Malta. I instantly determined on setting off; but tried whether I could not take my honours with me. I found that I must wait a "couple de jours." This is a deceitful French phrase, indefinite in its intention. I therefore considered it a duty not to linger a moment, and went to take leave of Baron Thugut. He felt for my situation, and said that, as the Emperor had signed the book, I might wear the cross a week after I left Vienna. This was a hazardous instance of his regard for me. I had wished to shake him by the hand as an honour to reflect upon; but when I made my bow the good old man snatched me to him, embraced and kissed me, while the tears rolled down his cheeks, twenty times. I felt the honour, the affection, the fondness, the mournful sensibility of this act. My feelings gave way, and I cried—as one oppressed with pleasure gratitude and sorrow at our parting. To the last moment of my life I shall think this the greatest honour I ever gained, the most flattering food for my vanity. Delighted and grieved I left my benefactor, and in the evening set off for Trieste, having obtained the esteem and friendship of many valuable men; Lord Minto, in particular, having honoured me with these and with his confidence.

I did not arrive at Trieste until the 11th in the morning, although I travelled day and night. Accidents, four in number, detained me some hours. I passed through a very fine country; and my astonishment ceased at Buonaparte's having made the treaty of Campo Formio. He had pushed there over a champaign country, but now he had mountains and capes before him, naturally defended by snow and other impediments. This and his precarious situation from Joubert's defeat in the Tyrol, were indisputably the causes and are now generally known to have been so, of his checking his career and not adding to his titles that of the Conqueror of Vienna. I have no hesitation in saying that the last eight posts to Vienna defended by eight thousand men, are more difficult to get through than the thirty from Mantua to Gratz covered by an army of eighty thousand.

The weather being quite calm no vessel could sail; particularly as in this country such weather always breaks up with a storm called a Boreas; but the next night after my arrival, the Vice-Consul Mr. Anderson told me that an oxen-boat was about to start. I instantly accepted the offer to go in her, and embarked at eleven at night. We had not enjoyed our calm long when the Boreas began to blow. Forty-two oxen were below, and there were thirty passengers, Jews, Turks, and Christians. The voyage was miserable; but early in the morning our cares were ended by the sight of land: at ten we made Venice, and entered the first port over a very dangerous bar on which the sea beat violently. As I was a courier and an officer I was not searched at the custom-house, though long detained there and at the town-hall by the stupid Venetian regulations. I had the pleasure of convey-ing safe for a poor Turk two pounds of tobacco, which he told me would be his food during the Ramazan.

The arsenal of Venice is very fine ; but the French have done it much damage. It was a melancholy sight to see the Doge's barge destroyed, sixteen ships-of-war cut in halves, and all the cannon taken away.

Petrillo, the landlord of my inn, having a little car-riage and wishing to go himself to Verona, I embarked with him in a gondola for Mestre, which is about six miles from Venice and we landed there about 2 A.M. on the 14th. From thence we went in our carriage to Verona. The road to the first post was lined with wrecks of houses which the French had pillaged : they had been the property of Venetian nobles who had here their " maisons de campagne." About five in the evening we arrived at Verona and I went and found Lord William Bentinck and his brother, who were very kind : I then went to General Bellegarde and delivered my despatches, &c. I here learnt that the armistice was broken and that it was hoped that Sir Ralph would come to Italy.

The next day General Bellegarde did me the honour to confide to me the whole plan of operations, and his wishes with regard to the operations of Sir Ralph. Lord William went with me again next day, and everything was decided. In the night of the 17th I left Verona, and returned to Mestre on the following day. I made the very good acquaintance at Verona of Major Nugent and Captain O'Ferral ; also formed,

if possible, stronger friendship with Lord William
Bentinck. The Austrian army I left with great confidence; since they loved their general, were well
clothed, in high spirits, and recovering from their sickness. I never saw them in finer order. The officers
received me with much kindness.

When we arrived at Mestre we found a very heavy
swell on the lagunes owing to a storm at south-west.
However, as my despatches were important I determined to proceed. The postmaster of Treviso embarked with us in charge of money to the Government; but he was soon so frightened that he offered
it all to us to put him on shore. As his agony was
so great we landed him on the first island. Here,
perceiving some soldiers in a boat in distress Petrillo
and I went to their assistance and with much difficulty
brought them safe. We then proceeded in our gondola,
and at great risk reached a port of Venice, not the
regular entrance. Petrillo is a very brave, fine fellow.
Englishmen in these countries are esteemed sea-gods:
and I gained and shared great applause for our perseverance and resolution from the spectators on shore.

When I got back to my inn I found the flattering
letter* of Lord Minto, announcing the gracious consideration of the Emperor in ordering the cross to be
sent after me. I received another at the same time
from another quarter, which assured me that my
leaving Vienna without it had pleased the Emperor
and every one. As my getting to Ancona as soon
as possible was of the utmost consequence, I waited
with the greatest anxiety for the weather to moderate, for no vesssel could leave the harbour in the

* See Appendix No. 3.

present storm. I employed my valet to find out some
ship that would go, but all refused. The captain of
an imperial vessel was waiting to sail with two German
couriers at the first possible moment : but he assured me
that he thought it might last, if it did not clear up in
twenty-four hours, for five or six days; as was frequently the case. I waited thirty hours with impatience,
but there was no amelioration : I therefore determined,
if the desired change did not happen in twelve hours
more, to try another plan—being sure that my getting
to Ancona alone was enough for the service, as I knew
every particular of the contents of my despatches.

Finding that the weather continued so bad, and
knowing the importance of my despatches, I determined to send the written ones to General Manfroi,
the commandant of Venice that they might be forwarded by the first conveyance, and myself set off in
an open boat for Ferrara, hoping to get from thence
by land or to pass in a fishing-boat the French line
of coast. I left Venice at about twelve o'clock at
night on the 20th of November, and arrived in safety
at the canal which leads into the Po; although we had
to cross two harbours where the sea rushed in with
prodigious violence and swell. One of these ports
was Chioggia, a town apparently well worth seeing.
Except in crossing these harbours the water was quite
smooth, as the lagune continues as far as the canal.
It was a tedious passage through the canal though
not very long, and we soon got into the Po, a broad
and rapid river here. With much difficulty my boatmen combated the stream, for we could not use a
sail the wind being contrary. Towards evening we
got out to refresh ourselves at a fisherman's house,

but were alarmed while at our meal with the report
made by a little girl that our boat was adrift.   My
situation was ridiculously unpleasant.   I saw all my
baggage floating away from me with great rapidity,
and I was unable to follow it.   By accident we found
a boat, and with great exertion recovered our own.
One hour would have carried her into the sea, and
six minutes' longer ignorance of her having broken
from the bank would have rendered every effort to
overtake her vain.   The next morning we arrived
at Pontelagoscuro.   Thence I procured a carriage
to Ferrara, four English miles.   Ferrara is capable
of lodging eighty thousand inhabitants, but has only
twenty thousand; therefore it is comparatively desolate.   I was obliged here to get quarters, and had
my billet on Louis Bosco: a very good man, extremely
kind, who would make me live with him, and who
had the only clean house I ever saw in Italy.   His
family were rather encroaching, however.   They compelled him to ask me for the appointment of Consul
and British resident at Porto di Goro; to apply for
his continuance as President of the Lottery in the
Ferrarese, a situation which he held under the Pope;
to get him a post of honour from the courts of
Tuscany or Naples; and to free him from the possibility of having requisitions made on his house and
property in the country.   I obtained the last for him,
and wrote to Count Sauran the Minister of Finance
about the second.   I hope that the application may
be successful for I esteem the father much: it was
the sons who were to blame; they made a rule
always to solicit some favour from every officer who
dined with them.

The town is too large for defence, but the citadel is very strong and has casemates for three thousand men.   The Austrians here, as in all their other new acquisitions, have added considerable works.

I was in daily hopes of being able to pass by Bologna.   The necessity of haste was, however, removed by my being assured that my despatches had gone to Mr. Windham, as I had directed; but, to my great astonishment and mortification, I received a letter from Lord William Bentinck which obliged me instantly to set off for Sir Ralph, as he then thought, at Elba.   I immediately started for Pontelagoscuro; and then, by virtue of an order from the Marquis Bellacqua the President, a very accomplished nobleman, at once obtained a boat though it was eleven P.M., and floated down the Po with great celerity to Porto di Goro.   Here, although I had important despatches from General Sommariva as well as from Lord William, and a letter from the President, I could not obtain a fishing-boat without paying down two hundred florins.   The admiral of the port (a mariner) could not enforce my orders; he therefore sent for a military force to Mesola.   In the interim I was agreeably surprised by seeing a Tyrolean officer arrive who had orders, in case I could not get a vessel, to send word back to Mesola: with the assurance that one should instantly be sent from thence.   However, he did not arrive till twelve at night, and we could not embark till the next morning, when we sailed with a fair but strong wind.   This continued to blow so heavily that we were obliged to go within three miles of Rimini and one of Pesaro, where the French were.   At two o'clock on the morning of the 2nd we made Ancona where I instantly disembarked, to the great alarm of my sailors who every moment expected a shot from the fortress. I carried my despatches to the General and went to seek Mr. Windham. He gave me information and advice which induced me to await the arrival of a messenger from Naples who was hourly expected. I, however, from my information got Captain Ricketts to sail directly for Rimini and Pesaro; and hope to have suggested for him a successful expedition.

My opinion about the land passage proved to be correct. Had I waited twenty-four hours I could have accomplished it; but without vanity I may say that I never felt a moment's hesitation to incur any inconvenience and peril when I thought the service could be benefited by my undergoing either; and I, who detest the sea, have often been astonished to find that all my aversions and apprehensions end the moment duty makes it necessary for me to embark; that an irresistible impulse urges me, and drives out of my thoughts those prejudices which I had perhaps the moment before entertained.

At Ancona I had the satisfaction of hearing that I had escaped being taken prisoner. A vessel in which I should have gone from Venice, had I not taken another course, was driven on shore on the French coast, and two German couriers were made prisoners. As I had written to say that I was coming by this vessel, Mr. Windham sent word to Lord Keith and Sir Ralph that I was taken.

On the sixth of November, Pozzoloni, the messenger, having returned from Naples and brought word that Sir Ralph was at Malta preparing to sail for Egypt, and at the same time a letter from Lord Keith to the effect that all hope of a descent on Italy was annihilated, I determined to set off that evening; and at ten o'clock left Ancona, cautioned against the dangers of the road from banditti. I purchased of the consul a pair of pistols for my defence, and felt no apprehension.

I will relate a circumstance which redounds little to my credit. I was induced to shave my poor poodle which I brought from Vienna; consequently all through the Apennines he shivered in misery; however, I endeavoured to make amends by incommoding myself very much, and keeping him warm in my lap. At Loretto I got out to see the holy house. It is a very fine building; a new Virgin had just been made, instead of the one which the French took away.

On the night of the second day's journey, just as it grew dark, I perceived a hill with a wood on each side, which I pointed out to Samuel * as a probable place for robbery. When we came there, the postillion, who had observed me priming my pistols, gave several whistles and said some words. The whistles were answered, and we heard a rustling. I instantly jumped out, and, to the great consternation of the postillion, walked by his side. I am convinced, from every circumstance, that he had prevented an attack of the banditti by his signs. It was the very spot, I afterwards learnt, where the consul's son had been plundered.

At Terni I breakfasted, and lamented much that I had not time to see the waterfall, especially as Jemima had sketched it. We went on as the day before,

_____
* Sir Robert Wilson's servant.—Ed.

dining in our carriage on bread and figs. At night we had another alarm about the same time as the previous evening. We saw five men, armed with long guns, standing at the bottom of a hill. I jumped out holding my pistol in one hand and my sword drawn slung on the wrist; Samuel also made a display of his pistol. When we came within two yards, one of the men advanced. I made a sign for him to keep off, and proceeded in great anxiety till we reached the top of the hill. I have often since reflected that this conduct of mine was rashness. Had there been a contest, five long guns must have beat our two pistols: —but then, these fellows were Italians.

About midnight we reached Rome; and while our baggage was settling at Zacharias's I went at two o'clock in the morning and knocked up Mr. Jackson, our minister to the King of Sardinia, and delivered my despatches.

The city of Rome is a very bad one; nothing but its antiquities can claim any person's regard. The houses are wretched, the streets unlighted, the people miserable, and there is an universal want of cleanliness and comfort. I was much disappointed with St. Peter's. The building does not look so vast, so grand, or so lofty as St. Paul's. Its front I think paltry. The colonnade, however, is very fine: but it has this fault, that it diminishes perspectively in the distance, so that the eye does not recognize the true dimensions of the columns; and the church, which forms the centre, partakes of this apparent diminution. The building looks as if sunk by this cause below the standing level of the spectator. In comparing St. Peter's with St. Paul's, I speak, of course, only with reference to the

vision; the facts of comparative dimensions are greatly
in favour of the Roman cathedral.   The Pope's palace
itself—the famous Vatican—is but a poor building.
I forgot to mention my opinion of the Apennines and
the Papal territory.   The towns are bad; the inns
abominable, and ridiculously dear—so much so that a
traveller must not ask, "What is to pay?" but offer his
own price, according to his own estimate of just due.

In Rome, as everywhere else, the French have made
great devastation.   In seven hours I saw everything
worth seeing,—though antiquaries will tell you that
it requires as many months. However, I am perfectly
satisfied, and never wish to return for closer scrutiny.
In the course of the morning I visited General
Dumas, who commanded the Neapolitan army.   In the
evening, my despatches having arrived from General
Dumas for the Viceroy of Naples, I left Rome about
six P.M.   Notwithstanding advice to the contrary, and
the example of the three officers of the *Mutina* who had
been robbed a few days before on their way to Civita
Vecchia by thirteen armed banditti and excessively ill-
used, I determined on journeying night and day ; but
I took the precaution, on leaving Rome, to change the
engaged and fixed hour of my departure, for the
postillions are in league everywhere with the banditti.
Nothing remarkable happened.   On the evening of
the 10th I entered the Neapolitan territory, and had
some difficulty, as my passport did not specify my
servant.   I was conducted with a guard to Itri ;
where I explained that in England and in Germany
it was taken for granted that a gentleman took his
servant with him if he chose; that as an officer I
insisted on passing him through, and as an English-

man, I bade them stop him at their peril. My menaces had their effect.

The road here was very good; indeed I cannot complain of that over the Pontine marshes. The entrance into the Neapolitan territory is very strong. At first there is only a road with mountains on each side; it runs so for two posts, when the mountains recede and a beautiful champaign country, but a very unwholesome one, opens and extends to Naples.

At night, in going out of the town of Itri, my horse fell down; in about half-an-hour he did the same thing again; when, it being evident that he was dying, I was obliged to wait an hour in a solitary wood until another could be brought.

At Mola di Gaeta a violent storm commenced; but I determined to persevere. When we suspected ourselves near the port, a flash of lightning followed by a tremendous peal of thunder had the extraordinary effect of putting out our light; and at the same moment the horses fell through fear and in their struggles dragged us into a pool of water. I instantly jumped out, but falling was completely immersed. Samuel kept his feet but was equally wet. With the greatest difficulty I gained the road. The lightning was so vivid that little or no advantage could be taken from its flashes, from the effect which it had on my eyes and from the contrast of the following darkness.

At last, however, in the glare of one of the flashes I thought I saw a turret, and towards it I made my way. My voice after a time brought out a man, and at the same time directed the postillion, who had got up his horses, to me. It proved to be the post-house; that is a stable for the horses and a hovel for the pos-

tillions and ferrymen. I never saw such a filthy hole:
so filthy that, wet as I was, I preferred sitting and
sleeping in the calash, until I was so cold that I was
obliged to enter and crouch before a miserable fire.
It was impossible to proceed and I remained in that
state till daylight. We then crossed the ferry, and I
found the turret which I had seen in the lightning to
be really the remains of an old ruined castle.

At about noon I reached Naples and at once went
to the Viceroy, who received me most graciously and
was much pleased with the news which I brought.

Naples has three strong castles—St. Elmo, which
commands the whole city and is not domineered by
even a distant height, particularly so. It struck me
that the French commandant did not defend it well.
In passing to inspect it I was filled with horror at
seeing a large grate, the only place of entrance for
light to the numerous dungeons, many feet underground, which were then filled with victims. Secret
tribunals, private murders, confiscations, bribery, now
desolate Naples. When and where this will cease is
beyond the speculation and even the hope of any one.
The Russians, to the amount of 3000, garrison the
fortresses. The Neapolitan troops do not even mount
guard in the palace of the Viceroy.

I went last night, December 14th, to a ball in the
palace of a nobleman who was weak or patriotic
enough, although possessing £80,000 per annum, to
engage in revolution. The French, after making him
pay two hundred thousand dollars, sent him at his own
expense as ambassador to France from the new republic. While he was there the king got his own
again and of course confiscated the property, and

would, if he could catch him, take the head of the
Prince of Angri, who is now a fugitive in Genoa.
His wife, having a pension of 8000 Neapolitan ducats
per annum, is allowed to live in the attics of her
former palace.   I thought it must have been a melancholy sound of music that she heard last night if she
has any feeling; for, in addition to the calamities
stated, most of her family have perished on the scaf-
fold or in prison, while part are doomed to perpetual
hard labour and bread and water in the islands, where
there are above three thousand of such sufferers.

This is the only instance of a country where the
nobles are democrats, and the poor—wretched as
their condition is—aristocrats.   They continue still
to love their king, exult in all the executions of the
noblesse, approve of the secret banishments, and are
arming against the French with the greatest enthusiasm.

In the morning I received a note from Mr. Locke,
to the effect that the corvette *Aurora* was going to
sail, and that the Count de Thurne, the minister of
marine, was on board.   I was to have gone in an
English merchant brig if the corvette did not sail.   I
instantly packed up, drove down to the Mole, got
into a felucca, and in a short time entered the corvette,
which I found a very fine vessel but badly manned.

It is a singular circumstance that in the cabin in
which I am now writing there are the prints of " War "
and " Peace," as copied by Jemima, represented by a
soldier leaving and returning to his family.   They
call up many feelings: hope inspires me and ambition
keeps me towering.   On quitting the continent of
Europe I feel as it were a strain on the chain which

binds me to England, and which seems reluctantly to
allow of extension; but no distance, although the drag
may be heavy, can break it.   God grant that I may
be able to wind myself up again by it to the hearts
by which I am attached to life, fame and virtue.

Dec. 20.—I arrived at Messina about daybreak,
and had the mortification of learning that the
Astræa frigate had sailed the evening before for
Malta.   Anxious to get forward, I hired a spolmira,
an open boat, for which I am to pay fifteen pounds.
It was evening before she could be got ready, when
we left this port in a calm my mariners rowing.   But
about seven miles off the weather began to get foul ;
the wind directly contrary and blowing strong, and the
sea momentarily rising.   I was asleep, tired by the
labours of the day, when the master woke me and
explained that it was impossible to proceed.   I wished
him to persevere until we could reach some port, but
found that there was none nearer than eighty miles.
As the difficulties even of returning now began to
increase rapidly, I at last consented that the master
should do as he thought best.   The permission
brightened up every countenance.   The boat was
immediately brought about and we reached Messina
in about three-quarters of an hour, the sea running
very high and the wind blowing in strong squalls.
On my return every one congratulated me, for they
had foreseen the storm that was brewing and has
continued with tremendous violence.   Ships that had
sailed two days before were driven back yesterday.

My anxiety is very great : but every hope is to be
entertained that Sir Ralph has not yet sailed, as the
supplies from home cannot have reached him.

"Everything is for the best." By getting back I found a government ship yesterday morning which is ready to sail for Malta with the first fine wind.

Perhaps a history which I am going to relate may prove that humanity was benefited by my disappointment in not arriving in time for the *Astræa*.

I had letters from Mr. Locke to an English merchant at Messina—Mr. Broadbent. On the morning of my arrival I went and breakfasted with him, and found him to be a character exactly answering to his name—plain in manners, honest and steady; in appearance a Quaker.

In the course of conversation I asked him after the unfortunate Dolomieu, saying that I had heard that he was sentenced to die. He started, seemed agitated, and asked particulars. I soon found that this was the man who had been the friend of humanity and of philosophy, who had visited the prison—nay, even discovered it—of this injured Frenchman, who had removed him from his dungeon, and performed all the duties of an Englishman.

It appeared doubtful to me whether my information was correct: but I expressed a strong wish to Mr. Broadbent to visit Dolomieu,* as I conceived that the more countenance and protection he received from individuals, the greater would be the check upon the tyranny of an unjust and unscrupulous government.

* Son of the Marquis de Dolomieu. He had devoted his life to science, and in 1798, with Monge, Denon, Berthollet, Fourier, Redouté, and other members of the "Institut," joined the expedition to Egypt by command of Napoleon. On his voyage back to Europe the vessel sprung a leak; the passengers and crew were saved with difficulty and landed at Taranto, where Dolomieu was immediately seized by order of the King of Naples and thrown into a dungeon at Messina. He was released at the peace of 1800, after the battle of Marengo.—Ed.

I was in the uniform of a British officer; with a rank
which alone was ostensible, but in the situation in
which I am so flatteringly placed as *Commandant of
the Cavalry* doubly consequential. I argued that my
going thus would prove that I was conscious of doing
a thing which would be pleasing to my government
and country; that the general interest of mankind
was excited in behalf of one who had benefited it so
much, and that they were determined to enforce the
rights of justice and acknowledge the claims of gratitude, undeterred by the menaces and unseduced by
the favours of profligate or frenzied sovereigns.

We went to the governor and obtained a shabby
assent to our application for admission, being restricted
to " converse in Italian ;" the order positively stating,
" that the gaoler might hear what was said." This
was illiberal; as, in the first place, I could not speak
the language, and in the second it was unhandsome to
suppose that an English officer would forget his honour.
Had I not been in regimentals the governor might
have been justified in acting with such caution.
However, I was glad on any terms to get permission,
and we went directly, attended by Captain Culver-
house.

Dolomieu's present cell, for until Mr. Broadbent
interfered he was in a dungeon, is on the second story.
When the door was opened he came forward and
shook hands with Mr. Broadbent. We were then
introduced to him. He immediately asked whether
I spoke French ; with an expression of eagerness which
too plainly proved how much he had suffered from
being so long deprived of the power of conversing in
his native language. I answered in Italian, Yes, and

then begged Mr. B. to explain the restriction imposed upon me. Mr. B. then, at my request, repeated everything I said. I began by saying, on purpose that the gaoler might repeat, that as an Englishman I had thought it my first duty to visit him, not only on account of the services he had rendered to mankind but as a testimony of our abhorrence of the unjust and injurious treatment he was suffering. I assured him that the strongest representations had been made to the British Government by every learned society in England, and an universal interest excited in his favour: that I offered my feeble services to render him every assistance possible; actuated by these motives and combining with them respect to my father's memory, who, as a member of every learned academy in Europe, must have been gratified by seeing me anxious to render aid to a man to whom the sciences were so much indebted. He thanked me much, and his manner fully proved the sincerity of his sentiments for the attention I had paid him. He spoke with a dignified gratitude of those Englishmen who had endeavoured to alleviate his misfortunes, and added— " War is a lamentable necessity but England and France know how to humanize its horrors. Bravery, humanity, and honour are their reciprocal characteristics. They fight like heroes, they treat as philosophers; but in other countries, where courage if it does exist is barbarism, faith is a mockery. My unjust detention is the act of that sovereign who knows no laws but his own caprices. Still, though his prisoner, I deny his authority and defy his power."

I asked him " Whether he wanted anything that I

could procure him?"—"whether books, pens, and ink were allowed him?" He said the last were not. As for the other parts of the question he delicately said, "Perhaps you will be good enough to interest yourself with the governor that everything may be allowed me which is possible." I asked him whether I could do anything for him at Malta. He said, "No! That all his friends had left it; but that there were some old servants of his to whom, if they asked after him, he should wish to be remembered." On his understanding that I was proceeding to Egypt to command the cavalry, and on my offering, as the events of that war would probably give an opportunity of interview with some French officers, to deliver any message to his friends in France that he might wish relative to his wealth, property, or philosophical objects, he most gratefully thanked me and nobly said, "Sir! you will find there at the head of the army a man who is a soldier, a philosopher, and one of my best and worthiest friends. He will fight on while there is a possibility of success; he will force your esteem by his courage; but when it may be necessary for him to treat you will find him a man of integrity, honour, and faith. Pray, if possible, go with the first flag of truce—tell him you have seen me: it will give him a pleasure which perhaps you may have felt when conversing with one who has lately been in the society of your dearest friend." Much more passed on this subject. I found all he said respectful and manly—no servility, no fanfaron impertinence. I left him gratified at having been the means of affording him much happiness which would not, I am assured, terminate with my visit. Some hours would he reflect on it with pleasure, since trifles must afford comfort to a man in his situation.

I was not disappointed in this opinion, since I have seen a letter which he subsequently wrote to Mr. Broadbent, supposing that I had sailed. He appears about sixty years of age; is six feet high; very upright; his hair long and grey; his countenance very expressive. His face remains a proof that he has been a very fine man; but ill-health, confinement, service, &c., have now drawn strong lines in it. His cell is about 12 feet by 8. The light comes in through a trellis grated opening of such a size as to admit enough fresh air. His bed seemed clean and tolerably comfortable. A few books were in his room. His provisions I did not see: I understood that as far as eight Carolines a day he was allowed to receive and expend, but not more for fear of his corrupting the gaolers: this sum is equal to about two shillings. He is allowed to walk out into a covered passage in the morning. In short I must confess that his treatment, if he were a criminal, is not *now* to be found fault with. But to him confinement is torture. In a book in the possession of Mr. Broadbent, in the margin of which he has written his will and notes addressed to his sister, he laments that he who has often without being an astronomer sat up whole nights to contemplate the heavens, should now be deprived of the sight of the sun at midday.

Sir Joseph Banks, Colonel Graham, and others have been very kind to him. I contributed my mite, conceiving that Mr. Broadbent ought not to be too great a sufferer from his generosity and humanity. I also sent him my pencil-case privately, the second gaoler being our friend.   Before he got this he was obliged to write with the black deposited by the smoke of his lamp.*   On the pencil-case are English inches marked, which I thought might be of service to aid his mathematical calculations.

Messina is a very curious city, beautifully situated. The old town must have been very fine : nothing but ruins remain ; an earthquake having destroyed it about sixteen years ago.   Two thousand people of both sexes and of every rank and age fled for shelter to some low ground near Scylla.   They drew their boats up on this marais and lived in them two days ; but on the third day of the earthquake the sea burst its bounds, and, almost literally boiling, swept everything away ; not one soul was saved.

The gut of Scylla and Charybdis presents the same dangerous and frightful navigation as when it was described by Virgil : full of whirlpools, the water seems furious at being confined between the mountains of Sicily and Calabria, and hisses continually its indignation.

The arsenal is very fine, the port dangerous, the citadel strong.

Dec. 22.—I embarked in the *Anne* transport at Messina.   I bought some very fine figs and mean to take them to Egypt, as with bread I can at any time make a dinner of them.   The wind is fair, but the ship's bottom so foul that she cannot sail fast.

Dec. 23.—The wind about two this morning became foul.

---

* In this manner he wrote in prison on the margins of his books and on scraps his " Essai sur la Minéralogique," published after his release. His pen was a piece of bone sharpened.—" Biographie Universelle."—Ed.

In the night of the 23rd the wind became very violent, and we soon found ourselves on a dangerous lee shore. The captain indeed called me and Captain Pemberton, a passenger, and told us that he had little hope of saving the ship. We continued crowding sail as the only chance left of bearing up against the wind, and at last enough was set almost to blow her masts out; but as they stood and the vessel was heavy laden we kept from the shore some time: when destruction seemed inevitable from the impossibility of clearing a cape, Providence interposed and saved us. In a moment the wind changed from south-east to west. The ship was instantly taken aback: the accident which lost the *Ville de Paris* and has wrecked many other vessels, but which *destiny* converted into the means of our preservation. The confusion on board was dreadful—scarcely a single person could stand above or below deck. Trunks, furniture, ladders, a horse, birds, dogs, men and women lay tumbling together. At last, with indefatigable exertions of the mate and Captain Grant— the best seaman I ever saw—together with those of Captain Pemberton, the sails were set right and we drove off to sea. The captain and all say it was one of the most terrible nights and miraculous escapes they had ever witnessed. We beat about, sometimes getting within eight leagues of Malta, for three days, the sea always in a tremendous state and we continually apprehensive of her masts going overboard from the motion and strain. At last it was discovered that the foremast was sprung: this, the weather still continuing dreadful, determined us to put back to Syracuse. With much difficulty we accomplished it and arrived about evening in the harbour, very thankful to God for our safety.

I do not know that I ever suffered so much in my life: the continual toss almost made me mad: the apprehension of losing my life was but a secondary consideration. I would not however go through all this again voluntarily for I dare not say what. The mate tore his hands dreadfully that memorable night: his brow at last was grated by the ropes. May I never have again to record such scenes!

Syracuse is one of the strongest places I ever saw. It has five long lines of fortification towards the land, and four wet ditches. Still I think I found a point for easy attack, least guarded because considered as defended by nature. About a mile from the town are the ruins of the ancient city. Here still exists to a great extent a famous aqueduct, and here is the tower in which Archimedes used to work and from which he watched the flotilla and the operations of the enemy. Here too is a prison which has a wonderful echo and the properties of a whispering gallery. Over it is the room in which Dionysius used to live for his own security, and for the purpose of listening to the conversation of state criminals who little suspected such treachery. Further to the right are the remains of the first Christian church in a very perfect state, and the chair in which the first bishop was enthroned. From thence you descend into the catacombs: vast sepulchral excavations extending above forty miles in length and ten in breadth. The coffin of Dionysius is shown. The coffins are not detached but hewn in the rock. The little children were put into the sides of the walls of the grand passage.

When the Christians were persecuted by the Saracens they were obliged to fly for refuge to these mansions of the dead, and formed a town underground. The vault devoted to the apothecary's shop and to the care of women in childbirth is pointed out, and bears proofs of having been thus really used. To what a dreadful state must these poor people have been reduced, doomed to occupy alive the coffins of those whose bodies had scarcely decayed! I thought this the greatest curiosity I had yet seen.

We left Syracuse on the evening of the 29th, and beat about till the morning of the 31st when we entered the harbour of Malta. Destiny seemed to prevent my reaching that point, and my immediate departure from it was equally curious. With much pleasure, however, I left the *Anne*, believing her to be the worst sailing vessel on the seas.

As we were beating off the harbour's entrance on the 30th I had the mortification of seeing a frigate just leaving it, and steering for Egypt. It is very singular that at Naples I arrived a morning too late for the *Greyhound*, at Messina for the *Astræa*, and here for the *Tiger*.

On the morning of the 31st we entered the harbour, and at the same moment a fleet of ships with troops to join Sir Ralph passed out. My anxiety of course was great. I got a boat, rowed to shore, and ran up to the top of the hill of La Valetta where the governor's house, the ci-devant palace, is. I there saw Governor Pigott and Captain Ball, who instantly gave me an order to embark in any ship of war or transport I could reach. I hastened back, nearly breaking my neck in running down, for the streets

are a slippery pavement, got my baggage from the
Anne, and rowed to join the fleet but could only reach
a brig.   Mounting her sides I presented my order to
the master.   Some officers of the 12th regiment
Light Dragoons were on board who did not seem
well pleased at my coming; but to that I was indifferent; and in answer to their representations that
there were already three in a small cabin and that I
should be ill accommodated, I told them that the exi-
gency of the service did not admit of etiquette, and
that I was too old a soldier to regard my own comfort as essential.   I afterwards found them very kind
indeed; it was with difficulty that I could prevail
with them to retain their own bed-places and allow
me to lie upon the floor, but upon this I insisted.   I
was obliged to live at their table for I had literally
not an article of my own : my figs I gave to the mate
of the *Anne*, being rather ashamed to carry them
about with me—a modesty which I and my comrades
here since regret.   It is true that I had arranged to lay
in a stock at Malta ; but time was too precious, and I
thought of the fate of the king of France whose appetite cost him his head.

We proceeded at once, under convoy of the *Flora*.
The fleet consisted of nine ships, having on board the
12th and 26th Light Dragoons from Lisbon.   The
brig I am in is the worst in the fleet, but was the
best.   She is now obliged to carry always a press of
sail when the other ships are under reefed topsails.
The *Braakel*, our stern commodore, has often saluted
us with a shot; but it is not the fault of our captain.
The sheathing, from the rapidity of our passage and
that she made from Gibraltar in only six days, is

entirely torn off her bottom, and she begins to leak; however, she is still better than the *Anne*.

I had scarcely finished the above when a tremendous squall came on; the sea was furiously high; our ballast shifted, and we were obliged to carry a press of sail. To add to our miseries the 12th Dragoons were very careless about their fires; the sparks flying everywhere, although there was loose hay lying close to the fireplace. Indeed I cannot but consider our escape as providential. A spark flew into the cabin; we ran out, and found thousands on every part of the deck and some smoking in the hay. In a few moments more the ship must have taken fire. And yet these indiscreet men murmured when we ordered water to quench the fire entirely; and at night smoked their pipes between decks.

On the 6th we saw land, which we supposed to be Rhodes; but towards noon were much surprised to see the commodore tack and stand off. The next morning we were still more astonished to find ourselves between two capes. The master did not know where he was, and we soon found that every captain in the fleet was equally at a loss. The commodore, however, kept standing in, and at night laid to. The next morning I took a boat and went on board the *Braakel* where I found Colonel Brown of the 12th Dragoons. Captain Clark told me that he was waiting for the return of the commodore who had gone ahead to learn where we were, and that he did not positively know on which side of Rhodes he was but had sent his boat to the shore, seeing some houses, for intelligence. In the evening the boat returned, and brought the information that Rhodes was to our left; which proved that

when to our surprise the commodore hauled his
wind, he had overshot the port fifteen leagues :
had night come on before the error was discovered,
we should all probably have been lost in the gulf of
Satalich.   Probably such an instance had never been
known before : the master of the *Braakel* said that in
thirty years' service he had never experienced it.
The cause was that the currents are strong and the
charts inaccurately laid down.   At night the *Flora*
rejoined us.   The next morning we saw Rhodes and
got within a league, expecting to enter the harbour,
when the *Pitt* sloop of war came out and directed us
to another harbour in the gulf of Macri.

On the 12th, as the ships were becalmed, I left the
Braakel and got into a Turkish boat to proceed to
the harbour.   In the evening I entered it and went
immediately on board the *Kent*, where I saw Sir
Ralph.   From thence I went in the *Kent's* cutter to
the *Chatham*, where my detachment was.   I found
that my people were on shore.   Making efforts I joined
them, and was received with great marks of attention and hearty welcome.   As soon as I got my
letters I went to Lord Keith, who received me
very kindly and asked me to dinner.   The captain
of the *Flora* here told me that he expected every moment to see the brig's masts rolled overboard ; and
Lord Keith said that her captain had always been
notorious for carrying sail, and told us many stories
of him which did great honour to his intrepidity.

My time was chiefly employed between the *Kent*,
Foudroyant, and my huts which we enter to-morrow.

The bay of Marmorice is very singular but excellent.
When you are in it there appears no outlet but one,

which is not so. Very high mountains environ it. At the head is a little town and a castle, both wretched. Provisions are very dear and bad; but there is plenty of game in the mountains. My men in cutting wood found also immense numbers of tortoises, which they eat; boiling them, I am sorry to say, as they do lobsters. Chameleons are also found; camels abound. Certainly it is a curious country, and it is gratifying to have been in it.

Jan. 25.—On the 16th I landed. Our huts were placed about a mile from the shore and as much again from the town. Wolves, which came close to our encampment making most hideous noises, disturbed us much at first, but we are now accustomed to it. The howling continues generally for half an hour together along the whole of the mountains in our rear.

On the 19th our horses arrived; and our disappointment was beyond description to find such animals as they appeared to be, even by moonlight, for they did not come till ten at night. The next morning confirmed our fears. Never were seen such wretched creatures; I could compare them to nothing but the turf-carriers in Ireland. The whole army was shocked. Sir Ralph, at the inspection, acknowledged that it was impossible to see worse, or to expect anything from us; but yet he was obliged to mount us with as many as could possibly be ridden. After many subsequent examinations my detachment will only keep seventy of them, and the 11th Dragoons thirty. Most of them have frightfully sore backs. The artillery are to have what we cast; but many of them will be shot. Seven were shot yesterday.

The 12th and 26th landed on the 21st, and received the same kind of animals.

The weather is terribly bad and our huts are deluged; but we have got some straw by unroofing a Turk's house and I now defy the storms.

I yesterday had my men out for an hour; and I am better satisfied with my prospects, as they are very expert; but I fear we can never hazard a charge on such rips. However, we have the consolation of knowing that the whole army is aware of the impossibility: therefore if we do anything their approbation will be in proportion.

By great good fortune I purchased, for 12*l.* 10*s.*, a very good little horse, something like my chesnut but smaller. He has good action, is well made, and very handsome. Of course he is much admired, and many of the generals and others have endeavoured to get him from me by observing that he is too light for my weight: but as long as a horse can career with me as he does I am satisfied that he is fit for my riding. His only fault is that he is too small to charge with.

I was obliged to leave off writing at this instant by a torrent of rain, which forced through my roofing. The camp is deluged. There is every appearance of a repetition of the storm: I am therefore preparing against it by throwing mud on the top of my hut.

There has been a sale of a ship's cargo, taken on her way to Alexandria.

Jan. 27.—The storm continued till this evening with unabated fury. On the morning of the 26th I rode down to the sale. It was very various. Among other things there were some very *extraordinary* fans

indeed; but they had been bought before by the
amateurs.   It is a most singular instance of French
character.

I happened to mention that I regretted much that
the dolls were not sold by auction.   There were two
dressed in the French reigning fashions.   Sir Richard
Bickerton's secretary, Mr. Boyle, who had the
management of the sale, asked one of the officers
whether I was a family man.   Upon his answering
that I was he very kindly came up and offered me
one of them, regretting that the other was already
promised.   I thanked him, and accepted the present,
pleased in the anticipation of the pleasure that it will
give to my dear little Charlotte when she receives it,
and really grateful to Mr. Boyle—a stranger till
then—for his unsolicited attention.

This night, at eight o'clock, I went to shoot jackals
or wolves.   Money of the 11th and Captain Duval went
with me.   We posted ourselves in the ruins of an old
house in the mountains, just behind some dead horses
which we had shot some days before.   In five minutes
an animal about the size of a Newfoundland dog came
within fifty yards of us, but then sheered off.   In ten
minutes more we saw thirty or forty of different sizes in
every direction, while the mountains resounded on all
sides with the screamings and growlings of others.   We
were rather disposed to be alarmed: but Money observed that their love language was as musical as that
of the Germans, and we laughed so loud that we
scared the wild beasts away.   However, they soon
returned and I fired at one within twenty yards.
I think that to-morrow I shall see by traces of blood
that the shot took some effect.   Money also fired his

gun, and thinking that after such a volley it would be
useless to stay longer we returned. An hour afterwards these animals, setting up in the same quarter a
loud and long yell, determined Birch and Boucher of
the 11th to try their skill. They were already inflamed by curiosity from our account. The night is
bad, for there is a great deal of thunder and lightning;
but this is fine weather for those wild beasts.

Feb. 9. — As it was thought advisable to send
to Cudjas for horses I received two thousand eight
hundred dollars from Sir Ralph, and with Birch,
Money, and Mr. Oliver of the 10th but acting as
volunteer to the 11th, I set off on the 1st of February.
Our party was increased by a guide and three dragoons,
so that we were in all nine horses and eight men. We
travelled for many miles, with every obstruction and
no track, over precipices and through deserts. When
evening drew on the guide wished to leave us at the
entrance of a wood: but when he saw me draw my
pistol to menace him he artfully gave me his own gun
as a pledge, and dismounting began to say his prayers
towards the setting sun; first washing his head, face,
arms, and hands in a rivulet. The operation was not
enough in earnest to remove any dirt: indeed, I have
generally observed that Mahomet's laws, which strictly
enjoin these washings as a ceremonial but were wisely
intended to preserve the cleanliness which the ceremony signified, are now solely obeyed with the first
idea.

Our guide having resumed his seat we pierced into
a wood, up mountains, over rocks which seemed
impassable. About eight in the evening the guide
discovered some huts, in which he explained that we

were to sleep; and in half an hour, after a march of certainly more than twenty-five miles, we dismounted from our horses, all tired and two of them lame, at a caravanserai.

This was a hut supported at the expense of the Grand Signor, who finds wood and a scheik or priest. The inmates were at prayers when we entered; but after this was over we found our way into a corner, and there deposited our money and ourselves. The fire blazing up, we were able to take a survey. The room was about 24 feet by 16. There were sitting on the ground fourteen people—Greeks, Turks, negroes, and others—travelling to sell fowls, &c. at Marmoras: but such dirty, miserable people I never saw. The room was filth itself: a mat full of vermin covered the floor. Here were four English gentlemen obliged to seek shelter. Strange destiny! We emptied our basket of provisions, and then entered into a kind of monkey conversation with our wretched companions. I pass over incidents which shocked us, for we were not then accustomed to the depravity of these barbarians nor had any conception of its existence. They saw our expressions of aversion and horror, but treated them with derision.

As this month is the feast of Ramazan, in which the Turks are enjoined to fast all day and pray six times in the course of the twenty-four hours, our sleep was constantly interrupted—mine at least, for the others found their floor too hard for slumber. I had thus an advantage over them, having always since I left Italy slept on the cabin floor at sea and the earth on land.

Each time of prayer the scheik repeated the same

words, but sometimes the people prostrated themselves oftener than others.   I counted seventeen prostrations in one prayer.   They fall down very adroitly, and never hurt themselves.

In the morning at daybreak we again mounted, and after some mischances proceeded on our way through the same kind of country and with the same dangers as the day before.   Now and then we met long trains of camels, and here and there saw a hut, which the guide cautioned us to avoid lest the women should inadvertently be exposed to the sight of Christians.

About 4 p.m. we reached Cudjas, after a march of fifty miles in which we saw only three fields cultivated.   Cudjas is situated on a bay; but on the southern side of it, so that we made a grand détour to reach it.   The town consists of about twenty miserable houses, but each was a shop in which slippers are sold.   At the entrance we had a glimpse of four fine-looking women dressed, as is the custom of harems, in an uniform pelisse.   They retired when they saw that we observed them.   They belonged to one of the Aga's chief people.

We were conducted by one of the inhabitants to the Aga's palace, which is exactly like an English farm-house and yard.   The square was filled with geese, chickens, &c.   On one side was stabling; on another a long range of wooden buildings, in which the servants, &c., slept; on the third side was the harem, which looked like a granary; and on the fourth was the wall of a garden; but at the extremity of the two long ranges were two very pretty buildings in the Chinese style.   We alighted and ascended the stairs leading to one of these : where we were shown into a room at the further end of which sat a Turk, who received us and explained that the Aga was out shooting; but desired us to sit down and await his return. Around the room were sofa benches, and the floor was covered by a beautiful Turkey carpet. There were two rows of windows ; the upper one had painted glass, the lower no glass but wooden shutters. After a time we saw the Aga arrive on horseback, dismount, and, although he saw us, run quickly up the stairs of the building on the other side. The Turk in our apartment said that he was gone to pray. The sun being now set we demanded food, and a servant brought us three dishes one of which only we could touch.

At about seven o'clock the Turk, who was ill of a fever and was curing himself in their way by eating ice, informed us that he was going to pray and that another room was preparing for us. We were soon ushered into it—a most wretched apartment, evidently long uninhabited except by rats. Some dirty cushions were thrown on the floor for our beds, chairs, tables, &c.

We now insisted on delivering our letter of introduction from General Campbell*—or *Mustapha*—to the Aga; but it was not till near nine o'clock that his secretary came and desired that one of us would go with him. Birch went. In the meantime we amused ourselves with one of the chief Turks who endeavoured to tell us the mysteries of the harem, informing us that the Aga had four wives and two concubines in it.

In about half an hour the secretary returned, and desired that another of us would go with him. I went to put on my sword but he attempted to prevent it

* A Scotchman ; but the Turkish Bashaw at Marmoras.—R. W.

This and the circumstance of his taking us one by one
gave me some suspicion, and Oliver determined to go
with me—both armed. We insisted, and went.

Our surprise was very great when, upon ascending
the stairs of the opposite building, we entered the hall
of audience—a very fine room, furnished with sofas,
carpets, &c. On the walls were suspended swords,
pistols, and other arms. At the bottom were the
servants drawn up behind a railing; on the sofas sat
the chief Turks; at the top on the right of the fire
was the Aga, and Birch on the left. We were compelled to take off our boots on entering the room.
We then went up to the Aga and made our obei-
sance, and afterwards took post by Birch.

The Aga was a man of about forty, with a remarkably fine black beard. He ordered us coffee and
pipes. In about twenty minutes Money came in.
Finding that we did not return he became very uneasy, and leaving a sentry over the dollars determined to follow us. We continued in the room about
an hour, talking by signs and with the few words of
their language that we could command; but we perfectly understood each other. We were not a little
surprised to hear one of the chiefs say that the
" French were good." This, in the presence of the Aga,
we thought strange: but Birch and Oliver, animated
by the scene and anxious to promote the service for
which we were sent, gave a pistol and a sword,
which were instantly suspended in the armoury.

We took leave perfectly confident of success. On
our return we wished to retire to rest; but events
occurred which compelled us to keep watch all night
with our swords drawn. Indeed otherwise the Turks

made such a noise with their psalm-singing, prayers, and shouting, that sleep would have been impossible.

I must draw a curtain over the night and morning till eight o'clock: suffice it to say that never was a night of such anxiety and misery passed. We welcomed daylight—for in this country no candles are used. The next morning we found a sensible difference in our treatment. The Turks would give us no wood, and only one very small cup of coffee for breakfast, without bread.

We now determined to try our fortune with the horses and to bring matters to an issue, as our situation became every moment more embarrassing and perilous.

The Aga's horses were all brought out into the yard. They were certainly very fine animals, the number about twenty; five or six of them true Arabians. To our consternation the Aga asked one thousand dollars apiece, when even for general officers we are commissioned only to give two hundred dollars. The other inferior horses were extravagantly dear also; for the most miserable which the country people brought in they demanded one hundred and fifty dollars.

Finding that nothing could be done with such a set, and fearing to expose ourselves another night to these barbarians, irritated as they now were at our refusing to buy their horses, we resolved to sound a retreat. At one o'clock everything was ready, and under some apprehension of an attack we sallied forth. Birch and I had previously attempted to see the Aga, but his guard threw down the trap-door at the top of the stairs at our approach. After escorting the horse with the dollars through the river at the entrance of the village, Money and I returned to buy bread for ourselves and men. We overtook our party about a mile off afterwards, and found Birch buying a horse which we took on with us.

Our poor horses had only had one feed of corn since they left Marmoras. We had no straw for them now; nothing but bread, and a little piece of pork, undressed, for ourselves; twenty-five miles to go before we could reach our caravanserai; and night coming on without a moon to assist us.

We pushed on as fast as possible and fortunately passed the most intricate and the most dangerous part of our route, fourteen torrents in the space of one mile, just before night closed in. Our guide with great attention brought us safe to our caravanserai about nine o'clock at night. The landlord, however, did not wish to receive us and opposed Money's entrance; but on his calling out I went and we made our way good to the fire, and showed them that we were true Englishmen by turning our backs to it and keeping it from them. At length a truce was made and we sat down quietly on the floor. The Turks went to prayers, which this night were very long but not very devout. After the service was over we began to think of our dinner, and Oliver took the direction of roasting the pork, which we ate after all half done tearing it asunder with our hands. The men found two fowls which they killed and ate. The horses had no corn; but by putting a pistol to one of the Turks' heads we forced some straw for them. Our company were rather worse and more numerous than the first night: a dirty rascal was next me, more wretched in clothes and appearance than I can describe. I as usual fell asleep; but snoring, a negro gave me a push and took my cloak even from under my head to awake me. This was an impertinence that nearly cost him dear; for we were irritated at the treatment we had received at Cudjas and, knowing that we were never to return by the same road, we determined to alter our former system of submission. All night we were obliged to watch the dollars, and to keep the Turks in check as they often attempted to encroach and take the fire from us.

The next morning we set off again at daybreak; not giving anything for our lodgings: as the landlord, when we passed on our way to Cudjas, had charged us two dollars—nine shillings—which rather than make our return disagreeable we consented to pay. We returned partly by a different route, but though shorter it was much worse. I declare that I went over precipices and rocks that I never could have conceived practicable. Our dollar horse fell down two or three times, being quite worn out; four others were dead lame. At ten o'clock in the morning, when the intense cold began to yield, we determined to stop and breakfast. Fortunately we saw on our way the remains of a fire where some Turks had passed the night. Here we alighted, and made a most delicious repast on some milk which Birch had procured at the caravanserai, and some figs which we bought of a Turkish jackass driver. The remainder of our bread we gave to the horses. We mounted again, and at two o'clock reached the top of a mountain from which we saw our fleet. We involuntarily gave three cheers, and with hearts refreshed proceeded on our way.

The four days of this expedition were certainly the

most miserable of my life ; in the power of barbarians ; separated by impassable barriers from the humanized part of the world ; exposed to insults abominable and mortifying ; in cold, hunger, and the most nauseating filth.

Our return excited much surprise, and disappointed many of the generals, who had calculated on our bringing them horses ; but they congratulated us on our escape. Sir Sidney Smith, when he heard the story, said that he wondered at our safe return ; that the Aga of Cudjas was a notorious rebel who had a few years before fought a battle with the Aga of Moughla, in which he had lost five thousand men.   It is very singular that the chief Turk at Cudjas accused Sir Sidney Smith to us as a traitor.

Sir Ralph approved much of the line of conduct we had adopted : and said that he had been in some apprehension ever since he learnt the disposition and acts of this rebel chief.

Ptolemy, my new horse, bore the journey to Cudjas remarkably well ; and thus gained my esteem and general admiration.

Feb. 11.—Yesterday the most violent storm of thunder, lightning, and hail came on that perhaps ever was known since the Egyptian plague.   The hail was lumps of ice, some—on the honour of a man—thicker than any walnut and much longer ; the lightning as rapid as one flash could succeed another ; the thunder loud and awful as the imagination can conceive.   In ten minutes our camp was a sea of ice : which without stockings or shoes I waded through, and felt as if my feet had perished in the attempt to pass from my own to Money's hut.   My hut had four feet of water in it ;

his had more.   In an attempt that I made to go round
the lines, in order to render every aid in my power, I
was almost struck blind by a flash.   Till then I had
looked at it with astonishment and admiration; for it
played and darted on the hills around us like the fluid
in electrical experiments, which are kept up for some
minutes together.   Never was such a scene of devastation in a camp.   At last about three o'clock it
abated, and we ran to the horses almost beaten and
frozen to death, and rode them about for half an hour.
One had been struck by the lightning and killed.
Captain Clarke* of the *Braakel* had given me some
rum: this saved me a serious illness, for I was
obliged to go all day barefooted, and enabled me to
do much good.

The day continued partially bad, but at evening the
wind rose and blew a hurricane.   During the whole
night it raged with tremendous severity.   All the
tents were blown down and most of the huts unroofed.
Signal guns of distress firing the whole night from the
ships driving in the harbour, and the confusion of noises
from the horses men and officers exposed to the fury
of the storm from the tents being blown away in a
moment, made it a perfect night of horror.   The
lightning was one incessant flashing of the most vivid
intensity.   At four o'clock in the morning a gust came
which threatened universal destruction.   The confusion on shore revived, and the distress-guns again
re-echoed.   Nothing could have borne up against it
five minutes longer; but this proved the last effort of
the wind, and in a moment all was calm.   Many
vessels are totally dismasted.   During the height of

* Brother of Clarke the traveller.—R. W.—*See below.*

the storm poor Sally, who has been a soldier's wife
these seven years and who is now with her husband
in the 7th Dragoons, miscarried. The dragoon told
me that she was lying in bed and the water rushing
over her in a torrent. I mention this as an instance
of the suffering which these poor creatures endure.

Feb. 13.—This morning I went round all the polacres
in which we are to sail, and fixed upon No. 13 for myself,—a Russian brig manned with Greeks. Captain
Chollet, and my adjutant Lieut. Barnard, accompanied
me. On my way I learnt the certain intelligence of a
Russian war. The 11th and 12th embark to-morrow ;
we the next day. My family is increased by a beautiful white horse which I mean to ride in action : I call
him Octavius.

Feb. 15.—Yesterday morning we marched to embark, but only half the troops could do so as the
other ships were not ready. In the evening Money,
Hutchins, and I went into the country to buy lambs.
An old woman followed us from the mountains into
the camp: when there she went up directly to our
kitchen and seized a large pan: the cook struggled
with her: it was ridiculous enough to see the fight,
as the Turk always kept her hand to her face to hold
the clout on it. At last I interfered and, finding her
pretensions just, ordered restitution: this pleased all
the bystanding Turks excessively, and I could perceive by their manner that it was a trait which will
not soon be forgotten.

Feb. 22.—The day before yesterday the remainder
of the troops embarked. Foul weather has detained
us. The captain has just returned from the commodore, and we sail to-morrow morning. It is impossible

to say where we shall land ; but I believe near Alexandria; probably near the tower of the Arabs where
there is a good bay.*

* The journals from this date to the 27th of April are lost. It is no
part of the Editor's duty to fill up the details of the intervening history, as
Sir Robert Wilson's share in the operations does not appear in his own
narrative, from which the general outline will be taken at the beginning of
the next chapter.—ED.

CHAPTER IV.

[On the 23rd of February, 1801, the British army fifteen thousand three hundred and twenty strong, twelve thousand effective, on board of one hundred and seventy-five vessels under the command of Lord Keith, sailed from Marmorice Bay for the shores of Egypt.

On the 1st of March the leading frigate signalled land, which proved to be the coast near the Arabs' tower, and on the following morning the whole fleet anchored in Aboukir Bay; "the men-of-war riding exactly where the battle of the Nile was fought."

The memorable landing was effected on the 7th.

Lord Nelson has left a proud memorial for the army and its gallant chief in the following letter, addressed to Sir Robert Wilson in acknowledgment of the receipt of a copy of his "History of the Expedition" published in the following year:—

LORD NELSON TO SIR ROBERT WILSON.

DEAR SIR,   Merton, December 23, 1802.

I FEEL most exceedingly honoured and flattered by your present of your valuable book of the Egyptian Campaign.

I really have always said, and I do think, that the landing of the British army was the very finest act that even a British army could achieve. Aboukir will stand recorded in both our services; and I can assure you that I always hope that both our services will, with pleasure, enjoy the deserved success of either, and that our only emulation will be who can render most service by their exertions to our king and country.

The very handsome manner [in which] you are pleased to speak of my services demands my warmest thanks. Your gallant, and ever to be lamented chief proved, by the manner in which he fell, what an old French general said when asked what made a good or a bad general. He replied, "Two words—*allons—allez*." Your chief and myself have taken the first and victory followed; and the medal which you so deservedly wear proves that you have imbibed the same sentiments. With every good wish,

I am, dear Sir,
Your most obliged servant,
NELSON AND BRONTE.

The approaches to Alexandria were successively made good. On the 13th, the British troops attacked the French posted on a ridge in advance of their main position on the covering heights in front of Alexandria; dislodged, drove them back over the intervening plain into their own intrenchments, and occupied the position. The castle of Aboukir was taken. Intelligence was received on the 20th that General Menou had joined the army of General Friant with his whole force.

At three o'clock on the morning of the 21st of March the French general moved from his post of advantage on the superior range of parallel heights, and attacked the British in their lines.

Before ten o'clock the battle of Alexandria was fought and won. "Honour to the brave!" On that field of his glory the gallant veteran, Sir Ralph Abercromby, received his mortal wound. He fell * as a soldier must desire to fall, if death is to be met in battle, conscious of duty nobly done and in the triumph of a momentous victory.

On the 26th the Capitan Pacha landed in the bay of Aboukir.

Sir Ralph Abercromby lingered till the 28th and died; Major-General Hutchinson succeeding to the command in chief.

An attempt upon Rosetta was soon determined

* The well-known engraving from the picture by Sir Robert Ker Porter represents the moment when the hero, long after he had received the fatal wound, sunk exhausted by his efforts in the field. Around are portraits of his brothers-in-arms. Among the rest is that of Sir Robert Wilson—the only officer in a hussar uniform. The painter has very skilfully represented his characteristic energy in the forward pressure of the attitude, and his sympathy of heart and spirit in the action of the hand.—ED.

upon in order to obtain the command of the Nile; and for this service General Hutchinson detached a small force to act in concert with four thousand Turks of the Capitan Pacha's army, the whole under the command of Colonel Spencer. The detachment marched on the 2nd of April.

Rosetta was taken on the 8th after a faint resistance and Fort St. Julien invested.

On the 13th, the embankment of the canal of Alexandria was cut. General Hutchinson consented to this destructive measure with great reluctance; but it seems to have been necessary for the attainment of the objects of the expedition. In a few hours the vast tract, anciently the Lake Mareotis but for centuries rescued from the dominion of the waters and subject to the cultivating hand of man, was covered again with the wasting "inundation."

The garrison of St. Julien surrendered on the 19th after a gallant defence, and the command of the Nile was secured. The easy accomplishment of this enterprise determined General Hutchinson to direct in person the further operations in the interior which he now resolved upon; and leaving General Coote in command of the forces watching the French at Alexandria, he joined the Rosetta army, which had been already strongly reinforced, on the 26th of April.]

April 27.—On the 23rd I left the camp and went to Aboukir. The next morning I rode to Rosetta, arrived in time for Birch's dinner, and determined to take up my quarters with him and join his mess. The house is miserable beyond description—mosquitoes, fleas, filth. The service has affected me in some de-

gree; but most have felt a feebleness and pain in the
bones since they came here. In the evening I went
and called upon Mr. Hammer, Sir Sidney Smith's
Turkish interpreter. I found him in the house of
Madam D'Arcy, sister-in-law of Wortley Montagu
who lived in Rosetta many years. This Mrs. D'Arcy's
maiden name was Dormer. She came from Italy with
Wortley Montague when she was very young, and
was educated in his harem; for he always lived in
every country in which he resided exactly as a
native. M. D'Arcy, a French merchant settled
here, married her: he died some time ago; but she
proposes to pass the remainder of her life in this
wretched country, to which twenty-one years' residence has habituated her. She has the remains of
good looks, appears to be about forty, and has preserved the English dress, manners, and language.

Captain Clarke, his brother,* and a Mr. Cripps, who
have been travelling all over Russia, Turkey, &c.,
arrived yesterday, and I was much amused with a
conversation respecting the existence of Troy. They
and Mr. Hammer, who have been there, convinced
themselves that they saw everything exactly as
Homer described it: contrary to the opinion of Mr.
Bryant, who has written a book in which he describes
the history of the siege although he never visited the
spot; and against a Mr. Carlisle, who was there at the
same time with them but whom they abused most un-
mercifully because he could not imagine the place "ubi
Troja fuit." Which is right and which is wrong it
is not for me to determine; but as many inscriptions
are brought from the plain itself by Mr. Clarke,

* Edward Daniel Clarke.—ED.

which he intends to present to the University of Cambridge, the learned may have an opportunity of forming their own judgment.

Yesterday a transaction was discovered which exposes the system of Turkish government, and affords a melancholy prospect for the territory returning under its yoke. The Caia Bey, or general of the army here, sent his chief into this town: he summoned the merchants, laid on them a contribution of fifty purses, each purse to contain five hundred piastres, and threatened them with the bowstring if they discovered the transaction to the Capitan Pacha or the English. The poor frightened merchants instantly promised obedience and in five days paid the money. Accident discovered the affair, and it is to be reported to General Hutchinson, who will find it a very delicate one.

This day a good regulation will be made as to the value of money and the price of provisions. The extravagance of the English and the avarice of the natives have raised everything to an exorbitant price. A maximum is imperative when an army is quartered among a people who have no idea of justice. An Arab would rather have eaten one of his own fingers than endeavoured to impose thus during the domination of the French.

April 30.—On the 26th General Hutchinson arrived, and said that I was the only person who had given him a true description of this town.

This morning I finished a letter to Lord Lansdowne.

I am now going to call on Sir Sidney; who unfortunately for the army and the country is in consequence of some low intrigue, but on pretence of the

French fleet being expected, ordered on board his own ship. The French fleet was seen dismasted, on the 24th inst., going into Toulon.

May 4.—I learnt Arabic the whole morning. On the 1st we heard the news of the deaths of the Emperor Paul and Mourad Bey. The following letter was received from the latter by Sir Sidney Smith in April, by the hands of a messenger :—

TRANSLATION OF A LETTER WRITTEN BY MOURAD BEY TO SIR SIDNEY SMITH.*

Dated Girgé, the 2nd April, 1801.

MY HONOURABLE, DEAR, AND OLD FRIEND COMMODORE SMITH.—It was always one of my most ardent wishes to keep up a continual correspondence with you, and to express to you the sentiments of friendship which I nourish in the secret of my heart for you; but not knowing in what part of the Mediterranean you were cruizing, I was obliged to interrupt my correspondence with you. Now I have received your letter through *Abdul Gawy*, by which I have learnt the two victories of the British, and the reduction of the castle of Aboukir, the garrison of which were made prisoners. All these news have affected me with as great joy as the tidings of the revenge against my enemies may be supposed to give me. God be praised for these victories, and with his assistance you will, I have not a doubt, destroy the

---

* With reference to this letter, after a short quotation from it, Sir R. Wilson thus writes in a note to the "History of the Egyptian Expedition:" "Many reasons forbid the publication of the whole of this interesting letter, but it is preserved as a very valuable document, which hereafter will reflect considerable credit on the character of our country as esteemed at that time in Egypt."—ED.

rest of our enemies.   God knows that my good wishes accompany you.

A real friendship subsists between your Court and the Sublime Porte; your countrymen are celebrated for courage and valour far above all other European nations.   Myself, I am attached to you for this long time, and have therefore a great many reasons to pray God to give you more victories and to destroy all the French.

I wrote to you formerly by *Abdallah Bachi* and *Arnaut Selim Cachof*, another letter you will have received by the hands of your secretary. *I have never begged anybody's protection*, but I solicit that of the British, for I have ever considered them as more faithful to their word than European Courts.   I have considered them as my friends, " *therefore I put myself under your protection.*"   You know very well that I fear nobody but the Sublime Porte; as the proverb says, "The arrow stuck in the eagle's wing was an arrow made of an eagle's feather."   It is known that the Sublime Porte does not always delight in its most faithful servants—those who are the friends of its friends, and the enemies of its enemies.   Having put myself under your protection you should act in a manner becoming your honour and glory.

You have heard and you know that since the arrival of the French at Alexandria until this time I have served the Sublime Porte with the utmost sincerity; that I employed gold and blood, flattering myself to be recompensed at least with an imperial office; that I was wholly occupied in opposing the enemy without rest or sleep day or night; that I destroyed more than twelve thousand Frenchmen, and lost more than five thousand Mamelukes and Cachofs, and after all this you have heard yourself what was said on my account at the Imperial camp.

In you I have confidence. I beg your Court's protection and fear nobody else. God knows that I wish to send you all the provisions of Upper Egypt, but you know that all the Arabs and all the peasantry of this country are in accord with the French, and that it is impossible at this moment to send you anything by land or water. You may convince yourself of the truth of this by the reports of others. As soon as you approach Cairo, with the assistance of God, I will furnish you with anything that is in my power and provide you everything you desire.

One of my men is arrived from Djedda with the news that the 1st Chaoul (13th February), twenty English ships had entered that port, and that twenty others were at *Moka*, and that forty were seen under weigh off the Persian Gulf.

(Signed)   MOURAD BEY, Sangiak.   (L.S.)

First P.S.—I send you this by *Sheik Ibrahim*, son of *Abdallah Bachi Mogrebi*, by whose verbal relation you will be informed of the rest. I beg you to send me an answer instantly.

Second P.S.—My dear friend, I have no better friend than you; I have known you a long time; I am afraid of the fate that hangs over me; I am apprehensive of the Sublime Porte; I request you will give me security by a friendly letter. As long as I enjoy your protection I fear no danger from the Sublime Porte. I pray you give me a letter which gives me this guarantee from you.

The army on the whole is very healthy, but ophthal-
mia from the sirocco, and dysentery have prevailed to
some extent.   This morning it blows a gale.   I never
was in so windy a country.   Above twenty sailors
have been drowned at the entrance of the Nile within
this week.   The sand-bar shifts continually and the
sea, in bad weather, breaks on it furiously.

I leave Rosetta with pleasure, for I shall not see in
camp so many horrible objects as swarm in this town.
I am now going to ride out and meet the seven hundred Turkish horse expected to cross the Nile from
the Grand Vizier's army.

May 6, 3 P.M. Camp near Deroute.

In the evening of the 4th I went to camp : in the
morning of the 5th the army marched, at five o'clock.
I went with San Luz, some Turkish cavalry forming
the advanced guard of the right column.   Muley
Mohammed, Prince of Fez, joined us on the march
with some horsemen.   He is remarkably good-looking,
and was picturesquely dressed in white edged with
red, and a gold pouch belt over his shoulders.   The
people regard him as a saint.   To please me he performed his manœuvres on horseback, both with musket and sword, with a dexterity which was admirable :
all his attitudes were graceful.   His sword was the
best and finest I ever saw.   He is considered the
bravest man in this country ; performing such feats
that all people regard him as invulnerable and sacred.
He headed the insurrection at Rahmanieh, when Buonaparte was in Syria, and where all the French garrison
was destroyed.   Although a price was set upon his head
he has just passed through their army, coming from

Mourad Bey. The commandant of the Turkish cavalry has promised me a fine sword which I shall value highly.

We arrived on our ground about three o'clock, taking up our position within sight of the enemy. This morning I got up at four o'clock as the army was to march to a better position; but we did not move till six. I went out in front with General Hutchinson to reconnoitre and did not return till twelve. We are now about three miles from the enemy who are strongly posted. We wait for the main body of the Turkish cavalry, who certainly join us to-day or to-morrow, before we advance to the attack.

Savary says there is *no rain in Egypt:* yesterday it rained heavily.

May 8.   Camp near El Hafa,
French Position.

Yesterday I went out with Birch to patrol, and to our great astonishment advanced to the French position which we found already occupied by some Turks. The French left it in the night. It was not defencible against our superior force. The Turks cut off the heads of six Frenchmen whom they found in Fouah, put them into a sack, and presented them to their general. General Hutchinson has remonstrated against this practice.

This morning I saw a return, found in one of the French huts, of the state of the army which had been here. It amounted to three thousand three hundred and thirty-one men, including officers, sappers and marines; but exclusive of five hundred cavalry. This is another proof of the danger of keeping papers. In the evening another letter was found, from the commandant of Cairo; stating that within a fortnight he had lost one hundred and forty men by the plague, and that within the last forty-eight hours his wife and three servants had died. In the morning I went over with Colonel Cole and Major Maxwell to Fouah, the ci-devant capital of Egypt but now the most miserable town in the world.

We received the melancholy intelligence of Mr. Keith's death. He was a great friend of mine and we were to have gone together to the Mamelukes. It is a sad destiny to be drowned in such a pitiful river as the Nile after so many escapes. I lament him much.

The Turkish cavalry so long expected is at length arrived and is now crossing the Nile. The Capitan Pacha has also come to Fouah, and crosses over to us to-morrow.

May 11.—On the morning of the 9th the army advanced. I rode on at the head of the right column but soon joined the advanced guard. When we came near Rahmanieh we found some cavalry on the banks of the canal of Alexandria, but I discovered that they were not French therefore advanced myself and was presently surrounded by about a hundred Bedouin Arabs who crowded about me to shake hands; a proof of friendship which I could have dispensed with. Colonel Murray went along the canal, and I confiding in my new friends went alone with them within half a mile of Rahmanieh on Colonel Murray's right. I advanced to within a hundred yards of the French vidette and remained about a quarter of an hour re-connoitring their position; when the Arabs made me go back as the French cavalry were turning out and galloping along the canal. I got back on the other side safe, and found Colonel Murray also retiring. I galloped off then to General Hutchinson and reported the extraordinary bad position of the French: they had their right, centre, and left upon the Nile. The French cavalry to the number of six hundred advanced upon the plain, which made it necessary for our army to form. A great deal of skirmishing went on between the Turkish cavalry and the French. At length the 12th and a detachment of the 26th (our whole cavalry did not amount to four hundred men) were ordered to advance with two pieces of cannon. At this moment an Arab coming in reported that the French were retiring, which induced Colonel Abercromby to ask me to ascertain the fact, if possible, by going to the canal. I was obliged to make a considerable détour and had nearly lost my horse in a bog; but at last reached it and found that there was no truth in the report of their *retiring* towards Alexandria. On my return I was obliged to pass under a cannonade directed against our dragoons, the first shot of which took off the leg of Captain King of the 26th and killed three horses.

General Hutchinson, not thinking it desirable to attack that night, prepared to take a position. In the interim the Capitan Pacha arrived and held a conference for some time; after which he went to the Turks on the left, and I with him, to see the attack of our gun-boats cannonading the French position.

Meeting Captain Brice, who was going over to Colonel Stuart's column, I got into his boat. We crossed out of fire, but as we landed saw the sailors who had just buried Lieutenant Hobbs of the *Delft*:

he was killed by a twenty-four pounder, which entered
at the bow of the boat striking off the heads of two
sailors and wounding three others severely. We had
a walk of a mile and a half to get to Colonel Stuart,
and had many shot whizzing around us. We found
him and Lord Bury within half musket-shot of the
enemy's battery on the opposite side. The soldiers
were lying down under cover of an embankment.
The Turks, as is their constant practice, had burrowed
in intrenchments thrown up by their own hands
without spades; but their standards were placed in
their front, attracting all the fire. They particularly
complimented Colonel Stuart with a number placed
in front of him, which he in vain endeavoured to
remove. The 89th greatly distinguished themselves
this day; advancing to their position under a very
heavy fire of grape, and driving before them three
hundred French and some cavalry. The Turks can
scarcely cry out "Bono John" enough—this is their
mark of esteem for us. I do not know whether they
allude to "John Bull." We in return say, "Bono
John Turk."

After a complete view of the rear of the enemy's
position we went back, but on our way ascended the
minaret of a village from which we saw the French
column retreating. The information was too precious
for delay; we therefore proceeded as fast as possible,
got into our boat very tired and faint, for it was the hot-
test day we had yet experienced in Egypt, crossed over,
mounted our horses, and galloped to General Hutchinson. We found that he had advanced to the canal
with the army, whose flankers were warmly engaged.
The Turks were really under a hot fire and were ad-

vancing most gallantly to the very intrenchments of the French, when an order was given to retire as it was getting dark. The Turks, who were within a hundred yards of the works when this order was given, went back precipitately, almost breaking our line which was their support. It was not deficiency of courage, but of practice and discipline, that made them act in so unsoldierly a manner. As their retreat made a feint of coming between us and the Nile the whole army was obliged to move to the left, and as it was dark this was done with some confusion. The Turks kept us in alarm as they, determined not to be surprised, fired volleys at shadows.

The next day, while I was riding with Birch who was ordered to dispose some troops for the attack on the left, Captain Brice came by and said that a French officer had just come over the water from the fort with a letter. I went immediately to General Hutchinson, who ordered me to go to the fort and keep back the Turks from entering lest they should murder the garrison. I found a vast number of them already on all sides as they had seen the flag of truce; but they went back quietly at my desire. I then rode to the fort, where I found Colonel Anstruther and Murray in conversation with the commandant. From thence I proceeded to General Hutchinson, who was waiting for the Capitan Pacha's consent to give the garrison a capitulation. While I was there the French officer who had come with the letter arrived. He was an artillerist, and a very gentlemanlike man. Colonel Brown soon after came into the tent with the report that a French party of forty dragoons had just been taken by a party of his own. The prisoners were soon brought in. The French captain who commanded informed us that he was coming from Rahmanich to Alexandria, which he had left four days since having been detained so long by the inundation; that he was escorting an aide-de-camp of General Biron carrying despatches; that they were attacked by a party of Bedouin Arabs about half a mile from our right, who shot a sergeant and mortally wounded the aide-de-camp; that at this moment they saw to their great astonishment a party of English twice as strong as themselves charging towards them. They had no idea that the British troops were in the neighbourhood, for the inhabitants and Arabs had deceived them and said that the French had not even retired from Rosetta. They saw now no alternative but death or surrender to our dragoons, as the Arabs were crowding in upon them: they therefore held out the white handkerchief. The head of the sergeant had been cut off but the aide-de-camp was brought in. There were five others also wounded. The detachment was of the 22nd Dragoons, the best and heaviest regiment here. They are known to the 15th as the horse-hair cap regiment whom we charged at Duffel.

The men were delighted at being taken, saying that they had long desired such an occasion to return. The officers were by no means dissatisfied. They were allowed to sell their horses.

As it was of importance to recover the despatches which the aide-de-camp declared he had lost in the affair I galloped off directly, and with much trouble and four dollars recovered from the Arabs about forty letters, but not the principal despatch. They promised to get it for me, and also the aide-de-camp's sabre, which I hear is a magnificent one.

I hastened back with my prize and we opened all the letters; but they contained little intelligence, as all declared that they were "forbidden on any pretence whatever to write about anything that occurred in the army"—a sufficient proof that Menou is in no pleasant situation—and "that they can scarcely speak without being liable to cashiering." They complain much of our cutting the dyke, and say that the water has penetrated far into Libya. Sir Sidney has been a three days' cruise on it. They state that some sailors escaped out of a vessel driven on shore by us report that Mr. Pitt has accepted the portefeuille: and that Mr. Fox is gone to Paris and Buonaparte's brother to London to treat on the subject of peace. They seem totally ignorant of our movements on this side.

After reading these papers I rode to the fort and French position, and I am convinced that the general would have done wrong, without the most positive certainty of what did actually happen, if he had attacked on the first day; although I know that many differ in opinion. The French evacuated the place in such confusion that they were obliged to leave much valuable property behind. They threw over into the water all the cannon on the works near the Nile, and out of their gun-boats; but they will be recovered. There are many valuable brass guns. They destroyed vast quantities of ammunition, and abandoned to us about sixty dgerms and eight gun-boats. In the first were seven cannon and great stores of flour and biscuit. No English went into the village of Rahmanieh, but the Turks defied the plague and orders. The French did not leave in their pest-houses any of their own people, but they left many Arabs. It struck me that the most melancholy circumstance of this dreadful malady is the necessary exclusion from all friends and attendance while the faculties remain perfect. It is a tragic preparation for the grave.

The name of the French commander was Lacroix— a very good man. The officers were all of the better sort; but they complained bitterly of their soldiers, and said that they were so mutinous that they could scarcely be brought into action.

The French having gone to Cairo it was judged necessary for us to follow them, as otherwise they might beat the Grand Vizier and our troops at Suez and prevent the Mamelukes from joining us.

Their whole force is thus distributed in Egypt. Four thousand infantry and eight hundred cavalry at Cairo, and on march thither three thousand infantry and four hundred dragoons; also three thousand sailors at Alexandria. The British force following the French is five thousand men.

It is certainly a daring enterprise to advance into a country on a sudden resolve, unprepared in any way, ignorant of the ground we are to pass over, and very little superior in numbers to the enemy. But what may not be expected from an army which has gained such miraculous successes? which when unprovided with artillery or cavalry has effected a landing, maintained its footing, and almost acquired possession of a country where from first to last fifty thousand Frenchmen have been thrown in, and where a very superior force still remains to oppose it? The expedition

to Egypt was an ill-advised one, but the troops have
deserved all gratitude from England.   Such an army I
never served with before.   Brave the British *always*
are; but such an order and discipline reigns here
throughout this army that one might suppose every
individual to be a noble gentleman.

This morning we marched at eight o'clock.   I went
in front of the Turks to see the cavalry.   It is not
composed of Turks, but of Arabs and all the vagabonds
of Syria.   Such a crew I never saw.   None of them
have swords, and but a few have muskets.

The villages through which we marched, and their
inhabitants, were wretched in the extreme; yet the
Turks plundered all they could even from these
miserable beings.   The exertions of the English
officers saved much cruelty; and I hope that the
punishment of one Turk, whom the Caia Bey must
execute, may have a good effect.   This day, however,
his men seemed very riotous and even hooted him as
he passed.   He said to General Hutchinson : "They
are a set of impertinent fellows whom I can scarcely
command."

Nothing can exceed the high character of the
British, or the love which the inhabitants and the
Arabs show towards us; but the Turks do the cause
much harm.   Their thirst for plunder is so great that
this morning they even entered and rifled the pest-
houses, or straw huts, where the infected people are
abandoned to death.

May 13.—Yesterday we marched about ten miles,
passing over the ground where Buonaparte beat the
Mamelukes.   The sirocco parched us to extremity.

General Hutchinson has just sent for me.   I am

going off to the Grand Vizier with despatches, and
have not a moment to lose, as my guard is ready. I
am also sent for to the Capitan Pacha to receive
despatches from him.

May 19.—On the 13th I started at seven P.M. from
the general's tent. At nine we crossed the Nile. My
guard was a Mameluke of the name of Mahomet Aga
a great friend of Mourad Bey's, and four Arabs. On
the other side we were joined by an armed detachment
of infantry, which, however, I refused to take ; but an
old Mameluke, wounded at the battle of the Pyramids, would proceed with me.

On the 14th, after travelling all night, we entered
the town of Sais. Here I found that I had lost every
shilling I had out of my pocket. It was no agreeable
thing to find myself penniless in a strange country,
with a long journey before me. However, money was
not wanted, for the people everywhere fed me with
bread and milk. The joy at seeing a British officer
was universal and most sincere. I travelled on the
whole night, but with difficulty got my guard to proceed as they were not accustomed to such exertion.
As it was, they would frequently stop to wash, and
then I found it impossible to do anything with them,
as they used only their hands to divide their meat and
take up their rice. I have seen seventeen hands at
once, black brown and tawny, in a large dish. This
formed a horrid contrast with the rice. My diet was
milk and bread. My friend Mahomet Aga one evening indeed took up a bone from which he tore a bit
of meat and thrust it into my mouth ; but I spit it out
again, nauseated beyond endurance.

The next morning, I crossed the Damietta branch

of the Nile at Zephta. It is nearly as broad as the
Rosetta branch. This was the fourth body of water I
passed through, including the canal of Menouf.

About four in the afternoon I arrived at the Grand
Vizier's camp at Balbeis. This Turkish camp was a
scene of universal confusion — horsemen galloping
about in all directions; pachas and agas moving with
vast suites to show their parade rather than inspect
their troops; others in their tents smoking, and surrounded by their numerous slaves; firing of pistols,
neighing of the stallions, dead carcases, pestilential air,
clouds of dust.

I was first conducted to the Caia Bey, the Grand
Vizier not being in his tent. He is a good and very
affable man: his character for courage stands high.
From him I went to the Reis Effendi, who was in London with the first Turkish ambassador. Here I saw
Major Hollowell who has been attached a long time
to their army.

The news had just arrived that the French had left
Cairo the same morning and were at El Hanka.
There was consequently much confusion. When the
Grand Vizier came in I went to him, and was received
with great marks of attention. He is a very fine old
man, with a most beautiful beard soft and glossy as
satin; his dress most magnificent; his tent correspondingly so.

When the state ceremony was over everybody returned but the Reis Effendi, Major Hollowell, Montresor who was on his way to Suez, and myself.
The despatches were read, but the advice contained
in them from circumstances could not be followed.
The Turkish army had mutinied the day before, be-

cause they were not allowed to go and fight the French under the walls of Cairo.

Reports coming from all quarters that the French were still advancing, four thousand cavalry under the command of the Caia Bey were ordered out, with instructions to charge the French columns during their march in the night.

The Grand Vizier became very anxious that General Hutchinson should be informed of his situation as soon as possible. I therefore thought it my duty to offer to return to him instantly. The offer was, of course, accepted with great satisfaction.

I waited however till twelve at night in hopes of a battle, but then set off as no firing was heard.

The Grand Vizier sent me two horses as a present, but I would only accept one. The Reis Effendi assured me that his Highness was in the greatest possible distress, because he could not make me the presents he wished as all his valuables were packed up.

It was no small exertion that I was about to make, as I had taken no rest for two nights and had been constantly on horseback; but a sense of duty and *love of praise* animated me.* I stopped at the Seraskier's tent on my way, and found him a man of most determined character and soldier-like spirit.

I found it necessary to make the greatest efforts to convey my information to the general. Our route lay by El Hanka. I passed within half a mile of the French; saw them all plainly; was a little alarmed once at our horses neighing, which might have discovered us. My friend Mahomet Aga—the finest character I ever knew—would return with me, though

* "Vincit amor patriæ laudumque immensa cupido."—*Virgil.*—Ed.

he was much fatigued. The whole of that night and until eleven on the night following I was on horse-back, except while crossing the Nile and the Menouf canal, and for one hour when I baited my horse. The Arabs were obliged to give up the journey, for I insisted on proceeding during the heat of the day and the sun was blazing indeed. Poor Mahomet Aga was nearly overcome; never before had he made such a journey. When we reached the Nile we found ourselves close to the advanced posts of our army in the Delta. There were no boats to take my horses across, but we hailed a gun-boat which sent a boat for us, and in this Mahomet and I crossed the river. The sailors told us to keep along the banks, but never said a word of the Desert. I soon, however, found myself surrounded by sand. We pushed on for two miles but still never reached the Nile again. Mahomet now began to be in great agitation. He kept crying, Allah! Allah! and threw himself on the ground. With difficulty I made him get up. He put my hand upon his forehead and arose. The sweat fell in great drops from him, and he trembled violently. At last, after wandering about some time, I perceived in what I thought must be the direction of the Nile something black. We pressed forward and found it to be earth not sand. I knew therefore that we were on the border of the Desert.

I felt certainly much relieved; for the moment I thought that I could get no water I thirsted for it, and the deep sand momentarily increased the sense of drought. In another hour we saw the Nile, and Mahomet leapt for joy like a child. Soon we hailed our gun-vessels for a boat and crossed over to the other side, lying all the rest of the night on the ground. At daybreak we went down the Nile three miles and arrived opposite head-quarters, when I re-crossed the river. The general was surprised at my return : and of course when he heard my intelligence appreciated the expedition I had used.

After breakfasting with the general, I went into the Nile—a most necessary purification. While I was dressing again some Arabs reported that a French convoy was passing the Desert: the cavalry and in-fantry were ordered out : I felt no longer any fatigue, and determined to go also. In vain I endeavoured to borrow a horse ; I was obliged to take the one which had conveyed me from the Grand Vizier's—the best animal I ever rode, for he seemed as eager as his master and to partake of his anxiety to get up to the enemy. At an immense distance we saw a dark mass on the horizon. Colonel Abercromby and I quickly passed our columns and, trusting to the Arabs who swarmed out in all directions, we went at full speed for seven or eight miles.

I was the first who got up tolerably close. It was my wish to make the Arabs fire on the front and flank of the enemy's column, but they would not venture within musket-shot. I was, however, compelled to ascertain the strength of the column and got very close, when two or three tirailleurs gave me the benefit of their shots ; one of which was nearer to me than I wish another to be in Egypt: the man who fired it afterwards told me that he was glad he did his duty in endeavouring to hit me, but equally glad that destiny had averted the direction, for at the same distance he would engage to hit an apple. I perceived some confusion among the enemy, but saw a very formidable force indeed. I knew that our cavalry alone could get up, and that for the infantry it was impossible. I thought of Sir Wm. Erskine, who with a very few men took two battalions by only asking them to surrender; and I took my resolution knowing that at all events delay was a considerable object. I therefore galloped to Colonel Abercromby, and begged permission to go with a flag of truce and ask the French to surrender. He approved much of the idea. For some time I could get no white pocket-handkerchief. At last a Major of the 12th lent me one. The cavalry, 240 in number, were by this time come up; also two pieces of cannon. I stuck the handkerchief on my sword but when I got near the French it blew off. However, I galloped on and asked for the commandant, observing everything at the same time most carefully. The commandant, Cavalier, chef de brigade and of the dromedary corps, advanced. I said: "I am come, sir, to propose that you should surrender to the English. Our columns are advancing against you, and it is humanity to offer you permission to go to France after laying down your arms." Cavalier replied: "You must retire from our columns. It is our duty to fight." I answered: "Then, sir, the responsibility rests upon your head; and remember that it is a dreadful one. You sacrifice your people." I turned my horse to go away. I heard the soldiers ask whether I had not said the words "return to France." I was presently called back, but pretended not to hear. An aide-de-camp galloped after me, and said that the commandant wished to hear my proposals again. I repeated them. He said that he must consult with

his officers.   There was a visible sensation in the corps.
I saw the termination of this affair.   In a moment
Cavalier came up to me and said that he would consent to give up the camels and baggage, but demanded
that the troops should go to Cairo unmolested.   My
reply was : " You, sir, must have a poor opinion of our
judgment or yourselves if you suppose that we will
allow the army at Cairo to be increased by a force of
five or six hundred men."   At length it was settled
that they should lay down their arms at head-quarters ;
that all private property should be respected ; and
that, in conformity with the King's direction to the
commander-in-chief, all men taken by his army should
be sent free to France and not considered prisoners
after their arrival.

The Arabs began to press in, but I ordered a squadron to surround the column and keep them back.
General Doyle and General Hutchinson—the latter
had by this time arrived—ratified the terms : and we
found ourselves masters of above seven hundred
camels, eighty men of the dromedary corps, one hundred and thirty dragoons, some hair-cap men as
stated before, three hundred and fifty infantry and
officers, artillerymen, &c. ; amounting in total to five
hundred and ninety-seven Frenchmen, and about three
hundred Arab camel-drivers : also of one piece of
cannon.

The convoy had left Alexandria to get provisions
at Rahmanich ; but finding that place taken was
proceeding to Cairo for the same purpose, which
proves Alexandria to be in want.   Some Arabs had
followed them the whole way from Alexandria, harassing them much and sending word to us of their

march. These useful allies have been well paid.
This shows the danger of making the natives hostile ;
but how can they be otherwise when the French allow
that in Upper Egypt they have killed thirty thousand
Egyptians—when every village that they have passed
in this country has been destroyed by them ?   Even
within a hundred yards of the place where I am writing are the ruins of a large village burnt by them,
where all the women and children were put to the
sword.

The successful issue of this enterprise was most
flattering to me. I rode to head-quarters with Cavalier,
who, after depositing his arms, came with General
D'Estaing's aide-de-camp and a colonel of infantry to
dine with the general.

As this journal is only intended for my own family
I may, without being charged with vanity, state all
this : I do not mean to claim any extraordinary
merit, only I had recollection enough to try a thing
often tried before : by the same stratagem Buonaparte
once in Italy succeeded in taking four thousand men.
Certainly Cavalier might have got off, for our cavalry
could not have followed a league further having
neither water nor provisions; but Cavalier did not
know this. He knew, however, that if he was beat the
Arabs and Turks would kill every man; he had a
desert to wander in ; water only for one day ; and he
must strike very deep into the Desert indeed to avoid
falling in with other troops of ours. It was a desperate situation.   On the other hand France their
native country, return to friends and relations, all was
within their reach. The officers confessed afterwards
that the words I made use of, "revenir en France,"
told like an electric shock on their minds.   Pleasure

gleamed in the flash of the imagination, dispelling their miserable anxiety and the scene before them.

The men of the dromedary corps were of the finest in form and countenance, and most beautifully appointed. It was an unique spectacle and made a powerful impression on all. The whole of the men taken were such as one might suppose the élite of the army of France to be.

Cavalier condemned the conduct of many general officers, and said that if Buonaparte or Kleber had been here we should have been opposed on our landing by eight thousand men instead of two; and that we should have found an intrenched camp at Rahmanieh.

I could not help, when Cavalier accused the Turks of barbarity, taking that opportunity of asking whether Buonaparte did really, as the Turks urge in their defence, massacre the garrison at Jaffa after it had surrendered three days. He answered that he was not at Jaffa at the time having gone on towards Acre: he confessed that he had heard it stated, but expressed a hope that Buonaparte had grounds for his justification before God and man.

I went to take leave of Cavalier at his embarkation with his men. He gave me his dromedary: and the commissary of war insisted on my accepting a costly marquee. All the officers said very flattering things, which made me almost feel shame; but I have the pleasure of reflecting that I have certainly obtained or increased their esteem for the English character.[*]

* Du lazaret de Rosette, le 10 Prairial, an 9, ou 30 May, 1801.

CAVALIER, CHEF DE BRIGADE, à MONSIEUR LE MAJOR WILSON.

Je suis, Monsieur, si convaincu de l'intérêt que vous prenez à nous, que je viens avec confiance vous prier d'engager Monsieur le Major Général

Isaac Bey on my return jumped out of the Capitan Pacha's barge, kissed me with a very hard beard, and told me that the Grand Vizier had beat the French. I galloped off instantly on a horse that I got without saddle or girth to the Caia Bey, and brought him to Isaac Bey who gave us the particulars of this important victory.

Camp, Chebreisse, May 23.

I went yesterday, after an interview with the Capitan Pacha, to the army of the Grand Vizier. The camp was forty miles distant. I was five hours *en chemin*. Delivered my despatches. The Turkish army was encamped near very high hills. The only position of heights in Egypt originally thrown up by the Romans.

This morning at eleven o'clock I was sent for by the Grand Vizier; when, after communicating to me some important information, he presented and invested me in due form with a beautiful Mameluke sabre of great value, and added costly gifts in embroidered silks, &c. I told him that I was a married man and mentioned

---

Hutchinson de donner de suite les ordres nécessaires pour l'entière exécution du traité que j'ai eu l'honneur de faire avec lui : depuis deux jours que je suis ici je n'ai pû faire exécuter une seule des conditions qui étaient à notre avantage. M. le Colonel Montresor, pour qui vous m'avez chargé d'une lettre, nous traite comme les Français qui ont été forcé de se rendre prisonniers de guerre. Vous connaissez, Monsieur, les conditions qui ont été librement contractées de part et d'autre ; je n'en réclame que la stricte exécution.

Je n'ai jusqu'à présent trouvé que peu de personnes qui vous ressemble, aussi moins le nombre en est grand, et plus les sentiments d'estime et d'affection que vous m'avez inspiré sont fondés et sincères. Je vous prie d'en agréer les témoignages. Le Commissaire de Guerre se rappelle à votre souvenir.

Je suis avec affection, Monsieur, votre dévoué serviteur,

CAVALIER

the number of my family, saying that his silks were therefore of higher value to me. He laughed much at my having so many children; and was much pleased when I answered to his observation that I had " married too young," that " this was impossible as I had only known real happiness from that moment."

His Highness ordered me an escort on my return, although I had come in perfect safety alone; however, I contrived to take only one Mameluke. We were five hours riding—or what is called steeple-hunting—about thirty-six miles, including the time lost by our horses knocking up for the last five miles.

When I saw the Capitan Pacha he was much pleased with my diligence. He took me in his barge to General Hutchinson, where I communicated my despatches; and, at his desire, wrote down all that I had verbally delivered. I used much caution in this, from a sense of the responsibility.

I am sorry to say that my horse, which I rode home this evening, or rather the dragoon's, is dead. I believe that the sailor who brought him up from the pontoon when I went into the Capitan Pacha's barge gave him too much water. It would distress me to think that I had ridden him too hard.

English Camp, May 29.

Thermometer 112° in the shade—the heat almost insupportable. The Capitan Pacha and the general arrived: they were received in great state by the Grand Vizier. Here I saw Ibrahim Bey—a fine old man, with a quick, sparkling eye: but the prince of the Mamelukes is Suliman Aga. The Mamelukes under

Ibrahim are in number about five hundred and sixty; very superior, in manner dress and appearance, to the Turks, but by no means mounted in the style that I expected. Indeed we have been grossly deceived as to the horses in this country. There are some handsome parade horses, bitted up with their severe bridles, but none can keep a high rate of speed for any distance: indeed the Grand Vizier told me that they do not value horses as Englishmen do for that quality, but only as they were strong and active. In Arabia Felix there is the species of blood horses which we admire, but they are very rare and exorbitantly dear. Of all those presented to General Hutchinson by the Grand Vizier and others, Ibrahim Bey sent the only two good ones. One, very small but elegant and thorough bred: the other, the largest black horse I ever saw, of the Nubian race; very active for his stupendous size, and so excellent, in my opinion, for the improvement of our English breed that I mean, if the general will not take him home, to ask for him that I may present him to the King. We hear that his Majesty is better—*grâce à Dieu.*

The Grand Vizier told me that it was his intention to ask that I might be allowed to remain with him: I of course thanked him, but I did not much wish it. He did so when on the following day I went to take leave of him; but the Capitan Pacha, who was then present, would not allow it. The next day we all set off. The general's brother and Proby, with a long retinue of led horses, were put under my convoy. After a seventeen hours' ride without food or drink we arrived here.

May 30.—Last night I went to pay my respects

to the Capitan Pacha—afterwards to the general,
where I found a man who had just come from Ibrahim—the Caia Bey of Osman Bey—to whom at nine
o'clock at night the general sent me off. He was
distant from our camp seven miles. He was much
surprised to see me, and much pleased as I was
the herald of security to him. He is an Upper
Egyptian—a man of extraordinary powers: indeed it
was necessary that Osman Bey, when he committed
himself and his Mamelukes to the conduct of an individual, should select the ablest. I returned about
twelve at night, and set off again this morning at five
to meet him; but after a ride of six miles I found
that he had passed on, taking the direct road in order
to avoid the Capitan Pacha till he had seen the general.
When I came to the general's tent I found Ibrahim
already there with some Mamelukes most superbly
mounted indeed.

Osman Bey, with near three thousand Mamelukes,
has advanced within eighteen miles of us. He passed by
the French troops at Djezzar, opposite Cairo, but they
did not dare to attack him. This defection of theirs
from the French is of the most important advantage to
us. We have reason to believe that it was the enemy's
intention to retreat from Cairo into Upper Egypt.
They will find there now a very formidable body of
troops ready to oppose them. If Sir Home Popham's
expedition lands at Cossir the friendship of Osman Bey
will be of still more essential value.

The Capitan Pacha yesterday asked me to go in
his ship to Constantinople when we are about to return
home—an offer which I shall probably accept.

June 1.—The army marched. The Capitan Pacha

the evening before sent to ask me to go up in his
vessel. I dined with him tête-à-tête, Isaac Bey being
the attendant slave and not admitted to eat till the
Pacha had dined. The Capitan Pacha pulled my
meat to pieces with his fingers, and I was under the
necessity of playing the courtier's part and appearing
much pleased with the attention. He however very
nearly made me forget my courtesy by asking whether
I could write. Nothing could exceed his kindness and
solicitude to do everything that could be gratifying.
Hearing that we wanted wine, he yesterday ordered a
large Russian transport to go to Cyprus and bring
back all that she can purchase as a present to the
British army. The munificence of this extraordinary
man is unbounded. He is a character formed to
replace the sinking Crescent in its meridian glory. If
life is prolonged—but many think him in a rapid consumption—mankind will behold with astonishment
events planned by his penetrating intellect and executed by his daring hand. Firm perseverance is a
principal feature of his character, and his former
failure has only rendered him more eager for success.
It is not right to commit more to paper.

June 3.—I rode to the Mameluke camp yesterday.
Osman Bey is a noble-looking man; the Mamelukes
striking troops, richly dressed and beautifully mounted.
Their horses are all well bred, but small in general. Individually they would beat any cavalry in the world;
but collectively a squadron of British dragoons must,
from its superior weight and strength, ride down an
equal body of them.

There are about a hundred French among them who
had been taken, and who, averse to being exposed to

the shame of returning among their comrades after
their *humiliation*, preferred remaining in the service of
their Mameluke masters. Yet country is an overpower-
ing sentiment: one told me that he would prefer death
in France to the honours of a Bey of Egypt. I am
endeavouring to rescue them, and am intriguing at the
pride and interest of those who have the power to
release them. Last night I represented to the Capitan Pacha the impolicy of allowing Frenchmen to be
Mamelukes: urging that among the number there were
some clever men who might aspire to and probably
gain the dignity of Bey, when of course they would be
influenced by French politics. This day I shall use
much the same language to General Hutchinson, whose
humanity and generosity will induce him to do all in
his power.

Mahomed Bey Elfi —the last name signifies "a thousand," and implies that a thousand sequins was the price
given for him when a boy by Mourad Bey—invited
me to coffee in his tent. Syphax, the name I gave to
the Caia Bey from his exact similarity of character and
appearance to him as he is represented by Sallust,
was in the tent. Mahomed told me that Regnier came
to him when Cairo after the defeat of the Grand
Vizier was capitulating, wishing to prevail on him
who was the only one desirous of holding out longer
to accept terms. His answer was, "No! I am an
Englishman." Upon which Regnier replied, "You
are wrong; it is true that the English are superior to
us at sea, but by land they are not even respectable;
therefore why attach yourself to a power that can
never aid you?" Mahomed answered, "Is not the
sea considerably larger than the land?" Regnier

acknowledged it. "Then," said Mahomed, "as the dominion of the English is larger than yours so must they be greater; therefore I continue English."

Heard of a thousand men landed at Cossir.

June 5.—The army marched to Sinai, nine miles; thence, on the following day, ten miles, to Verdam. The army sickly.

June 9.—In the evening of the fifth it was arranged by the general and the Capitan Pacha that I should go at daybreak to the Grand Vizier's camp. I set off at 4 A.M. and after a ride of thirty miles found it; he had moved without our knowledge. Next morning, taking twelve men with me, I went and patrolled within two miles of Grand Cairo; took a sketch of it, and made on my return an official report that the citadel was not defensible it being commanded by a very high hill.

Suliman Aga, the prince of Ibrahim Bey's Mamelukes and the handsomest and noblest of them, presented me with a very fine chesnut horse. Ibrahim himself gave me another. Afterwards the Grand Vizier gave me my despatches, and I set off on my return and found our army at the head of the Delta.

The Capitan Pacha desired me to patrol till I found the enemy. After riding about four miles I met a Mameluke Bey who had just returned from Gizeh, where he had been sent on an important secret mission the purport of which was only known to the general and myself; therefore not to be mentioned or even hinted at at home. He assured me that there was not a Frenchman out of the works of Gizeh. I therefore returned to the Pacha. Our camp is at the head of the Delta. The Pyramids, although eight miles distant, appear close.

June 11.—I received a report from Aboukir that ten of my men were dead of the plague, and fifteen in hospital. The army has four thousand sick.

Tanash, four miles from Cairo, June 14.

We marched yesterday morning at daybreak, but only a league in advance. I rode on in front to within a few hundred yards of Cairo, or rather Boulac which is its suburb. We had a beautiful view. It is the only picturesque scenery in this country; but does not realize the ideas we form of the Elysian fields which the poets placed here.

This morning the general told me that he wished me to go and patrol this night towards Gizeh and, passing it, ascertain whether the French bridge on the other side may be attacked. His selection of me to perform this service is very flattering. Mamelukes alone go with me: my guide is a French deserter.

June 16.—The Mamelukes behaved ill; would not go as far as I wished but left me alone. I saw Gizeh and its bridge; found that it might be attacked with 12-pounders; returned at ten at night. The general much pleased with my report.

June 18.—I went yesterday with the general to show him the bridge of Gizeh. Placed him at a point from which he could see everything, and then went on with Captain Duncan of the artillery to reconnoitre its defences. Got close to the works; found them strong on that side, as there was a fortified palace of Mourad Bey. Two hours after, when all was quiet, I went out again and saw the other front: here the attack will be made. The French cavalry tried to cut us off but we kept too good a look-out.

A letter was brought in, found on an Arab who was killed in his flight by the Saint—the Prince of Fez. It was addressed by Monsieur Belliard to Menou at Alexandria.   He tells him falsehoods, of course, and represents his shameful retreat from the Turks as a victory ; affirms that he killed five hundred and took two pieces of cannon, and that his cavalry sabred two Beys.   "*Risum teneatis amici.*"

A shameful circumstance came to light yesterday. On the general desiring the surgeon to be in readiness to receive wounded, he confessed that he had only bandages for two hundred and that he had been so provided even when we left Rosetta.   A commissary and a * * * * * * * certainly ought to be hung.

I hope to arrive in England six weeks after the receipt of this,—"*Fortunâ favente.*"

Camp, 1½ mile from Gizeh, June 23.

I was sent on the morning of the 21st a long way off to the right and was ordered—at seven at night— to post four hundred Arnauts in the village in which I was this morning, and where the batteries are to be made this night.   I returned at one o'clock, night, having posted the Arnauts within half musket-shot of Gizeh but covered by a wood.

On the 22nd a flag of truce was sent in from the garrison, and a conference asked for to settle terms of surrender.   General Hope was sent.   The Congress at Rastadt was nothing compared to this.   Never, in the presence of four armies of the troops of so many nations, on such interesting ground, on a more important subject, was a military council held.   General Menou unequivocally declared that the object of his instructions was the evacuation of Cairo, and the return of the French troops under the command of General Belliard to France. . What further passed I do not know.

June 27.—This morning I went to see the Pyramids. The great one only strikes you with wonder when you are immediately under its base : this is prodigiously vast, but the altitude is by no means imposing. The stones of which it is built are enormous; but certainly I think hewn from the rock on which it stands. Formerly it was cased with granite and marble : vast ruins of these still remain ; and near the summit of the centre pyramid some thirty yards of this casing still exist, with hieroglyphics engraved. There are a great many smaller ones, and ruins of about forty. From this circumstance, and from observation of the holes or catacombs in the rocks, also from comparison with the pyramids at Saccara and the places of mummies there, I have no doubt of these being sepulchral edifices.

The French endeavoured to open the smallest of the three pyramids, but without success ; indeed they were always obliged to work protected by a large corps, which rendered the operation more difficult. The difference is great with us. An Englishman can ride alone there. I did not descend into the vault of the great pyramid, having no flambeaux ; but I am convinced that Strabo's statement that the door in his time was in the centre of the pyramid is erroneous, as the base is now visible on the solid rock on which it is built. Moreover, it is not probable that the sand would cease to operate when the door was brought near the level ; it would soon have blocked it up.

The Sphinx has a gigantic head of a woman hewn out of the solid rock : her back is like a fish's, hewn out of the rock also : the tail is not visible. The French have dug down to her breasts, but have not discovered her legs. It is the most stupendous stone I ever saw or imagined. The Egyptians or Mamelukes have defaced her eyes and nose, but every feature is still visible.

Conference proceeded. Articles agreed to and signed. The delay of twelve days for the evacuation, and as many for the march to Rosetta is very disastrous, as our operations against Alexandria will be so long stayed. The Capitan Pacha seriously insisted on the French giving up all the negresses in their possession ; and Madame Menou in particular, "*as he wished to present her to the Grand Signor!*"

The Mamelukes are not satisfied with the state of things. Osman Bey threatens to go in person to the King of England, *if his written promises are not fulfilled.*

Camp near Gizeh, July 4.

Yesterday I went with Hutchinson and others to visit the pyramids and catacombs of Saccara. We first descended into the catacombs of birds. We were let down by ropes into a dry well about sixty feet deep ; but when I saw the entrance at the bottom I dreaded suffocation so much that I climbed up again. However, as the party seemed determined to persevere I went down a second time. The entrance would only allow of a person crawling, not on his hands and knees but literally, *ventre à terre.* In that position we slid backwards above eighty yards, till the vaults opened sufficiently to admit of our standing upright.

Here we saw millions of mummied birds — the feathers in many remaining perfect. We were glad to get up again soon and crawl out of our graves. We saw afterwards a vast variety of pyramids and found an immense number of idols and a sculptured head as large as life : I brought away also a necklace of beads, worn no doubt by some fine lady three thousand years ago. I design it for my little Charlotte.

There has been no repetition of the French* *feu-de-joie* for the capture of Ireland. The French say, with reference to that announcement, " *Il est permis quelquefois mentir un peu—mais Général Menou a menti très-hardiment.*"

The French fired minute-guns for General Kleber, whose body they were removing from its grave on board a dgerm to convey it with them to France. The procession was a very solemn and affecting sight ; for never was a man more adored than Kleber. General Hutchinson's brother, who dined the day before in Cairo with General Belliard, says that when his name was mentioned almost every officer present was moved to tears. It is singular that the Grand Vizier should have been present to-day. If he was really the instigator of the assassination every shot must have pierced his heart : but I watched his countenance and he seemed perfectly tranquil.

The Grand Vizier was much pleased with the appearance of our army : indeed notwithstanding what it has undergone it is in very fine order. On his return he played the djereed ; and the same folly and childishness was practised by his whole suite. Men affected to receive from his hand repeated blows, to

* " Expedition to Egypt," Vol. I. page 200. 4th Edition.

scream at each, and at last expire at his feet, with all the mummery of a death scene in a French farce.

July 8.—Marched yesterday to change our ground nearer the Nile. I got from Cairo eight beautiful ostrich plumes, the best that could be purchased. Shall I see them waving this winter on the head of my dear wife? If human calculation can be depended upon I may answer yes.

Yesterday, the French having evacuated Cairo during the night, I passed the river very early at Imbaba and rode to see it. The feebleness of its works did not surprise me, but everything else did. Boulac is a mass of ruins; the entrance into Cairo no better, and the city itself miserable. The streets, however, are better than those of Rosetta; the main street being at least four yards wide. Never was such a wretched place as the citadel: a dozen shells would have brought down ruins that would have overwhelmed the garrison: the heights also commanded it at half musket-shot. In short there is no doubt that it must have surrendered at discretion. Our troops had occupied the citadel: on our descent from it we met the Grand Vizier's army which had mutinied to come into the town. They fired in every direction particularly as they passed us. Our situation for some minutes was very unpleasant.

At Cairo I found a most interesting and valuable letter from Regnier to Murat, after his being sent on board the *Lodi* in arrest.

July 14.—Despatches arrived yesterday morning from England. I rode immediately to the Capitan Pacha, who begged me instantly to go to the general at Cairo. He presented me with a beautiful enamelled gold box, sent by the Grand Signor from the seraglio. It is a most elegant present and of rare value. I arrived before the despatches.

Franciscan Convent, Cairo, July 16.

On the 15th the army marched. First the Turks, then the British, then the French, with an escort of our dragoons in the rear. The French column consisted of about five thousand men, including artillery and cavalry. About one thousand were in dgerms, and one thousand sick had previously gone off.

On the 18th the Grand Vizier entered Cairo in great state. He has turned Ibrahim Bey, &c., out of their houses; but his consequence is going in half an hour to be taken down a little. My regiment has not yet marched out.

The general wrote to the Grand Vizier that unless he reinstated the Beys in their houses, &c., he must do it himself by force: reminding his Highness that he has twenty thousand men to execute his orders; and adding that he would rather lose his head than break his faith pledged to the Mamelukes.

On the 20th I rode to Gizeh; called on my way on Osman Bey Tambourgi, and found him much alarmed at the conduct of the Grand Vizier. I reassured him by telling him of what the general had done to protect them.

Rosetta, July 30.

I left Cairo on the 26th by water and reached Rosetta on the 29th. The French army is encamped between the Turkish and the English at the distance of five miles from hence, ready for embarkation to-morrow. The number to be embarked each day is two thousand.

The embarkation went on admirably. The whole two thousand were on board by twelve o'clock. It was a pleasant sight to behold; and pleasant to reflect that our march to Cairo had terminated so successfully. The world will scarcely believe that six thousand men surrendered so easily. The army at Alexandria, not knowing what number we had to oppose, at first murmured at the capitulation; but now they are more satisfied.

Aug. 6.—Preparations for the siege are going on. General Menou refused a flag of truce yesterday.

Aug. 8.—Saw our chief engineer's plans of the enemy's works. They are very strong in their front, but not so much so to the westward: however, the attack will be made on both sides and both flanks of their position. We shall first make an attack to gain possession of a ridge of hills necessary for our operations advanced in front of the right of their main position; but this will be connected with the landing to the westward.

Aug. 10.—A letter came this morning from the general desiring me to hold my detachment in readiness for embarkation. This was the consequence of an application from me that if the detachment could not be remounted, and the service did not require it, they might be sent home. Twenty men had died of the plague, and eighteen were in hospital at this moment; so that their number was reduced almost to insignificance. But every principle of honour and duty makes it requisite for *me* not to leave this country until the expedition has issued in the siege of Alexandria. By removal of my people first I have performed to them my most sacred duty; yet I trust that it will be the last to be exacted of me as major of Hompesch. The detachment has been an unfortunate one indeed: but individually, apart from the loss of my command and my feelings on this account, the service has been most favourable to me in every other point of view. Nothing could be more flattering than the attention and consideration shown me by the highest in rank everywhere, and more particularly by the recommendation which the commander-in-chief has sent home.

Aug 17.—Yesterday evening the troops embarked and sailed for the westward: I changed my intention of going with them, as I heard that the ferry on this side would be the best. We received an account of Saumarez's great victory by a ship from Gibraltar. This morning at three o'clock the line was under arms; at daybreak the columns moved to the attack on the right and left. Both perfectly succeeded; indeed scarcely any resistance was made. But although we got easy possession of the hill in front of the left of their works General Moore did not think it prudent to retain it: he therefore withdrew to the proper distance for making the first parallel, which the men soon covered notwithstanding that the fire was very great from the main position and from the pharos upon our troops. We lost but very few men. On the left, after taking possession of the green hill, our troops were not molested except by cannonade; when suddenly the French sallied out in a column of about one thousand men, and ran towards it. The 30th, a very weak regiment, was the only force we had to oppose them; but when the enemy came near they rushed upon them with the bayonet, met and drove them instantly. The French behaved miserably ill. Our loss on that side is about thirty or forty wounded and a few killed. The French had many wounded and above a hundred certainly killed. Twenty prisoners were taken. Nothing could exceed the eagerness of our troops to be engaged : had it been prudent to permit them I am sure they would have stormed the main position with delight. Never was a finer sight for its extent, or a more gallant charge than that of the 30th regiment.

Thus I have " lived to fight another day."

Aug. 23.—In the morning of the 20th, after detaining Byng to his great anger for my despatches two hours, I embarked, and after three hours' sailing without a shot from the French batteries, landed five miles westward of Alexandria where our army was encamped. The moment we got upon the sand-hills to view Marabout the tower fell. The French never returned a shot, but we kept up a heavy fire the whole day : in the evening the commandant capitulated. The garrison was one hundred and ninety-five men.

In the morning at daybreak the army moved in three columns over the ground and isthmus by which Buonaparte advanced to Alexandria. The columns were scarcely in motion when the French sharpshooters fired upon our advance. General Byng and myself volunteered to act as General Coote's aides-de-camp, and were so employed. The French were posted with a force of about twelve hundred men on the narrowest part of the isthmus. Two gun dgerms and two 12-pounders defended their right; seven 24-pounders their left ; field-pieces their centre. The men-of-war flanked

our left, and the gun-boats our right. The French
offered a sharp resistance to us at this point; but
nothing could check the onset of the advanced guard,
supported by our columns closely. The grape fire was
very heavy, but our guns played on theirs with great
success. Everything was carried literally *au pas de
charge*, and notwithstanding their very heavy fire we
drove the enemy over a space of four miles, and took
post within a mile of the walls of Alexandria and a
thousand yards from Fort des Bains.

The immediate result of this success was the capture of six pieces of cannon, and about two hundred
of the enemy killed, wounded, and taken. Our loss
was trifling; about fifty; two officers wounded. The
French have three severely wounded, and taken. For
the extent of the action I have no hesitation in saying
that it was the most beautiful sight, in picturesque
circumstances, that I have yet seen. Our men-of-war
brigs, and the *Diana* frigate, with their armed launches,
behaved remarkably well; as did the gun-boats on our
right. The troops showed the courage which has ever
distinguished them.

For two hours and a half every man was under
severe fire of artillery, but the swelling sand-hills prevented the enemy's directing it well. General Coote
showed a coolness and conduct which astonished me.
His courage I had never doubted. He was always
with the advanced guard, and exposed his person as
much as the most intrepid soldier of the army. I
thought, indeed, that he should not have done it so
much, and that was the opinion of everyone.

We were all highly delighted to find ourselves so
near the walls of the town, as we thought it was pro-

tected by such a line of defences as that which kept us so long in check to the westward. We now find that there is only one fort to be attacked before we are actually at the walls. This fort is not strong, being commanded by the heights which we have taken.

Batteries will open against it to-morrow. Our fleet of frigates, &c., is anchored within a cannon-shot and a quarter of the town, and French ships are lying close hauled up to it. These we might destroy by our batteries from shore, but we look forward to a share of them as prizes.

There are altogether about one hundred sail in the harbour. It is a noble sight to see them, and the harbour of Alexandria, so completely in our possession that there is no possibility of the smallest boat going in or out without our licence. The worst of the position is that fresh water is only to be had at a distance of two miles in the rear, but we hope to find wells.

General Coote gave me the despatches after the action was over to carry to General Hutchinson. I went in a man-of-war's cutter; we ran the distance —sixteen miles—in about an hour and a quarter; but when we landed I was obliged to walk far before I could get a horse. The general was delighted to hear of our success, as he had been very anxious for the event. On my observing that I thought General Coote's position so near the enemy required a rein-forcement, he instantly ordered eighteen hundred men —Colonel Spencer's brigade—to embark.

I went to the Capitan Pacha to report my intelligence, and of course was welcomed.

In the evening, as I thought it probable that the

French might attack General Coote in the night, Byng and I set off again, and arrived here about eleven at night.

This morning all was quiet on our side, but a firing of artillery and musketry was heard to the eastward. I breakfasted with General Coote and was asked to dine with him, but declined as I wished to get back early. He made me many compliments for my attention, &c., to him yesterday.

The wounded French officers all agree in describing the garrison as discontented, and living only on rice and oil. They allow that by this movement we have discovered their feeble point, and say that the place is ours either by siege or by assault. The colonel, who has lost a leg, complains bitterly that he should have been deprived of it merely for the caprice of General Menou, as every other person wished to surrender long since. Eleven gun-boats are sent round from Lake Mareotis this day to enter the harbour. Messieurs will have a warm berth ere long. A corps of Mamelukes, from Damanhour by the Desert, arrived yesterday at the ground from which we marched. We do not want them now.

Read newspapers to the 16th June. Saw the Gazette; but, although my friends here style me accordingly, I believe nothing till I see my letters from England.

Camp before Alexandria, August 26, 1801.

On the 23rd General Hutchinson came. General Coote kindly recommended me to his approbation for my conduct in the action. The firing of musketry and artillery to the eastward was a feint on our part to ascertain the enemy's whole power of fire. It answered completely, as the batteries played for an hour and a half incessantly, aiming at nothing.

In the evening of the 24th a flag of truce was sent in by General Menou. As this was the first he had honoured us with expectation ran high, but it proved to be only a complimentary letter to the general for the humanity shown to the wounded French officers and men, and a recommendation of the garrison of Marabout to " a *brave* and loyal army." However, this must be considered as a preliminary letter.

Yesterday morning the batteries to the westward opened on Fort des Bains. The French returned some shells into the camp itself. The general sent me with despatches to General Coote. I went in the Capitan Pacha's barge. The general detained me, as he said a movement would be made in the evening. At eight P.M. a battalion of the 20th with unloaded muskets, and about fifty cavalry, advanced, attacked, and got in the rear of the French posts in front of Fort des Bains, surprised a battalion, and took sixty prisoners—eight officers—and killed and wounded about thirty men. I myself saw fourteen dead in a very small compass. Everything appearing quiet the troops were ordered back, only posting pickets on the important eight hundred yards we had just gained. I was in the boat going to the general with the intelligence when suddenly musketry began on the left with violence: I immediately landed, and mounting a horse found General Coote at the scene of action. The French, thinking that the support was withdrawn, had endeavoured to recover the lost ground. The pickets alone, although opposed to eight hundred men, kept their ground until the 20th, &c., again arrived, when the firing of every battery, theirs and ours, also that of the gun-boats, illumined the whole horizon. The roar of cannon, the rattling of the small arms, the shells in the air, the whistling of the cannon balls, with the flashing fire, made this night-scene one of extreme interest and beauty; though the shots came too thick for any but a distant spectator to regard it with unmixed admiration. The shells burst in every part of our camp, but I do not know with what execution; as when the action ceased, which it did in about an hour, I set off instantly to come here where I arrived at day-break. Our loss was trifling: I should reckon that of the French at two hundred men, but the returns are not yet sent in. I did not go to rest but, communicating my good news to the general and the Capitan Pacha, went to take a view of our batteries, which opened on this side at the green hill.

The batteries ceased playing at mid-day as the French withdrew their guns. About 7 P.M., while I was in the general's tent, a French flag of truce, brought by the first aide-de-camp of General Menou, arrived to propose terms of capitulation and an armistice for three days. The propositions of General Menou seeming sincere the cessation of hostilities was immediately agreed to. The aide-de-camp supped with us, and ate like a man who had not had a dinner for some time.

He told us that the whole garrison had been up and in arms for the last five nights, and that the night before (General Coote's attack) they had most seriously expected an assault. General Menou, he said, wept bitterly when he wrote the letter to propose terms, feeling as a man of honour and a lover of his country;

and added that the general would go without a shilling from the country, his probity being remarkable, although a man burdened with debt. We told him that this eulogium was the universal statement even of his enemies in the army which marched from Cairo.

Thus terminated an expedition which reflects new and lasting glory on the British arms ; an expedition which, originally planned by ignorance, has been conducted with surpassing skill and success incalculable.

General Menou in the defence of Alexandria has done his duty. The inferiority of his numbers, which rendered it impossible to oppose resistance on such a vast line, the prostrating fatigue and almost famine of his troops, justified him in surrendering at that precise moment. A longer delay would neither have done credit to his judgment nor to his humanity; unless his garrison had volunteered to die in their works, devoting themselves to fix some lustre on the memory of the army of the East.

General Coote has been kind enough to mention me to the general, but none of these things must come to public knowledge from myself. They are related only for those who are so very dear to me as to be interested in and entitled to the relation ; and therefore I request that these communications may be kept strictly within my own family. Nothing is so ridiculous as an eager anxiety to publish by the means of friends one's own reputation.

• I did not mention that our army to the westward is encamped in the ancient necropolis, or city of the dead. Immense catacombs are open in every part. The temple of Diana and the baths of Cleopatra are also in our possession.

Aug. 31.—Yesterday evening the final terms of capitulation were agreed to. They are highly honourable to the army; as they obtain all the just points of demand without too much depressing a fallen enemy.

Sept. 1.—We are to take possession of the lines to-morrow.

Sept. 3.—Yesterday, at 11 A.M., the grenadiers, with drums beating, colours flying, and firing of cannon, marched to take possession of the enemy's lines; the bands playing the Grenadiers' March. It was a noble sight. The French did a shabby thing: they cut the halyards to prevent our flags being hoisted on the flag-staff in the centre battery and on Pompey's Pillar.

The enemy's line is very strong in itself, and defended by a second line of redoubts well built, which would have poured a most destructive fire on our troops after they had gained the first position. Three of the batteries were *miréd* in the first line. The Arab town—the old Alexandria—is nothing but a heap of ruins enclosed by walls, with very large flanking towers at the distance of a hundred yards from each other. The wall itself is of immense extent. In the centre of it throughout pillars are placed horizontally at distances of ten yards. These are of the finest granite; but whether they are placed there for strength or for ornament I cannot pretend to determine. The beautiful ruins of the towers and some fine architectural remains, particularly the gate of Rosetta, afford a spectacle pleasing even in the midst of desolation. On the right, close upon the sea, stands Cleopatra's Needle. As I have been at Rome, it does not strike me with surprise. Certainly it is a fine monu-

ment; though in a bad situation, by which its altitude
is lost. From its being placed in front of the old
harbour, *i. e.* opposite to its entrance, I conceive that
it originally served as a land-mark for ships. It is
covered with hieroglyphics. After observing this
well I went to Pompey's Pillar, passing over immense
fragments of broken columns, of marble, granite, &c.
The distance from one to the other by the wall of the
town is three miles. This famous column is the only
celebrated thing which I ever found to answer my
expectations. Its magnitude, height, and beauty of
proportion are beyond conception by means of description. On a flag-staff placed on its summit is the
cap of liberty; it will baffle every effort to remove
this until another rope can be fixed to enable a man
to ascend. The batteries and forts from this pillar to
Cleopatra's redoubt (where the needle is), and from
thence to "Fort Triangular," are immensely numerous; some of them very regular and full of cannon.

I expect to be out of this country in a fortnight.
My detachment has not yet sailed. The whole army
will leave within a month, with the exception of some
cavalry.

Sept. 6.—Yesterday I rode into Alexandria, and
saw General Menou, who gave me permission for free
range. He is a little fat man, very eloquent. He
abused General Belliard, and declared again that he
would make him lose his head. He wished the general to give him a frigate, justifying the request by
alleging the handsome terms given by Buonaparte to
General Würmser!

Alexandria is a miserable town, very small. The
French have destroyed all the suburbs since our arrival.

There is a good Grande Place, in which Menou is encamped; a very handsome wall, just finished by the
French, forms its rampart and protects the isthmus on
which the town is built.   The Pharos is connected
with the mainland by a causeway a quarter of a mile
in length with walls on each side.   The fort Pharos is
very strong: thirty-five pieces of cannon are on its
walls—some beautiful.   The other forts are not so
strong against regular approaches: the guns very
bad.   About five hundred pieces of cannon are in the
works of Alexandria, and there are about sixty field-
pieces in park.

The greatest prizes are, however, antiquarian.   Two
remarkably fine statues, now in General Friant's house
—one is that of Maximus Severus—the fist of the
Colossus of Memphis; two sculptured marble sarco-
phagi of great size, brought from Thebes by General
Desaix; a marble mummy case covered with hieroglyphics; the famous stone with hieroglyphics, Coptic
and Greek inscriptions; and many images, &c. &c.

The French army effective in Egypt at our landing
was twenty-two thousand men: exclusive of one thousand nine hundred marines, near four thousand sick
embarked in the Cairo army and at this time at
Alexandria, and several thousand auxiliaries.

The British army landed was twelve thousand eight
hundred men; and it never received a reinforcement
until Cairo was taken, with the exception of five
hundred convalescents from Rhodes.

Buonaparte's campaign in Italy was nothing to this.
He descended the Alps, it is true, without a commis-

sariat; but we invaded a country with such inferior force, without the means of dragging cannon, or more than ten pieces, with only two hundred cavalry, and literally without a camel or baggage-horse. Now we are masters of more than fifteen hundred pieces of cannon, three thousand of the enemy's horses, and three thousand camels; besides magazines, stores, and ships.

Sept. 7.—I dined with the general. He said many flattering things about my leaving him; and told me for the first time that he had once mentioned my name in the Gazette, twice recommended me privately to the Duke: and added that he should do it again, not only in his own name but in that of General Coote. If everything else had been unfortunate I should still have considered this expedition fortunate as relating to myself, because it has given me the valuable friend-ship of this excellent man.

This morning I am going to announce my departure to the Capitan Pacha; it will be distressing to me after his great kindness.

Aboukir Bay, Pique, Sept. 11.

Yesterday I took leave of the general, who was most kind, then went to the Capitan Pacha, who showed the same feeling, and made me promise to visit him at Constantinople.

This morning I parted with my officers and took leave of my detachment; obtained a Greek boat, and embarked, after a two hours' row, on board the *Pique.* With ecstasy I leave Egypt, and pray that I may never set foot on its shores again. The *Pique* is a beautiful vessel; Captain Young commands her. The fleet now sailing with us consists only of men-of-war—no trans-ports—seven sail of the line, one frigate.

Beating about. Captain Young is one of the most hospitable, generous, amiable men I ever met with.

This morning, at eight, while we were on deck, looking at the *Termagant* sloop of war coming down with a press of sail to speak the admiral — she had left Aboukir after us—the sky became suddenly overcast to the east, and we saw a tremendous squall coming down upon us. We had only time to haul the top-gallant sails when it reached us. It began to blow very hard and to lighten vividly. On a sudden, to the north-west, we saw an immense foam on the sea, and in a few moments a waterspout of enormous dimensions advanced rapidly against the wind towards us: we waited for it with much anxiety, and loaded all the guns to fire at it; but to my great joy and admiration it broke ahead of us, ploughing the sea into mountains and abysses. A similar one then formed, and marched onward against us like Ossian's Genius of the Storm : but the whole atmosphere being now charged with moisture, it broke in every part, falling in torrents, melting away our menacing danger, and driving every one who could not be useful off the decks. For about ten minutes darkness brooded on the face of the waters, and the flashes of the lightning alone gave light to the daytime. The wind blew a hurricane, but it was of short duration. When day broke again through the black horizon, the *Termagant* brig was lying a wreck on the sea, with all her top-masts hanging over her sides. We sent a boat in aid.

General Moore was in the *Termagant*; Captain

Young went on board the admiral, and brought back intelligence that "Lord Nelson, with fifteen frigates, has succeeded in burning and destroying the French armament at Boulogne."

October 7, at Sea, 50 leagues from Malta.

Nothing has occurred, except that I beat the second lieutenant, who boasted that he would go up to the top-mast-head and come down again before I could get into the main-tops. I reached the main-tops before he had even got to the top-mast-head. I had never gone aloft till then.

Malta Harbour, October 8.

Arrived this morning, to my great joy, in Malta harbour. The thought of being so much nearer to our country and our home; the animation of the scene, so beautiful in contrast to that which we had left; the firing of cannon; the triumphant music of the bands; the acclamations of the people hailing the conquerors of Egypt; all lift the spirits and stir the heart.

Oct. 11.—I find that the Gazette* has not done me justice as to the capture of the convoy; but Hutchinson gave me reasons which in part satisfy me. He knows well that I was never ordered in with the flag of truce, but volunteered on my own judgment and

---

* "On the 17th, when encamped at Alkam, we were informed by the Arabs that a considerable body of French, &c., &c., were advancing towards the Nile. The cavalry were immediately ordered out with two pieces of cannon under the command of Brigadier-General Doyle, &c. &c. Col. Cavalier commanded the French convoy. The cavalry came up with him after a march of about three hours. *A flag of truce was sent in to them by Major Wilson of the Hompesch, requiring them to surrender, &c. &c.* With these terms they complied," &c. &c.—*Extract from "Bulletins of the Campaign of* 1801."

hazard to go in with one when General Doyle was scarcely in sight. Abercromby, however, has acted, and will act, most honourably in the affair. Delicacy to General Doyle has been the cause why facts are not stated to the public exactly as they occurred. This is a lesson to all *aspiring young men* who seek "glory in the cannon's mouth," as the handbills say.

Oct. 19.—A report circulated on parade this morning that peace was concluded.

Oct. 21.—Yesterday a French corvette brought intelligence that the articles were signed on the 1st. Terms not officially made known.

Pique, Malta Harbour, October 23.

The *Pique* being ordered to Marseilles Captain Young offered me a passage. I embarked this morning. Sir Alexander Ball is on board : a most agreeable, sensible man, and my friend.

Oct. 24.—We sailed this evening. I must tell a curious anecdote. At General Fox's table the other day the captain of a twenty-four-razee, which arrived at Malta from Toulon with English prisoners on board taken in the *Swiftsure,* clapped the general on the shoulder saying, " Why, general, you ought to go to China; the people there would adore you as a saint. They always choose the fattest and most purse —— fellows for their worship." The effect of this speech may be conceived. This captain is a disgrace to the French navy; he sells wine and confectionary. When he dined with Lord Keith he set before him two bottles of his claret as a sample for the company, and actually made his bargains at that time !

Toulon, November 3.

We made the harbour of Toulon this morning, and are working in under Fort La Marque. I defer my opinion of the strength, &c., till my more near inspection. The town is so commanded that I am surprised that any officer could think of defending it. You might throw stones from the mountains upon it. Sir Alexander Ball landed with me at the quarantine house, where the military intendant and the adjutant-general of the fleet Matard—whom Sir A. Ball saved at the action at Aboukir—came to us. They were very civil, and Matard expressed much gratitude; but they could not save us from twenty days' quarantine. This was a thunder-stroke little expected. We determined to go and see the lazaretto. It lies at the opposite side of the harbour, three miles from the town; situation pretty, but no words can describe the bestiality and misery of the house. Two rooms were shown to us as our quarters; they were sickening, and we unanimously resolved that it was better to sail to Minorca.

Lazaretto, off Toulon, November 8.

Notwithstanding my resolution I was persuaded by Captain Walker to remain and perform quarantine. Colonel Cole and Sir Alexander refused. The *Pique* sailed with them on the 5th inst. On the same day I went on shore to give directions for preparations at the lazaretto. Fortunately we found a *washed* and comfortable room with a fireplace in it; so good that I am sure Sir Alexander would have stayed if he had seen it. I regret that it was overlooked as he is a most worthy, good, and agreeable man. We returned on board a little brig, the *Calypso*—with French prisoners doomed to the same quarantine—to give time for the chamber to get dry and in readiness. Our cabin was wretched and full of vermin. At night a most dreadful levanter blew: we drove, but another anchor brought us up. The night was as terrific as any I ever passed, not excepting that off Sicily in my way to Malta. The master expected every moment that we should go on shore. This morning the gale abated, and we landed and came to our lazaretto. Chairs, a table, litter, and a fire, make it habitable.

There are six ships of the line here, one frigate and two sloops: in various conditions. These are the remains of the proud navy which once rode here. It is very interesting to recall the scenes which have been acted in presence of the silent witnesses around us. The battles fought; the dreadful conflagration of the fleet, and the subsequent fusillading of fourteen thousand souls; the present gloom; the aspect of woe and ruin offering itself in all that I can see, cannot be passed over without serious reflections. Jean Bon St. André is in the lazaretto. What may his reflections be?—the friend, the agent of Robespierre!

Nov. 15.—On the 13th Captain Bourne came on shore, and told me that the captains of the navy, and officers commanding regiments and corps were made Knights of the Crescent. How true it may be I know not, but it gives me small pleasure. The Order of Maria Theresa wants not this additional ornament. Yesterday Matard came to see us. The *Dido*, with General Menou on board, anchored this morning. About an hour ago I was sent for to the barrier, and found there Captain Macmurdo of the 8th regiment, who has determined on staying and performing quarantine; taking our apartment when we leave. Fourier, Monnet, Redouté, all members of the National Institute, are his party.

Nov. 19.—The last two days have been made agreeable by the society of Fourier and Monnet; though a little under restraint for fear of touching. The former is a very amiable clever man. I have had the opportunity of being attentive to him by supplying a few things that they wanted. This has been of service to me in its consequence: as Fourier promises me a letter to Berthollet, which will insure my introduction to Buonaparte, the Abbé Sieyes, and others. He told me that in Upper Egypt he discovered a temple,* with the signs of the zodiac so represented as to prove its construction eight thousand years. His delicacy, however, is so great with regard to any injury that he might do by shaking the religious faith of the people in the Mosaic chronology *as received*, that he is doubtful whether he ought to publish this curious fact.

General Menou came on shore here the other day. Admiral Gantheaume and all the administration came to visit him. I could not help observing with a smile the gilded oars and royal decorations of the admiral's boats.

Nov. 21.—At last our imprisonment is ended. We leave to-morrow morning. Our last five days have been passed most agreeably in the society of Macmurdo, Fourier, and the savans. This morning we

---

* At Denderah. The planisphere of this zodiac was removed to Paris in 1822.—Ed.

saw the drawings of Redouté; they excel everything
of the kind I ever saw—particularly the fishes of the
Nile. From Fourier I heard much of Buonaparte:
especially his reasons for the massacre of Jaffa and for
poisoning his own sick at Acre. He talks well on all
subjects, and is one of the best-informed men I ever
met with.

Fourier has reasoned himself into the publication of
the facts respecting the chronology of the world: but
means to write upon them scientifically, leaving it to
others to render the information more simple and generally comprehensible. I think that he is acting in compliance with duty to society in giving currency to
matter so interesting and instructive.

Nov. 23.—Yesterday we set sail in a boat from the
lazaretto, and in about half an hour landed at Toulon.
I called upon Admiral Gantheaume, and paid the customary visits to the different commandants, &c. Dined
with Gallois, and was introduced to a most charming
and amiable family. They are of Brittany. Madame
is beautiful, and much like Jemima. They were
greatly pleased to find that I thought their physiognomy like the English. *England is still the envy of
France.* In the evening I went to the theatre; the
play was Hippolite and Phædra; the house small; the
company numerous, and well dressed. The gentlemen
all wore powder, and the servants were more magnifi-
cently clothed than the king's body coachmen on a birthday. They sat in front of their respective masters'
boxes. The play was well acted; Madame Racour,
the first actress of France, playing the part of Phædra.
I did not like the subject of the tragedy or its jingling
rhymes. The former is certainly not fit to be re-

presented before modest maidens; but the French are
not particular in this respect.   The too celebrated
Grande Place, where so many thousands were executed,
is the only picturesque part of this town.   The quay
is miserable.

Fourier gave me a most elegant letter for Berthollet
which will be of much service to us at Paris.

Nov. 26.—Matard visited us yesterday.   Dined with
Gallois.   Since my stay here I have learnt much of
French ideas and manners—not to the credit of the
nation.   I have some thanks to receive for my representations of English manners, women, and husbands.
Madame Gallois is a most charming person, and re-
sembles Jemima so much that I could sit and think
myself in her company : but I fear that such grace
and loveliness cannot long bloom in the pride of
virtue and honour, in such an infected atmosphere.

Royalty has friends everywhere in this country—
that is to say, a monarchy chosen by the people themselves.   The common language everywhere, even
among the employés of government, is, " France is
too great a country for a republic."   The booksellers'
shops teem with Royalist publications, and abuse of
the revolution and its principles ; and these seem to
receive the sanction of Government.   The novels are
full of the distresses of the royal family : and the
" Orpheline " is the favourite work of the ladies, who
weep over its affecting pages and exclaim against
their savage persecutors.   Buonaparte is universally
liked—but a little suspected.   It may be thought
strange that I should see so much in so short a time,
but those who know me will not conceive my relation
to be less the truth.

Q 2

Marseilles, November 27.

I went on the 26th to Admiral Gantheaume ; dined
with him, and met General Leopold Berthier. Left
Toulon and our charming friends, who parted from us
with tears. Gallois walked with us out of the town.
While we waited for the coach he showed us all the
English positions, &c.; and told us that to save his
father's life he had acted in the Republican army.
We arrived here on the 27th. This is a fine city, but
much decayed. Few ships of any size in the port ; no
defence of consequence. The fort is only remarkable
because the Duke of Orleans was confined in it so
long. In the theatre this evening, strange to say, I
was saluted by three of the officers of the dromedary
corps which I took in the Desert : nothing could exceed their expressions of gratitude.

Lyons, December 4.

On the morning of the 28th we left Marseilles, and
have been travelling ever since. Infamous roads. At
the inns generally sumptuous fare and exorbitant
charges ; but everywhere welcome to the English, and
abuse of the revolution. All regard Buonaparte as the
benefactor of his country by giving it peace, but are
not insensible to his usurpation or blind to the extent
of his power.

Five miles from Marseilles we were shown a natural
curiosity ; a mountain exactly resembling the head of
a man. At Orange is a triumphal arch, built in the
time of Julius Cæsar; a beautiful monument of antiquity in good preservation. Near Pillau we overtook
an old clergyman who had been banished from his
flock nine years, and had only returned a week before :

the people who passed all saluted him with great respect, and in his own village they ran out of their houses to show him honour. Further on we passed the ruins of a beautiful château : the master and three of his daughters had been guillotined, his wife went mad, and the château had been sacked by brigands. Buonaparte, we learn, is coming to Toulon ; so I fear we shall miss him. I much wish to see him on account of his celebrity ; not from esteem.

The people of the Hôtel de la Table Ronde at Vienne are of the better sort. They told us some affecting anecdotes of the siege of Lyons. They sheltered numerous unfortunate Lyonnais after that event ; and a little girl was shown us who saved many people by pretending that she could not read. This gave her liberty to look over the lists of denounced names.

Lyons is one mournful mass of ruins : everything that was once grand or ornamental levelled to the earth : all the houses rifled with bullets : no activity, and all-pervading gloom.

Dec. 8.—I left Lyons for Paris. Nothing remarkable but the universal meanness and griping extortion of inn and shop keepers. We have passed through a charming country, but until we arrived at Fontainebleau saw not one tolerably decent village. Fontainebleau is beautiful, but melancholy from contrast of present desolation with past grandeur. In the palace riots a school of a hundred boys, educated at the expense of government.

Hôtel de Toscane, Paris, December 9.

Arrived this day. The reflection that we are in this city, so famous and so infamous, causes a singular feeling. I shall write my impressions of it—as it is interesting—setting down everything without prejudice. It does not strike me at first sight as I expected.

I first called upon Mr. Jackson and the Austrian minister, not—as I supposed—Count Cobenzal : but he received me in a very friendly manner. I called also upon the Prince and Princess Beauveau. Berthollet is absent from Paris. I fear that my judgment of this city will not be deemed honest by many, yet I know it to be impartial. The spectacles, the gaieties, and the vices of Paris intoxicate the senses perhaps, and obscure the discriminating powers of most English travellers. I have driven over the whole town, and seen certainly all its exterior beauty : I have now only to examine the rich interior of its palaces and museums. Any person who has been in Dublin can form the best idea of Paris : magnificence and meanness are only more frequently contrasted. The hotels are superb edifices ; the Tuileries the noblest palace I have yet seen; the Louvre grand ; all public buildings calculated to inspire admiration. But Paris has not a street so good as our Cheapside ; all are narrow, dirty, unpaved; the houses old and mean in general, the shops without brilliance, and the tout ensemble bearing a strong resemblance to the worst parts of the City of London. Here are no open squares, no streets denoting wealth or comfort. Few equipages in the streets ; but abundance of fiacres and cabriolets. The population seems scanty, and both sexes are badly dressed. The women wear a costume which contrasts unfavourably with English neatness and decency in the clothing of the lower limbs. However, I must allow that they are beautifully made, and walk well.

The ruined state of the great hotels, which are almost all either converted into solitary offices of government or advertised to be sold, gives the town a very melancholy and sombre aspect. Paris is built aristocratically, and seems to pine for royalty. The traces of this bloody revolution are still too visible. When I passed the ruins of the Tuileries I felt a glow of admiration, softened by sorrow, for the fate of the brave Swiss. When I passed the place of Louis XV., and halted for a moment close to the spot, round which a rail is fixed to mark it off as consecrated, where the fatal guillotine took the life of the unhappy king, it was an effort to refrain from tears. Death on that spot, within sight of his royal abode, must have been peculiarly horrible : and memory must have embittered his last moments. Coming out of the opera in the evening I met General Pigot and Lord Cahir, and went home to sup with the latter. His wife is looking beautiful and is the admiration of the Parisians.

The word *sujet* introduced in the Russian treaty has given rise to much speculation ; but all agree that Buonaparte's " Je le veux " is decisive.

I learnt Dolomieu's death to-day. He is a loss to science, and I shall miss a grateful friend.

Dec. 13.—Yesterday I saw many public buildings, and in the evening went to a subscription ball. The society as to *men* is very bad—sad, ill-looking fellows indeed. The women are by no means handsome ; dressed vilely ; a profusion of diamonds, but worn in bad taste, and much vulgarity. Madame Tallien was present. I was much disappointed in her. She is very large, and has a full face—" ox-eyed "—but eyes *very expres-*

sive indeed. This is the only ball at which she has been present for a long time, as she is not received in general: even Madame Buonaparte is not allowed by the First Consul to admit her visits. Lady Cahir was by far the most beautiful woman in the room.

Dec. 15.—I visited the Temple and the Bastile with Mrs. Bosville and Edward,* whom I met unexpectedly in Paris. The porter was offended by my asking for the chamber where the unfortunate king and the great Sir Sidney were confined, and would not let us see anything. The site of the Bastille alone remains; there is not a vestige of the prison. I dined with Lord Cahir; and yesterday visited various places of note and interest; the assemblage of monuments among the rest. The tomb of Abelard and Heloise alone is worthy of admiration, and commanded reflection. As works of art the mass are without interest. Dined with Duponville; Edward was there. Afterwards went to the Marquis Bellairs: thence to Lady Cahir's. This morning breakfasted with the Prince de Beauveau. Rode with Lord and Lady Cahir to the Bois de Boulogne—a charming resort, but too distant for public convenience: it has suffered much from the revolution. Among the company I have met here were Mr. Wombwell a great friend of Bosville's, Lewis, Madame Collard a very handsome woman, and Madame de Noailles. Lord Henry Petty and Mr. Seymour are the only English whom I have seen; except Doyle nephew of the general.

I have now seen Paris completely; and pronounce that even its profligacy has neither gaiety nor elegance of dissipation to attract the youngest men. Society is in

* Sir Robert Wilson's sister and brother.—ED.

the most abandoned state.   There is no smile on the countenances of men.   In short France is enduring all the miseries of the most despotic government, and is verging fast to a fall.   Organized as the country now is it is impossible that it can hold together as an empire.   Peace, however contradictory it may appear, has been the ruin of France; and within a few months the government will be no more.   The English government ought certainly to grant all the passports that may be asked for.   The state of Paris—so different to expectation—the expense, the gloom, and the consequent *ennui* will soon sicken our eager travellers.

Calais, December 19.

On the morning of the 16th, we left Paris: but in the evening before I went to the Théâtre Français, and saw Talma.   He has a more expressive countenance than Kemble: but rants rather too much.   Supped at Lord Cahir's, and met the Duchess of Nevers and Madame and Mademoiselle Coligny.   The latter gave me a cup of Angoulême china to take to the Marchioness of Hertford.   At seven o'clock the next morning we were on our journey.   I left Paris without regret.   Twelve at night we reached Amiens.   Here I got out and called on Lord Cornwallis: but he had retired, and I could only see Colonel Nightingale who expressed much gratification at my attention.   We continued our journey the whole night, breakfasted at Berney, then passed on to Boulogne where we stopped only to buy food to eat in our carriage, and at six o'clock in the morning arrived at Calais: drove to Quillac's, ci-devant Dessin's; the best hotel I ever saw, and where the only sign of royalty in the whole coun-

try we passed through was visible—a fireplace, on
the back of which is a crown with fleurs-de-lis.   All
the churches, châteaux, &c., from Paris are in ruins.
The noble palace of the Duke of FitzJames is utterly
destroyed.   At every step of our course we have
heard curses against the revolution, and its barbarous
traces are everywhere visible.   At last we came in
sight of our happy land: where all that remains of
nobility in man or virtue in woman has found a refuge
from all parts of the world.

Home, December 22nd, 1802.

On the 20th, Citizen Margaux Prefect of Calais
having given us leave to embark, we went on board an
English vessel, the *Minerva* packet, and sailed at mid-
day ; it was blowing hard, but we made Dover Castle
at four P.M.   The wind increased to a gale, and we remained on board all night : anchored in the Downs.
The vessel drove in the night, though we had two anchors
down, but happily brought up after a time.   Most of the
ships also drove, and two went on the Goodwin Sands ;
but as the wind moderated in the morning I hope the
crews may be saved.   At daylight a boat came off to
our signal : and after paying each two guineas and a
half to the boatmen to take us on shore, besides the
ten for our passage, we touched in safety the beach
of Old England : though not without danger, as the
surf on shore was tremendous.

I kissed the pebbles with ecstasy.   I hailed with
delight that country which is not only the perfection
of the universe, but also the home which contains all
that is dear to me in life.

I hurried on ; slept at Dartford ; breakfasted in

London with Bosville, who received me most affectionately; thence posted to Winkfield. On arrival I found
that Jemima was at Windsor. I immediately sent Hold-
ridge off for her, and now am awaiting her coming
with all intensity of love and gratitude after an
absence of fifteen months: proud in the consciousness
of virtue, which I feel to be not unworthy even of *her*
affection.

CHAPTER V.

[SIR ROBERT WILSON returned to England, as related
in the last chapter, at the close of the year 1801.
The preliminaries of peace were ratified while he was
on his passage home, and the treaty was signed at
Amiens on the 27th of March, 1802.

Soon after his arrival he arranged for publication
the materials which he had collected during this service: and in a few months published his first work,
" The History of the British Expedition to Egypt."
It commanded immediate attention. Edition after
edition was called for; it was translated into
French for foreign circulation; the press of the
day acknowledged its permanent interest and its
merit as a military work; and distinguished persons
and private friends testified their appreciation:—

EDWARD DANIEL CLARKE TO SIR ROBERT WILSON.

DEAR SIR,

I BELIEVE you are not acquainted with the handwriting of a man to whom you showed much civility in Egypt; but that you have not entirely forgotten the brother of Captain Clarke of the *Braakel* is evident from the handsome manner in which you have handed his name to posterity.

I have received the greatest pleasure in reading your work. Everything conspires to make it interesting. The subject would have given it *that salt* even had the narrative been dull; but it is written in the best manner, and having some little acquaintance with books I think I can venture to assure you that your work, like the "Memorabilia" of a second Xenophon, will be read when the army of Egypt and perhaps the nation that supplied it is no more.

I suppose another and another edition will soon appear, and therefore I lose no time in making known to you that the name of the gentleman who accompanied me in my travels is not *Harvey*,* but *Cripps*. You saw him often at Rosetta, and he feels himself indebted to you for the civilities he received there. In the note to page 175 of your work Harvey has by mistake been printed instead of his name.

As you have done us the honour to notice our journey in so flattering a manner, it may perhaps be pleasing to you to know the real extent of our travels. I shall immediately state it, and you are at full liberty to mention them.

The discovery of the ruins of the city of Sais, in

---

* Corrected accordingly in subsequent editions.—ED.

the Delta, was made by us after the departure of the
French; and it is some pride to Englishmen that
after the researches of the French savans so considerable a city as that of Sais whose ruins cover a great
tract of land, should be reserved for the travellers of
our own country. I brought from the ruins of the
Temple of Isis, in Sais, many curious monuments of
antiquity, and more beautiful sculpture than is usually
found among the works of Egyptian artists.

The ruins are situated about a mile from the eastern
bank of the Rosetta branch of the Nile, very nearly
in the situation laid down by D'Anville, and a little
beyond the canal of Belkin to the north, joining the
Rosetta with the Damietta branch. The village is
called Silhadger, and is opposite to the point where
the battle of Chebreissa was fought. It was D'Anville's
position of the city, joined to the account which some
Arabs gave us in Cairo, that led us to the ruins. They
exactly correspond with the description given by
historians; the water of the Nile being admitted
during its inundation into an area surrounding the
Temple of Isis.

The extent of our travels was over 39° of north
latitude, viz., from $29\frac{1}{2}°$ to $68\frac{1}{2}°$; and 45° of east
longitude. Our limit to the north was the frontier
of Finmark; to the south, the pyramids of Saccara
in Upper Egypt; to the east our travels extended as
far as the most eastern course of the Don, the ancient
Tanais. We passed through Denmark, Sweden,
Norway, Lapland, Finland, Russia, the deserts of the
Don Cossacks, Kuban Tartary, Circassia, and the
Crimea. Afterwards in Turkey we visited the plain
of Troy; and as you have mentioned this, it will be

as well to make known to you that the tombs of the heroes slain in the Trojan War had already been noticed by M. Chevalier. What I have undertaken, in opposition to Mr. Carlysle, is to prove the identity of the plain; and the truth of Chevalier's observations. Some new discoveries I made there: which, as they have never been published, might, if you think proper, give additional novelty to your remarks upon that subject.

I discovered the *mound of the plain*, and the *tomb of Ilus*, and the *city of New Ilium*. I *ascertained the temperature of the sources of the Scamander*, which has been noticed in France by M. Chevalier; and was the first traveller who ever surmounted the glaciers on the summit of Ida, and ascended to Gargarus the highest point of that range of mountains; at whose base I found the ruins of the Temple of Jupiter Liberator.

Afterwards we visited Asia Minor, Syria, and Egypt. Thence returning we went to all the Grecian isles: to Athens, to the Morea, and to the plains of Marathon. Then we ascended the summits of the mountains, Hymettus, Helicon, and Parnassus; and passed through Bœotia, Thessaly, Macedonia, and Thrace, to Constantinople. From thence through Bulgaria, Wallachia, Transylvania, Hungary, Germany, and France, to England.

If there is anything in the University that you want, either to enlarge your work or to elucidate any subject which you choose to write upon, I hope you will apply to me. In the mean time I have the honour to be
    Your obliged, obedient servant,
                    EDWARD DANIEL CLARKE.

Cambridge, Jesus College, Feb. 2, 1803.

COUNT WORONZOW TO SIR ROBERT WILSON.

Londres, ce $\left\{\begin{array}{l}\text{25 Novembre,}\\ \text{7 Décembre,}\end{array}\right\}$ 1803.

MONSIEUR LE CHEVALIER,

S. M. l'EMPEREUR ayant reçu votre ouvrage, m'a chargé de vous communiquer, Monsieur le Chevalier, sa satisfaction et sa reconnaissance, et combien il était charmé de l'avoir lu.

C'est avec le plus grand plaisir que je remplis les ordres de l'Empereur pour exprimer ses sentiments à votre égard, et pour y ajouter les miens.   Je vous prie de croire à l'estime et à la considération les plus particulières avec lesquelles j'ai l'honneur d'être,

Monsieur le Chevalier,
Votre très-humble et très-obéissant serviteur,
S. C. WORONZOW.

When Napoleon in 1798 determined upon attempting the conquest of Egypt as a means of assailing the British power in India, and fitted out an expedition for that purpose, he associated with it an illustrious band of sixty men of science, instructed to explore the hidden wonders of that land of fabulous antiquity. Too much credit cannot be given to him for this design, either on account of its far-seeing policy for the advancement of general knowledge and civilisation, or on the ground of its patriotism.   The fruit of the labours of the French Institut is one of the most valuable publications in the whole range of literature : a noble and imperishable monument to the genius of Napoleon, the learning and research of those famous

men, and the intellectual eminence of the French
nation.

But while the conqueror swept through the marvel-
lous land with his armies, and while the members of the
Institut unburied its mighty relics for the admiration
and instruction of mankind, two acts of a savage barbarism in Syria cast a shadow upon Napoleon's name.
Sir Robert Wilson heard the cry and sympathised with
the suffering of outraged humanity, inquired with
characteristic justice whether the alleged facts were
true, found them to be so upon unquestionable evidence, and then boldly proclaimed the truth to the
world. In his history he openly charged Napoleon
with the massacre of 5,000 Turks at Jaffa, and with
the poisoning of 580 sick in his own army at Acre.
For the support of the charges he appealed to the Regiment of Bon, whose muskets shot down the Turks,
and to the members of the Institut, who held a debate
upon the poisoning in their assembly at Cairo ; to
Assalini, in his work upon the plague ; and to a certain physician who had refused to be the instrument
of murder at Napoleon's bidding. He challenged the
accused to demand his prosecution in the English
courts, proudly conscious that even Napoleon would
find equal justice there : but he firmly and constantly
refused to give the individual names of other witnesses ;
because he knew that men whom Europe and the
world had reason to hold in honour, would be im-
perilled in their lives and liberties by the power of a
vindictive tyranny. Desgenettes was that noble-
hearted physician : and Fourier's immortal name may
now be added as an unimpeachable witness. The
following letter exhibits the terms of familiar regard in

which Fourier and Sir Robert Wilson communicated
with each other: and the indorsement fixes Fourier as
one of Sir Robert's authorities for the accusation:—

FOURIER TO SIR ROBERT WILSON.

MONSIEUR LE CHEVALIER,   Paris, le 13 Mars, 1802.

J'AI des remerciments à vous faire pour les expressions obligeantes dont vous vous servez dans la
lettre que vous m'avez fait l'honneur de m'adresser.
Lord Henry Petty, votre ami, vient de me remettre
cette lettre, et je regrette beaucoup que l'obligation où
je suis de quitter Paris, ne me permette point de
cultiver sa connaissance autant que je le désirerais.

Pendant le peu de temps que je resterai dans cette
ville si je puis lui être agréable en quelque chose, il
me trouvera tout disposé à le servir.

Je vous avais entretenu à Toulon du service que
Sir Sidney Smith m'a rendu en Egypte, en offrant
d'être dépositaire de mes papiers; et M. Perregaux a
eu la bonté de m'apprendre, après votre lettre, que
Sir Sidney Smith était dans l'intention de m'adresser
ces papiers aussitôt qu'il aurait reçu les informations
nécessaires.   Je vous prie de continuer vos bons
offices à cet égard, et de transmettre à Sir Sidney
Smith la lettre et la note ci-jointes.

J'étais déjà persuadé de la douleur qu'a dû vous
causer la mort de l'illustre M. Dolomieu, pour qui
vous aviez beaucoup d'attachement.   C'est une satisfaction pour ses amis d'apprendre que sa mémoire est
honorée du souvenir de personnes aussi distinguées
que vous pour leurs lumières et l'élévation de leur
caractère.

Je vais quitter Paris; le Gouvernement m'ayant

confié l'administration d'un département méridionale ; et à tous les motifs qui me rendraient agréable le séjour de la capitale, il faut que j'ajoute le regret de ne point vous voir dans le voyage que vous vous proposez de faire à la belle saison.　Je vais prévenir M. Berthollet et lui donner l'espérance que vous lui ferez visite à cette époque.　Quant à moi, j'espère que vous me dédommagerez par votre correspondance, à moins que vous ne poussiez votre voyage jusqu'à Grenoble ce qui serait plus agréable pour moi.

Je conserverai toujours un vif désir d'entretenir avec vous des relations que vos qualités personnelles rendent infiniment précieuses.

Je suis, Monsieur le Chevalier, avec tous les sentiments de la considération,

　　　　Votre très-humble et très-obéissant serviteur.

　　　　　　　　　J. B. FOURIER.

Thus indorsed by Sir R. Wilson :—

" Fourier's letter from Paris."

" *This man was secretary to the National Institut : and cut out, as he told me himself, the pages, by order of Buonaparte, which contained the dispute in the Institut when Desgenettes made his charges against B——.*"

In the year 1821 Sir Robert Wilson visited France, and while at the house of the Duke of Vicenza, at Caulaincourt, General Gourgaud being present, the conversation turned upon these charges.

In a note-book Sir Robert Wilson writes :—" The duke and Gourgaud both admitted the massacre of the garrison at Jaffa ;* but they denied the actual

---

* Sir Robert Wilson was said, some years afterwards, to have retracted these charges. *He never did so.* And his own answer to the assertion shall be given hereafter in its place.—ED.

empoisonment of the sick at Acre, though they were
prepared to defend the proposition as one made in the
interests of humanity; considering the misery to which
the sick were exposed from capture by a Turkish
enemy. The answer of Desgenettes, as he related it
to me, from reference to a journal, was :—'I am a
physician, not a philosopher. My duty is to preserve life ; not to take it away upon abstract theories.'
I have since lived to see a Russian prince cut a French
officer's throat to terminate his miseries."*

In Dec. 1802, Sir Robert Wilson sent his history to
the Emperor of Austria, with the accompanying
letter :—

SIRE,

EN ma qualité de Chevalier de l'ordre de Marie
Thérèse, je sens qu'il est de mon devoir de sou-
mettre à votre Majesté un ouvrage militaire redigé
par moi-même ; mais, Sire, j'ai encore d'autres puis-
sants motifs qui m'engagent à vous offrir ma relation
historique des événements qui ont eu lieu en Egypte.

J'ose espérer que comme militaire, votre Majesté
éprouvera quelque plaisir en parcourant les détails
d'une expédition dans laquelle les troupes d'une nation
intimement allié à la maison d'Autriche par les doubles
liens de l'amitié et de l'admiration, ont démontré
qu'elles n'avaient pas oublié les leçons et le noble ex-
emple qu'elles avaient reçus des armées Autrichiennes.

Comme Anglais, j'ai désiré ardemment d'éclaircir la
conduite de mes braves compatriotes, et de refuter,
par la seule vérité, les imputations envieuses de ses
ennemis ; comme ami de l'humanité, j'ai voulu faire
connaître au monde civilisé la barbarie atroce qui a

* See " Russian Campaign," published by Murray, 1860.

souillé et couvert d'infamie le Général-en-chef d'une
armée Française ; comme ennemi de toute tyrannie et
de toute usurpation, j'ai désiré dénoncer des actions
qui devraient unir du même sentiment tous les
souverains et tous les peuples de l'Europe.

Toutes ces considerations, Sire, ont contribué à
me décider à offrir à votre Majesté mon histoire de
cette campagne ; mais indépendemment de ces motifs,
la gratitude que je resens pour l'honneur qui me fut
conféré par votre Majesté, lors de mon séjour à
Vienne, en me rendant à l'armée d'Egypte, joint à la
manière flatteuse dont ces honneurs me furent
accordés, à moi personnellement, m'eussent toujours
décidé à vous rendre tous les hommages de respect et
de reconnaissance dont je me sens capable.

Que le règne de votre Majesté puisse être de longue
durée et couvert de gloire ; que l'Autriche et l'Angle-
terre puissent continuer à être étroitement liés par des
sentiments réciproques d'attachement et d'intérêt ; que
tous les ennemis de votre empire puissent être bientôt
confondus et anéantis ; et que je puisse trouver de
fréquentes occasions de prouver mon zèle et mon
dévouement pour le service de votre Majesté, sont et
seront à jamais les vœux bien sincères

Du très-fidèle et très-reconnaissant
serviteur de votre Majesté,

ROBERT WILSON.

Chevalier de l'ordre de Marie
Thérèse, et lieutenant-colonel
de cavalerie au service de Sa
Majesté Britannique.

A Londres, ce 10 Décembre, 1802.

In the summer of 1802, as appears by comparison
of dates,* he was quartered with the regiment at Dorchester.   In a memorandum headed "Anecdotal Remarks," he writes : † "Having determined to pay my
respects to the king at Weymouth, I arrived in the evening of the 2nd of Sept., and posted myself with my wife
at the pier-head when his Majesty was promenading
in that direction.   We attracted his notice, and after
some few remarks, he desired me to go on board his
yacht next day that he might question me more about
Egypt, and turning to Lord Hawkesbury, he observed :
' These are atrocious crimes with which he has charged
Buonaparte : I believe them all; do not you, my
lord ?'   Lord H. declined an answer.   We went on
board (next day), but not a word was said about
Egypt."

On the 16th of May, 1803, war was proclaimed
with France.   Immediately upon this Sir Robert
Wilson was appointed inspecting field-officer, under
General Simcoe, in the counties of Devon and
Somerset.   In the summer of the same year the
Prince of Wales, dissatisfied with remaining a
mere spectator of the continental strife, addressed to
the king through Mr. Addington ‡ his minister an
appeal for permission to serve in the army in defence
of his Majesty and the realm.   The correspondence
was published in a pamphlet and is preserved in the
Annual Register of that year.   Upon a copy of the
pamphlet among Sir R. W.'s papers is this note in his
handwriting :—

* Sir Robert Wilson singularly omitted dates of years, in frequent
instances giving only those of days and months.—Ed.

† See Appendix No. 1.

‡ Afterwards Lord Sidmouth.

"This first letter * was written by R. W., the remainder with the assistance of Lord H⁰." (Hutchinson.)

"The idea of this correspondence was suggested after dinner at C⁰. H., and the order for execution given on way from thence to the opera in the r¹ carriage, Sir W^m. Keir being also present."   "Tempora mutantur."†

For two years Sir Robert Wilson continued in the comparative retirement of this local home service, but far from inactivity.   In 1804 he prepared and published his "Inquiry into the State of the British Army, with a View to its Reorganization."‡   The title expresses the general scope of the publication; but it involved the expression of his opinions with regard to the volunteer force, the favourite scheme of Mr. Pitt.   He did not, of course, object to the force itself; but contended that in order to its efficiency it ought to have a military organization, and that it should be regarded only as subsidiary to the regular army, for the large increase of which he also strenuously contended. The principle is generally acknowledged in 1862.   Mr. Pitt, however, complained to the Duke of York of this as an attack upon his system, and Sir Robert Wilson was ordered to India.   This he regarded as a sentence of banishment: and he appears to have made a personal appeal to the king, always his friend.   He writes: "I was ordered by the Duke of York to India, and only by the king's *positive command* obtained a revocation of the edict."

In this work he made his first public effort to obtain for his humble companions in arms redress of the grievance which in his first service so powerfully

* Dated July 18, 1803.

† The proximate date of this note is indicated by these words. It most probably was soon after 1821. —Ed.   ‡ London, 1804.

moved his sympathy and indignation. "Educated," he says, "in the 15th Light Dragoons, I was early instructed to respect the soldier. That was a corps before which the triangles were never planted; where each man felt an individual spirit of independence and walked erect as if conscious of his dignity as a man and a soldier; where affection for his officer and pride in his corps were so blended that duty became a satisfactory employment, [and the acquisition of new distinction the chief object of each man's wishes]. With such men every enterprise was to be attempted which could be executed by courage and devotion; and there was a satisfaction in commanding them which could never have been derived from a system of severity."

"Corporal punishments never yet reformed a corps, but they have totally ruined many a man who would have proved under milder treatment a meritorious soldier. They break the spirit without amending the disposition. While the lash strips the back despair writhes round the heart, and the miserable culprit, regarding himself as fallen below the ranks of his fellows,* can no longer attempt the recovery of his station in society."

This is a noble protest. And one letter of approval from a friend, written at the time, will convey the sentiments of just and well-judging men:—

SIR F. BURDETT TO SIR ROBERT WILSON.

My DEAR WILSON,   Piccadilly, Aug. 13, 1804.

I CANNOT refrain from sending you a hasty line to convey to you my sincere thanks, not only for your

---

* "Fertur . . . *ut capitis minor*
—— humi posuisse vultum."—*Horace.*—ED.

expression of attachment, which I so highly prize, but principally for your excellent publication, which I regard as one of the most material services ever performed for this country in particular and for humanity in general.

You have done it bravely, wisely, and ably; and whatever else you may do it will ever command and insure my esteem.

In haste, yours sincerely,

F. BURDETT.

From the subjoined letter it appears that at this early day Sir Robert Wilson was disposed to make his father's advice, that Parliament should be the object of his ambition, a rule of guidance. His employment in the western counties, and the political influences which ruled there, probably suggested to him to become a candidate for the representation of Liskeard :—

COLONEL M'MAHON TO SIR ROBERT WILSON.

MY DEAR WILSON,   Carlton House, March 5, 1804.

I DO assure you most heartily that my past silence has not proceeded from any want of friendship or regard; but the fact is, I have scarce had a moment to myself for these three weeks past, during which time the occurrences of one day have so entirely changed the face of affairs of the former that any communication I could have made would not have tended to enlighten the subject: besides which I have observed throughout the greatest care in not being quoted for anything—a matter extremely difficult in these days.

The king for the first time saw the chancellor yesterday for a quarter of an hour; and the bulletin to-day is—" His Majesty continues in a favourable progress of amendment." I therefore have no doubt his convalescence will be proclaimed in a day or two, and no change will take place in the royal functions.

I showed both your letters in confidence to the prince, because they best spoke the fairness of your sentiments. He commanded me to say he should have been happy to have thrown a mantle over you for Liskeard had his interest there, whatever it may be, not been long bestowed on Tom Sheridan who is again a candidate on the present occasion; and that, in case you do *not* stand yourself, he wishes you, as he cannot assist you *there*, to throw whatever influence you have into that scale. Write to me what you know at Liskeard for the p.'s information.

Adieu, my dear Wilson, and believe me always most sincerely yours,

C. M'MAHON.

At the same time he sought for military, and perhaps diplomatic, service in different directions. He applied to Lord Mulgrave under the idea that he had the appointment of the Lord-Lieutenancy of Ireland. And failing this, and possibly other applications for active employment in the British service, the European armaments then going on seem to have suggested to him to offer himself as a volunteer in the Russian army. The answers of Lord Mulgrave and of Count Woronzow are added :—

LORD MULGRAVE TO SIR ROBERT WILSON.

Harley Street, May 14, 1804.

DEAR SIR,

ACCEPT my best thanks for the flattering manner in which you express your offer to serve with me, of which I should readily have availed myself had there been any foundation for the report of my appointment to the Lord-Lieutenancy of Ireland.

I am, dear sir,
Your most obedient and faithful servant,

MULGRAVE.

COUNT WORONZOW TO SIR ROBERT WILSON.

Londres, ce 28 Novembre, 1804.

MON CHER CHEVALIER,

EN arrivant de Bath hier j'ai trouvé la lettre que vous avez bien voulu m'écrire. L'estime que j'ai pour votre caractère et votre mérite, et la franchise avec laquelle vous me parlez, m'obligent de m'expliquer envers vous avec la même candeur au sujet qui vous intéresse si vivement.

Quelque désir que j'eusse de voir à notre service un homme de votre mérite, mon cher Chevalier, connaissant la réputation que vous vous êtes si justement acquise, ma sincérité éloigne tout espoir de voir accompli ce désir, et je ne puis que différer complètement de l'idée que vous avez formée de notre service militaire, par les considérations suivantes : l'Empereur ne prend qu'avec beaucoup de difficulté des étrangers à son service, quelquefois avec le même grade, quelquefois un grade moins de celui qu'ils avaient porté avant d'entrer dans l'armée Russe : les appointements du militaire Russe en général sont si modiques, qu'un

officier de l'armée Britannique à demie-paye reçoit
plus qu'un officier Russe en service actif; on est
moins payé chez nous que dans aucun autre pays de
l'Europe, parce que la noblesse chez nous, riche ou
pauvre, aime à servir et a toujours quelque chose à soi
qu'elle dépense ; et en général les officiers non-riches
qui sortent du service, trouvent leurs biens assez
dérangés.   Ainsi bien loin de gagner quelque chose
quant à la partie économique, vous y perdriez encore
beaucoup plus par la cherté excessive de vivre chez
nous. Ajoutez à tous ces inconvénients le désavantage
qu'un étranger doit toujours avoir dans le défaut de
la langue : le service en Russie exige une connaissance
au moins suffisante de la langue du pays ; toutes les
ordonnances et toute la discipline de l'armée sont dans
la langue Russe ; et vous auriez été bien embarrassé de
vous trouver dans la position de ne pouvoir non-seulement avoir un commandement convenable, mais de ne
pas même comprendre notre service : sans cette connaissance de la langue vous ne pourrez avoir aucun
commandement non-seulement d'un bataillon, mais
pas même d'une compagnie.   Les considérations que
je vous présente ici, mon cher Chevalier, sont trop
puissantes pour que je puisse tant soit peu encourager
votre projet d'entrer dans notre service ; je vous les
donne avec cette franchise et sincérité qui sont la suite
de l'estime et de la considération toutes particulières
avec lesquelles je serai toujours

Votre très-humble et très-obéissant serviteur,

I. C. WORONZOW.

A Monsieur le Chevalier Robert Wilson.

His perseverance and zeal were at last rewarded :

and after two years' labour as inspecting field-officer he was "allowed to purchase a lieutenant-colonelcy in the 19th Light Dragoons, and to exchange into the 20th Light Dragoons.

" The effective part of the regiment was in Sicily, but he organized the remaining troops so rapidly that they were in a short time reported fit for service ; and he was sent with them, and in command of the cavalry detachments, to join the expedition of Sir David Baird then rendezvousing at Cork."* At this point the autobiographical memoirs are resumed.]

Memoranda.

I embarked at Southampton on the 4th of August, 1805, with two hundred and thirty dragoons, divided in the ship *Whitby* and the *Union* brig. The vessels proceeded to Spithead. On the 18th, Lord Nelson, in the *Victory*, anchored at the Motherbank, and I went in a boat to see the *Hero*—the ship that led the van in Sir R. Calder's action. She was much injured.

August 19, Whitby Transport, Spithead.

The commodore—Captain Downman†—hoisted a signal for all masters of transports to go on board : when he gave notice of his intention to sail this evening.

On the 21st we were off the Start; with a fine breeze and fair. The *Britannia* yesterday evening bore down upon us in a most unwarrantable manner; so close that had our captain not changed his course we must have been struck by her.

* Introduction to " Russian Campaign."
† Of the *Diadem*.

Latitude 49°, Longitude 20°.

A miserable calm—loss of ground. I employed myself in finishing a memoir long since begun on outpost service. It is a collection of instructions acquired by my own experience, without reference to any other writer; every idea is probably, however, already in print, for unless the truth of the positions were obvious to every military man they would have no value: but I doubt whether any other person has digested with so much care the results of his observations in that service for the improvement of others. I have taken much pains to elucidate the subject, in order that the young officers of the 20th may not be unprepared for this essential duty. The ignorance or misconduct of a single individual now hazards my own reputation.

August 26, Twelve, Night.

Wretched night—heavy gale—no sleep till six A.M. The kettle-drums and trumpets which I have ordered to sound in the cabin in order to rouse the lethargic were this morning to myself unwelcome.

Cove of Cork, August 27, Nine P.M.

We anchored at one P.M. in the Cove. I went on shore and saw Sir David Baird. He was very civil, but made no communication. I saw General Ferguson : wrote to Lord Hutchinson : met Godfrey Macdonald, and dined with him in a hovel dignified by the name of an hotel. In the evening I went on board; expecting to sail as the order to that effect was most urgent, occasioned by the report that the French fleet was at sea. Sir David Baird feared to be detained by orders from England. The

Britannia, last night, nearly foundered the *Union.* She, as Arbuthnot informs me, was so near, that many dragoons were prepared to jump into her for safety. In consequence, I went to the *Diadem* in order to report to Sir Home Popham this repeated misconduct of the *Britannia.* Sir Home was not on board, but the ship was in very high order indeed. Sir David Baird sails in her.

At anchor, Cove of Cork, August 29.

The signal was made to sail. All the convoy were soon under weigh. Signal to anchor outside the harbour. I went in the evening, with Captain Eustace and Cromwell, on board the *Diana* Indiaman, and obtained some good intelligence as to our destination. Colonel Adams's brother is private secretary to Mr. Pitt, who has written to him that the Indian troops are to be under Sir D. Baird's orders. Went next day on board the *Northampton* Indiaman—a small extra ship: found there, in the 24th dragoons, a sergeant whom I had dismissed from my regiment for theft, without punishment; he has acquired again a very good character. Thence I went on board the *Union,* and returned shortly to my own ship: There I discovered that our Madeira and porter had been pillaged by the ship's cook, a sergeant, and a regimental cook. Court-martial ordered. The ship's cook I shall at all events send on board a man-of-war; the sergeant will be broke; and the regimental cook, as he is an old man, I shall punish by a very strong emetic and the inscription of " rogue " on the left sleeve.

August 30, 1805.

Captain Butterfield, agent of transports, came on board to receive the sailor who had stolen our wine:

he congratulated us on our destination, and offered
each of the captains 200*l.* for his share of the prize
money.   The sailor was taken on board a man-of-war;
our soldier sconced of grog; and the old sinner, who
is very like Silenus, had a strong emetic given him by
way of reprisal for our Madeira.   When he was very
sick the band played the " Rogue's march " to him.
The opportunity for addressing the men was not lost,
and I had reason to feel satisfied with the effect of my
oratory.

September 2, 40 leagues from Cork.

In the evening of August 31 a breeze sprang up from
the northward; when the commodore fired his signal
to weigh.   When passing his ship I directed our men
to man the yards: and they gave the general and him
three cheers, which the men-of-war returned in the
same manner.   I wished by this attention to show
a proper respect to our commander-in-chief and pre-
possess the soldiers in his favour, as well as to attract
a beneficial notice to them.   The effect was very good :
our men being well dressed and well placed.

In the Atlantic, Sept. 5, Five P.M.

All the wild fury of a storm is raging : to increase
the misery our course is scarcely true.   " Ye Gentlemen of England," and " Blow high, blow low," are
appropriate tunes, if I had voice, or heart, or stomach,
to sing them.   In the middle of the night a sea broke
into our cabin : all hands were employed on deck, so
there was no relief.   All darkness, except from the
phosphoric gleam of the spray.   Many vessels dismasted.   The soldiers worked in danger which made
others, more alive to its nature, anxious.

About ten ships are missing in the fleet.

Sept. 10.—Yesterday I went on board the brig, and was obliged to sleep there in consequence of our ship shooting too much ahead. I was very angry: since had the breeze sprung up I never could have got on board again. Newland and the captain of the *Whitby* were with me: the latter became furious. Arbuthnot was as gay as a young sparrow, and is the life of the brig's company.

Sept. 11.—Yesterday Sir Home Popham sent a midshipman in his boat for me, with a very kind invitation to dine. Sir David Baird received me in a very flattering manner, and assured me of his marked protection; but I could not gather much from his manner as to our eventual destination. I discovered, however, that Sir H. was not to have gone with the fleet, but to have proceeded in accordance with his own desire. I learnt that the *Diana* Indiaman was disabled and could not proceed from Cork; but the 59th, on board of her, were ordered to embark in the *Diadem* and *Diomede*. Returned to the *Whitby* at eight P.M., and found as great a difference as if I was removing from Portland Place to Hockley-in-the-Hole.

Sept. 12.—In consequence of a fear that we might not have water enough, I directed that no linen should be washed at sea.

I saw some hanging up yesterday: at this I was angry and issued an order on the subject, but found afterwards that some of my own formed part; I therefore reprimanded myself in the following order:—

"September 12, *Whitby.*

"The commanding officer having learnt that some of his own linen was washed, contrary to the order on that subject, is sensible that the reproof directed against others recoils with more than double force upon himself; since he is responsible for the act of his servant.

"The preservation of the water is essential for the general welfare, and therefore no infringement of the order relative to the washing must henceforth occur."

Sept. 16.—Beautiful mild weather, which has enabled me to complete the detachment with every appointment; and we are in very high order. I should not now fear the inspection even of the Duke of Kent. I keep my boys regularly to school, and in no voyage was ever so industrious myself. I have written volumes, and read until the materials for reading are exhausted.

The men have just caught a large fish with a harpoon; but he is full of sea vermin. I have prevented his skin being stripped off while alive—the proposal of an epicure.

Sept. 18.—Arbuthnot's brig was run foul of by an Indiaman some days back. One of her sailors with an axe prepared to cut away the mainstay of the brig's foremast. Arbuthnot seized an unloaded carbine and presented. The sailor was so frightened, that he threw himself under the yard-arm, and our men followed up the success by cutting such of the Indiaman's ropes as were lashed with the brig's. This was an admirable display of presence of mind. Three hundred miles from Madeira—probably our first point of rendezvous. The fleet dispersed: but collecting.

Sept. 21.—I composed yesterday, finished and copied

fair this morning, a discourse, which I propose to read
to-morrow—being Sunday—if the weather permits, to
my dragoons.

Sept. 22.—Preached my sermon after reading
prayers.

Sept. 24.—Yesterday, Arbuthnot came on board
with the major and Hartwell. The major is oppressed
with that dreadful malady the "blue devils." Indeed,
our passage has been bad enough to beat down all our
energies. The sea rises, the wind howls, and the ship
rolls : triste! triste! triste!

Sept. 26.—In the last twenty-four hours we made
twenty-two miles—for us an extraordinary progress.
To-day, instead of twenty-two miles we have only made
six. Can human fortitude endure this without a
murmur?

Sept. 27.—Calm all day and night—not one yard of
progress. I went this morning on board the *King
George* to General Yorke of the artillery, for ammunition. He expects that we shall only touch at Madeira
and proceed to the Cape de Verd Islands for water—
distant now about twelve hundred miles. In this case
we must either be destined for the Cape of Good Hope
or for South America. He is employed in altering
the shafts of the artillery tumbrils and cannon, so that
they may be converted into poles for oxen to be
yoked.

Three, P.M., September 28.

Land! land! land!—huzza! huzza! huzza! Such
was the cry a minute since, and it is justified by the
sight of Porto Santo, a few miles distant from Madeira.
All well, all gay ; notwithstanding that none of us may
disembark, and that we have still so many leagues of

s 2

ocean to traverse. The mere sight of *terra firma* will always cheer us landsmen.

Oct. 4.—On the 29th we anchored in the road of Madeira. Here we found the *Leda* frigate and the West India fleet. I landed with difficulty and peril. I reserve an account of Madeira, and a narrative of our proceedings during our stay, for a separate paper.* On my return on board I found great irregularities in consequence of intoxication : but a young cornet being involved in the same offence, I pardoned all on account of the officer's bad example ; hoping that shame would be his correction.

The next morning I was early with Arbuthnot and Godfrey Macdonald on board the commodore : he and the general were most kind. The latter informed me that I was to have the cavalry on board the East India ships attached to me, and that my command would be still further increased. At dinner with the consul, Sir David Baird, the adjutant-general, a son of Lord Minto, several captains of the navy and of Indiamen, were present. General Beresford afterwards came. I was introduced to him by Sir David, next to whom I sat at dinner and with whom I had a very interesting conversation.

In the morning I procured a boat and went on board my ship. I there learnt that a man, a farrier, at twelve o'clock of the last night, being drunk, had fallen overboard. In the six or seven minutes during which he was in the water, the boat was lowered and he was picked up ; his eyes, however, were so sealed with sleep and gin that he did not awake until he had been on deck some time. He now remembers

* See Appendix No. 7.

nothing. How delightful this turtle-sailing must be! He was, however, in my opinion an unlucky fellow, as he did not sleep through the voyage. This fact is still more extraordinary than what occurred to a sailor on board Sir Home's ship in the heavy gale: he was washed from one of the yards into the sea, and brought back again by the next wave.

We learnt here, after some days, that the fleets were to separate; and the signal was made for them to divide. Sir David Baird will now probably style himself commander-in-chief, instead of major-general in command. All the men-of-war saluted his flag and cheered as he passed. The transports followed; we leading the van and cheering. We then had instructions to steer S.W.—a course for Teneriffe, the Cape de Verd, or the Cape of Good Hope.

Oct. 5.—I purpose to go out to the different ships whenever I can, for a change of scene is necessary to divert the thoughts in so long and uninteresting a voyage.

Oct. 7.—Steering for the Brazils.

Oct. 8.—Latitude 27°. Many of the men are ill. I have ordered flannel for them : to be made up in bandages for the waist. I procured it at Madeira for them. The *Narcissus*, sent to reconnoitre, returned at six A.M. this day. The commodore, who was steering W.S.W., immediately changed his course to S.W.: so conjecture is at fault as to our first destination. The ultimate object is doubtless the Cape. Many of our men, ill of dysentery, have cured themselves by drinking the rust of the anchor-stock in brandy!—a new form of steel medicine to me. The Brazils two thousand miles distant.

Latitude 10° 26', October 17.

I went on board the commodore, transacted some important business for our future projects, and ascertained the whole progress of our voyage and enterprize. The kindness of Sir David Baird is very great, and he seizes every opportunity of gratifying me. Sir Home is not less well-disposed. General Ferguson came on board when I was in the *Diadem*, and was very civil.

Oct. 19.—The men practised ball-cartridge firing. We are ordered to pursue this exercise unremittingly. Arbuthnot and I went on board the commodore, as I had a communication to make to Sir David Baird respecting horses at S. Salvador. On my return I found cause for displeasure. The position of a commanding officer is not a bed of roses.

Oct. 22.—A circumstance occurred which would have assured me of the proposed objects of the expedition, if I had not been previously informed. When I entered Sir Home's cabin suddenly, I found him and the adjutant-general employed in reading " Barrow's Travels in Africa," vol. 2, which treats altogether of the Cape of Good Hope, and before them was a treatise on the winds upon that coast. An observing eye may thus often discover mysteries. I am ordered on board the *Northampton*, to inspect the dragoons attached to us, and to see the quartermaster-general in his ship and General Yorke, relative to our supply of ammunition. We have been firing again this morning, and made excellent practice.

Oct. 20th I went on board the brig, where I am now writing and propose to sleep. Several artillery officers are expected to dine here, on which account

Arbuthnot is stuffing a turkey and making dainty puddings. My chief reason for leaving my ship to-day in the worst weather, was that I had cause to be displeased with the conduct of some officers in her. I paraded the 25th, 12th, and 19th detachments; found them but a motley crew, and shamefully neglected in their equipments. Instructions received to make the port of S. Salvador, where the fleet is to procure the necessary supplies.

The climate in these latitudes is really terrible : they seem condemned to an alternation of calms and storms, thunder, lightning, and deluges of rain. We suffer much, and make little way : indeed, we only make any progress during the tornados, and are forced to desire the frequent return of that which we cannot enjoy when it arrives. I shall endeavour to get back to the *Whitby*. The two young gentlemen whom I wished to reprove are probably come to their senses. They offended, and I gave them a severe reprimand. There has long been a jealousy, and they have been irritable on account of leaving England. Their observations on this subject have exposed them to my animadversion. There is no offence that I can forgive so little as a public declaration of disgust at service, and desponding language respecting the result of an enterprize. One was a militiaman, and is, I fear, now so in spirit; the other was a heavy dragoon and never proposed to be a soldier : but when at the theatre for exertion I hope both will " deform fair nature with hard-favoured rage," and show a desire to earn distinction : this conduct alone can make me feel an interest in promoting their views when the service has ceased.

Oct. 26.—On the 23rd I went with Arbuthnot on board the *Belliqueuse;* and learnt that the *Diadem* was to go to S. Salvador with the *Leda* and probably twelve of the best-sailing ships. A heavy squall separated the brig from us, and we are obliged to remain. Arbuthnot is in full *réjouissance,* and has just devoured half a pig for his luncheon. On the 25th the *Leda* bore down upon us, and I was ordered to go in her on board the *Diadem.* I left Arbuthnot with Captain Byng of the *Belliqueuse,* the brother of Edmund: one of the most hospitable and excellent men I ever met with. This morning we made the commodore, and I went on board and received instructions relative to the purchase of horses. Returned through a mountainous roll of waters; and was nearly swamped in getting on board through mismanagement of the *Leda's* sails: I was very glad to find myself again on her quarter-deck. The wind has been so violent during the last thirty-six hours that both gun-brigs are almost disabled, and several vessels have lost their topmasts. I expected calm weather in these latitudes, whereas we have an everlasting gale. I have much to do now, and my responsibility begins at S. Salvador, where active exertion will be needed. The *Leda* has an excellent captain (Honeyman), pleasant society, good accommodation, and a bath; so that my position now is to me a resurrection from the infernal regions, compared with the *Whitby's* cabin.

October 28, Latitude 1° 59'.

The east trade has reached us and we proceed rapidly. This morning, the *Whitby* being found too heavy a sailer we bore down upon her, and I went on board for my portmanteau. I heard that a man whom we had sent to the brig from her was dead, and the sergeant-major's child, an infant, was no longer a passenger on the surface of the waters. I have ordered the commanding officer to apply instantly for a surgeon's assistant, and hope that, although several men are poorly, no serious illness will break out. It has been, however, too bold an experiment to send troops so far in so small a transport.

The little uneasiness which I spoke of is now removed, and we parted very good friends. I returned to the *Leda* to proceed to S. Salvador. To-morrow we expect to reach the equator and arrive at Neptune's capital.

October 30, Latitude 0°.

This morning, at four o'clock, we passed the line *without breaking the ship's back in the leap.* At eleven A.M., a voice was heard at the bows inquiring what ship this was; who commanded her; and whither bound? To all which questions the officer of the watch returned suitable answers. A car then advanced, drawn by painted men, who looked very much like chimney-sweeps on May-day. In the car were seated Neptune, Amphitrite, and their child; attendants and Nereids followed. They advanced to the quarter-deck, and there Neptune with a trident in his hand and a crown of feathers on his head, and Amphitrite with a bottle of cordial approached the captain, whom they saluted, and afterwards paid us all the same compliment. This ceremony being over, the car proceeded with the party round the deck. Unfortunately the rapidity of the motion overset the god and goddess, without, however, any injury; except to Neptune's pigtail which was supported by a servant whose body was smeared all over with tar. The order of procession being restored, they descended to the mid-deck where a tub of water was placed with a small board across it, on which the stranger was to be made welcome to Neptune's residence. The unfortunate guest, seated on the board, was first covered with a wet cloth and swab to keep him warm. He was then hoodwinked with another cloth. Neptune next asked what brought him to his domain? Some appropriate answer being given Amphitrite was desired to salute him, which she did with a very harsh scrub of her beard. The barber was then ordered to do his duty. A large brush dipped in tar was first applied over his nose, mouth, &c., which lather was afterwards well rubbed in with the hand, when a wooden or iron hoop razor was applied according to the direction of Neptune. This operation being over the guest was asked some question, or desired to hail the ship through a speaking-trumpet; down which as he opened his mouth a bucket of water was dashed, the board under him was removed and he soused into the tub of water; while numerous buckets from all hands inundated him until he could escape. Such is the extraordinary custom, which is rendered venerable by antiquity. The officers this day escaped, but in general they must submit to the ceremony. Above two hundred men are to be initiated this morning; buckets of water are flying in every direction, and the mid-decks are inundated.

We are proceeding rapidly with a fair trade wind.

Latitude 3° 46', November 1,
Off the Roccas, or Pimental Shoal.

I little thought when I finished my last journal that the next would commence with the melancholy narrative that I am now about to write; and yet when I left the *Whitby*, after directing her return to the fleet, a thought crossed my mind that what the officers considered a misfortune might, perhaps, be destined for their good. Probably she has been preserved by her absence from us.

The weather continued fine, and nothing material occurred yesterday. The chronometer in the evening being found at variance with the dead reckoning, the master of the frigate directed a proper course, as he supposed, to avoid all danger by too great dependence either on the one or the other. He hoped to pass the island of Noronha to the eastward. On going to bed I said—half serious, half jesting—to Captain Honeyman, "I presume that we shall have notice in the night of land being ahead." On which he observed, that he should be "glad to hear that notice, as then we should know our longitude to a certainty," adding that he had "ordered a good look-out."

About half-past three, the officer of the watch came into the cabin and said that breakers were close ahead. The captain ordered the ship to tack and fired a gun for signal of danger to the convoy. He went also himself on deck. In a few minutes after the first gun was fired another gun followed, and we tacked a second time : the sure evidence of imminent peril. The man on the look-out had never seen land or heard breakers until the ship was close upon them; he first cried out "land!" and immediately afterwards "breakers!" An attempt was made to tack the ship before the officer of the watch had come into the cabin, but she missed stays; and when the captain got on deck the master advised, as the ship had entered the breakers S.W., that she should be brought out by a N.E. course. This was natural enough; but no sooner was the tack effected, than the forecastle look-out cried, "Land round the bows, high and dry!" At the same moment, the quartermaster heaving the lead sang out, with admirable presence of mind in order not to alarm the crew, "seven fathoms!" but came and whispered to the master—"only five." The ship was instantly put about and happily wore; had she again missed stays we must have perished. The stern turned within ten yards of abrupt and craggy rocks. From so perilous a situation few vessels ever escaped. She darted almost immediately into thirteen fathoms, and care for ourselves no longer occupied our thoughts. That misfortune had befallen some of the fleet was now but too certain. Signal-guns of distress were heard from several quarters; and when a reluctant day dawned we saw three ships on shore—the *Britannia*, the *Europe* Indiaman, and the *King George* artillery ship with General Yorke on board.

Breakers and rocks seemed to forbid help in order to secure the victims to the greedy waves. Two islands of white sand, on the summit of which was discovered some verdure, and flanked by a ridge of low rocks on each side stretching to the westward several miles, were the theatre of this distress. The *Britannia* was the most distant from us. Several Indiamen were lying off in order to discover any means of promoting the safety of the vessel or her crew. When we went

down to breakfast her mizen-mast had been cut away
to lighten her aft; on our return she had totally disappeared.   We fear that she had succeeded in forcing
over the surge, and sunk when she came into deep
water from the injury she received.   Thus, probably,
has been overwhelmed one of the richest Indiamen
that ever went out.   She had on board a very large
amount of specie, besides a most valuable cargo and
numerous passengers.   She was, however, a very old
vessel, this being her thirtieth voyage and intended to
be her last.   On arriving in India, she was to have
reposed as a guard ship in the Ganges.   The *Europe*
to our great joy was soon relieved, with the loss of her
fore-topmast, by her own efforts.   The unhappy *King
George* stranded on the extreme point of the reef, presented and still presents a most wretched spectacle.
About seven o'clock she fell on her beam ends, the
spray of the sea bounding over her topmast head.
The bowsprit was covered with her unfortunate crew
and the artillerymen embarked in her.   By degrees,
we saw their number reduced: a flag on the sand
island directed our view to about two hundred of them,
who had escaped and who made signals to us for relief
by holding out white handkerchiefs, &c.   We are
now lying-to about three miles from them and have
sent, through a heavy sea and notwithstanding a brisk
gale, every boat in the ship to bring them off.   When
the people on shore discovered the boats, we could
perceive them throwing up their caps into the air in
an ecstasy of joy at their expected deliverance.

This has been a most affecting scene.   When I
reflect upon the wonderful preservation of the frigate,
the total disappearance of the *Britannia*, the wreck of

the *King George,* and the yet uncertain fate of the sailors and troops, I am oppressed with the various considerations which crowd upon my mind.

I cannot avoid mentioning an instance of great coolness in one of the sailors, who was employed in pumping in order to clarify the water in use for the ship. He continued his employment without a moment's pause, when the rocks rose around us on every side and each man was preparing for the shock that was to rend the vessel into fragments; for we had a great deal of canvas set.

Captain Honeyman has behaved with much steadiness and fortitude; his distress of mind is very great. No blame whatever can attach to him; but he has high feeling and a good heart.

Nov. 2.—The first boat returned with some of the shipwrecked artillerymen about one o'clock. From them we learnt that General Yorke was the only person known to be drowned. The ship had struck about half-past two in the morning. She filled about daylight. The men then lowered themselves from the spritsail-yard upon a rock which seemed to communicate with the island of sand. About forty men had descended when the general went forward. Previously to this moment he had been most collected, but when he attempted to fall from the rope his resolution forsook him; yet, notwithstanding, he refused assistance offered him. He remained suspended until he was heard to say that his strength had forsaken him, when he fell into the surge. A rope was then flung, which he in vain attempted to seize. Several of his men ventured into the surf to reach him, but every effort was fruitless. Exhausted by swimming against receding waves, he sunk and rose three times, always getting his head above water.

Thus perished an officer who had been considered the most eligible for the conduct of his department in the expedition : who had come out with leave, signed by the duke and Lord Chatham, to allow of his immediate return after the service was completed : and who proposed to pass the remainder of his years in the enjoyment of every blessing which an amiable wife and a sufficient fortune could authorize him to anticipate. But such is destiny that this man was forced to yield his life ; while a man with a broken leg, and a woman with a child born only two hours before the calamity, were saved !

The boats having brought off in the first instance all the helpless the women and children, of whom there were a great number, returned ; but were four hours the second time in reaching the shore, and did not get back to the ship until near nine o'clock. This caused us some anxiety as we dared not move nearer, and in these climes there is no twilight.

One hundred and sixty-three persons were thus saved from a miserable destruction, for the island afforded no water and is the abode of sea birds ; its encompassing waters are the resort of sharks. Fortunately for the wrecked men a little cove was discovered into which boats could pass, or they could never have got into them ; and by a happy fortune they had saved one of the boats, which enabled them to pass from the rock on which the wreck was left to the high land, over two pieces of water which flowed between. Not an article was saved by any person, except by an officer who secured his wife's picture. General Yorke had his plans in his pocket; but his body was not thrown on shore, so they are lost. This island of rock has evidently been the scene of similar catastrophes, as three old anchors and some planks were found upon it.

The men behaved uncommonly well, and at no moment forgot the respect due to their officers and obedience to their orders. The master of the ship—a fine old man—was the last to embark. He was pulled into the boat by *his own son*, who had not been known to him for ten years: having been idle he went into the navy, and is now a sailor in the *Leda*. The men were somewhat bruised but are doing well. Several have their legs much inflamed from the salt water, the sun, and the sand, but are not seriously hurt. The officers have suffered most in this respect, and especially the naval officers who went in the boats to bring off the people. One man only is missing: it is to be hoped that he is drowned; there is some fear, however, that after very great exertions he drank some wine out of a cask thrown on shore and was asleep in some sheltered place.

The vessel went to pieces about twelve o'clock. She was the finest of her class in the transport service.

We could hear no tidings of the *Britannia*. The master of the *King George* saw her drift by him with the loss of her mizen-mast, and with the ensign reversed—the sad signal of distress. The universal belief is that she has foundered in deep water. The argument is too much against her chance of preservation; nevertheless I will not abandon my hopes until we have communicated with some of the ships which sent boats to her, for that we know was done by two Indiamen. If she be saved the loss then is not so serious as we feared, as the *King George* had discharged her ordnance stores previously. The safety of the *Streatham*, after the loss of her fore-topmast, is a cause for great satisfaction; and our own preservation is allowed to be one of the most remarkable circumstances that ever happened. We owed it probably to the darkness, as a drunken man often owes his life to the effect of the liquor that first exposed him to hazard. But how we got out by the means and in the way we did is miraculous. The *King George's* crew considered our destruction inevitable, for they saw us in the moment of most imminent danger. The captain of the *William Pitt* Indiaman came on board in the middle of the day to offer any assistance in his power, and took a boat-load of the men on board as they passed on their way to the *Leda*. We made sail last night, and stood to the N.E. thirty-nine miles in order to get to the windward of the fatal Roccas; when about four this morning we fell in with the main convoy standing on a course that must inevitably bring them near to the danger and, if the wind fails upon the rocks, since the current is so very strong. We are now beating up to the *Raisonnable* to warn her of them, the *Diadem* not being with the fleet. The first ship I saw when coming on deck this morning, was the *Whitby*. What must be her surprise! No doubt conjecture is everywhere busy. Every one is on the look-out for breakers. We must pass very near our well-known terror within an hour!

Such are the charms of navigation, particularly on a coast but little frequented and inaccurately charted. I feel much for Captain Honeyman; but no human prudence could have averted the catastrophe. He has done much in preserving so many lives by his example of coolness; and yet I would not like to tell the tale as it must be told to Sir Home. Who will draw Priam's curtains and disclose his Troy on fire?

November 4, 5° 58' South.

We found that the *Diadem* had not left the fleet as we expected. Captain Honeyman went on board and related the misfortune. The general and commodore were much affected; but the latter, who is unquestionably one of the first navigators in Europe, had made the Roccas to a mile and was aware of the danger. He was, however, probably the only officer in the fleet so informed, and I believe that even he did not know the whole extent of these perilous shoals.

We were sent to find the *Verona*. The next day we saw her to leeward, and her captain coming on board confirmed the melancholy intelligence of the *Britannia* having foundered. All her people were saved, except one man who obstinately refused to quit the ship, being drunk. As she went down he sprung from her, having cut away the life-buoy to save himself; but in vain. Captain Birch, her commander, at four o'clock in the morning went on deck and ordered his mate to shorten sail. He had scarcely given the direction when he perceived a large ship bearing down upon him on the other tack. The *Streatham* rushed upon his bowsprit and, falling round almost unripped the side of the *Britannia*. The *Streatham*, losing her fore-topmast and top-gallantmast, stood on; but the *Britannia* instantly drove upon the rocks, which she had at the moment discovered. She hung by her stern upon them a quarter of an hour; then cut away

her mizen-mast and soon floated, with the loss of her
rudder. The water was then found to pour in ; but the
pumps reducing the leak, Captain Birch ordered his
boats to the aid of the *King George's* people. They
had scarcely left the ship when the leak gained so fast
that the safety of the vessel was deemed impossible,
the boats were recalled, and the signal of distress
hoisted as before stated. The *Verona*, the *Europe*,
and the *Comet*, being near sent their boats directly ;
and four hundred people were brought away, with
twelve chests of treasure out of one hundred and fifty
each containing 1000*l.*, before nine o'clock in the
morning ; when the ship settled to the water's edge
for a quarter of an hour ; and then giving a heavy
lurch went down head foremost into the unfathomable
deep, only seven miles from the Roccas. Her decks
at the same time blew up, and the spars rose fifty feet
into the air. This caused the spray which we had
remarked when the vessel disappeared from our sight.
Captain Birch remained to the last moment in the
· execution of his duty, and springing from the quarter-
gallery into the sea, was, as we are told, picked up by
the *Europe's* boats. Not an article of property or of
clothing was saved except what each individual wore.
Mrs. Russell, a very handsome woman, just married,
could not even save her diamonds : they were in a box,
but it was refused admittance into the boat. Her
distress of mind since the accident has been very
severe ; but happily, on board the *Verona* are two
female passengers from whom she may obtain garments as well as the offices of friendship.

Great as has been the public loss on this occasion,
the vessel altogether being of about five hundred

thousand pounds value, still I cannot but deplore most the ruin of those who for such a distant voyage had embarked all their property; and have thus lost, perhaps, their station in life and been reduced to poverty never to rise again.

We sent provisions on board the *Verona*, and such linen as could be spared; but the officers of the artillery had previously reduced the stock much, and my small portmanteau contained but a soldier's kit.

About four o'clock yesterday we made the land off Rio Grande, and found the current still very strong. The land, which a little to the eastward is guarded by an iron frontier of rock seventy miles in extent, is a degree nearer than it is represented to be in the charts. Here, by such unknown dangers, was Captain Elphinstone in the *Egyptienne* once nearly lost; and here probably will many more vessels terminate their course. A general gloom prevails, which will only be dissipated by brilliant success.

Off S. Augustine, Nov. 5.

Yesterday, a signal ordered us to bring on board the commodore the crew of a boat on our lee bow. After searching in vain for some time, we discovered two men on what we supposed to be a wreck, but which proved to be a catamaran boat in use on this coast. The singular construction of these boats excited our admiration, both on account of their simplicity and the hardihood of the mariners who first ventured on them.

Five spars, each about eighteen feet long, are fastened together by bolts of iron-wood: these are cut at their extremity, so as to be thin and pointed. In the centre of the spars a board descends about four feet, upon the principle of a lee-board, to prevent the raft from upsetting or making too much lee way. The mast is about eighteen feet high, and the sail triangular; a small bench, in which a hole is cut to receive the mast, crosses the raft about four feet from the fore end of the spars; about six feet further astern two sticks of iron-wood are fixed, three feet high; another stick is laid across them, and another stick, upright with a forked end, is attached to the centre of this cross-bar. This whole apparatus is used to suspend the fish-basket, the lines, and other tackle. Four feet from this is a small stool without any support to the sides or back, but which crosses the raft. On this the steersman sits with a rudder much like a paddle, that acts against two little sticks placed on each side of the raft at the very extremity. He also manages the sail. The other man seems generally to stand upright, but he can sit down with the steersman. A stone is their anchor; the rope or cable is made of grass, and their fishing-line of cotton admirably woven. The sea here is high, and the wind blows strong from the S.E., so that white horses cover the ocean; the waves, however, can make no fatal impression on this vessel, if so we may call such a contrivance, than which there probably is none more primitive in form in the history of navigation in the world. The waters roll over the spars and wash the knees of the mariners, but without any hold they remain firm; or if by accident they should be washed off, they instantly swim again on board their never-injured bark.

We hoisted the catamaran on deck, and bought the

fish, which proved very good. The two men who came on board had copper complexions; the hair of one was curly but long; that of the other was very silky, but his features had a negro character—yet the countenance was engaging, and he might be called very handsome. Their teeth were white, their eyes expressive, and their limbs well-proportioned. At first they had shown some apprehension, but were soon reconciled. They came that morning from Flor, in the Bay of Fermozo.

We now carried a press of sail to reach the commodore: when at dinner the officers reported the foremast to be sprung; it had given way with a considerable explosion. The commodore being informed by telegraph of our misfortune, lay-to, and about nine at night we ran alongside and sent the Brazilians to him. At the same time I sent a note to Sir Home; in which I offered, if the good of the immediate service could be promoted or more distant objects be beneficially effected by an officer traversing the Brazils overland, to embark on the catamaran with the men sent to him, and from their place of abode proceed to S. Salvador through the country—a distance of about five hundred miles. I was excited to this offer by various considerations: and had I been permitted to undertake the enterprise I might have rendered much service to the country, and certainly secured some advantage to myself. I was satisfied that, although the catamaran was to me a novel it was not a dangerous navigation, since the use is general on a large tract of coast. Sir David at first consented, but afterwards said that sickness having broken out in the *Union* among the 20th my superintendence would be necessary. I have, therefore, on every account, to regret this unfortunate and hitherto unknown evil, which has sent above twenty men to the hospital. I am very anxious to get on board, and examine the extent and cause of the mischief.

The Brazilians returned this morning. We hoisted out their catamaran, and they quitted us loaded with presents, highly delighted at their treatment, and full of pleasure in anticipation of returning to their homes and giving their wives the treasures which they carry away. They dwelt much on this and seemed to suffer great regret at the distress they must have felt at their absence; soon, however, to be converted into a cause for joy—

> "O'er the vast globe still woman holds her sway :
> The prince and beggar equal homage pay."

S. Salvador, November 10.

After a rapid run in very bad weather we anchored in this bay at half-past nine last night. The fleet are expected to-morrow. I shall reserve a description of S. Salvador for a separate paper,* and only say that a more abominable place does not exist. Filth, horrible figures, and ruins meet you in all the streets, which are in fact mere lanes. It is a medley of the worst Italian and Turkish styles of city. The blacks are all of enormous size—the black women hideous. The proportion of blacks to whites is as thirty to one ; the whites are but semi-men in appearance, and a disgrace to the dignity of Europeans.

Nov. 11.—I have just returned from an expedition, most entertaining if no mischief follows. Having

* See Appendix No. 6.

gone on board the *Diadem* we proceeded to the shore in grand parade, with the general, commodore, and staff, under a salute, to call on the governor whose palace commands the town from an eminence of very great height. Seven two-wheel carriages were on the shore to receive us. The general and commodore entered the first, drawn by six mules; General Ferguson was in the second, drawn by four; I was in the fourth, with Captain King. When we had nearly reached the summit General Ferguson's carriage ran back, and one of his mules fell. The third carriage unable to resist receded, and another mule fell. Our charioteer attempted to take advantage of a little open spot on the right, but the pavement being as slippery as glass our off mule also fell. King roared to me to jump out. I was so pleased at his fright that my limbs were immovable from convulsions of laughter. He got very angry and attempted to pass me; but my sword getting between his legs held him back, and my mirth increased with his distress. At last the servant made us dismount, when we saw the fifth carriage completely overset; Captain Honeyman and Captain Gordon (nephew to Sir David Baird) were in it. The latter received a very violent contusion on his temple. Our order of procession was completely overthrown. We attempted to proceed on foot; but the severe heat and great height still before us overcame our resolution, and we seated ourselves again in our crazy vehicles. Never was a cavalcade dispersed more ludicrously, save the last accident. Astley's never presented so good a scene, nor could the tailor riding to Brentford cause so much amusement.

Having reached the palace we passed through rooms lined with officers to the grand saloon, where the governor was waiting. He received us with great affability and good manners. He was dressed in a red coat, had a sallow complexion but good and mild physiognomy, with all the characteristics of a gentleman in appearance and address.

The officers were admirably uniform, and the levée would not have disgraced an Austrian headquarters. The soldiers looked extremely well, and all was conducted in a very military style to my great surprise; for I had no idea that any Portuguese troops were in such high order.

The palace has a superb suite of rooms sufficiently furnished for a tropical latitude, and the view from them is beautiful.

Having exchanged assurances of esteem, cordiality, &c., we remounted our cabriolets; and passing through the town over frightful ways, proceeded to the quarters prepared for the general and commodore, about two miles. The eye could not regard a nobler prospect. Lofty mountains, deep ravines, covered and connected with the mango, the jack, the banana, the cocoa, the plantain, the coffee-tree, stretched along the whole route. No scenery of imagination could rival its grandeur and beauty.

The *Whitby* arrived the day before yesterday. The report of numerous sick on board was quite erroneous.

I visited several monasteries; some magnificent and on a large scale, but the fathers ignorant and inhospitable. We slept at night in the apartment prepared for us: in the course of it we were awakened by a dreadful yell, proceeding from some unknown quarter but certainly given with a negro's voice. It lasted twenty minutes. So devilish a sound I never heard.

Yesterday I went on board the *Diadem* by signal. The conversation with the commodore was highly satisfactory as evidence of his sincere friendship; but I cannot at this time communicate its object.

In the evening I received a note instructing me to lose no time in the purchase of horses. I went to see a person with whom I had business; he was absent, but I found his wife—the largest, *cranest*, and most vulgar Irishwoman I ever beheld. The Lord have mercy upon her husband, *in the tropics!*

S. Salvador, November 16.

Colonel P—— is the owner of the houses occupied by the generals, and the possessor of large property here. He acquired this by marrying a Brazilian lady whose parents he outwitted. They insisted upon a man of fortune as their son-in-law. P—— borrowed of his friends ten thousand pounds. He went to the mother, informed her of his intention to visit Portugal, and said that he wished to lodge this sum in the hands of her banker for safety, requesting her husband to be trustee that he might not spend his fortune in his intended tour. The money was deposited; the day fixed for his departure; when the old lady offered her consent to his marriage, provided that he settled the ten thousand pounds upon her daughter. The bargain was completed and he came into immediate possession of a very considerable estate, with the income of which he has paid all his debts, now lives like a prince, and at his father's death proposes to quit S. Salvador for ever, as he pines in the midst of grandeur for associates of equal consequence. His wife is *very, very* far from handsome; but she appears passive, and therefore his domestic cares are light. A more generous candid foreigner I never met with.

This morning I went to Sir David Baird. We walked together some distance, and reached a beautiful spot from which we looked upon the richest forest scenery and the water of an extensive lake; but the total absence of grain cultivation is remarked with pain by Europeans, who connect with the sight of immeasurable woods ideas of an uncivilized population and barbaric government.

All the ships as they get ready assemble at the harbour's mouth. This is a good arrangement for fresh air; since this place is unwholesomely sultry, and oppressive to the highest degree from the filth thrown and left in the streets, as well as from the exhalation from the labouring blacks, which taints the otherwise refreshing gale.

Here I have found the greatest advantage from masonry. No sooner had I declared myself than houses, horses, servants, all things, were put at my disposal; for the institution is held in the highest estimation, because the laws and bigotry persecute the professors with fire and sword. I dare not now mention the names of those who devoted themselves to my service: but some of the chief members of government have in private made me their acknowledgments.

My passage is not yet fixed. I am anxious to go in a man-of-war rather than in a transport, because the latter is not sure of arriving at the first moment and I may be served again as I was in Egypt: whereas if the man-of-war arrives I am at my post, and ready to act with the first detachment that lands.

Nov. 19.—At two this morning I am going with Captains Harding and Newland to an island some leagues distant, where horses, as I am told, are to be procured. Hitherto I have met with some success, and have bought several tolerably good.

This morning I went to Sir David Baird's and rode up and down a flight of twenty-six steps; not to show off, for Captain Gordon only was present, but to ascertain the activity of my horse. I have toiled most severely, being always on my legs or on horse-back for the purchase of horses; besides the trouble of getting money from the commissariat, and that of writing drafts for payment, arranging for forage, &c. I have lost no opportunity of promoting the public service by want of activity or diligence, and indeed my own honour is much implicated in the success of my present efforts.

I cannot help remarking here that my cross renders me the greatest service, for the people consider me as of their own faith. Arbuthnot's bald head entitles him to the distinction of a *padre*. He improves the claim and secures great advantages; for imposition upon a *heretic* is here regarded as a commendable action.

Verona Indiaman, Nov. 29, Lat. 14° 53'.

On the morning of the 17th I proceeded with Captains Harding, Cromwell, and Newland, with a party of five dragoons and two sailors, in the *Whitby's* skiff to Taparica. My object was to procure horses;

and although I had been forbidden by the governor to make purchases out of S. Salvador, I undertook the responsibility of violating this order: Sir D. Baird had informed me that he would be obliged to disown the proceeding as sanctioned by him if any remonstrance were made by the Portuguese government. The importance of success determined me to incur every hazard, for if I failed in mounting some men on the first disembarkation how could I hope to participate in the active service of the enterprise? I could not tolerate the idea of being a mere spectator when fortune presented me with an occasion of being a distinguished actor. I could not bear the thought of having left my family and passed so many thousand miles with various anxieties, to reach the goal without being noticed as one of the emulous competitors for the prize of honour.

The governor had consented to the purchase of a few horses: but his permission had been granted with reluctance, and his manner operated as a restriction upon the sale: for, notwithstanding that Arbuthnot made every zealous effort and had an unlimited order for money, he could only buy eight horses in the town in addition to the six which I had purchased; and eventually we could only bring from thence nineteen horses altogether.

We reached the island of Taparica in about three hours, landed with difficulty, and pitched our tent. The blacks brought us abundance of fruits, and gave notice to the Portuguese that our object was to buy horses. Several were soon brought, some of which we purchased, and I appointed two of the inhabitants to act as my agents, promising a commission on every

horse which they sent and which became mine. I
soon discovered that I should not be disappointed in
my object; for on the island resided a class of Portuguese farmers who all kept good horses, and who
being good horsemen had them very well broken.
In no country out of England have I ever met with
such a class of independent yeomanry. They had all
decent houses; many very superior to our English
farmers' houses. They dressed very well, and with
their jockey-boots resembled our young sporting
farmers. Nor was the English horse-dealer without his rival here in habits, manners, and craft.

The first day I bought fourteen horses: but money
failing I determined to go in a canoe to S. Salvador.
I left Taparica about five P.M. This was the first time
in my life that I ever sailed in a hollow tree; and no
one would choose such a vessel for comfort. The
wind blowing fresh, and the sail being extremely high,
the two mariners and myself were obliged to sit all
the way on the sharp edge of her side. In about two
hours I reached the opposite coast, mounted my horse
as soon as I could get him saddled, and rode to Sir
David Baird. He was much pleased with my success. Afterwards I went to the commissary for
money, but none was to be procured till the next
morning. I therefore arranged with him that the
adjutant should bring me 200l. the next day, and at
twelve at night re-embarked in my canoe. We were
three hours getting back. The night was dark; and
when we passed the breakers there was much awful
grandeur in the scene, from the whiteness of the foam
in contrast with the black shade of the surrounding
waters; while the lightning, which is here continual,

occasionally exposed the forests of Taparica. I found
my party asleep, and joined them. At daybreak we
rose and recommenced our bargains. Although the
adjutant did not come till late with the money I
found no difficulty in inspiring confidence for the
fufilment of my engagements. When he did arrive
and the gold was laid out upon a table the fame
reached all quarters, and horses flocked in. Those
who before demanded higher prices than I would give
could no longer resist the charm of possessing such
coin, and now pressed to accept my terms. Darkness
interrupted our proceedings that night, or Taparica
would have been unhorsed. The next day, having
sent back the adjutant for more money, I with Newland rode to the town of Taparica distant three
leagues along the shore, over rocks and occasionally
through deep waters. We reached it in an hour;
but the town afforded us no satisfaction, with the
exception of relief from thirst by a glass of sangaree
and a water-melon. We were coming back at the
same pace, when one of our jockey friends met us, and
requested us to go and look at a horse belonging to
a Portuguese near the road. He was admirably
mounted, and led us across country in a style I never
saw equalled : it would have daunted us if shame had
not fortified our hearts and rendered us superior if
not insensible to danger.

Fox-hunters have no longer cause to boast their
daring exploits. I will answer for it that Leicester-
shire never saw such an intrepid leader as the Portuguese horse-dealer. But he found that we were capable
of the same exertions; and selfish vanity insinuates
that our performance had more merit, since to us the

character of the country was unknown and the powers of the horses untried. We both lost our stirrups, and the saddles were only kept on the horses' backs by the pressure of our knees and the just equilibrium of our bodies; for in this strange country they never draw the girths for fear of breaking the leather. Such is the condition of the equipment that in the trial of three horses I broke fourteen stirrup-leathers, and my companions nearly as many. The jockey succeeded in selling his own and his friend's horses well to us.

We returned to our tent in good time. It had been removed during our absence by my directions to the grounds of a whale-man, in whose boats we were to embark our horses. This was necessary too for security, since we had only five men to guard thirty animals, whose violent passions raged with inconceivable fury at sight of each other : for although they were all fathers of families they indulged in the most vicious propensities; making night hideous with their wild transports.

The next morning we embarked ten of the horses. Having received an order from the general not to purchase more than fifty in all, I determined to go off directly in a whale-boat to be rowed by eight men. We had scarcely passed the breakers when she was found to leak so much that one of the men was obliged to leave his oar, and for the seven miserable hours that we passed in her during a heavy gale he was obliged to bale out whole pailfuls of water momentarily with a bucket. The wind was so high and the tide so strong out of the harbour that every effort to reach S. Salvador was vain; and at last, when all were nearly exhausted, we laid hold of the rocks at the extreme point of the bay, and were saved from drifting God knows where. We slowly moved towards the town along the shore, and reached it half an hour after midnight. Sir David Baird the next morning was highly satisfied with what I had done, and directed me to purchase a hundred horses, if possible : but many were lost to the service by the contradictory orders issued previously.

On my way back to Taparica with 300*l.* I visited Sir Home on board the *Diadem* to make arrangements for the conveyance of the horses in the transports, and then returned to my island.

In the middle of the night I was roused from sleep by a voice familiar to me, and found the purser of the *Leda* with a drawn sword in his hand : he told me that he had been robbed in the house of a black man two miles distant, that he had fled, leaving all his property, and he requested me now to assist him in recovering it. He had come on shore in the morning with Mr. Parker the second lieutenant, a Portuguese merchant, and two servants, to buy stock.

I was very tired, and yet unwilling to commit the execution of this business to another, for I was afraid that some indiscretion might interrupt the harmony that subsisted between me and the people of the island. I therefore sallied forth with the purser, well armed ; but as I passed the house of one of the principal residents I thought it would be prudent to request him to send some of his people with us. I knocked him up and explained my business ; for from my knowledge of Italian and Latin, and indefatigable perseverance in speaking with the Portuguese, I had acquired the power of holding a conversation. The master of the house determined upon proceeding with us himself; and, brandishing an old rusty Toledo, he claimed the post of honour to march in front. When we arrived at the house we found only a woman in it: she protested her innocence and delivered up the clothes of the merchant; who had run out of the room and left them when the purser discovered the robbery of his pistol and the attempt to take his watch out of his fob.

The pistol alone was now missing, so we returned with the recovered baggage.

The next morning we proceeded to embark more horses, and in the course of the day our Portuguese commander brought the missing pistol.

A letter from the adjutant informed me that eight Englishmen had been attacked in a boat by blacks, and two officers, with a servant, murdered. Seven dragoons were sent me at the same time as a reinforcement, and as they brought pistols the master of the vessel expressed great alarm. Some of the inhabitants spoke to me on the subject; but I told them that there was a regulation in our service that all soldiers when on duty should carry fire-arms or sabres. I added that in Taparica the measure was useless, as I gave proof by never wearing any weapon. This observation satisfied them immediately; and indeed I had reason to repose every confidence in their attachment. Few British officers ever gained the good-will and opinion of foreigners more thoroughly than I did here, as future circumstances may one day testify. Whites and blacks all sought opportunity to evince their esteem, and I certainly did all in my power to acquire theirs.

Z——'s mad imprudence alone endangered the mutual good understanding: for a Portuguese privately told me, "That captain is not a good man; he is not like the colonel; yesterday evening he took a crucifix and gave it to the dog in scorn." The fact was that Z——, seeing a crucifix in the hands of one of the inhabitants, took it, under pretence of a respectful consideration, and then thrust it into Pacha's mouth. I took pains to investigate the matter quietly, and learnt the particulars from an officer present who felt deeply for the act at the moment. I could not speak to Z—— on the subject; the matter was too serious for mere censure: but on account of this and his intolerant disposition to the inhabitants I determined to send him off the island, and never to give him any trust of responsibility while he is under my command. At the same time I had it intimated to him that I was not altogether ignorant of his conduct. I fear that this young man is destined to be the victim of his own imprudence: but I will not urge his ruin.

At twelve o'clock on the following day, having embarked fifty-six horses many of which were of an excellent species and had admirable properties, I prepared finally to evacuate Taparica; and sailed for the fleet now under weigh, with Newland, in a boat which had been sent to carry horses but was not well adapted for that purpose. After various difficulties and dangers we laid our bark alongside the commodore's ship, in which I deposited as a present two very fine turkeys, fifty pineapples and melons, and a sack of mangoes. I had also purchased for Sir Home two noble horses, so that I have had some opportunity of expressing my sense of his kindness. I gave considerable quantities of pines and melons, and some Muscovy ducks, to officers in several of the ships: but I was only liberal by the liberality of others, for the greatest part of them were given to me.

The commodore sent me to the *Verona* to report her state. I executed the commission; then went back to the island, and bought five more horses and one mule. At two P.M., I went to Sir David, who regretted that I had not bought more mules as he wanted to put two guns under my command. I said nothing at the time, as I did not like to promise success when I knew that several officers had for many days been in search of these animals—far more valuable here than horses and of greater strength. Later in the day the commodore weighed anchor and proceeded towards the harbour's mouth: this alarmed me lest I should not be able to complete my intention; but he dropped anchor again, when I went on shore and instantly prepared my plan for the purchase of four mules. After a walk of three miles I procured them and another horse, which gave me great satisfaction.

I must mention that, notwithstanding the murder of the English in a boat, I walked without any weapon of defence: which may be considered as some proof that there was no general hostility against us in the minds of the Brazilians. On the contrary I that night experienced more than ordinary testimonies of goodwill.

The officers were massacred chiefly on account of their own misconduct. They forced off a boat, with two black men in her, who refused to go but at last agreed to take them if they would pay them first:

instead of money they gave them blows, when both
jumped into the water. In a few minutes, a canoe
with eight men paddled alongside; the men sprang
upon the English, killed three, and wounded all. Mr.
Parkinson was dreadfully beaten about the head, and
a cadet's body when found was also in a frightfully
mangled state. On searching his pockets, all his teeth
were discovered tied up in a handkerchief. He had
evidently secured them, when beaten out, in this
manner, and afterwards received his mortal wound.
When I came away several of the assassins were
arrested.

Having completed my object, I had now to embark by daybreak the mules and horse. Before it
could be effected the signal was made for all ships to
sail. Vessel after vessel weighed anchor, and I had
much reason to fear that I could not reach any ship in
time; but my good fortune prevailed and I came up
with the agent of transports, who instantly ordered my
cargo on board two vessels which were standing out
and which received them. I then went on board the
Verona, all my wishes happily executed. From thence
on board the *Diadem* when I reported and proposed
my arrangements to Sir David. He approved of them
and pointed out the bay for my disembarkation, and
the first object to which I was to direct my operations—
viz., the seizure of all the horses and draught cattle in
three farms under the Blueberg hills.

I have a painful duty of friendship before me. I
heard of the death of Arbuthnot's brother on the
morning of my leaving Taparica, from the paper of the
25th September brought to S. Salvador; where we had
also intelligence of the continental war from French

papers. Arbuthnot is the last man to whom I should
wish the herald of misfortune to approach. He is
indeed a most amiable and worthy man; and as a
proof of my high but generous regard I shall seize the
first occasion to restore him to his friends.

Dec. 7.—Nothing remarkable occurred on the 4th.
On the 5th the fleet laid-to in order to collect all the
horses scattered in the transports on board the *Maria*.
I superintended this service.

Yesterday I received my orders for the landing. A
gun was made over to me, and I was directed to take
in charge a young cadet—a native of the Cape—who
had volunteered his services. Sir David gave notice
to the officers assembled for orders on board the
Diadem that he should summon us all again for final
directions. I was made very happy by finding that
my detachment is to be disembarked with the van
division.

A gale has blown heavily, and, unfortunately, we
have lost by sickness three dragoons and five horses.

The transfer of men and horses to the *Maria* was
completed. This is a great relief to my mind; as by it
I have now secured the services of the best men in the
regiment in those first enterprises which are to be
executed by the cavalry, and which require the
greatest efforts of gallantry and intelligence for success. Not only our own credit, but the serious
interests of the expedition are much concerned in our
conduct.

We have, as I am informed, to act against the
counter efforts of three hundred excellent cavalry,
commanded by able officers. I am very far from
despising my enemy, but I hope that events will justify

my confidence in ourselves. Under no control but
that of the commander-in-chief, intrusted with an independent power of action, my responsibility is considerable : but if I can procure horses my means will
not be insignificant, since I can then bring into the
field three hundred good dragoons and two pieces of
cannon, with light infantry occasionally attached. My
hope is that I may eventually obtain the command of
all the outpost duty. The enemy, if not strong
enough to fight and unwilling to stand a siege in Cape
Town, may retire into the interior of the colony and
for a long time protract the war; but this I do not
expect from the description of force.

Verona, December 14.

On the 9th I was ordered on board the *Verona,*
as the horses were not well. I went on board just
in time to see one die. This day we hailed the
commodore to demand better water : men and horses
refused that which we had on board; it was foul from
having been put in wine and beer casks not properly
cleansed.

Dec. 15.—The *Belliqueuse, Leda,* and *Diadem* sent us
water. Two horses were raised from the agonies of
death by oatmeal, gin, and hot water. All the horses
on the windward side, without exception, have been
well, and the lee side has never wanted air but for the
first three days; still the animals suffer there from
great pain in the bowels, and as I suspected inflam-
mation of the kidneys—from whatever cause—I determined upon trying diuretics. The remedy has so far
proved infallible.

Dec. 22.—Foul wind for several days, and heavy

sea ; it has been impossible to keep the port-holes open
for air.   Several horses dead.

Diomede, December 30.

On the 23rd Captain Cunningham of the 25th
came on board the *Verona* to show me the minutes of
a court-martial, directing the punishment of a thousand lashes to be inflicted on four men ; for disobedience
to orders and refusing to stand at the wheel until the
grog had been reissued, which had been generally
stopped in consequence of the bread-room having been
broken into by some person unknown. As I was
aware that the greatest order had not prevailed on the
Northampton among the cavalry officers, I determined
to go on board myself and investigate all matters with
a view to their satisfactory arrangement.   Upon full
inquiry I found that although the men were culpable
they had been aggrieved by the detention of the
spirits ; since the captain of the ship had no right to
stop their allowance on his own authority. I therefore
addressed the whole corps ; and giving the merit of
interference in mitigation of the sentence to Captain
Barker, whose authority I felt obliged to maintain
notwithstanding his error, I directed the most culpable to receive a booting from their comrades who
had been disgraced by the transaction : and then I
added further remarks on the necessity of maintaining
discipline and subordination under any circumstances.

Having effected this to the satisfaction of all parties,
I proceeded to hear the unpleasant complaints of some
of the officers urged against each other.   These after
long conversation and many interviews I completely
settled, and had the pleasure of witnessing an honourable and cordial reconciliation.

I could not avoid giving it as my opinion that, instead of stopping the grog, with respect to which no offence had been committed, there would have been more justice and appropriateness in withholding the biscuit until the quantity stolen had been made up by this means.   I do not extenuate robbery when I lament that the men should be tempted to such acts: but I pledge myself, if ever I obtain a seat in Parliament, to use all my efforts to procure for the soldiers the same quantity if not quality of food as the sailors receive.   They both keep the watches alternately, and work for the service of the ship : and both have the same stowage for reception and arrangement of food.

On Christmas-day, after dinner, all the dragoons on board began to dance, and passed a very merry day. This gave me much pleasure, for I delight in the decent amusements of those who are under my command.   At night they had an extra allowance of grog given them by Captain Barker, and they sang many excellent songs.   The Miss Brownrigges danced on the quarter-deck for half an hour, and I was the partner of one.   In the evening we had a sumptuous entertainment, and a fine round of English beef was highly relished.   Captain Barker's liberality is unbounded. In no situation in life did I ever meet a man better informed on every subject, and as a navigator his merits are allowed to be pre-eminent.

Yesterday (Sunday) we had prayers; and afterwards I addressed the dragoons in terms of approbation of the regularity of their conduct while I had been on board, and of encouragement for the future to continue in such habits.   I never was more lucid or fluent and felt disposed to speak at length : but I thought concise pithy sentences would be more appropriate and useful.

Last night I left the *Northampton* to go on board the *Diomede.* As I went down the ship's side the dragoons gave me three cheers, which could not but please me with reference to the past and inspire me with hope for the future.

Verona, January 3, 1806.

Land descried this morning. Standing in : an animating sight. We are all in high spirits : more impatient than anxious.

Jan. 5.—Yesterday evening we made Table land; this morning stood into the bay. The fleet anchored to the westward of Robben Island, about four miles from the mainland. I, with my detachment and the 38th and 39th, entered the boats. We rowed seven miles and approached the shore within three hundred yards ; but the surf was declared too heavy for landing and we returned to the ships. Sir David Baird and Sir Home then determined to carry the army to Saldanha Bay, and General Beresford, with the 38th and the dragoons, was sent forward to form an advanced guard and secure the first port where water was to be obtained. On the 7th we anchored in Saldanha Bay, when General Beresford sent for me and told me that he proposed that I should land with three companies of infantry and such dragoons as I could embark, to march immediately and occupy Tea Fonteyn, said to be distant about fifteen but in reality twenty-five miles from the spot at which we were obliged to land. I was to maintain myself there, and endeavour to procure all possible supplies for the army ; seize the landlord, draught oxen, horses, &c.

The wind blew a very heavy gale, so that no boats could reach the usual place of debarkation four miles distant, and I was ordered to land in the open bay. At three o'clock the signal was elevated for casting off from the ships; and I in a man-of-war's boat with Newland in her, and towing our long-boat with ten horses, bore up for the shore. Expert management was required as the gusts were hurricanes, and I could not help feeling again that the elements were not in unison with my fortune: so much persecution as I have experienced from winds and waves is very remarkable.

The infantry landed without opposition, but up to their middles in surf. The boats with horses could not approach the shore, but cast grapnels some way off. The horses were forced over the sides, and sailors carried our men and accoutrements; but three horses were lost after they reached the shore. About five o'clock the whole were landed, and we marched under the conduct of a sergeant of my own who, having been quartered in this neighbourhood before, undertook to be our guide. We continued our progress along shore for a mile and then turned over a heath and marched on it about four miles. The ground being covered with thick and high brushwood, the infantry suffered much.

My sergeant having fallen upon a path informed me that we had now got upon the direct road. About twelve at night the infantry began to flag, and I halted all such as wished for rest that they might repose and come home in the morning. About eighty remained; but I thus prevented straggling. At two the advanced guard informed me that houses were

near. I took seventy men of the light infantry and
dragoons and surrounded the houses. A Hottentot
came out, who upon my asking him where cattle and
horses were undertook to guide me to his master. I
went on with twenty dragoons a league when we
came to a large farm; here I found a team of noble
bullocks, fourteen, but only one horse. The farmer
hid himself as I learnt afterwards in the wheat-
stack, but his wife, a very delicate pleasing woman,
remained: I did my best to calm her fears, giving
a receipt for the waggon, oxen, and Hottentots.

On my return I found to my dismay that we had
come all the way wrong. I was reasonably angry
with the sergeant for having undertaken to guide us,
and we retraced our course; the men muttering their
indignation, and I in great distress of mind. After
marching until six o'clock I was compelled to halt, as
the infantry neither could nor would proceed.

The halting-place was about five miles from a high
rocky hill, where the sergeant assured me water was
to be found and the right road to Tea Fonteyn. As
the stragglers had come on about nine I assembled
the infantry and pointed out the place where I proposed to refresh them till night. They willingly
consented to proceed, as water was to be hoped for
there and the day began to be intensely hot. We
crossed the intervening heath at leisure, but I went
forward to examine the house from which a desert of
white sand, two miles in extent, separated us. My
horse being least fatigued I got on before the adjutant
(Harrison), and when near the house saw two men
on horseback. I galloped on to intercept their retreat.
They saw me and attempted to fly. I drew my sword

to intimidate them, and they drew up, but seeing that
my horse was blown they dashed by me.   I then drew
my pistol.   One of them cried out for mercy, but continued his flight.   I could have shot the poor fellows,
and should have been justified in doing it, for they
were armed against us and the country would by
their escape gain information of our approach; also
their horses were objects of importance: but other
considerations weighed more with me, and I replaced
my pistols in their lodging without regret.   The
adjutant missed me, and concluded that I had retired
instead of advancing.   Had he not done so we should
have secured our prize without risk: but this is a
lesson to me never to proceed in such cases alone;
as a single man may meet with disasters that must
shame his enterprise, and he can seldom effect any
great object.

The infantry came up soon afterwards, fainting with
fatigue, heat, and thirst.   I shut them up in a barn,
and would only allow each at first a small proportion
of water, for it was very bad in colour, and putrid in
taste and smell.   This afterwards we little regarded.
The throat wanted moisture, and the nostrils and palate
could not be consulted.

The owner of the cottage spoke English, and I sent
him to General Beresford, distant, *after our sixteen
hours' march in heavy sand, only five miles!*   Job never
showed more patience than I did in these vexatious
and cruel circumstances.

Having refreshed three hours I resolved to proceed
with the dragoons, and if possible twenty-five infantry, to occupy the destined but yet unattainable
post.   Twenty-five men turned out.   We carried

their coats and even their muskets. After marching two miles in sand and heat more oppressive than I had ever experienced, the light infantry spirit began to droop. One man became sick. I put him on my own horse, and taking his musket marched six miles in great pain, for my boots galled me severely. About five P.M. we reached a hill from whence our guide showed us Fonteyn. In order to conceal our movement I halted the troops till dusk, and we all slept in luxurious forgetfulness of care. At eight we marched again four miles over still heavier sand, without water; but by management, such as making the men fix bayonets and using other precautions as if I expected to find an enemy posted here, I kept them together. When we neared the houses I hastened on as fast as our gallant horses could move, for gallant-hearted indeed they were and since have proved themselves, and surrounded the kraals. Some Hottentots ran out. I saluted them in friendship; but one man continued his flight in anxious haste. I rode after him, laid hold of his head, and throwing him back went to the spot towards which he was so eagerly moving, and discovered a pen full of oxen. The sight rewarded me for some of our vexations, and was a compensation for the injury that our non-occupation of Tea Fonteyn earlier might have done the army. Our joy, however, was somewhat damped by finding that the place was called Elands Fonteyn, and that Tea Fonteyn was still ten miles distant.

It was impossible to proceed. The men and horses could not stir, and the cattle required a guard and convoy to Saldanha in the morning. We therefore lay down and slept in the sand: it was very cold. Two oxen were killed for the men, and after a brief repose one hundred and twenty oxen, under an escort of three dragoons, were sent to Saldanha, and eighteen were left in the pen for the troops that were expected to follow. The greater part were draught oxen of a beautiful breed; there were a few cows among them of the same breed and even more beautiful. The remaining dragoons, having received a share of raw meat to cook at their journey's end, marched immediately with me towards Tea Fonteyn. Arbuthnot was left to bring on my twenty-five light infantry when refreshed, and the rest of the infantry who arrived at daybreak were to march on the following night.

On our route a vast number of ostriches passed us, but not within our range.

When we approached Tea Fonteyn our horses were nearly exhausted; but although they lay down at the shortest halt, they rose and moved again when the march was ordered with a courage that entitles this race to noble consideration.

Arrived at Tea Fonteyn, we found a house with very large premises. A steward who proved most friendly to us was left in charge. There was abundance of corn, some wine, horses chiefly wild or unbroken, but no cattle, as the greater part had been removed the day before. When we appeared in sight armed boors were engaged in taking away what little stock remained; but they fled upon our advancing.

A post of thirty dragoons and ten regular infantry were within an hour of Tea Fonteyn, but no other troops were in the neighbourhood. My position therefore required vigilance, but I resolved to march at midnight and carry that post; particularly as the cattle from Tea Fonteyn and other farms were assembled there.

At night we all turned out. No infantry had arrived: this made me uneasy for Arbuthnot, and an alarm had excited all our attention; so that each of us lay down with our horses in hand, depending upon the vigilance of our patrol to guard against surprise. I drew up my people as well as I could for defence, barricading some of the avenues with carts. About midnight Arbuthnot arrived and found me on my dunghill, and announced the approach of General Beresford with the whole 38th regiment who, in consequence of notice that the English army had landed in Table Bay, were moving there with all speed. The general indeed arrived with about thirty men, but the 38th regiment never could muster as one until three o'clock the next day, and then above two hundred men were missing. They came in by ones and twos, exhausted and careless of everything in the world but water.

Among the unfortunate sufferers fifty of my dismounted dragoons endured the most: in heavy overalls and boots they had struggled over this terrible desert, and kept up their resolution until their physical powers denied co-operation. Such a woful march as this I never witnessed. The flight of the 18th of May in Flanders—the retreat through Holland—the movements in Egypt—offered no parallel. Fifty good cavalry would have annihilated the whole force. Why such a detachment did not occupy Tea Fonteyn is a question which one day I hope to ask the Dutch general. Their absence on all accounts appears a most faulty disposition.

General Beresford had received intelligence of the army's landing, which chagrined him much. It vexed me equally but did not surprise me; for the vicissitudes of fortune must be expected in war, and I always anticipate the most decided departure from that which appears most probable. The chief engineer, the chief commissary, the cavalry on which so much depended in calculation and for which so much expense had been incurred, all were absent at the moment when their service was most needed. We yet rue the mischance of their being sent to Saldanha, because had they been present the guns of the enemy must, for the most part, have fallen into our hands.

Had General Beresford been sent away alone the appearance would not have been favourable to the commander-in-chief's integrity. Beresford was an Irishman, and Colonel Baird succeeded to the brigade in his absence. Thus prejudice argues *even now*; but, I believe, without any truth. Sir Home positively declared that a lull which he did not expect determined the attempt at midnight; and that he had resolved, when we were sent away, to sail the next morning with the army to Saldanha. Nor will I believe that my presence was an indifferent object on military grounds: Captain Smith's was still less so on the score of private friendship.

The next day, the 9th, General Beresford, Arbuthnot, Hartwell, the adjutant, and I, proceeded with thirty-three dragoons to make the best of our way to the army. We marched until two o'clock in the morning, when we came to Groene-Kloof a large deserted house. Two wretched Hottentot slaves only guarded this mansion of misery, and we took possession and slept there. At daybreak, while the general and I were deliberating upon our course on a high hill which we had ascended for survey, a boor appeared coming towards the house. We lay down until he had entered the plantation—the first trees we had seen in Africa—and then I ran down the height, arrived in time to conceal the men, and secured him and his horse as we entered. He was much frightened, but told us that the English had advanced to Riet Valley after a severe action.

We directly mounted and marched to Brach Fonteyn distant twelve miles, where we found horses, oxen, &c.; but as a proof of our forbearance I must mention that we would not take two fine stallions for fear of injuring the breed of horses at the Cape, although we were not then certain of being masters of the colony. At Elands Fonteyn, too, we gave back four cows of a particular species with the same motive.

Having obtained fresh horses here, General Beresford, Captain Smith his brigade-major, Arbuthnot, and I, with ten dragoons, hastened forward at speed. When four miles from Riet Valley, two boors whom we met informed us that Cape Town had been taken two days before.

I will not dwell upon our feelings—they were selfish—nor will I murmur at fate; for who can read beyond the present page?

We now increased our pace although fourteen miles were still before us, reached the outworks of Cape

Town just as the army was entering to take possession, and joined the line of march. The sight was brilliant, and the view of the town as we passed the castle delightful; particularly to us who had crossed so much desert.

The next morning I was sent for to Sir David Baird; and finding that he wished to despatch an officer on particular service, I offered to go, notwithstanding our late harassment. I went directly off to General Ferguson, posted at Wynberg, with directions to him to march a force instantly to secure one hundred Frenchmen who had stationed themselves in Hout Bay. They proved to be sixty only, and they all surrendered immediately. On my return I dined with an English merchant, and met Mr. Patterson the brother of Madame Jerome Buonaparte—a fine, indiscreet, honest young man, tired of life because he has no care, as he says himself. I had a long argument with him about the military character of General Janssen. As a man, I never heard of a chief and public character who stood in such high estimation.

On the 12th I had a long round to make in a dreadful south-easter, which blows more severely here than in Egypt. On the 13th all horses were put in requisition for the cavalry: and in a very hot day I was kept five hours examining three hundred horses, of which we took one hundred and forty and the artillery sixty. In the evening I had a parade to examine them again. At ten at night I had orders to march and join General Beresford at Stellenbosch with all the men I could mount, and to move at two o'clock in the morning. Various orders had been given before so that we were distracted with the confusion. About three miles from the town we passed the place of execution : here one man was hanging by the neck; another, with his head off, was suspended by one heel ; a third was lying upon a wheel on which he had been broken ; and two heads were elevated on poles. About twelve o'clock in the day we reached Stellenbosch, distant twenty-eight miles. The ground we passed over was deep-white sand and desert. I found General Beresford in the house of the land roost—a very good man, his wife somewhat pretty and amiable, his eldest daughter good-looking, but his youngest a *third horse*. We watched until midnight for Sir David Baird. He arrived soon after. About three o'clock General Janssen's secretary came, and General Beresford was requested to meet the governor next morning at Holland's Kloof.

At five I was suddenly ordered to march, and lead eight mules and twenty-seven cast horses to the next station. This annoyed me very much. Who can bear such confusion and contradiction of orders as cavalry suffer from under infantry officers ? From such dreadful control the good Lord deliver me !

Marched to Klapmut, distant ten miles ; the latter part of the way with an Englishman—Mr. Watney— resident at the Cape, in a waggon with eight horses driven by one man at a rapid rate. English charioteers ! hide your diminished heads, for your skill does not equal that of a Hottentot.

Jan. 17.—This morning a farmer came to acquaint me that some soldiers had broken open his wine vaults and were plundering. I galloped two miles with him, and found three of the 72nd and one of the 59th in the act of drinking from the hogshead. I attempted to

secure them : but the soldier of the 59th, mad with
liquor and mutinous in heart, resisted; and I was
obliged to point my sword at his breast as he menaced
me with his musket.   When I had forcibly wrested his
musket from him his language was so daring that I
was obliged to knock him down with my cane, which
I did most effectually; and also with my fist one of
the Scotchmen who came to his assistance.   At this
moment my orderly man came up or I might have
received some mischief, as three out of the four were
capable of action and had loaded arms.   1 now took
the arms from them all, with the muzzle of a pistol at
the head of the man of the 59th who was the most
outrageous, and putting them all in a waggon brought
them to Klapmut.   As I respected the regiments I
would not bring these men to a general court-martial,
but sent them to their own corps under escort.   The
man of the 59th was, however, again so insolent to me
as I was ordering them into the cars, that I was under
the necessity of dashing him to the ground, giving him
a severe blow with my sabre, and tying his hands
behind him.   I had previously asked pardon for him
and the others from their commanding officers ; but he
must now be contrite indeed before I can be justified
in extenuating his offence.   I have just received an
order to send a sergeant and twelve men to Stellenbosch, and march myself to Groene-berg, distant twenty
miles, this evening.   General Janssen has sent in to
offer terms.   An ultimatum is returned.

Jan. 21.—I waited all night in expectation of another
courier: one came in the morning to order my march
back to Stellenbosch, as the business was settled.   On
arrival at Stellenbosch I was directed to proceed to

Hottentot Holland's Kloof. Here I posted myself within a mile of the Dutch videttes. General Janssen was at Hottentots' Holland, signing the capitulation. At night I escorted him through our lines to his own. Next morning I met Mr. Klüpp who commanded the Dutch post which fired upon King at Saldanha and the troops which I was preparing to attack in Tea Fonteyn. He very civilly offered to conduct me up into the mountain; and I was the first Englishman in this army who ascended the lofty summit and entered this extraordinary pass. It is not in my opinion unassailable and impregnable. Almost eternal vapour rests upon the whole ridge. The troops looked miserable. Shakspeare's description, in the mouth of a Frenchman, of the appearance of the English army before the battle of Agincourt would well apply to their state; with the additional circumstance of an iron rocky scenery.

After I had descended I was moved about two miles further back, and directed to escort the Dutch troops to Simon's Bay. At ten o'clock General Janssen came up with the advanced guard of his army and, when I approached to salute him, asked whether he had " not the honour to address the officer who had gained so much reputation in Egypt?" My reply was becomingly modest; and I only relate the circumstance to prove that General Janssen is no great friend of Buonaparte: indeed, the whole tenor of his conversation afterwards assured me of the fact.

The condition of the army was wretched; but the Waldeck yägers still looked military. There is something so naturally martial in a German that the character cannot be destroyed. The Hottentots seemed

mean : nevertheless they are excellent soldiers for service, and very faithful. But their women are horrible
to the sight: hideous in countenance, and clothed
only with a sheepskin undressed, the raw side exposed,
they excite inexpressible disgust and dishonour the
human race. The want of water renders this land the
most terrible in which war can be carried on ; and so
heart-sick and heart-weary have the unfortunate exiles
here found themselves, that General Janssen himself
assured me that above twenty of the Waldeck regiment
had destroyed themselves under this insuperable de-
pression. His own son was one among seven officers
who perished by their own hands. Yesterday we
marched ten miles to Hottentots' Holland ; this
morning marched again at five o'clock to Zoute river,
about nine miles. After breakfast the general's passports were brought to me for his passage with suite
and baggage into Cape Town. We parted in great
friendship. I had done all in my power to show
respect to his misfortune, and he was very sensible of
attentions which contributed to relieve its weight.

The destination of the Dutch troops was changed
with consent of General Janssen, and now they were to
embark in Table Bay instead of Simon's Bay, which
from the continued south-east blast was rendered unsafe
for shipping. Our marches had been painful to Rondebosch, three leagues from Cape Town. The heat was
excessive, the sand over the ankles and even then no
firm bottom, progress slow : the bullocks dragging the
cannon all knocked up.

Jan. 22.—Yesterday received at five A.M. the arms,
colours, guns, artillery and cavalry horses. I was
obliged severely to reprimand the captain commanding

the artillery—the only Dutch officer who has acted with any degree of opposition, or shown unworthy enmity to British interests. My rebuke was much approved by his brother officers. I rode into the town; dined with the general; then rode back to my station. The night was very dark so that I lost my way; but at last, notwithstanding a most perilous road, arrived without accident. This day I have employed every moment that I could spare from my excessive duty in writing. Went into the town; returned at night, and lost myself again exactly at the same point. After I had put up my horse two shots were fired and we all turned out, but our patrols could gain no intelligence.

Sir Home tells me that he is daily discovering more prize money. 200,000l. is already secured; the army shares. This is the only circumstance that relieves our melancholy, for the prospect is very sombre. Joy has no influence here. I cannot describe the pleasure of travelling in the country better than by stating that waggons without springs are the *chaises de postes*, and that the lightest vehicle never moves without eight bullocks or more, and that even these can sometimes scarcely pull through the sand.

The women seem pretty, but every one admits that they are totally unfit for social companions. In truth, this is a real colony of shopkeepers. Plutus is their only god; they do not pretend to raise temples to any other. In the whole country there are but two churches—so unfavourable have priests found this soil.

Feb. 11.—Since the date of my last journal, variety and multiplicity of business have so crowded my time that I have not been able to employ a moment in private matters; and now I can only concisely state that I was ordered to leave my command of the Dutch camp, and fix head-quarters at Cape Town. But I have been employed six days on an important court-martial for the trial of an officer accused of cowardice; and have been on several committees to fix the price of requisition horses, which is at last settled by an average of 26*l.* The Cape horse is not in my opinion of high qualities, but we have a roan troop of uncommon beauty.

The principal public events that have occurred are the punishment, and the most severe one I ever saw, of an East India Company's soldier for robbery; the departure of the India fleet, which relieves the colony from the supply of four thousand people—a very important object; and the issue of an order this morning for every officer in the garrison to wear *black leather stocks!*   ·

Before dinner on the day on which General Janssen gave his public entertainment, the news arrived of Lord Nelson's victory. As the company entered the saloon the guns of rejoicing were firing, but a sense of impropriety prevented any expression of triumph. After dinner the band of the 38th began to play "God save the King." There could not be a more unfortunate concurrence of seemingly disrespectful circumstances.

When I first reached this town I thought it a paradise: but the sense was deceived by the sudden transition from a desert country in which we had been enduring extreme misery from fatigue, heat, thirst, and sand. The houses are good: but the offensive smells, the furnace heat of the atmosphere, the blast of the south-east wind which rages here with inconceivable fury and violently drives with it clouds of sand and gravel, the mercenary character and the stupidity of the inhabitants, the excessive dearness of every necessary of life, all render this place one of the worst stations on the globe and particularly for military men. The measures of our commander will establish it for us as the Cape of Despair. Officers and men are discontended beyond expression. The balance or *goose* step introduced for their practice excites a fever of disgust, and disease makes formidable havoc in our ranks. I have fifty men sick, and the proportion is moderate when compared with other regiments. The principal cause of this destructive sickness is, I believe, bad wine, and the want of every comfort for those affected. As yet, I have not been able to get a room for my regimental hospital, and the same confusion and want of arrangement pervade every branch and department of the service. The requests for leave of absence have already enraged the general, and the resignations meditated will bear evidence that the feeling is such as I have described.

Every officer in the regiment but myself has been ill. I have not had a moment's uneasiness on account of health; but I turn my eyes to the sea with a longing look and envy even the Dutch prisoners, who resolve to continue such and go to Europe. With a view to forcing them to enlist into our service their stay is prolonged and they are kept in the strictest confinement. This mode of crimping does not accord with the dignity of the English nation nor with military honour.

Feb. 13.—Yesterday a most violent south-east wind blew the whole day. It seemed as if the air were striving to dislodge the lofty mountains that overhang the city, and the clouds of sand produced the darkness of night.

I have had many painful embarrassments rendering it difficult to preserve my system, from the mad fury of different officers: but I persevere undaunted.

Feb. 15.—I applied yesterday to be exempted from the wear of the *black leather stock*, and stated the king's order* on the subject, but was refused my petition; so that I have nothing to do but bear the yoke with as good a grace as possible. I shall transmit my protest to General Calvert, for we have a right to protection from such troublesome caprices and local commands.

I was field officer, and to keep my eyes open till midnight, went to a party at the paymaster-general's, where I found an assemblage of Dutch ladies who soon began to trip on the cumbrous toe. All the beauties of the Cape were present. At midnight I went my rounds—no pleasant duty: the distance about five miles, and the road most dangerous from uneven surface and very difficult to find. Every time I lost my way, and every time have had to report the dreadful state of the burying ground through which we pass.

---

* Sir Robert Wilson remonstrated personally with Sir David Baird on this subject. When he spoke of the "king's order," Sir David answered, "I, sir, am his Majesty here." Wilson, with his significant smile, and with a profound bow, replied, "Very well, *King David;* your Majesty's orders shall be obeyed." This anecdote, related to Sir Provo Wallis by an officer who was there, is preserved as an instance of Sir Robert Wilson's tact and readiness. The good-humoured sarcasm was not resented.—Ed.

The bodies lie almost uncovered, for wood is too dear to allow of coffins.

I was obliged to rise at five o'clock to superintend the punishment of four men of the staff corps, sentenced by garrison court-martial. The first man received three hundred severe lashes, the others one hundred each: but to show how much officers should consider before they bring men to this disgrace for slight offences, I shall state that I was obliged to punish the first man without any officer of the corps to which he belonged being present, and none came until the second man was tied up.

After the punishment, the general asked me if no application had been made by the commanding officer of the corps to remit the sentence of two of the men. On my answering in the negative, he informed me that the commanding officer had been with him only the day before to obtain their pardon; and that he had granted it but desired him to attend at the punishment and mention his own wish to me publicly—the general's sanction privately—so that it was to appear as if the whole was impromptu. The commanding officer, however, slept soundly, and forgot his victims. I have been very angry and shall insist on the most serious notice being taken; for the same inhuman indolence might occur in more capital cases. The duty was most unpleasant, and spoilt my breakfast appetite.

March 4.—At twelve this day a signal was made from the Lion's Rump for an enemy's vessel in sight. I rode to the Monille battery, and arrived in time to see a French frigate strike to the commodore who had just returned from his unsuccessful cruise for Linois. He fired but one shot. I went with Sir

David back to the Chavan, where the *Diadem's* boat
landed an English officer who proved to be Captain
Wilson of the Queen's, taken with three companies of
his regiment and two of the 54th on passage from
Gibraltar under convoy of the *Tunis* frigate, by a
squadron of eleven sail of French line from Brest
commanded by Admiral Villaumez.   They were first
sent on board the admiral's ship and plundered of
everything, then sent on in the *Volontaire* of forty-
four guns.   When they were brought to by the commodore the French captain said to the English
officers, " Chacun à son tour," and surrendered immediately.   Fortunately for his comfort as a prisoner
he had treated the English with great kindness.

The strictest secrecy was enjoined by Sir David
after reading Sir Home's letter, but enough transpired
in the first rush of curiosity to convince me that the
French expedition is coming here ; so that I, who
lamented my absence from the Blueberg entertainment,
may yet be gorged with the martial banquet now
cooking for us.   I only hope for a fortnight's delay,
as there has been too much attention to the goose-step
for warlike arrangements.

March 6.—Instead of eleven sail of the line only
six are coming.   Jerome Buonaparte commands a
seventy-four in the expedition.   I must relate an
anecdote truly characteristic of the French national
feeling.   When the *Volontaire* was lowering her
colours, the second captain of the *Atalanta* French
frigate stranded here was asked by Patterson
whether he knew her name.   He attempted to look,
but rubbing a few tears from his eyes said, " Ces
bêtes larmes me défendent de voir."   The French

captain and his officers are permitted to return to
Europe in consequence of their good conduct to the
English officers and soldiers on board the *Volontaire*
as prisoners.

March 10.—Last night I was roused from my bed
with an alarm that the French had landed in Saldanha
Bay. On going to Sir David he confirmed the news,
and showed as his authority a man who had just come
from thence. This man spoke French well, and declared that he had conversed with the French officers
on shore, and added every probable particular. Nevertheless, I depended so much on Arbuthnot's conduct
in such a case—and from him I had received not a
line—that I persevered in disbelieving the informer
and requested Sir David not to act upon the report.
Mr. Rheinveldt, the chief magistrate, divided with me ;
the generals and chief engineer against me : and
Newland was marched, with two guns and thirty men,
instantly to Saldanha. This morning, the reporter
confessed the whole story to be a drunken fabrication.
He may rue his humour, for his life is in danger ; and
I suspect that there was an object in the tale. The
French here naturally wish to give their countrymen
every chance, and a division of our force may be of
serious detriment in case of a vigorous attack on Cape
Town.

March 12.—I dined yesterday with Sir Home ; he
made me most happy by the invitation and by under-
taking to give me a passage in the *Diadem* to Europe,
where he expects to be in August at the latest.

I received a report from Arbuthnot which I sent to
head-quarters, and Sir David has sent him a very
flattering letter of approval.

The man who told the falsehood about the French at Saldanha had a severe whipping yesterday, at six different places. He was scourged with rods; one of which was held in each hand of the executioner, and the blows were given as fast as possible. A severe punishment—but he merited death.

April 14.—On the 12th it was announced that an expedition was determined upon against Rio de la Plata. Sir David consented that the 71st regiment and General Beresford with a few artillery should undertake that expedition, which appeared to me indiscreet.

Yesterday Sir David Baird, at drill, asked me to dine with him. The 71st embarked. After breakfast I went on board Sir Home's ship with Arbuthnot who wished to go on the service. When on board I conversed with the carpenter, who gave me information relative to the Rio de la Plata in which settlement he had lived some years. I obtained from him a draught of the place by which I had more reason to be satisfied that my original idea of this enterprise was correct, and that in all human probability it would be a failure. After dining with Sir David I walked away with General Beresford, and could not help saying to him that I hoped he would look well before he leapt. I promised to send him a copy of the sketch given me by the carpenter, and the Spanish army-list given to me by John Kemble in England, by which the force in the country appeared far more considerable than was allowed by Sir Home. Sent both this morning. Drummond told me that Sir Home, who had yesterday mentioned my anxiety to go to England, was gone to ask that I might go with him and carry despatches to Europe. Presently Arbuthnot came running to me, and said that I was instantly wanted by the general. The report circulated that I was going with the expedition. On entering the government house I found Sir Home at the door very gloomy. He followed me into the passage and said, " So, sir, you have entered a protest against the expedition—drawn your plan—as much as to say, after this go now if you dare." I denied it. He said that " what I had actually done amounted to this." Sir David came out and received me most graciously—droll enough—and desired me to walk up stairs. General Beresford showed equal courtesy. Sir David then asked me where I had obtained, or from what information I had drawn my chart. I told him. He then inquired about the book which Kemble had given me, and concluded by expressing his acknowledgment for my information. I answered that I thought it my duty to produce whatever might tend to elucidate the question, either for or against an enterprise in which the national honour, the reputation of the army, and the safety of friends were concerned. Both Generals Baird and Beresford repeated their thanks continually; while Sir Home remained silent. They then all went on board the ship again to see the men, with my sketch and the army list in their hands. All is still suspense, for the council is not yet returned on shore.

The events of this day prove how uncertain all human operations are, and on what trifles great events often depend. John Kemble's accidental gift and my curiosity have suspended in balance and may perhaps have prevented, a plan that interests nations and involves the lives, fortunes, and happiness of many individuals. I think that I ought to send the book to the British Museum. I am seriously pained that Sir Home should be displeased: still I think that I have done my duty honestly to my country; and I have such little opinion of naval-military schemes of enterprise, that I am in my own mind certain of his being injured only in fancy if the expedition does not proceed.

April 14.—The expedition was decided upon, but with very restrictive orders. Yesterday morning it sailed. Sir David sent for me to tell me that he had been over-persuaded. Sir Home wrote me several very friendly notes, and left with Sir David the expression of his wish that I should go to England when the fate of the detachment is known. This wish will be complied with.

April 24.—A vessel arrived in Simon's Bay brings news of peace between France and Austria. I dread to hear the terms.

The general came into our barracks and was highly satisfied with their cleanly state. In one troop, however, he observed a horse that was not very clean, and asked the quartermaster why there was neglect in this case. The quartermaster answered that he was " too vicious to be cleaned." The general replied with unbecoming severity. A man was called out to clean him: he rubbed one side with some difficulty, when the general ordered the quartermaster into arrest and retired; but no sooner was the horse touched on the side where he had no eye than he became furious, and in an instant cleared away men and horses in all directions. When I was made acquainted with the affair I represented that the horse

had been reported to me as too dangerous to be
cleaned some time since by Captain Cromwell: that
Captain Arbuthnot and Mr. Odell, who had been in
command with him, had also made the same report:
that he had kicked and bitten several men: and that
General Beresford had cast him for such vice three
weeks since, but ordered him to be kept in our stables
until a bruise on his back was well. At the same time
I wrote to Colonel Vassal, now commandant of the
town, that I recommended the quartermaster's libera-
tion as I foresaw that his trial would be attended
with unpleasant results, the evidence being so strong
in his favour; a hint which colonel Vassal could well
comprehend. He will, I believe, in consequence be
restored to liberty: but I shall order a court of
inquiry to be held for the sake of the man and the
credit of the regiment; so that the transaction being
upon official record may not be liable to erroneous
relation.

April 29.—I went on the 27th with Brownrigge to
a party in the country, where the contract of marriage
—an event which must take place eight days before
the actual marriage—between a Miss Hunter and
General Munich was to be celebrated. We were the
only two English officers, but there might be eighty
persons altogether. The dancing literally lasted all
night. The destined bride was about sixteen; a
very fine country girl, unaffected, and very interesting
from her simplicity. She was surrounded by relations
and friends who all seemed happy and fond of each
other. The old joined with the young in the festivity,
and the scene resembled the description of the former
manners of England. I was highly gratified as the

welcome was most hospitable, and no circumstance occurred that could be recorded to the disadvantage of our hosts. Personally, I had every reason to be satisfied with the attentions paid me; but I was equally pleased to observe an honest freedom of manners without any affected refinement. The fetters of social distinctions were not permitted to interfere with this entire freedom : and I mention as some proof of it, that in a company where an officer of high rank and more particularly with my additional distinctions might be presumed to command some preference of courtesy, and where his attentions might be supposed to gratify the pride of the parties to whom he offered them, I could only dance the fifth dance with the bride; her kinsmen and acquaintance claiming her hand till then. At supper the health of the bride and bridegroom was drunk in large glasses and gaiety of heart prevailed, but the strictest decency and propriety were never infringed upon. A bishop might have been present and never had reason to avert his eye or ear. I confess that this correct behaviour astonished me, as I had been induced to form a different opinion by reading the books of travellers.

About daybreak some of the nearest neighbours went home to dress and return to dine, which is the custom. We passed a very pleasant morning. Four old people danced a very regular and perfect minuet, notwithstanding that one lady was of immense size. I joyed much in this sight, which completed the scene of domestic felicity, and reminded me of Old England, where in the middle classes of country society primitive modes of family happiness still find a place.

Y 2

Nor were the emotions which this amiable display of antiquated vanity excited in the youthful portion of the company less creditable. Every eye glistened with satisfaction and every voice cheered with affectionate ardour. A very pretty girl standing next to me observed, " I am so glad to see the old people so happy !" and I believe she felt the remark as deeply as she spoke it energetically. When such goodness of heart is general the writer is too severe who lashes, with fierce rudeness, a deficiency in those accomplishments which are common in Europe ; unless he confines his censure to those who have neglected foolishly to observe the advancing graces of society and to cultivate them in their children. At dinner, two o'clock, almost the whole party reassembled. The merry wine-cup was introduced again to the " health of the host and hostess," and once replenished to the " welfare of the place." The company then retired to the hall, and the rest of the day was passed in various rustic amusements, tea, and supper.

Women all over the world I find are equally able to support the fatigue of dancing. Although there were some girls who from seven P.M. to seven A.M. danced incessantly—each dance without a moment's interval succeeding the foregoing one—except during the one hour devoted to supper, and although the floor was paved with bricks, yet they seemed fresh and quite ready to prolong the exercise ; shaming, I will confess, all the men. There was no waltzing, only country dances and French dances.

I have been thus particular because the manners of a country are always interesting, and I have felt it a duty to render justice to the people of the colony.

I flatter myself that I shall be the bearer of my next despatches. My absence from Europe at such an interesting period is an unparalleled misfortune in my history.

May 12.—Nothing extraordinary happened until the 10th, when some vessels were signalled. They proved to be the *Porpoise* sloop of war and two store ships from England, which they left on the 28th of January. The news transpired yesterday, and such a catalogue of woful disasters I never heard. Pitt's death has been felt here as the worst of the calamities. We are all sad and desponding.

May 15.—Fortune and I can never meet kindly again. To be absent from Europe when such great changes were in progress, and when the elevation of my friends to power offered opportunity for advantageous employment, is a hard destiny. The public news which I have been devouring all this morning, and an English November day, have quite oppressed me; and I do not wonder at Wright's suicide or the breaking of Pitt's heart.

As soon as news is received from government of the disposition of the forces here I shall strenuously urge my return home. Lord Hutchinson, the papers say, has an appointment. I am satisfied that he will have some good employment; and I calculate upon his friendly offices, at all events to remove me from hence.

There is scarcely any expedition from this place that would employ me satisfactorily, unless Spanish America is to be vigorously attacked; for from the intelligence that Sir Home's convoy has been separated, and that a French fifty with two frigates has gone to

Rio de la Plata so that their crews will secure a garrison to Monte Video, I consider that Sir Home's enterprise has failed.　A war with North America would probably be chiefly maritime, and I have no inclination to fight with Yankees whose resistance scarcely offers military honour.

May 27.—On the 24th, I wrote to Sir David that I wished to return to Europe.　On the 25th, he sent for me and said he knew that I had family reasons, and that my friends were come into office, so that he would not detain me if I made a strong application.　I did this yesterday and it is granted; but the red flag is this moment hoisted and the signal repeated that an enemy's fleet is off Simon's Bay. Fortune may yet be disposed to make me amends even in Africa.　The drum beats to arms—thank God! —Huzza!

May 29.—Disappointment often mortifies hope. The repeatedly signalled enemy turned out to be neutral vessels.

June 10, Adamant, 3 degrees from the Cape of Torments.

On the 4th of June the troops were reviewed and looked admirably well.　Next day I paraded my detachment, and took leave of them in a short address.　The major and adjutant could not speak to address the men. I was much moved at this instance of their affection : indeed I felt the pleasure of my departure from this detestable colony greatly impaired by the thought of leaving men who I had reason to know were much attached to me ; but I had the satisfaction of reflecting that I had taken every precaution for their comfort and future interests.　The next day I took leave of

my good friends, and particularly of Colonel Vassal
whose kindness I shall never forget; and after settling
all affairs I mounted my horse and rode to Simon's
Bay.   There I found that Captain Styles of the
Adamant, who had offered me a passage, had determined upon sailing the next morning at daybreak.
I then discovered that my writing-case with keys was
left behind.   I was very uneasy on this account and
resolved to go back myself.   I set off about six
o'clock.   The night was very dark and a great plain
of water divided me from Cape Town : but after losing
my way and recovering it I got safe, mounted another
horse, and returned; riding thus above fifty miles at
night over a solitary tract, with wolves howling,
quicksands menacing, and a heavy writing-case under
my arm as I came back.

I got on board just in time; but it is a singular
circumstance that the boat which conveyed me to the
ship sprung a leak, and I had nearly lost my passage.
Captain Styles received me with a hearty welcome
and we sailed immediately.

June 27, St. Helena.

On the 22nd, after a tedious passage of fourteen
days, we reached St. Helena.   On shore I slept at
Captain Cox's, who married a sister of Lord Essex.
A most extraordinary event which happened twenty
years before brought me to his recognition the moment
he saw me.   I dined with the governor at his country
house and rode with Captain Styles and Colonel
Halket, a fellow-passenger on board the *Adamant*, to
see the island.   We were all much astonished and
pleased at the interior country; but we hope not to

stay here long as we are all heartily tired of the place.*

June 29.—We have dined repeatedly with the governor and slept one night at the plantation house; a great relief to us, as our rooms in the town are an abomination from their condition and closeness. We heard on the 27th of the loss of the *Burgess* Indiaman by the *Walthamstow* and *Lord Nelson* just arrived from England. The gallantry of the crew of the *Burgess* in saving the ladies is admirable. There are two cadets here who were preserved by clinging to a Newfoundland dog and a pig.

July 10, at Sea.

We sailed yesterday. The China fleet arrived on the 2nd under convoy of the *Lancaster*, 64, after a passage of four months. By considerable exertions they watered in eight days. One of the captains was the celebrated Wilson who was cast away on the Pelew Islands. He is a fine old man with a most pleasing countenance and a reverend head, seventy years of age. Another was a Captain Gribble commanding the *King George*, the ship which fought Linois in the action in which he was repelled by the China fleet. He recognised me as having inspected him at Barnstaple when he was acting as a yeoman. In another ship was the lover of Miss Jessy Patton the governor's daughter: he is a brother of Colonel Oswald of the 35th regiment, and chief mate of the *Exeter*. A finer young man is not to be seen in any service. In the *Lancaster* came Captains Heathcote, Christian, Williams, and Dare. In Christian I found an old acquaintance and the brother of Hompesch's wife.

* " Sketch of St. Helena." See Appendix No. 8.

His company has been a great amusement and pleasure to me, and he and Williams are now fellow-passengers in the *Adamant*. At ten yesterday morning, after breakfasting with the governor, Christian and I went down to embark in a boat of the *Lancaster*. The *Adamant* having stood off about five miles lay to, so that we were in hopes of reaching her : but when we approached she made sail again, to our great vexation as the weather was very hot, and the poor fellows who rowed us were exhausted by a ten years' service in India, and broken in spirit by the disappointment of not returning to England as they had been led to expect. The case of the *Lancaster* is indeed the most cruel instance of neglect that I ever heard of : no man could ascend her deck unmoved by the sight of a crew so broken-hearted and yet, in figure and coun- tenance, the most admirable specimens of a veteran marine.

Resolved not to pursue the *Adamant* on account of the men who had so far to row back, we went away to the *Hope* and got on board of her ; from whence we were quickly sent for by the *Adamant*, which now lay to in order to receive us. I should have preferred remaining in the *Hope* for a few days as Captain Miniski, a Russian officer who has been learning naval tactics for some years in British ships, was a passenger in her, and is one of the most excellent foreigners I have ever known. I have been highly pleased that I have had opportunity to show him some attentions.

July 22.—I went on board the *Warley*, Captain Wilson. He was bringing home an animal of exquisite beauty and unknown species from Malacca. It has the expressive eye and delicate limbs of the antelope, the tusks of a young boar, the throat and body of a stag, two sinews upon the nose, and two holes under the eyes through which he breathes when oppressed in the chase.

A stone was shown us which, when dipped in water, becomes elastic and tractable as putty, but cannot be cut through; and a map used in China which country occupies the whole surface, while round the edges England, America, France, Germany, &c., &c., are introduced as very minute islands. A variety of rare and costly articles of Japanese, Chinese, and Malacca manufacture were also in Captain Wilson's collection.

August 9.—Yesterday I went with Christian on board the *Windham*, Captain Steuart, and dined there *en fête*. Afterwards we amused ourselves with rowing to the *Exeter*, the *Ocean*, the *Howe*, the *Warley*, and the *Cootes*. In the *Howe* I rode round the deck on a magnificent Arab horse, an event probably not of frequent occurrence on the Atlantic. On board the *Ocean* was a bull three feet high, not altogether so large as York. In lat. 32° 14', long. 37° 30', I sent to the deep, in charge of the *current post*, a bottle containing a paper with the following words: "*Adamant*, August 9, 1806. If the bottle containing this paper is picked up six months after this date, let the finder acquaint Captain Christian, R.N., or Lieutenant-Colonel Sir Robert Wilson, stating when and where it was found."

I have done this in order to ascertain the direction of the currents, as we see around us vast quantities of seaweed supposed to come from the Gulf of Florida and to return there.

August 20.—On the 17th I took advantage of a calm to visit several ships. The *Adamant* shot ahead and did not shorten sail for us, but as I was determined to get on board if possible, Christian and I got into the boat at eight o'clock P.M., when it was quite dark and the ship was going five miles an hour. We hoped that, by means of lanterns and firing muskets, we should make the *Adamant* see us. However, after rowing hard for twenty minutes, we were obliged to give up the chase. Fortunately, the *Warley* bore down and picked us up.* This was a most unpleasant adventure, might have terminated fatally, and has given me cause for great displeasure. The next morning we came on board. The same day a man from the maintop lost a knife overboard. Four hours afterwards a dolphin was caught, with two flying fish *and the knife* in his stomach.

August 29.—A furious gale. I am indeed but an unlucky mariner. In the height of the gale York and Pacha rushed for shelter to me and could not be driven from the cabin, although never permitted to sleep there. In York, this is more remarkable, as he never comes near me at any time, having enough amusement with the crew, but instinct told him that in trouble his master would prove his best protector.

August 31.—Yesterday, at three o'clock, we saw the *Lizard*, an American. She hinted that there was great news of peace. The ship's crew cheered notwithstanding the menaces of the officers.

---

* This was the occasion to which Sir R. W. refers as one of the imminent perils of his life, in the memoir quoted in the preface to the "Russian Campaign," p. 2.—ED.

" A word to the wise"—reflection to the thought-ful.

This day off the Start. The boats are employed in the melancholy service of pressing the crews of Indiamen who have now been absent two years. What a farce to these poor fellows is the freedom of Britons! How sorrowful to them is public utility!

APPENDIX TO VOL. I.

No. 1.

HAVING determined when at Dorchester to pay my respects to the king at Weymouth, I arrived in the evening of the 2nd September,* and posted myself with my wife at the pier-head when his majesty was promenading in that direction. We attracted his notice. After some few remarks he desired me to go on board his yacht next day that he might question me more about Egypt: and turning to Lord Hawkesbury he observed, "These are atrocious crimes of which he has accused Buonaparte—I believe them all—do you not, my lord?" Lord H. declined an answer.

We went on board but not a word was said about Egypt. The king was apparently agitated, and was more rapid in his delivery than formerly. Towards evening he desired the band to play some music from Handel, set to words among which the line occurs—"We never will bow down:"—I presumed "to images,"—for the king immediately cried out, "Now let the Roman Catholics come on! I wish they were all here!" He then lapsed into a devotional reverie; as might be inferred from the motion of his head and his hands but his eyes were closed. The next day he was much calmer, and still more so the third. He nevertheless once showed much irritation and harshness towards Princess Augusta; who was taking care of Princess Sophia, seized with her usual spasmodic complaint. From his countenance at the instant his appearance when in a frenzied state might well be imagined.

* Probably 1802.—ED.

Again, before many people he abused General Dundas in
coarse terms; and declared that he "Gave him Chelsea to get
rid of such a troublesome burden." In his political observations he was also very indiscreet; saying before the sailors
that he "hated all reforms," that he "loved the constitution
with existing abuses better than if they were removed:" and
he was very severe against the Parliament for the Aylesbury
Election Bill. When he was at the theatre one of the
actors said to another on the stage, "You think yourself a
great man because you represent all the silly fellows of the
shire." The king clapped his hands and seemed delighted :
but generally he slept there a great deal, or talked so loudly
as to disturb the performance. One ludicrous incident
occurred which occasioned much laughter. The queen and
Princess Elizabeth retired from the box while the king was
asleep. The audience feared that one of the princesses had
been taken ill, as all were not present. When the king
awoke he asked "Where the queen was gone." Princess
Augusta whispered the answer. The king roared out, "Then
why did she not take all the playbills with her?" The
house immediately apprehended the whisper: and it was
convulsed.

At the wedding fête it was presumed that the king would
be allowed to sleep in the queen's apartment, which hitherto
for several years had not been the case: but the usual precautions were taken to prevent his occupation of the room.
These precautions are, first, the entrance of two German
ladies at an early hour: next, on the retirement of the
queen, two of the princesses attend her and stay until the
king withdraws. He sleeps in the next house; for he declares
that he never will have a separate apartment in the same
residence with her.

The advice of the physicians, the entreaties of the
ministers, have all been in vain. The queen is inexorable.

The morning after the fête the king was very unwell.
One of the princesses told my informant, "We have had
quite a scene this morning with the king." I afterwards
learnt through the same channel that the king had been
very outrageous; and had abused Mr. Pitt and all his party

violently. That the king was much attached to the Adding-
tonians I had before an opportunity of ascertaining: for when
Nat Bond came to the rooms the king watched till Lord
Hawkesbury was turned away; and then went up to him and
paid him and his former colleagues the most flattering compliments, and on various occasions repeated them.

On board the yacht the king lent Sir W. Parsons the
"Life of Handel," with notes by himself.   I asked Sir
William whether these notes were written with any ability
and knowledge?   He answered, "Not in the least degree.
There is one however very much against Lord Cardigan, the
Duke of Queensberry, and Lord Galloway; in which they are
called fools for liking Italian music."   When Sir W. Parsons
returned the book with courtly expressions, the king said, "I
am glad you like these, for I wrote them during the time they
chose to say I was ill last winter."

At the parade of the evening on the 16th the king was so
remarkably lively as to attract general notice, and particularly
among the German officers present: one of whom observed,
"Ich habe niemals den König so lustig gesehen "—"I have
never seen the king so gay."   I replied, "The arrival of the
Duke of Sussex has animated him."   For the next two days
his physician, Sir F. Milman, entertained very serious apprehensions; as there were increased symptoms of returning
malady, which more and more engaged public attention.   It
was a melancholy sight and most painful to all about him, as
they were thrown into continual embarrassments.

The character of the king under this affliction seems totally
changed.   Occasionally he is more liberally disposed: but in
most cases malignantly; hating those whom he best liked,
wishing the death of supposed enemies, and taking into great
aversion his old and faithful servants.   He affects to be
totally foreign, which formerly he could not bear any one to
be: and he now stalks about with gauntlet gloves on his
hands, in the biggest Hanoverian boots. .

"O! vanitas rerum humanarum !"

Sept. 22.—The king after dinner was more petulant and
excited than ever.   It was the anniversary of his coronation.
He appeared in a Hanoverian general's uniform, and as

Count Woronzow remarked to me, was more " bavard " than usual : but in politics and in his memory I thought him more acute than ever. Towards night he became quite childish, and faltered much in his speech.

Sept. 23.—The king went on board the yacht to attend Divine service. He came to the rooms in the evening and appeared more staid than the preceding day. While the Duke of York was at Weymouth the king left off his gauntlets and big boots; but the duke was alarmed at other appearances. On Tuesday, the 25th, on board the yacht he was very wild and irregular. On the 27th he went on board again, and sea and wind were very high. Notwith-standing the fitting up of Windsor Castle at so great an expense, he now talks of living in Cumberland Lodge : but he takes much credit to himself for the following stratagem of economy.

Immediately after his illness he was informed that new furniture would be required in Buckingham House. It was always a custom that the old should be taken by the Lord Chamberlain; but the king precipitated Lord Salisbury's dismissal and protracted Lord Hertford's appointment that, as he said, " The furniture might in the interim be removed to Kew and Hampton, and thus escape the gripe of the Chamberlain."

On the 29th a fête was given on board the yacht. Some verses were recited by Elliston which affected the king and queen to tears. They contained a strong allusion to the king's former illness, and to death. A friend of mine wrote them ; and before they were given to Elliston they were sub-mitted to Princess Elizabeth and approved.

Sept. 30.—Sir F. Milman has warned the queen of his apprehension that the king may have an attack of apoplexy. For the last week it appears he has been suffering much from severe headaches, very dissimilar from his old nervous affections. With them he was very cold : whereas now he feels during the attacks burning heat in his face and hands. The king on the 26th had a fall with his horse : but his head-aches had come on previously.

The Hanoverian boots and gloves have not been resumed;

but the other day the king went into the market, bought himself six red mullets, and astonished the poissardes with his free conversation.

On board the yacht, on the 1st of October, the king came forward to the mainmast against which runs the division of the quarter-deck.   Princesses Augusta, Sophia, Amelia, and Sophia of Gloucester, Lady Isabella Thynne, Lady C. Strangways, Lady Georgina Bulkeley, and Mrs. Drax, were sitting upon the sofas.   The king commenced the conversation while taking some papers out of a green box, by observing—" Mrs. Drax! you look very well—very well indeed.   Dear, lovely Mrs. Drax! what a pretty ass you have got!—bring it here; how I should like to pat such a pretty ass!"   This was said twice in the same quaint manner, and with a voice which reached every part of the ship.   The confusion of princesses, ladies and gentlemen, officers, mids, and sailors was indescribable.   Some of the mids and sailors tumbled over one another into the hatchways, unable to retain their fits of laughter; as if they had been swept off by chain-shot.   This expressive outbreak did not proceed from any *sudden fancy*; but the king had overheard Mrs. Drax in the morning saying to a pretty little donkey much admired at Weymouth, " Oh! dear, pretty little ass! come here that I may pat you! How I should like to pat you, dear, pretty ass!"

On this day the king did not come on board till 11 o'clock, an hour later than usual.   On inquiring at the Lodge the cause of delay, as he was always most punctual to the minute, I learnt that the king had been disputing violently with the queen; and that every princess had been in tears.

On Tuesday the 2nd of October I quitted Weymouth, full of melancholy thoughts at such a picture of suffering humanity; and at the terrible future that awaits a good man, and in heart a truly British king.

> " There is no comfort to this great decay."

R. W.

The above was shown to Lord Moira, who asked me to lo him show it to the Prince of Wales.   The prince sent me a very civil message through Lord M. and added a wish that " I would make the memorandum as public as I could."

> " Thus would he needs invest him with his honours
> Before his hour was ripe."

R. W.

No. 2.

GENERAL COUNT STAREMBERG TO SIR ROBERT WILSON.

London, 13th October, 1799.

DEAR SIR,

I RECEIVED both your letters of the 23rd and 29th September and feel as I ought to do for your kind friendship and remembrance. The details you give me, and your judgments upon the whole of your military operations, are extremely interesting; and brought me a new instance of your talents and disposition for the career of heroes you began already to tread with such distinction under the emperor in Flanders: where you deserved by your skill and bravery the honourable and seldom conferred tokens of military valour and renown.

We were apprised yesterday, by the newspapers only, of a reverse sustained by the allied troops on the 6th. I expect anxiously the account you certainly will be so good as to send to me of that day: which I am afraid, if it proves as it is reported, would force to give up the expedition in that quarter.

From Hamburgh mails are due: we long for their arrival to know the certainty of a still greater misfortune related in the Paris papers, which mention the total defeat of the Russians in Switzerland, as well as the death of our gallant General Notze. Though deeply concerned by that truly very distressing account I cannot forbear to observe with regret, that whenever the Russians in the course of this war tried to attack the enemy by themselves they were always obliged at last to apply to the Austrians; in order to rescue (from) the dilemma their rashness had plunged them into. I hope our brave archduke will succeed as well on this present occasion as Kray and Melas did in Italy; and then everything may be well again.   Pray accept anew of my most sincere thanks, and the assurances of my sincere and everlasting attachment.

STAREMBERG.

No. 3.

LORD MINTO TO SIR ROBERT WILSON.

DEAR SIR,   Vienna, November 9, 1800.

I HAVE the satisfaction to tell you that I have this moment received the eight crosses of the Order of Maria Theresa, for the officers of your former regiment who have already received medals from the Emperor.   I have the pleasure to forward yours by this occasion, and as soon as I receive whatever writing or act belongs to this transaction I shall not fail to transmit it.   In the mean time the cross which I now send you has been delivered officially to me, *for the purpose* of being transmitted to you, *from the Emperor*, and being *immediately* worn by *yourself*.   I must once more repeat the gratification I feel in being the channel of this gracious act, which does equal honour to the hand that gives and those that receive.

I have reason to suppose that a considerable part of Sir Ralph Abercrombie's troops are gone to Lisbon, and the destination of the remainder does not seem determined. Pray communicate this to Lord William and believe me, dear sir,

Your obedient and faithful humble servant,

MINTO.

No. 4.

CAPE OF GOOD HOPE.

ORDERS OF SIR ROBERT WILSON IN COMMAND OF THE CAVALRY DETACHMENT PREVIOUS TO LANDING.

12th December, 1805.

THE commanding officer having procured at St. Salvador some horses for the service of the dragoons, has selected such non-commissioned officers and men to disembark with them in the first instance as from their experience will be best enabled to execute the duty intrusted to them; on which depends the efficiency of the whole detachment as cavalry. The commanding officer trusts that the detachment so selected will reflect that much is required of them, and that intelligence with the strictest regard to discipline must aid their gallantry; for they must expect to act against an enemy's cavalry, well commanded and having the advantage of local knowledge. But there is no superiority which may not be reduced if conduct does but direct zeal: while the very smallness of original numbers will add considerably to the distinction that every soldier values more than life. The British infantry from regard to their interests as well as from attachment to the cavalry will direct much notice to the character and execution of their enterprises: and on such occasions individual talent or exploit cannot pass unknown or unrewarded. The moment is arriving when the detachment of the 20th Dragoons may honour the reputation of their regiment, their service, and the British military character: when their actions may entitle them to the approbation of the commander of the expedition, the esteem of the army, and the gratitude of their comrades. For the sake of obtaining such brilliant results, the commanding officer trusts that each man will pay all possible attention to the preservation of the health of his horse now embarked, and think no sacrifice of personal convenience too great that tends to promote this object. Frequent attention to the management of the food most palatable to him, rubbing of his legs, and regard to his cleaning will secure an effective condition.

In the field the strictest silence must be maintained: any disobedience to authority in the moment of action, any expressions of doubt or dismay under any circumstances, would consign those who acted so criminally to the penalty of death and infamy. No dragoon, except when stationed as a vidette, must ever use fire-arms at night unless ordered.

No detachment of dragoons must ever retreat at a greater pace than ordered by the commanding officer.

Any dragoons continuing a retreat after a halt is

ordered are to be sent back as prisoners to be tried for cowardice.

All dragoons must consider the safety of their comrades to right and left as well as their own : if stationed to give an alarm on the appearance of an enemy they cannot fire too rapidly or retire too gradually ; but false alarms are disgraceful.

No dragoon must drink any liquor when in a village, or dismount, without leave ; for no excuse for intoxication from a small quantity having taken a strong effect will be admitted. The interests of the expedition, the safety of all detached parties, as well as the Articles of War, direct the kindest treatment of the peaceful inhabitants. Violence against their persons or plunder of their property is immediate death without trial. The booty taken by the valour of the troops from the enemy will be divided according to the orders already issued on that subject ; which orders are to be read again to the men when within 100 leagues of the Cape : the Articles of War are also to be read.

As a gun is attached to the dragoons, the artillerymen that serve it must experience the cordial friendship as well as the protection of the dragoons. The commanding officer is confident that the cavalry will never abandon the gun without orders from him. Till that moment they should regard it as committed to the charge of their courage ; and therefore consider its loss incompatible with their honour.

After a charge, if such an opportunity offers, all must rally again as soon as possible ; and form without any reference to exact plan in the division or squadron : with the exception of such division as may be ordered to pursue.

No success or retreat of the enemy must precipitate men into a pursuit, which from ambuscades or their scattered state may terminate in disaster.

Officers will be the best judges whether pursuit is necessary ; or whether such hazards are to be encountered as are exceptions to prescribed rules of warfare.

Having thus given an outline of the most important duties to be observed by those who may first land, the commanding officer assures the officers and men who cannot be mounted that he will make every possible effort to obtain horses for them : but in the interim he hopes and expects that they will zealously execute every service required of them, however unusual to their habits or however laborious. A soldier should feel a pride in contributing to the general success in any way that his commander may think essential; and the men may be assured that their officers will emulously share their fatigues as well as their dangers.—R. W.

———

The nature of the service on which we are to be employed will probably oblige me to divide frequently the small force we can at present calculate upon landing. In the first instance we are to make an effort, that may increase our force by the acquirement of horses and afford much aid to the army by the obtaining of draught bullocks. Independently of an able cavalry that we have perhaps to encounter, we labour under the disadvantage of presenting ourselves to the inhabitants for the first time with the intention of taking from them so valuable a portion of their effects. The established repute of British integrity will, however, allay their apprehensions of total loss, if by soothing treatment they feel assured that we come not upon them as freebooters : it is therefore an object of the highest importance to satisfy their minds, and if we cannot gain their active goodwill leave at all events a favourable impression of our conduct. Such officers as are detached will have with them blank receipts called *bonds* signed and sealed by myself; which they will fill up according to the number of cattle taken away, and leave with the proprietor : or if he should have fled, they will affix the other paper which will be given to them in some conspicuous part of his house. Cattle when brought away must be delivered up to the first post of infantry : a receipt from the officer should be required, and the officer commanding the cavalry, if there should be time, ought to have the beasts marked so as to know to what farm they belonged. Horses when obtained may be mounted by the party that obtained them if better than their own ; provided there is no danger or pernicious delay in making the exchange : but the supernumerary horses must be sent with all expedition to the dragoon depôt, or, if the detachment should be pressed for men, given up to the first infantry post, with orders that they be forwarded to the depôt.   If the detachment should be divided so as to occupy several farms at the same time, officers commanding each must regulate their movements for the general safety of the whole: taking care to keep up all possible communication and prevent any sudden irruption of the enemy, who are always to be expected.

But it must be impressed on the minds of all that on this service horses and cattle are our chief object; and that from this they are not to be diverted by false notions of engaging with an enemy unnecessarily, when we may weaken instead of augmenting our force: but this is not to prevent any enterprise that is justified by the hope of eminent advantage, or of impressing on the enemy a respect for the cavalry force acting against them.

At night combination of movement is difficult; but if any division is necessary the greatest caution, vigilance and silence are requisite: if attacked the greatest resolution and impetuosity, without regard to disparity of numbers.

Above all things a false alarm should be avoided, and any hint of insecurity.   A handful of men must be prepared to front any way, and can only hope for safety in extraordinary energy directed by able conduct.   You have with you many accustomed to service and fire, therefore you have no cause to apprehend any panic striking upon them; and be assured that if officers will only lead, such men will always follow: I can entertain no doubt on this head.

If orders cannot be issued to all detachments, officers commanding must act according to their own judgment.   Every detachment must move with an advanced and rear-guard and with flankers when possible; and have an established rendezvous in case of dispersion.

Examples must be made of all men who dismount to go into houses for drink, or who plunder any article; also those who manifest any licentiousness or neglect of discipline are to be dismounted and sent to the depôt.   The safety and credit of all is blended with the conduct of each individual.

When moving in front of the line to protect the infantry from the enemy's skirmishers, officers must not only keep their eyes towards the enemy but observe the directing divisions. As there may not be time to send orders, the commanding officer of the line of skirmishers and divisions must seize the idea of the operation intended whether from choice or necessity, and conform accordingly. If the commanding officer of the 20th should suddenly advance with any division to cut off any of the enemy's advanced parties, the other divisions must act to support him or secure his retreat according to their ideas of what is requisite : unless the signal for the whole to advance is sounded.

If the enemy should endeavour to cut off any of our parties the same judgment must be exercised. But above all things the safety of the gun attached to us must interest all, and no effort be withheld that can avert the disgrace of its loss. If an opportunity offers to seize an enemy's gun the moment must not be lost : a gun can but fire twice before cavalry should reach it, and its execution is seldom of any consequence.

If a man is wounded so badly as to be obliged to leave the field, a comrade in cases of absolute necessity may accompany him; but that man must return so soon as he has procured for him any surgical aid. I shall from time to time add such further remarks for your direction as our situation may require : and I feel confident that I shall have to thank officers as well as men for the support which they afforded me in every branch of the proposed duty both as to preparation and actual service : and that their conduct in the field will be distinguished for intelligence as well as courage.

THE commanding officer hopes that the officers of the 20th Light Dragoons, feeling those sentiments which should influence all military men when the reputation of their service and the interests of their country are at the hazard, will seek every opportunity to promote the success of the present expedition. They may give efficacious assistance by their example, by animating their men with zeal, and displaying an activity which may shame the most indolent and indifferent into exertion.

Those officers who cannot be mounted in the first instance may be called upon with the dismounted men to assist on other duties; which, although not immediately within the limits of their own service, are nevertheless essential when a more useful application of the force cannot be proposed. Zeal on such an occasion must insure a proper estimation, and will afford the best proof of the British cavalry's disposition to give the most effectual aid to the general service of the army. The commanding officer will make every possible effort to procure the means of mounting the whole, and he has not anticipated the possibility of a failure. He trusts that the dismounted captains will be actuated by a regard for the general interests of their regiment; and pay as much attention to the welfare, efficacy, and comfort of the attached men as to those of their own troops; and that they will co-operate with the major in disembarking the detachment in as great strength as possible. Every man must be landed that is not disabled by positive sickness; no dragoons must be retained in the service of officers as servants, nor at the mess interfere in the smallest degree with the efficiency of the mounted or dismounted detachment; nor must any servant appear here or hereafter, when out of England, in private clothes. No officer must land with more baggage than he can carry on his own horse: for dragoons are positively forbidden to take any of their officers' baggage on their horses.

Officers must disembark and land their men without confusion or injury to their appointments. Without regularity there can be no hope of a creditable appearance or satisfactory progress.

The commanding officer hopes that between this and the day of landing the most assiduous attention will be paid to fulfil all orders on that subject; that the major will supply all such as may have been omitted; and that captains will particularly regard the settlement of their books up to the 24th of this month, with the issue of the money as already ordered.

No. 5.

SIR ROBERT WILSON TO LORD HUTCHINSON.

Cape Town, January 11th, 1806.

MY DEAR LORD,

I DO not know whether I ought to accuse destiny : but no
man has experienced more the caprices of fortune than myself.
We made the land on the 3rd, and anchored on the 4th.
I was in the boats with my detachment—the 38th and 39th—
to land in the morning of the 5th; had rowed seven miles,
and approached the shore within three hundred yards, when
the surf was declared to be too great for the attempt. In
the afternoon Sir David Baird and Sir Home determined
upon carrying the army to Saldanha Bay; and General
Beresford with the 38th and the dragoons was sent to form
an advanced guard, and secure the first post where water was
to be obtained. The same night the surf lulled, and the
commodore proposed another attempt in the Lospard's Bay,
distant five miles from the former proposed place : it was a
much more eligible shore, since the first was surmounted by
a steep hill so that the gun-boats could command nothing
but the beach. General Ferguson was sent to reconnoitre
the surf as there was then much doubt as to the possibility of
debarkation : he daringly hoisted the signal " affirmative."
The boats pushed off and a footing was gained with the loss
of about fifty men swamped in one launch. The gun-brigs
dispersed the Hottentots and gazers who were stationed to
protect the landing-place, and only a few men were killed or
wounded on either side. On the 7th the army was landing.
On the 8th they marched in battle array, a single line *without
reserve*. When they ascended Blueberg Hill the Dutch
line—composed of about fifteen hundred regular infantry,
five hundred French sailors employed as infantry, two hundred regular dragoons, and seven hundred burgher and boor
cavalry, with twenty-four pieces of cannon—were seen *at the
base* of the hill: a position taken up by General Janssen for
the better effect of his artillery. No sooner did the British
line crown the height than the guns opened and killed or
wounded about sixty men of the 31st. Our guns drawn by

sailors also fired; but Sir David Baird ordered the Scotch brigade to charge. They gave three huzzas; the Dutch answered with nine. Colonel Grant was wounded. As the Highlanders moved on he got off his horse but mounted again, and a general burst of applause broke from the Scotch line at his determined gallantry. When they had advanced within a hundred yards they fired a volley and rushed on; but as the smoke dispersed the Dutch army was seen in full retreat, leaving behind three pieces of cannon. It was at this moment that a few dragoons might on either side have decided the fate of the day in a brilliant success. The English were exhausted by their efforts and from want of water, and by the sun burning with torrid heat on a white sand. The Dutch were exposed to equal disaster and must have lost all their artillery. The Dutch cavalry behaved like dastards. *The British were not there.* The only consolation I have is that if present we might not have answered expectation; and now our absence excites the deepest regret for presumed loss of gallant service: yet I should be unjust to doubt the merit of the small but meritorious detachment that were mounted. On the right the 59th secured the sand-hills, and a company of the 24th in advance suffered severely from some sharpshooters; but were chiefly opposed to the Waldeck Regiment who would not fire against our battalions. The Scotch brigade has certainly acquired great honour not more for their courage than for their steady discipline: so good was their spirit that no wounded man that could serve left the ranks: and after the action when a wounded French officer offered his watch as a recompence for conveying him to the hospital they *actually* refused the donation. The same day General Janssen retired towards Hottentot Holland's kloof, taking with him eleven hundred infantry, all his cavalry and light artillery, with an immense quantity of cattle, &c. The day after, the town offered to capitulate; and we took possession yesterday in *Asiatic pomp* of victory. In the action the English lost about two hundred men: the Dutch certainly above three, for the musketry was admirably directed. The French battalion suffered most and fled soonest, for all their officers except one were killed or wounded. The Waldeckers unfortunately lost also many men. Their conduct so exasperated the Dutch general that he struck the major, and shot one man with his pistol through the head. On their return into the town he broke the regiment and the night before last gave as the watchword to his troops, " The Waldeckers are dishonoured." But he forgets that the French had sold many of them, and that the Dutch governor had violated their capitulation as to pay in the most shameful manner; or he would not be surprised at their desire to change masters.

&c., &c., &c.

Believe me, my dear Lord,

Most sincerely and gratefully yours,

R. WILSON.

No. 6.

MEMORANDUM OF S. SALVADOR, OR BAHIA, 1805.

THE view of this bay after shooting from the eastward round the rocky promontory on which the fortress S. Antonio is situated is perhaps the most magnificent in the world.

On the right the land covered with wood rises to a great height. Among the woods appear the towers of various monasteries and the white stone walls of extensive edifices: while the shore, indented with numerous small bays, is studded round with the most picturesquely irregular villages. At some distance in the bay, and still on the right hand, the city crowns a lofty mountain and covers the base and sides with its streets.

Some low land richly wooded, apparently luxuriantly fertile, and which receives the most beautiful tints from a sky of far more than Italian splendour and hue, projects in an oblique direction: while the lofty and broken mountains of the island des Fradres stretch across the bay, and form the head in connexion with the island of Taparica, which constitutes the left boundary of this common basin.

Sandbanks confine the roadstead : but the channel is safe and the anchoring ground good. Men-of-war may ride within a few hundred yards of the town, and boats proceeding to the shore land anywhere in safety.

The fortifications which should defend the bay are insignificant, but the Portuguese are working at several batteries to command the roadstead near the town.   These, if well executed, may effect that object.

Opposite the arsenal a fort is advanced about a hundred and fifty yards into the water; but the guns are too much exposed, and ships of war might approach within pistol-shot. On the right of the town, and on the table land of the mountain, stands the citadel: a feeble work: ill situated, as it but very partially commands the city or any important line of communication.   The garrison, however, consisting of three regular regiments is in excellent order.   The uniformity of the troops, their equipment, cleanly appearance, steadiness under arms, and regularity in the execution of their duty would do credit to any service: and the inspection of their barracks has astonished the British officers who have been in Portugal and Madeira, and who did not expect to see such a contrast between the colonial troops and those of the mother country.

These regiments are never removed into Europe.   The officers exchange when they wish to retire from America: but the privates, satisfied with better pay, attached by marriage or connection to the soil, and inured to the climate, seldom seek to revisit Portugal where they can neither possess the same comforts nor the same consideration.

The militia force, consisting of about three thousand men, is well organized, but the officers and privates are not in favour with the military or the populace.   There is no cavalry; although all the inhabitants coming from the interior are good horsemen and ride good horses.

At the base of the S. Salvador mountain extends a line of streets about one mile and a half in length.   The houses are lofty, the streets narrow and wretchedly paved.   Several market-places branch out of this line towards the bay, and Billingsgate may on every account be jealous of a S. Salvador rival.

In the streets above noticed shops are to be seen, (if the sneezing passenger can open his eyes, for the atmosphere is full of pounding snuff), crowded with the multifarious articles supplied from England as well as with those of native produce. There is no tavern, and but one or two regular coffeehouses. The apothecaries' shops, which are numerous, constitute the places of rendezvous for those who wish to drink sangaree and play at draughts or backgammon. There are two buildings like London Exeter Change where trinkets and wares of all kinds are exposed for sale; and where British cutlery, &c., may be purchased cheaper than in England.

Topazes, sapphires, &c., are prohibited articles of sale; but they are to be purchased. Counterfeits however are most common.

Innumerable monkeys, parrots and parroquets amuse the stranger: and the exposed right breasts of the black women also engage his attention from the novelty of the spectacle. But if he has common civilized sensibilities he must feel disgust at the groups of black slaves of both sexes and all ages exposed for sale: while the mournful song of the blacks charged with their oppressive burdens pierces to the heart with its doleful tones.

Most of the black men are of uncommonly large stature, particularly those employed in carrying the sugar hogsheads. Their labour is excessive; and it is scarcely possible to imagine a more distressing toil than the carriage of one of these huge sugar casks up the mountain in a heat of ninety-eight degrees.

A stream of perspiration flows down the backs of the negroes: while the entwinement of arms round each other's necks, to form a rest for the bar on which the cask is slung, occasions a steam of heat around them that seems to threaten suffocation.

The government have enacted laws for the protection of these unfortunate people from the tyranny of brutal masters: but the thumb-screw, and the whip made of five thongs of a dried bull's hide, are notwithstanding cruelly exercised. Interest alone checks the full satiety of savage feeling. In some cases even sex can excite no pity.

Between seven and eight thousand of these blacks are annually imported into S. Salvador: for the mortality among the slaves is very great from bad treatment and careless arrangement.

The upper town is a more regular series and mass of building, and more order is preserved in the streets. There are several large open squares in one of which stands the governor's house—a great edifice without distinctive architecture or interior ornament. The rooms are spacious, and appear from some gold and silk remnants to have been once suitably furnished. There is an opera house open on all religious and civil festivals. The singing was very inferior, and there was no ballet from want of dancers. Most of the ladies present wore masks, or wound a white handkerchief round their mouths and throats, which produced an effect very disagreeable to the European eye.

Those ladies who had not boxes sat in what would be termed in England one shilling slips, from which all males are excluded. In general the ladies of high fashion do not frequent the opera.

The monasteries are very large and superbly decorated, but except in the Italian monastery there is scarcely a monk who knows any language but his own : and few even there know more of Latin than is contained in their pater-noster.

The Brazilian Portuguese experience no encouragement from their government. No native is allowed to hold any public office : their habits are thus confirmed in that indolence which the climate invites. They lounge in their cabriolets drawn by two mules, or are carried in their palanquins ; but they never adventure on any pedestrian exercise. An umbrella guards their complexion from the sun's rays in their passage to and from the doors of the houses they enter : and thus they languish through life in a state of quiescence almost amounting to torpor.

The European Portuguese functionary is a different being. He hopes to revisit Europe, and he protects his health without extinguishing his powers of energy.

The white population is very scanty.* The Portuguese

---

* Not above 200,000; while there are half a million of blacks. The length of the Brazils is about 2,500 miles and in some parts its extreme breadth is nearly as much. In this immense range climate varies much ; but in general

government is afraid of encouraging a colony which in a few years might disengage itself from all dependent connexion; of which design some symptoms have excited suspicion.

The principal produce of the colony is sugar. In a district of ten leagues circumference round the city it is said that there are five hundred mills: but the principal mills are situated in the districts of Cachoeira, Cobalto, S. Amar, and S. Maura. In some of these mills three hundred horses are employed.

Coffee is very scarce, rice abundant. No corn of any kind is grown, so that the horses are obliged to eat the sugar cane, plantain and grass, and occasionally cassada with molasses.

A good red wine is made in S. Salvador, and fruit of all kinds abounds. Poultry and oxen are plentiful, but mutton is scarce and not good: the fish market is supplied with an extraordinary variety of fish.

The country round the town is scarcely to be described. Nature here displays a scenery too gorgeous for adequate delineation. The splendour of the firmament by night and day, the beauty and vastness of the foliage, the gigantic features of the landscape, at all events require far more than common powers of language to bring them before the mind of the reader with pictorial fidelity. Few towns have such a commanding site or a grander outline. "Man—man alone dwindles here," from the want of proper political institutions.

At the base of the San Salvador mountain to the northward, a large body of water completes a view scarcely to be paralleled in the world.

The island of Taparica admits only of the anchorage of small vessels near its shores. A bar, very perceptible at low water, stretches from the entrance of the bay and forms the first barrier at about two miles distance from the beach; a reef of rocks within half a mile forms the second barrier; but neither of them reaches so far as the town of Taparica which lies at the westernmost point of the island. Poles with cocoa-nuts on them mark the channels of entrance which are

---

it may be said that the country is healthy; and it will be rendered still more so as the colonization extends.—R.W.

very narrow; and in front of each channel stands a large building erected by the whale boilers, who chiefly reside on this island.

The shore is covered with bones of whales which frequent this bay four months in the year.

Numerous detached cottages skirt the shore: and immediately behind them appears a continued forest of cocoa, mango, orange, banana, and other trees.

The white inhabitants are a peculiar class of people. They seem to possess with the comforts all the original independence of the English yeoman. Their dress, manners, and institutions are indicative of wealth and of a sense of its true value. The life of a Taparican farmer seems to glide on in ease and affluence. He appears also to merit his happiness: for the condition of the *slave* is here improved to the fullest degree that the institution permits.

The island of Taparica is sixty miles in circumference; and the most intelligent Brazilians affirm that it might produce cargoes for five hundred sail of shipping. But from the paucity of the population only a small proportion of the ground is cleared; and the export is very trifling. A small traffic is carried on by canoes that pass to the island des Fradres, and Cachoeira on the mainland. These canoes carry cocoa-nuts, pine-apples,* and other fruits to exchange against farina and rice: and S. Salvador is chiefly supplied from hence with fish carried across the bay in canoes formed of hollow trees. These frequently upset; but every inhabitant of the island of both sexes is an expert swimmer and therefore life is seldom lost.

Numerous torrents descend from the hills to fertilize the soil; which produces almost spontaneously.

The cattle are large. The horses, which are of a remarkably good race and very active, might with some attention be improved so as to remunerate export to India. Few riders are more daring than the Taparicans. With loose girths, stirrups they dare not rest upon for fear of breaking the leather, and free rein, they dart over the ridges of the

---

* The pines grow in fields like turnips in Europe, and are remarkably fine.—R. W.

rice fields, through the sugar-cane plantations, and over the most dangerously broken surface. Sometimes at full speed they twist among the cocoa-trees; where a false turn might insure the most disastrous consequences.

The town of Taparica is very small but neat; and there are several good shops. It is the only town of any importance in the island.

The morals of the inhabitants are in conformity with those of all others in climes where the sun glows and where slavery prevails. Passion and interest combine to excite and sanction unlimited indulgence: and in Taparica the human frame is so early matured by the climate that girls of twelve years of age frequently become mothers.

When a Taparican girl accepts a lover for the first time she presents a cocoa-nut to him, which her parents have suspended for some years previously for this occasion. It eats as if it were candied.

It was impossible on quitting the Brazils not to envy the possession: and the day that the fleet went to sea was perhaps the happiest in the governor's whole life; for he could not possibly divest himself of the apprehension that temptation to protract departure from a colony the most valuable in the world on account of its capabilities and position, might be irresistible: especially as *protectorates* are in fashion.

The East India Company has reason to wish that into whatever hands the Brazils may fall in these variable times they may continue inert: for the *terræ situs* would offer many anxious subjects for their consideration if an impulse were given to their powers of action and expansion.

No. 7.

Memorandum of Madeira, 1805.

On a course of south-west from Cork the small island of Porto Santo, flanked by lofty rocks called the Desertas, is first discovered in long. 17° 6′ W. lat. 32° 37′ N.

Porto Santo is habitable and has several harbours affording security to shipping except against strong southerly winds.

The soil produces corn, wine, oil, fruits, &c.

At the distance of about twenty miles, in the direction of east and west, rises the island of Madeira with a very lofty and abrupt elevation. The mountain appears to be about seven miles in ascent: but the capping clouds obscure its summit from distant observation.

At the base of the mountain and in a recess not sufficiently indented to form a port is situated the town of Funchal, built of white stone. It is the capital of the island, and the only town of any consequence.

From the roads the appearance of the island is picturesque, but the mountain, though covered with cottages, monasteries, and country houses, has a naked aspect from the want of verdure. A monastery half-way up the mountain and situated in the midst of a thick dark-green wood presents a pleasing exception to the generally barren features.

On the right of the town, and separated from the mainland about fifty yards, a rock about forty yards in height rises boldly from the sea. On the summit of this rock a fort has been erected of very insignificant strength.

The abutment of the mainland is of equal height and is crowned by another fort. This abutment perhaps should be described as another rock; since a ridge of low rocks connects it with the mountain: the Portuguese have constructed a causeway of about sixty yards in length to secure the communication. This fort is called the Loo: and here is to be found the only secure cove for boats; in which also very small vessels may anchor without risk.

The roadstead being in every part of the shore forty fathoms deep, and generally sixty, the surf falls so heavily on the beach that the island boats alone insure convenient or even safe debarkation. Ships' boats are constantly swamped and almost always half-filled with water: and in every state of the weather and of the surf the boats must be directed stern foremost to the shore. By going round to the Loo cove these hazards would be avoided: but the circuit is generally thought too tedious.

As it was found that even the island boats could not at all times approach the beach to take their cargoes on board and carry them off to the ships, the merchants subscribed for the erection of a very lofty brick column on which a crane was fixed to project beyond the surf. But the experiment did not succeed: and the column remains, a monument of the un-accomplished design.

A rock about sixty yards high, in the centre of the town, has afforded the Portuguese a good position for a citadel. This commands the roadstead also ; but a battery on the left of the town, a little elevated above the water's edge, is still better calculated to protect the anchoring ground.

From the base of the fort called the Loo stairs convenient for ascent are hewn in the rock : and a narrow path about a mile long leads to the town. This path is paved with very slippery stones, and is altogether dangerous and painful to the passenger. The devastations of the torrent, which in 1804 washed into the sea eight hundred persons, and over-whelmed whole streets, increase the inconvenience of the communications : and the open doors of an *admonitory* hospital, whose wretched tenants have not lost the appetite of curiosity or acquired a sense of shame, render the view extremely dis-gusting and loathsome.

The French hotel is the first house to which passengers arriving in the town from the Loo are conducted. The rooms are airy and spacious, with windows which command a view of the roadstead. The apartments may also be called clean : but the most extravagant prices are demanded for their use and for general accommodation. An Englishman keeps an inn in the centre of the town where the charges are more moderate ; but the locale is not so good. The town of Funchal consists of narrow streets, replete with filth notwith-standing that a stream of water runs through the centre of each street.

There is an abundance of shops filled with every species of commodity, and an extensive vegetable and fruit market crowded with pumpkins, tomatoes, bananas, cucumbers, chilis, grapes, &c.: but none of the fruits are remarkably good or highly flavoured. Pigs,* casks, cooperage works, and sledges

* The wine is brought from the mountains in pigs' skins.—R. W.

drawn by oxen, fill all the streets: and Funchal is truly a
vintner's town.   There is but one open space; where there is
a pump, and an avenue planted with orange-trees leading to
the great church.   This is a large pile of building only
remarkable for some silver railing round the sanctuary.

There are several convents.   That of Santa Clara is the
most visited, as there is a novice fifteen years of age in it
whose beauty is generally admired.   This perhaps appears
more favourably when she is placed by the side of the Lady
Abbess, seventy-six years of age: on whose upper lip a pair
of moustachios has been cherished which would make an
Hungarian warrior jealous.

The sisterhood affectionately imitate the Lady Abbess's
example: and even pretty Anna Emilia's upper lip is inflamed; as if an attempt had been made by some means or
other to animate the down.

The Portuguese women in general at Madeira are not what
the world calls handsome, particularly those of the working
class; their complexions being of a putrid olive colour.   And
the perspiration stands upon the face in bubbles, like water
upon a greasy surface.

On their heads rises a high toupee of coarse grey hair:
similar in appearance and quality to the horse-hair used to
stuff common chair-bottoms.

There was once seen however, in the superior class, a young
lady coming from mass whose form and expression made
observers think " she was not of the earth on which she
stepped:" but on inquiry it was found that she was a native
of the island—like another Miranda, " the top of admiration."

The male inhabitants of the country justly merit the
description of a fine race of people.   Employed from sunrise
to sunset in descending and ascending the mountain with a
heavy burden of wine on their shoulders, and walking at the
rate of five miles an hour, their muscles have acquired an
Herculean texture.   The burning rays of the mid-day sun
cause them no lassitude: the new wine or the fresh pressed
juice of the grape afflicts them with no malady.

For each load the carrier receives sixpence: and although
these loads are brought from great distances each individual

earns on an average three shillings and sixpence a day and sometimes four shillings.

The English merchants who reside here have country houses distant two or three miles up the mountain: for a continual residence in the town is from heat, stench, and noise insufferable. The walks to these houses have along the whole way a canopy of vines, and the *treillage* is lined with the most fragrant productions of the vegetable kingdom.

The house of Mr. Murdock is the most distinguished. The gardens are tastefully laid out, and with taste great comfort is combined. In this garden are also some of the highest flavoured grapes, pines, &c. But in general fruit is not much cultivated nor is the high condition and quality of the grape such an object of attention as might be expected: for every species is pressed in the same vat; with the single exception of the black Madeira grape lately introduced.

About forty thousand pipes of wine are made annually and the revenue collected by the government is considerable: while the merchants in many cases make large fortunes, and one—a Portuguese—is said to have amassed property to the amount of 10,000*l.* per annum.

If the Dutch would only undertake to be the scavengers of Madeira for ten years there would not be a more delightful spot for residence in the temperate zone. The soil, which it is said is formed or enriched by the ashes of a forest that covered the island and which accidentally taking fire burnt for several years consecutively, is capable of yielding every requisite produce: and the climate on an average is no more and no less than from seventy to seventy-five degrees.

No. 8.

MEMORANDUM OF ST. HELENA, 1806.

An exhausted volcano with a partial verdure which tempts settlers to encounter one of the most unhealthy and dank climates in the world. Passengers, however, notwithstanding that they pay at the lowest charge one guinea per day for frugal board and a bedroom, and half a guinea per day for a servant, eagerly seek refreshment here: and the governor's residence called Plantation House is from culture and surrounding foliage, but perhaps more from the agreeable character of the governor's family, a very fascinating abode. When it is remembered that this island is 1,200 miles distant from the nearest land, melancholy thoughts intrude: " and the waves which roll a girdle round:" " pelagi—urgentibus undis:" seem to be walls of exclusion from the habitable world.

The island is about 11 miles long and 7 broad: so small a feature indeed in the immense surrounding ocean, that East India ships have heretofore cruized as it is said in vain to find it notwithstanding that the pilot pigeons were seen ;* and after many days' search, have recorded in their log-books, " St. Helena sunk." Once missed, six weeks may be required to regain the position; as the trade wind blows with great strength.

The arrival of a fleet causes great sensation. It is the harvest season of all the inhabitants, and there is a satirical song which, denoting the effect of the welcome intelligence, commences by the words:—

> " Hark ! I hear the signal gun :
> Molly, put your stockings on."

There are those who say that in good truth hose is never worn by the females except on those occasions.

The island is well defended. There are guns the carriages of which are remarkable for depressing construction which enables shot to be fired with great precision: but stones or balls dropped down would be equally fatal ; as the precipices under which landing is practicable are almost perpendicular.

St. Helena is in long. 15° 55′ S.; lat. 5° 49′ W.

---

* Pigeons in pairs are always on the look-out about sixty miles from the island, and before it can be seen.—R. W.

No. 9.

CAPE OF GOOD HOPE.

THERE is little doubt that at some remote period, the mountains which now constitute the headlands of the promontory of Africa called since the discovery of the passage to India "The Cape of Good Hope" and previously "The Cape of All Plagues," were divided from the continent by a strait of the ocean; which rolled at the base of a lofty coast, distant about forty miles and now connected with the Cape mountains by a plain of sandy soil.

The receded waters do not appear disposed to encroach again upon the abandoned tract which Batavian industry was not, as in Europe, excited to recover from their dominion. And yet they do not suffer their right of occupancy to lapse from unsupported claims: for in the winter season they cover a part of the plain near Muyssenberg; though not to such a depth as to prevent the passage of cattle, or to render the ordinary communication of the inhabitants precarious.

The "Table Mountain" is the most remarkable of those which compose the headland. It rises above Cape Town to the height of about 3,600 feet :* but notwithstanding that the elevation is so considerable and the declivity very abrupt, no feeling of awe is inspired by the contemplation of its altitude. From the peculiar conformation of the ground, and perhaps from the conditions of the atmosphere, there is an absence of that "fearful majesty" which is generally associated with mountain sublimity.

The "Sugar Loaf," or "Devil's Peak," is contiguous, and rises to the height of about 3,000 feet. This mountain was probably once united with the Table Mountain nearer to their respective summits: but the torrents have separated their connection, and threaten to prostrate the lofty honours of the former; as they are sweeping through numerous channels and fretting their ruinous passages by vast and increasing fissures.

---

* Some of the mountains of the colony are 10,000 feet above the level of the sea. —R. W.

The " Lion's Rump " continues and completes the chain in the north-west direction : and an active imagination will trace in the shape of this mountain the idea of its name.

The shore round the headlands from the Lion's Rump to " Simon's Town " is steep ; and admits but of such difficult communication, that until lately the passage was deemed impracticable for a horse and dangerous for a foot-passenger.

" Table Bay " is formed by the point of land projecting from the Lion's Rump, by " Robben Island " distant about nine miles, and by a curving coast. From the month of November to May ships may ride here in perfect safety: indeed for the last three years the season has been so mild that the vessels have remained much longer without experiencing any hazard. And at the beginning of this war a large ship detained by the Dutch stood at her anchorage with a very bad cable through the whole winter.

When the south wind blows very strong * communication between the vessels and the shore may for a few hours be difficult. But even this interruption may be avoided by anchoring near to the town : since frequently a heavy gale of wind is blowing at the distance of a mile from the shore, when within this line there is mild weather and smooth water.

When Table Bay ceases to be considered a safe station, the ships proceed round to " Simon's Bay " in the Bay of " False." A navigation extremely uncertain : as the passage is sometimes effected in a few hours; and as frequently vessels are beating for three weeks, having not only to combat an adverse wind, but in that case a head-sea of almost unparalleled ferocity.

In Simon's Bay there is secure shelter : but the entrance is somewhat hazardous on account of the rocks ; on which the *Trident* man-of-war and *Colville* East-Indiaman were lost some years since.

Simon's Bay is, however, far from a convenient station for the conduct of the necessary communication between the shipping, and Cape Town distant four-and-twenty miles. Two-thirds of the way, and particularly the first nine miles,

* It generally blows six months in the year : and for six months not only rain, but sheets of water fall from the clouds.—R. W.

are almost too bad to admit of traverse: carriage is therefore tedious, and extravagantly expensive.

Decent accommodation may indeed be had at Simon's Town: which is more properly a row of houses erected at the foot of high and rocky mountains. There is sufficient ground to form a quay: but as there is not in the neighbourhood any land that can be cultivated, even for garden produce, the provisions brought from the interior bear a high price.

False Bay and Table Bay are the only roadsteads that are frequented by shipping: for, although there are several other small bays on the coast of the Cape, vessels never use them except from necessity. However, as they are practicable points of debarkation, they are interesting features in military surveys.

Between Simon's Town and Cape Town are two villages, or military posts, which afford refreshment to travellers. The first is Muyssenberg, distant nine miles over a track formed upon the rocky ridge of very high mountains; except where it traverses these sandy bays from the uppermost part of which the sea has retired. This track is so narrow that only one waggon can pass at any time: and the unequalled skill of a Hottentot driver is necessary, to conduct it in safety through the intricate paths and over the massive fragments fallen from the overhanging cliffs; which fragments have been driven by their weight and impetus many feet into the ground.

Muyssenberg is a pass formed by the near approach of a high mountain to the sea, which rolls at the base with a heavy surge.

From Muyssenberg to Weinberg, seven miles, the road passes through a deep sand, partly covered with heath. A very good inn distinguishes this station: and at some little distance huts are erected as barracks for seven hundred soldiers.

From Weinberg the road branches through Constantia, where the wine of that name is made, to Hout Bay; and this narrow slip of country is well wooded and picturesque. Another road leads to Cape Town, distant eight miles; of which road the first five miles present a view particularly pleasing, in a country whose general features are nakedness and desolation. On each side are the decorations of luxuriant plantations and rich verdure : while handsome public buildings designed with taste, and houses less stately but not less graceful, recall to the European the most pleasing scenery of his own hemisphere. The last three miles are divested of every charm, but the interest of approaching Cape Town as a relief from a wearisome journey.

A barrier-line of works, advanced half a mile but not sufficiently forward for military defence, and extending from the sea to the mountains, covers the site, and no more, of the town. From this point the traveller can see only a crescent of black hills, the ocean, a mass of flat-roofed white houses like those which children build with cards, and an old fort called the Castle. As he proceeds his eye falls upon no enlivening object ; and finally the angle of the fort intercepts even the traces of habitation which he had discovered ; with the exception of a great building full of windows and surrounded by a wall, which he may imagine either a barrack or a hospital. As soon, however, as he has passed this projection, in proportion as the spirits were depressed and the fancy disappointed, the breaking prospect will raise and cheer them : smiling as it is, and robed in magnificence. Instantly the traveller will be moved to admire a noble parade of considerable extent, planted with oaks, handsomely ornamented with masonry, and flanked by elegant houses with various-coloured frontages. His eye will range over the castle and the barracks : in advance of which is a large square, and further on numerous streets branching from the parades and regularly communicating at right angles with other streets. Nothing offends the eye : and if the whole design be not yet completed, it is so marked in outline that the effect is almost equally pleasing.

Nor does a more particular examination of the town diminish the force of his first impression : on the contrary, the observer will find increasing cause for admiration as he passes through the different streets, and sees that there is not one tenement which he can designate as the dwelling of want. The meanest houses are superior to those of decently conditioned persons in Europe, and are erected upon a uniform plan. The houses of the more wealthy are built upon a scale that few cities of Europe can vie with; and Holland alone can pretend to rival the neatness of the interior, and the cleanliness of the household arrangements.

The public buildings of Cape Town are not indeed remarkable. Had the Dutch government continued there would have been built a hall of justice, a granary, and a prison, after the best architectural models: but the execution is now problematical, as the English establishments already consume more than the whole revenue of the colony without the appropriation of any part to public improvements.

The government house is large and commodious. It is distinguished also for a handsome and safe staircase: an object totally neglected by the African builders, who first finish the apartments and then drop a perpendicular flight of stairs through the darkest corners of the chambers. But the chief ornament of the government residence is the garden: a space of ground a quarter of a mile in breadth and nearly half a mile in length, at the further extremity of which are two considerable menageries, wherein the wild tenants have sufficient room for exercise. Through the centre of the garden is a fine gravel walk, planted on each side with lofty trees; and other lateral walks (covered by the skilful direction of the branches, and with a foliage impenetrable to the sun) which offer an agreeable shade. These, however, are held consecrated as Cyprian groves, and therefore are not publicly frequented: so that the promenade of the inhabitants is confined to the principal walk, where every evening bands of military music take their station.

The admiralty house is small and not suitable to the rank of the inhabitant: but the locale is convenient as being immediately contiguous to the dockyard. The castle is a handsome model of ancient fortification against rude assailants: it contains large barracks and a house wherein the commandant and other officers reside. The timber of the castle was, as it is said, cut from the woods that formerly covered Table Hill, where now a growing stick is not to be found.

The theatre is neat, but theatrical representations have been rare. An attempt was lately made to substitute concerts: but neither the Dutch nor the English gave much encouragement to scientific musical professors. A common fiddle, accompanied with a pipe and tabor, fascinated them more than the exquisite skill of several celebrated amateurs who kindly endeavoured to improve their tastes.

The company indeed assembled to hear their performances: but it was on the assurance that their gloomy attention would be recompensed by a gay afterpiece. For if a dance had not always been promised as an allurement, the musicians, notwithstanding their merits, would have been left to express their own raptures and applaud their own skill and execution.

The town house is ancient but not ornamental. The library has excellent dimensions: but alas! the shelves contain only Dutch treatises on disputed points of law and polemical divinity.

The prison house is small and the external appearance reproaches the humanity of the government. At present it is woefully crowded: and such is stated to be the difficulty of administering justice in this extensive colony, that several prisoners are in confinement who have been detained for three years without any trial whatsoever. All criminal matter must be adjudged at Cape Town: and every one will approve the rule that the sword of justice shall never be placed in hands that are not capable of poising the balance. But as this procrastination is so great an outrage, some immediate measures should be adopted to correct an injurious system of delay, tantamount to denial of justice.

There is another evil in the arrangement of this prison which can exist only from culpable inattention to the unfortunate; and which might be in a moment abolished. The debtors are now confined in the same yard with the most atrocious felons. Nay, the criminal condemned to die for murder is lodged in the same, or in an adjoining, room with those who have only been the victims of misfortune or indiscretion: whilst the families of these latter are obliged when they visit their relatives to pass through the wretched hovel; to expose themselves to rude gaze and vulgar mirth; and to feel the additional misery of knowing that the objects of their affectionate anxiety are doomed to pass their whole time in the pestilence of such an association.

The slave house is a large building where 250 slaves belonging to government are lodged. I only notice this edifice in order to express detestation of the system, and to urge immediate improvement; since none of the present arrangements are calculated to promote the health and comfort of the slaves. This is the more reprehensible in a colony where the general treatment of the slave is most praiseworthy.

There are two churches of very considerable size, which are well attended. Although these belong to different persuasions religion is not disgraced by any animosity; and the clergymen who officiate are men of exemplary good character.

Amongst the chief private houses is an hotel on the Grand Parade kept by an Englishman. Here the principal officers of the garrison have established a club, to which every captain of the navy on the station belongs as an honorary member: and the Cape Expedition will be ever remembered by the military composing that force, as one where mischievous prejudices which might have injured the public service were rejected at the outset: also as one where the most friendly intercourse was unceasingly maintained between the services.

In the Heer Grasse is a subscription society consisting promiscuously of the garrison and inhabitants. Here the assemblies are given. They are much frequented; for dancing is an accomplishment of which the Cape young people are passionately fond, and in which they eminently excel.

Previously to the late arrival of the English almost every house appeared to be that of a private gentleman. The stranger would be much perplexed to discover from what quarter the wants of families were supplied, and how the establishment of such good houses could be maintained without any apparent source of income; since every one must be aware that Europeans who had independent fortunes would never traverse the ocean to reside in an African colony. But the excellence of the houses is the cause, not the consequence, of wealth. With very few exceptions every householder takes in lodgers and provides board either by the year, month, week, or day. Nor does this occupation affect in any degree their pretensions to association with those few who, by the bounty of Providence or the industry of their forefathers, are enabled to live upon the interest of their property.

Decency of manners and decorum of conduct alone distinguish classes in this community. All white people are esteemed equal. They consider that aristocratical constitutions are but official distinctions; calculated to maintain order, but not intended to divide mankind; that virtues or vices exalt or degrade men; that social qualities or unfriendly dispositions, similarity or dissimilarity of manners and habits, invite or forbid intercourse. The man, not the title, is the object of their consideration. The stranger who pays is treated as a guest and, although entertained with respect, finds himself surrounded by companions who are not discomposed by the presence of a superior nor inattentive to the courtesies of good breeding due to a reputed inferior. Their principle of action is mutual accommodation: and the proudest foreigner must be satisfied to contract with them upon the terms of mutual civility. His self-importance will never be exposed to an offensive shock if he adheres to these conditions; but his vanity will never be gratified by servile obsequiousness. England has already introduced the financial establishments of a kingdom into this colony; but she would do quite wrong were she to revolutionize the society: and those English of both sexes who proceed there should bear in mind that any contemptuous treatment of these honest people, now fellow-subjects, on account of their simplicity of habits and principles of equality, would be far from honourable to their own feelings or advantageous to the interests of their country.

Public auctions supplied the articles that in Europe are at any moment to be obtained in the shops: and as a tax upon them formed a material branch of the revenue, the government encouraged this practice; which was injurious to the general interest of the people, since a few wealthy persons monopolized the articles most wanted, and bought them in until a price set by extortion was offered. It is to be hoped that the present government may sacrifice the advantage of this mode of traffic ; and make such regulations respecting auctions as will enable the inhabitants to buy on fairer terms. By this means the consumption will be extended, and the value of increased exports to England may be checked against the diminution of colonial revenue.

The number of slaves in the service of each family is a cause of some surprise: and particularly as there are so many women and children. This is indeed a burthen imposed upon the masters by an honourable aversion to sell those who have been born under their roof.

The history of slavery is in general a mournful recital of oppression and sufferance. But detestable as is the usage still the condition of the slave is not at the Cape Town a subject of reproach to the master. Here, and here alone perhaps in the world, are the slaves treated with a mildness that would merit the admiration of a Howard. No rigorous toil excites compassion or indignation; no melancholy plaints pierce the heart of the passenger. The little children are even caressed by their proprietors with as much kindness as if they were the offspring of relatives ; and if they be not born in freedom they are for years unconscious of their shackles. They are associated in every amusement ; they share every act of tenderness with the white children. And although the European mother prefers her own race, she would think herself unworthy to be a parent if she could neglect an infant, or not treat it with kindness because it was the offspring of a slave. This indulgent conduct towards infants born in a state of reprobation, does, surely, more honour to these people than any imitation of those refinements in other colonies that too frequently render the heart insensible to offices of humanity. But in the discharge of these duties it is not pretended that there is no exception: that the lash never scores at the caprice of ill temper, and the sweat never pours in the service of a tyrant. Such cases must exist. The power that bad men have to be cruel is an insuperable argument against all slavery: but it is gratifying to reflect that here the record of cruelty contains but few memoranda of such crimes.

Whether slavery can be immediately abolished is a reasonable subject of question; because a great interest is vested in this property, and the whole of the agriculture is conducted by that system. But although the total emancipation may be procrastinated until an act of benevolence may not be at variance with the rights of property, still few countries possess within themselves more available means of accelerating this great work of humanity.

Until the first possession of the Cape by the English, the Hottentot had ever been repudiated as a being that dishonoured the human species; a heathen, incapable of civilization and of the practice of moral duties. The name was a term of reproach: and the naturalist, ashamed of his affinity to man, endeavoured to class him amongst the vilest of brutes. Sir James Craig first tried the experiment of his human qualities. He invited some hundreds of these people into the British service. He incorporated them into a battalion under the command of Major Campbell, whose judicious and amiable conduct justified the selection. After some months' experience, these reprobated Hottentots were found and pronounced to be a race of gentle and inoffensive manners, capable from physical energies of any bodily service, and possessing the ordinary mental gifts of mankind. Thus rescued from opprobrium and misery they have maintained the character so early relied upon; and their conduct has never ceased to do credit to the discrimination of their protectors and benefactors.

When the English restored the Cape to Holland, General Janssen continued the Hottentots on the military establishment. Their docility gained his esteem, and their military attainments his confidence. In the day of combat they did not forfeit, as soldiers, his good opinion: and when the fortune of war obliged that general to retire into the mountains, where he was suffering, with the remains of his feeble force, severe privations and extreme inclemency of weather; when it was believed by the corps that the general had resolved to continue the most desperate warfare; when Europeans were hourly deserting from their standard; not one single Hottentot was seduced from the fear of disastrous service or tempted by the rewards of the victor to violate the fidelity he had pledged. Patriotism could have no operation; with oaths they were unacquainted; enmity against the English was not in their hearts. Innate honesty and honourable principle were the guardians of their duty: and these virtues were their inheritance from those forefathers whom the colonists had so long disdained, and whom Europeans still held in scorn if not in abhorrence.

These Hottentots then might be employed as a principal instrument to facilitate the abolition of slavery and augment the defences of the colony. By being enrolled for military service they would be assured, under the superintendence of their officers, of protection from ill usage; and by being cantoned amongst the farmers they would gradually acquire agricultural inclinations.

The wild and independent Hottentots called Bushmen, who now, scared at the toils of compulsive servitude and jealous of their freedom, prefer a precarious subsistence to the bread of bondage, and a life beset with peril to one protracted by the selfish care of a master, would discriminate between voluntary industry and the task of slavery. They would observe the comforts that compensate for the sacrifice of a vagrant liberty; and would very soon be disposed to accept an establishment where their persons might be free, their families protected, and the profits of their labour applied to their own remuneration.

The African is not so incorrigible a savage as he is generally represented. The man who loves his wife and children, eats grain, and knows the value of money, can always be taught the advantage of a tranquil state of society. The Bushmen are not ruder than our ancient Britons: and a savage state is not more essentially adapted to their mental faculties or physical temperament.

When Ali Bey ruled in Egypt the Arabs swept, with desolating hand and without apprehension, the crops and the cattle of the fertilized lands. The toil was for the peasant: theirs was the tributary harvest They not only seized enough for their necessity, but they wantoned with redundance. The victorious Ali resolved upon the protection of the helpless. He defended the flocks and the tillage with his arms. He invited the assailants to merit the productions of the earth by contributing to their growth. No longer could the Arab seize his prey with impunity. Scanty subsistence was only to be bought with the blood of the tribe: and frequently this blood flowed in vain. Baffled by the vigilance, the courage, and the wise dispositions of Ali, the Arabs greeted him as their conqueror and accepted the conditions of peace. Part he received into his service as an auxiliary force against the hordes that might, from remote quarters, penetrate to Egypt. To others he gave villages where their aged and infirm might repose in safety, and where the grain of their own lands might be deposited. During his reign afterwards there was tranquillity and safety: but he fell in Syria too soon for the consolidation of his system and the happiness of Egypt. If then the daring bands of Arabia, shepherds and robbers from the time of the Patriarchs and probably long before, were thus moulded into habits more consistent with the safety and repose of regular society, can any reasonable argument be urged why the Bushmen should more successfully resist equal measures of vigour, wisdom, and humanity? why they should prefer the hazardous plunder of 20,000 head of cattle; where every hand is against them, and their indiscriminate destruction is lawlessly sanctioned by the laws? A wiser government will endeavour to mollify the hatred of the exasperated colonist and the vengeance of the Bushmen; will undertake the protection of property without imitating the crimes of the robber; and will seek to establish an intercourse with their chiefs and so familiarize them to the comforts of civilized society. Such a government will finally triumph by an union of policy, kindness, and power.

To render the Hottentot woman less hideous is beyond the power of legislation: but a change of attire may render her less nauseating. At present she is clothed with a raw sheep-skin thrown over her shoulders; the bowels of a sheep are twisted round her waist, dependent so as to hide that extra-ordinary conformation about which the curious reader may consult Vaillant or Mr. Barrow; and her cap is the stomach of some animal. Her locks are matted with grease, and her infants (they are generally numerous) are carried upon her back, in the sheep-skin so folded as to make a hood. Her features are all contrary to European ideas of beauty. Her limbs are well formed; but she appears bent in the spine from the immense rotundity of a certain quarter, which after childbearing becomes stupendous. Nature has indeed varied from the rule in the human species when moulding the Hottentot female: but such is the caprice of fancy, or such is the design of Providence to improve the race of these beings in exterior appearance—for they really are destitute of none of the amiable natural qualities of women—that the finest young men who ever left Europe do not revolt from their embraces, or reflect on these aberrations with disgust.

It cannot be urged that the Hottentot is unable to sustain fatigue. He is low in stature, but strong and active as the antelope. His diet is moderate, and he can bear either heat or cold. He is animated by an emulous spirit; or he never could have attained that degree of military excellence, which astonishes every beholder who remembers in what state he was born, and that the language which conveys instruction to him is but little understood. He is perhaps too fond of intoxicating liquors, but that unhappily is a vice of imitation. His diligence is equal to his powers: and now the post from Simon's Town to Cape Town is conveyed by relays of Hottentots.

When an extra post is employed a single Hottentot performs this distance (twenty-four miles) with ease in four hours and a half; and in ten minutes is ready to return with the same expedition. It is the intention of government to establish this system through the whole colony: a measure that is calculated to produce very beneficial consequences, as formerly letters were carried by the cavalry, which ruined many horses and was injurious to the general discipline. But it is not necessary that the colony should altogether depend upon the Hottentots for service: twenty-five thousand white inhabitants in possession of the whole property of the colony, could never want hired servants, when in the same territory

there were fifty thousand domesticated people of colour who
would have no other means of maintenance. Bad masters
would probably be abandoned by their former slaves: but the
greater part would continue from gratitude, and from a consciousness that they could not improve their condition.

In Cape Town there are about two thousand houses; in
each house there are upon an average six slaves, and of these
many are unnecessary; but they are retained because they
are for the most part born in service and have their nearest
kindred in the same houses. Now, if slavery were abolished
this burden would be no longer imposed; for there could be
no reproach on the free employment of them under other
masters.

The purchase of useful slaves demands a large capital. An
ordinary cook costs 200l. Life is precarious even with the
best treatment; and in a few months the death of valuable
slaves has reduced a respectable family to poverty. An affecting incident occurred lately in Cape Town which does
honour to all parties. Several slaves had died, and bank-
ruptcy ensued. The last survivor, and one for whom a considerable sum had been paid, is on his deathbed: he requests
to see his mistress; he begs her benediction; he acknow-
ledges her maternal care of him and his companions;
he weeps, and faintly articulates with his last breath:
"Edwards sheds no tears for himself; he feels only for
his poor dear mistress, to whom his death will bring such
ruin."

The proprietors are aware of the hazard of this property;
and would be easily persuaded to any arrangement that
might restore a part of the purchase-money already expended,
and establish the institution of hired servants. Even if no
part should be restored in money, if the only repayment were
by gratuitous service for some time, still the gain would be
great to the family of the proprietor: and it would be felt to
be so when sickness or death incapacitated former slaves,
and it was found that no demand was made upon capital to
replace them.

Morally, the abolition would be of great importance to the
community. At present every female slave who attains the

age of fifteen or sixteen years receives the visits of some
lover, by whom she becomes a parent: her second child, and
so on, has another father; and probably one of different
colour. These unhallowed births are far from being discou-
raged or kept concealed from the family. Such promiscuous
intercourse must surely not only be viewed as indelicate, but
must be attended with pernicious consequences to young
people, by familiarizing to their minds images which a
virtuous education is most careful to exclude.

The female slaves of the Cape are very handsome, particularly the Mustees: whose black eyebrows, hazel eyes,
ruddy complexion, and well-moulded limbs merit the pencil
of the ablest painter, or the chisel of the most accomplished sculptor. The Cape ladies are indeed unwilling to
acknowledge such pretensions to admiration: and consequently a man of gallantry, if he seeks to be favourably
received by them, would not hazard an opinion that might
indicate his sensibility to the charms of the slave. The Cape
people in their *theories*, not in their *actions*, consider that
nature has drawn a determinate line between whites and
blacks, and intended in her partiality that the latter should
be always dependents: under this impression they can
scarcely reconcile themselves to the sight of white servants;
but they do not extend their notions of supremacy to the
justification of tyranny. They hold that it is a sufficient
misfortune not to be born fair; and that it is their duty to
alleviate the calamity as much as possible. Their compassion
does them honour. Their vanity is as natural to them as to
the *hunchbacks* who, seeing a shipwrecked European sailor,
were about to murder him as a *monster with a straight back*,
when the philosophical chief of the hunches interposed and
said: "My children, if nature has ornamented you with a
beautiful elevation of the shoulders, be thankful to the
Almighty Creator for his preference of love; and preserve
this deformed man with a straight back as an object to excite
your gratitude: do all you can to comfort him for his misfortune in not being formed like yourselves."

If there was no further importation of slaves, in all probability the faintest trace by colour of an Angola or Mozam-

bique extraction would in a few years disappear.   The amalgamation is already rapidly proceeding.

Mr. Barrow recommends an importation of Chinese artizans and workmen.   If the colony should remain in the hands of the English, permission might be granted, when peace is made, to such English soldiers as should be willing, to settle, with certain limitations as to military service, in the colony.   The temptation of gain, the influence of the women, the detestation of a sea voyage—*on which a soldier for some unaccountable reason is only half fed, and therefore half famished*—would induce many to accept the proposal cheerfully.

The inhabitants of Cape Town live better than any people in Europe.   There is scarcely a family which does not, twice a day, sit down to a meal consisting of soup, fish, curry, meat, vegetables; and a dessert with Cape wine and claret.   Their diet is somewhat too richly dressed, but the English mode of cooking is being rapidly adopted.   All the markets are well supplied; and the gardens are loaded with vegetables and the fruits of all climates.   Bread has indeed recently been scarce.   No individual has been allowed more than a pound per day; and such grain of the farmers as was more than sufficient for a year's consumption in their families at this allowance, has been seized for the supply of Cape Town.   But active measures have been taken to import such a quantity as may relieve this serious scarcity.   If, however, provisions bear no extravagant price, the cost of raiment and articles of European manufacture is excessively exorbitant: as, upon an average, 300 per cent. premium is levied upon the necessities of the colony.   There is no probability of any great reduction, as the ships from Europe have an ulterior market in India should the Cape be so stocked as to offer a lower premium for their commodities.   Fortunately the climate is so mild that generally fires are unnecessary except for cookery: otherwise, from the price of fuel and clothing, the inhabitants would suffer the greatest misery.

The manners of the people have been much misrepresented. A picture has been darkly coloured that was susceptible of relief from the introduction of brighter, softer, more pleasing, and truer tints. A heavy denunciation has been registered against the inhabitants of the Cape ; as if virtue were here more rare or vice more licentious than in any other European colony. Another Gehenna has been declared, with more complete exclusion of hope. But the extravagance of calumny or satire is an antidote against its venom. Censors of national morals should be well acquainted with the state and manners of society in the several polite nations of the world, before they publish their remarks upon any particular country: so that the scale by which they measure public worth or depravity may be regulated upon an equal and intelligible principle. Some writers artfully advance the interest of their works, by insinuations which move the passions while they pretend to rebuke levity and immorality. But the honest and intelligent visitors of the Cape will find that its inhabitants afford no more matter for reproach and reproof than all civilized societies: and that, with the exception before stated, of the hiring out the persons of the female slaves, the same manners, opinions, teaching, and regulations as in other communities oppose an indecorous indulgence of the passions. It is an indisputable fact that, except in moments of extraordinary political disorder, civilized society is everywhere constituted and regulated by the same laws. Decency and decorum are always cherished, even by the professed votaries of pleasure, as the eternal and active principles which alone can command just admiration.

An exposure of partial frailties is ungenerous: and from such a representation to insert a sweeping clause against the whole community is uncandid and unjust. The dissemination of such aspersion is also extremely pernicious. On the one hand, that contemptuous deportment which is the consequence closes the avenues to an intercourse which might remove prejudice: on the other, an offended *amour propre* is excited to activity, and strengthens these feelings of dislike and enmity which misrepresentation had in the first instance engendered.

The men in Cape Town generally employ their mornings by attendance at their sales, or upon shipping concerns, and in the superintendence of their neighbouring farms. They dine about two; then repose; and in the evening resort to the society house, where they smoke, play backgammon, cards, billiards, and talk over their affairs. The younger men who have leisure are more gallant in their occupation; and they are not destitute of resources to pass their time pleasantly. Their manners are unexceptionable. They are cheerful companions, and adhere in their dress strictly to the English costume; which is indeed so much the attire of both sexes that an Englishman can perceive no variation from his own countrymen in this respect.

If the men of the Cape have not applied themselves more sedulously to literary pursuits, the neglect cannot justly be ascribed to any deficiency of talent, or to an indolent indifference to improvement. It is in reality owing to the absence of encouragement either by allurements of interest or distinction; since employment in the public offices was never the reward of their ability. But yet, secluded as they have been from Europe and restricted to a trading communication, there are many who speak French, German, and English fluently: and should measures be taken to stimulate application, should schools of instruction be opened for the youth of Africa, the masters will not have an idle situation from want of students; nor will the natives of the colony be long destitute of those attainments which embellish the social state of nations. Nature has with a profuse bounty bestowed upon these men her gifts of stature, proportion, strength, and all the properties that characterize an excelling growth of the human frame: nor has their Maker withheld those powers of intelligence which education unfolds and matures.

The Cape young women are particularly well formed, walk with grace, pay French and Spanish attention to their *chaussure*, and dress with great taste; notwithstanding that they have had no sight of European fashions for several years. But, whilst they display with advantage the elegance of their forms, they avoid that extreme which leaves nothing for a generous fancy to suppose. There is no regular beauty to be seen as in Europe; but their faces are pretty and pleasing. Their eyes are expressive; their complexions very fair, and blooming as the damask rose, without artificial colouring:

and if they would generally pay more attention to a most ornamental but too delicate part of the human structure they would rank high amongst the fairest works of the creation. They sing, play well, dance English and French dances gracefully, are lively in conversation, good tempered, quick to learn, and desirous to please from benignity of character as well as from natural female self-estimation. Indeed they only need instruction to be proficient in every female accomplishment. Before marriage they are generally light in figure: after they are mothers they become more *embonpoint:* and age advances with a rapid step after twenty-five; which is probably owing to the little exercise that they take, and the closeness of chambers which have no ventilation.

No doubt those discords and dissensions which violate the quiet of all communities have not been successfully repelled from Cape Town; but yet no place exhibits more natural scenes of domestic enjoyment and family union. During the late peace marriage had become a civil contract: but little abuse seems to have been the consequence of the facility of divorce. Since the last recapture the usual ceremonies are again instituted; and the land-roosts, or magistrates of districts, are empowered to officiate as ministers.

Heretofore those farmers who had lived in the remote provinces were unable to attend at Cape Town for the solemnization of marriage. Necessity, therefore, substituted the obligation of a mutual engagement: and the ratifying act was delayed frequently until the parties could find it convenient to visit Cape Town. Then, accompanied by three or four children they presented themselves at the altar of the church for the matrimonial and baptismal rites, which legitimated all past transactions : almost the only species of *ex post facto* law that was ever benevolently applied in any country.

The day of marriage, or more generally the day when the license is obtained, is celebrated as a festal holiday for all the kindred of the bride and bridegroom. They meet at the house of the nearest relations; dance the whole night, most generally upon brick floors; assemble again to dine. And they frequently continue the fête for three days.

At these gaieties from one to two hundred persons are present. The licentious will be much disappointed if they expect to be there entertained with indecent revelry. All is mirth, without an indelicacy that could stain with a blush the most virtuous maiden's cheek. Ingenuous in the expression of their feelings, the company honour with their cheerfulness the happy pair whose union they were invited to celebrate; without exposing themselves to the reproach of trespassing on social propriety.

The inhabitants of Cape Town are fond of society; and their doors are always open to receive their friends, without formal invitations. The ladies pass their evenings in conversation or amusements, but cards are very seldom introduced at their houses. The division of their day does not, however, agree with the habits of the English; and therefore there is little intercourse notwithstanding the best disposition.*

Few equipages are to be seen in Cape Town, and the carriages in use are those which were left by the English. But notwithstanding their antiquity the worst of them was not to be bought under two hundred pounds: and a prudent man would not insure a life for half an hour that was hazarded to their conveyance. A covered waggon without springs is the usual vehicle for the most respectable families. These waggons are drawn by six, eight, and ten horses. A Hottentot seated upon the fore part of the waggon, on a level with and sometimes lower than the horses, guides them with peculiar skill through the streets or in the worst roads; and can use the whip with such dexterity as to strike infallibly the smallest given spot. It is true that these animals have not the courage and force of the English breed, but nevertheless many of them are highly pampered and unruly.

Whether a Hottentot coachman in England could match an English coachman's achievements, may perhaps be disputed by his brothers of the whip in that country. But it is

* A variety of other circumstances rendered a more intimate association at that time impossible. And this the inhabitants regretted the more, as the remarkable improvement in English habits with regard to the use of wine had removed the only objection to such intimacy.—R. W., 1824.

almost certain that they could not rival his peculiar talent: nor would a French postilion be able to compete with him in the crack of the lash.

The variety of inhabitants, their shades of colour, their costumes, and their physiognomies, always afford a most entertaining and interesting scene in the streets of Cape Town.

People from all quarters of the globe are assembled at the Cape: and the different features of all the tribes of Africa may be here contemplated and compared.

Those who arrogantly and impiously defend the slave trade, with the blasphemy that the Almighty Creator stamped his indignation upon the unoffending posterity of Cain by a black tincture of the skin, rendering his generations also worthless and abject in mind, will not be pleased to see this theory exposed to confutation and ridicule by the evidence that fair complexions are in these latitudes changed to the darkest hue, and hair to wool; and that noses are flattened by slow and gentle gradations. If they had reason, but bigots never have, they would in future attribute to physical and not to spiritual causes the variation of shade in human complexion.

An Englishman, who is perhaps rendered too nice by the comforts of his own country, may be revolted by several of the customs of Cape Town. But neither Rome nor London were built in one day: nor were their subterraneous cities excavated in a single year.

There is one exception to the general cleanliness and decency of the city. Not only is the burial-ground over-loaded with tenants, but the corpses are interred so near the surface as to emit the most pestilential effluvia. The bodies are generally, on account of the scarcity of wood, buried without coffins; and therefore greater precaution is necessary: particularly as a high road much frequented runs directly through the burial-place. There are however canals in some of the streets.

General Janssen proposed a military place of sepulture in another quarter, upon a plan intended powerfully to excite those useful sentiments which the view of such a receptacle

is calculated to inspire. The troops had already formed the
area, when the work was interrupted by the arrival of the
English. If the design be not carried out, the military must
be consoled by the reflection " that sweet are the tears which
nis country sheds over the unburied head of the soldier:" as
they are daily obliged to pass their festering comrades; whose
carcases are exposed to be mangled by the vultures and the
dogs, which assemble on the ground of inhumation as at a
common hall of banquet.

The vultures in such a country would in ancient times
have been worshipped for their utility : and they are now protected from destruction by the service they render to the
town. They consume the carrion with an astonishing
rapidity and neatness; stripping the bones in a few hours of
every fibre. But the dogs are a dreadful nuisance : they fly at
every horseman; howl hideously; and are flayed by a most
malignant cutaneous disorder.

Unfortunately, the necessity of water supply obliged the
first settlers to select a locality for Cape Town, that for the
five summer months of the year is visited by a demon of the
atmosphere.

When the cloud embryo of the south-east wind is seen
forming upon the Table Mountain, then every door and window must be closed. The heated air within is more tolerable
than the malignant and wild blast that is about to rage. The
fleecy speck soon shapes itself to maturity : vapours roll on
vapours; and gathering from all quarters shoot their supplies
to feed the engendering war of elements. The masses piled
to the heavens and bellying over the eminence of the table
land seem bursting, indignant at restraint. At length the
signal volley is fired; and the dense cloud precipitates itself
half-way, down the mountain, when it disperses to fill the
opening space, and affords relief to the earth that seems
about to be cruhsed by the weight. In a few minutes, however, the storm resumes its action, and at the first onset every
fabric is shaken to the foundation. Gust succeeds gust until
the successive shocks become too frequent for computation;
whilst the light fragments of the loose soil are impelled with
such fury that the atmosphere becomes solid : and yet so

subtle are the fine parts of the sand that no joiner's art can resist its penetration; and so sharp are the coarser particles, that no living surface, if exposed, can be insensible to acute pain. Such is the violence, with such virulence does this wind urge its course, that the most philosophical temper can scarcely refrain from a frenzied clamour against its imaginary animosity; or from offering, like Lear in despair of sufferance, " mad defiance to the tempest."

The strength of this wind is expended generally in twelve hours: and about the same time is required for the organization of a new hurricane. But sometimes the magazines are so well stored as to lord it in the field without a pause for several days.

Four miles from Cape Town, when the point of the amphitheatre is passed, the south-east wind is much less violent and unaccompanied by any deleterious effects. Although the principal inhabitants have their country residences in this neighbourhood, still they cannot avail themselves of such asylum; because at this season of the year, as the ships lie in Table Bay, commercial transactions require their presence in the forenoon: and the blast is so formidable in the evening, that even the assurance of some hours' relief is not a compensation for the difficulty and, indeed, the danger of combating the adverse element in a carriage. Nor does the country at this season of the year possess the same inviting allurements as in the winter months. The extreme heat and drought destroy vegetation; the trees are destitute of their foliage, and the land of verdure. The living principle seems extinct.

When the European calendar denotes the winter, then the harvest smiles and the soil is decked with herbage. It is then that the air is temperate and the weather inviting to exercise. The rains that occasionally fall are indeed heavy; but they seldom continue above eight-and-forty hours together, and most frequently descend in the night: and ten or twelve days of European summer commonly intervene between these deluges of the sky.

Snow sometimes falls and rests on the hills; but in the low lands never. If the climate of the colony be salubrious as it is represented by many, still the atmosphere of Cape Town must be excepted. In the summer the confined and parched air, in the winter the excessive variations from heat to cold are pernicious to men and to cattle. The great sickness of a new garrison may in some degree be attributed to sleeping upon damp brick floors without bedding, severity of duty, exercise in a heat by thermometer of 120°, and bad wine: but not altogether; as many become victims to the climate who are enabled to avoid these inconveniences, and who are never guilty of any excess. Few officers indeed escape some serious illness. A consumptive subject perishes immediately: and numbers of the inhabitants die annually of this disease, to which there seems a disposition in the youthful system. If the young recover from it there is afterwards a proneness to fat. Phenomena of men weighing from 20 to 30 stone are frequent in every part of the colony: whilst the fatal flush glowing on the cheek of youth and beauty is a sorry spectacle that is too often to be seen. It is also remarked in the hospitals that, although wounds heal as in Europe, the backs of punished men require all the care and skill of the surgeon, and always excite considerable solicitude. Nor can men without imminent risk of life receive more than 300 lashes: even then the cases are long doubtful; so that in violation of the law the punishments were inflicted, in regiments where punishments took place, at separate intervals.*

The excessive drought of the air also affects the horses at Cape Town: and the English found when, last in possession of the colony that they were never equal, in heart or condition, to those of the country, notwithstanding equal food, care, and exercise. The south-east wind has an effect upon them similar to that of the same wind after it has passed the Desert in Egypt. The blast strikes them suddenly with paralysis, and death almost always ensues. Can a stronger proof be required that the air then must be detrimental to the human constitution?.

---

* It is to be hoped the day is not distant when this unmanly and cruel mode of punishment will be abolished: even Prussia has rejected corporal punishment, and followed the example of France, Holland, and Bavaria.— R. W.

The whole colony cannot however be designated as congenial to life, if longevity be a criterion. The age of man so seldom attains the verge of threescore years and ten, that an instance of this nature is long recorded as extraordinary: and there never has been seen by the colonist a human being in this part of Africa who had been in life 100 years.

The average of what is here denominated longevity is from 50 to 60, and few only are enrolled in either list. The general inactive habits of the people may partially influence the duration of their days; but no regimen or diet would probably avail much. Either the soil must be changed, the mountains sink, or an ecliptic movement give a new climate, before the " grandsire of threescore," as already described,* will be *often* seen in any condition; much less at the gambol of the dance. But there are some exceptions and extraordinary local variations in this colony as to salubrity: since without any yet ascertained cause in some spots health seems to have established her sanctuary; in others, and contiguous ones, mortal malady infects the atmosphere.

From Cape Town to Hottentot Holland is a dreary sand tufted with black verdure, over which the oxen toil with difficulty for near thirty-five miles. But the district of Hottentot Holland, embracing a circumference of about eight miles, is well watered, handsomely wooded, planted with vineyards, and displays a scene of comfort and beauty that would ornament any country. The Cape Madeira, the Stein, and more ordinary wines are made here. In all there is a nauseating sweetness like that of antimonial wine. The vintners are not satisfied with the use of sulphur to *fumigate* their barrels; they moreover throw into each a considerable quantity. This operates injuriously, by thinning the blood and producing those disorders which originate in the poverty of the vascular system.

The common Cape wine is of the most pernicious character; suddenly intoxicating, and occasioning most violent sickness and pains of the head; frequently inducing the worst species of dysentery, and at last causing death.

* See page 317.—Ed.

Above Hottentot Holland rises the ridge of mountains which is fairly presumed to have been at one time the boundary coast of this part of Africa.

On the right is Gordon's Bay, an eligible point of debarkation, as the ships can approach with safety. The troops would here find ample provision, horses, and draught oxen : and they might seize the kloof, or pass, to which General Janssen after the action at Blueberg retired ; and by which the important communication between the interior and Cape Town is much impeded, if not altogether intercepted. This pass is extremely lofty : the summit is almost eternally capped with clouds : but many entertain a doubt whether the position is unassailable.

On the left above Gordon's Bay is a still higher hill, divided near the apex. The security of this position was observed by the discontented slaves. They ascended, explored, and resolved to erect on this retreat their banner of liberty. They retired with their wives and families, and the flocks of their masters, to settle in this region. They built huts, arranged their arsenal of defence—ponderous stones —and not only bid defiance from their ramparts to the vengeance of their masters, but long made predatory descents upon the lands of the farmers in Hottentot Holland.

In tracing the country at the base of the mountains, Stellenbosch distant about ten miles is the next village, and is extremely well worth a visit. The site which it occupies is of great extent, the houses are sumptuous, and the finest oak-trees are planted throughout.

Unfortunately a fire three years since consumed a considerable number of these trees as well as of the houses. But by the beneficial aid of the government, and under the superintendence of an estimable magistrate, the ravages that it was in the power of industry to repair have been more than obliterated ; and time is alone wanting to restore the foliage. From Stellenbosch to Paarl is about sixteen miles : accuracy in regard to distance is in this country difficult to be attained ; as the roads are not measured, and each passenger calculates according to the tedium or agreeable celerity with which the time has been passed on the journey. An hour on horseback is, however, on an average understood to mark the distance of five miles, and a pedestrian's hour to comprehend three: but the African's computation frequently disappoints the traveller.

The Paarl is esteemed to be the prettiest village in the colony, and is doubtless deserving of admiration. Here is a school upon a small plan for boys. The master is intelligent and well qualified for his situation; but the encouragement of government is necessary to give the establishment protection and success.

From the Paarl to the Roode Sand kloof is about thirty-five miles. This pass is important, as by its occupation and that of the kloof of Hottentot Holland all supplies might be cut off from Cape Town. And this is a most serious consideration, as the district of the Cape does not contain sufficient resources of corn and cattle for its own maintenance exclusive of any garrison: but as General Janssen had not sufficient force to occupy both passes, had he remained at Hottentot Holland's kloof he would have been turned by a force moving to Swellendam, distant 200 miles; where an interior ridge of mountains, branching at right angles and running between the two kloofs terminates, and uncovers the whole of the flat country in rear of the general's position.

Had the English force which landed at Saldanha been ordered to turn off to Roode Sand, instead of proceeding to Cape Town when no longer required to act as the advance guard of the main army, General Janssen would never have meditated a stand; but must have capitulated or retired immediately. In military operations, however, it is often seen that fortune is a better friend than judicious disposition: and he cannot fight ill who fights chained to her car.

Beyond the Paarl there is no village worthy of notice. Scattered farms speck the country between Roode Sand and the sea, and along the Berg river which rises in Stellenbosch and falls into St. Helena Bay.

This river is not navigable. Some pretend that with little difficulty and expense it might be so made. The hippopotamus is found upon its banks: but the slaughter of this animal has been so great that a heavy penalty is exacted upon the destruction of one without permission of the government. The flesh is food of high flavour, and it is much esteemed.

St. Helena Bay is distant from Cape Town about 130 miles; of which the last fifty run through a wild and barren tract of country. This bay is only visited in cases of necessity by ships, as nothing is to be procured there.

Saldanha Bay, forty miles nearer to Cape Town, is more frequented, but is destitute of water, with the exception of what is extremely bad and barely sufficient for daily supply to a few men and cattle.

Consideration for the safety of the harbour, and the military objections so truly urged against the possible defence of Cape Town if assailed by a superior army, have induced a suggestion that the capital of the Cape should be transferred to this point: and the idea has been entertained that water might be conducted by an aqueduct or even by a canal to this point from the Berg river which runs within a few miles. The removal of a capital is a measure of most serious moment, and one that should command the most deliberate counsel: for the speculative welfare of the mother country should not too rudely clash with the settled interests of colonial subjects. To the farmers over the mountains the change might not prove detrimental: but the inhabitants of Cape Town must be ruined by it, as their property is vested in houses and in the shipping interest. The expense would also be enormous: and the garrison must be increased by at least 2,000 soldiers; unless Cape Town is to be abandoned altogether whenever an enemy appears in Table or False Bays.

If the colony should become an integral part of the British empire, and eventually prove a valuable possession, perhaps the erection of some forts at the entrance of Saldanha Bay and upon several commanding points might be judicious. But these would be useless if they depended upon any exterior supply of water. Tanks must be constructed within: and an enemy that attacked would then suffer that inconvenience of drought which would be a powerful impediment to his operations in the summer months.

If the prosperity of the colony should be such as to permit

a more extensive establishment, then indeed Saldanha Bay might with propriety be selected for a settlement. But it must always be remembered that, although Saldanha Bay is only sixty miles by water from Table Bay, when a south-east wind blows merchantmen *may be* a month, and men-of-war *have been* a week and more, beating that distance.

A small arm of the sea runs into the country in an eastern direction about eight miles. A league of this arm is navigable for small vessels keeping close to each shore. On the south side is the post-house: on the north a farmer's tenement, opposite to which the vessels lie and procure a daily supply of water, some cattle, and a few vegetables.

Five miles from hence under a hill somewhat remarkable is another farmer's tenement, where bad puddle water is to be procured. Ten miles further are several Hottentot huts upon a commanding spot of ground, close to which are several wells full of excellent water; and eight miles further is Tea Fonteyn, which is a large and well-watered farm. The road so far is over, or rather in, a deep white sand : no water is to be obtained but at the stations above mentioned, except in the winter season when various pools are formed by the rains. The column of the English proposed to be the advanced guard of the army was marched to Saldanha Bay, with the object of securing Tea Fonteyn ; a post essential for the supplies of water, grain, and cattle. Never was a force more favoured than by the unexpected inattention of the enemy to this point. It was thus enabled to secure possession of a large and fertile district, lying on the direct road to Cape Town and menacing Roode Sand pass distant only fifty miles.

A variety of unfortunate circumstances seemed to conspire against the success of this detachment, and a couple of guns with a hundred cavalry might certainly have annihilated the invaders.

The morning after the force was detached from Table Bay, and the ships conveying it had anchored in Saldanha Bay, Captain King of the Navy and Captain Smith of the Engineers had proceeded towards the shore with the hope of communicating with the portmaster: but a volley of shot as soon as the boat approached pierced several of her planks, and obliged her to sheer away.

In the afternoon General Beresford, being aware of the importance of the post of Tea Fonteyn, ordered the officer in command of the cavalry, with fifty dragoons mounted on horses brought from St. Salvador, and three hundred infantry of the 38th Regiment, to land and proceed to that point.

A heavy gale that ploughed the bay, and ignorance of the shore rendered the debarkation of the horses difficult: and the dusk of evening had set in before the party began to march.

The mate of an American ship lying in the bay was soon met; and he gave the information that the portmaster and the farmers residing on the coast of the bay, had already retired with all their cattle. After a march of eighteen miles over a sandy soil some Hottentot huts were descried. The infantry was halted; and the cavalry proceeded about three miles before they reached the kraal and a farmer's house: but already the Hottentots had given the alarm; and a waggon with fourteen oxen was seized at the instant it was starting to remove into the interior, in accordance with the orders of the Dutch governor who had commanded obedience on pain of death.

While the seizure of the oxen, and presumed arrival at the appointed rendezvous were exhilarating the captors, their joy was converted into despondency by the information obtained from the drivers that the guide had mistaken the road, and that thirteen miles were to be retraced before the right track could be recovered.

The infantry already wearied by a long march after several months' confinement on board ship, proceeded about eight miles to the rear; when fatigue and a favourable spot for the indulgence of some repose determined a halt. But in two hours the sun darted his fiery blaze with such power, and the want of water became so urgent, that the troops requested permission to advance towards a house that was perceived in the horizon, in order that they might obtain water to slake their thirst.

After six miles' march they reached the station; but there

suffered painful restraint, while an insufficient quantity of black and putrid water was being served out to them.

This station proved to be five miles from the original landing place at Saldanha, but in the direct road for Tea Fonteyn on which the detachment had been ordered to move.

Before the detachment had reached the house the commanding officer * and another officer had gone forward to reconnoitre, and upon their approach two armed men had galloped away from the premises. They were not fired at us they might have been; for it was an object not to exasperate the inhabitants of the colony and dispose to a jealousy which would co-operate with the governor in its defence.

The men who thus escaped proved to be officers of the government, carrying orders to evacuate the district.

No further time could be lost without great prejudice to the service.

The light infantry on being made acquainted with the necessity of an immediate advance volunteered at once to go forward, and the whole body of infantry became equally eager; but it was judged more expedient to oppose this wish, and prescribe rest till evening for all but the cavalry and light infantry.

After a most distressing march of eight miles in loose sand and excessive heat some cultivated land was discovered: and arrangements having been made to conceal as much as possible the advance of the party, a little after dark possession was taken of a large kraal where several hundred head of cattle were penned, amidst the cries of the terrified Hottentots who rushed out from the neighbouring huts.

This was a valuable acquisition; and a proportion of the cattle were immediately sent back to Saldanha. But still Tea Fonteyn was distant eight miles, and the possession of that station was of the most vital consequence to the expedition. The infantry were too much exhausted to move; they were therefore left at Eland Fonteyn, which this post proved to be, with orders to advance when their comrades left behind at the first wells

---

* Sir R. Wilson. See page 294.—Ed.

had come up to relieve them. The cavalry moved on to Tea Fonteyn, where they arrived soon after midnight, and had the good fortune to surprise the whole establishment: here they found provisions in abundance, some horses, and an ample supply of cattle.

In the middle of the next night General Beresford, with Colonel Vassal, a part of the 38th Regiment, and the light infantry detachment left at Eland Fonteyn and which had again lost its way, arrived and found refreshment ready provided.

The next day the remainder of the infantry arrived; and also the dismounted dragoons of the 20th Regiment, who had suffered most severely from such a march in boots and cloth overalls, with saddles and kits on their backs.

General Beresford had on the morning after his advanced guard had landed, received advice of the army having effected a disembarkation at Blueberg: he therefore resolved to effect a junction without any delay; but although forced marches were made, the general could only arrive with the mounted detachment just at the moment the troops were drawing out to take possession of Cape Town by capitulation, after the action at Blueberg.*

On the evening of the 5th the English fleet, after a voyage of four months, in which the *Britannia* Indiaman and the *King George* transport had been lost on the Roccas, off the

---

* From Tea Fonteyn to Groene kloof, twenty-four miles, hard road, little water *en route*; between the road and the sea were sand downs covered with strong, high, nutritious pasturage for cattle. Groene kloof is a pass over a ridge of lofty mountains extending from the sea to Roode sandhills and at right angles to them: ascent gradual for three miles. At the base on the Cape Town side is a large government house; and a farm where Spanish merino sheep are kept, and from whence the first ram of that breed was imported into New South Wales. The proprietor is a great agriculturist on English principles and a benefactor to the colony.

Groene kloof to Brach Fonteyn, nine miles, through a heavy sand without water. In the neighbourhood of Brach Fonteyn are several good farms and pleasant country. Brach Fonteyn to Blueberg, eight miles; Blueberg to Riet Valley, six miles; Riet Valley to Craig's Tower, the extreme outwork of Cape Town erected to command the ford over Salt Stream, ten miles. Total, fifty-seven miles.—R. W.

coast of America, arrived in Table Bay and anchored off Robben Island.

The *Narcissus* frigate which had been detached to St. Helena, and which was expected to be met with off the Cape, was not in sight: but information was obtained of the force of the enemy; and it was known that an attack was expected, by the arrival of the *Espoir* gun-brig which had been sent forward from St. Salvador, where the fleet had remained some days on its passage.

The chief engineer who was on board the *Espoir* had reconnoitred the coast; and had procured his intelligence from a neutral which had just sailed out of Table Bay.

Orders were issued for the 38th, 83rd, 59th and mounted dragoons to effect a landing the ensuing morning, at day-break, in a small bay formed by some rocks, and sufficiently wide at the entrance for the advance of two boats in a line.

The *Espoir* was anchored a quarter of a mile off, and the boats were directed to rendezvous around her: but as many of them had to row ten miles, five hundred men were not assembled before eight o'clock A.M.

This unexpected delay deranged the proposed operation: for it was found that the sea-breeze had occasioned too high a surf to allow of debarkation that morning.

It was also clearly perceived from the deck of the *Espoir* that a body of the enemy, with artillery, was posted on the lofty hill of deep sand that rose gradually from the shore; the summit of which was not musket-shot from the beach.

The enterprise was therefore necessarily abandoned for the day; and the disappointed troops were ordered to return to their ships.

The same evening it was determined that General Beresford should proceed with the advanced guard to Saldanha, and it was arranged that the whole expedition should follow the next day: but after the departure of General Beresford's detachment the wind lulled; and the sea became so calm that another attempt was resolved upon in the morning in a small boat bay on the eastern side of Blueberg, where the ground was far more favourable than the point of debarkation originally proposed, for the troops, after landing, to acquire and preserve a position.

General Ferguson's brigade was ordered to land. That officer proceeded to examine the state of the surf, as doubts of the practicability of the landing were still entertained: but when he gave the appointed signal the boats started forward, and forcing through the surge which upset only one boat, their prows were fixed on the beach.

The enemy had not expected debarkation at this point; or indeed anywhere on this part of the coast, after the preceding attempt had been baffled, and after the departure of the detachment of the fleet towards Saldanha; for this had been distinctly seen, and had confirmed their error. The only resistance experienced by the landing troops was therefore made by a feeble picket.

The whole of the day was employed in landing the remainder of the army, their guns, provisions, water, and stores. This an increasing surf rendered a very difficult service; and in the execution of it Sir Home Popham and Captain King narrowly escaped perishing.

The moment selected for debarkation had been extraordinarily favourable: for the weather at the same season had heretofore been considered a security for the colony against such an enterprise at this point; and for several days afterwards the landing on the line of shore from Saldanha to Cape Town would have been impracticable.

Early on the subsequent morning the army,* about four thousand strong exclusive of the marine battalion and sailors, moved forwards.

The heights of Blueberg defended the main approach to Cape Town: but these heights, terminating upon sandhills near the coast, left a pass open on the left flank.

The 59th Regiment was directed to move through the sandhills, while the main body ascended Blueberg; where it was presumed the enemy would be posted if they intended to hazard an action. The English however mounted the

---

* The regiments disembarked in Lospard's Bay were the 24th, 59th, 71st, 72nd, 83rd, and 93rd.—*London Gazette*, February 28th, 1806.—ED.

heights without opposition; and to their surprise saw the enemy drawing up in the plains below them in order of battle.   As the English crowned the heights they were saluted with three huzzas and a continued discharge from thirty pieces of cannon.

The British line without any hesitation descended.   When sufficiently near to attack, General Ferguson was ordered to charge with his brigade.   The compliment of three huzzas was returned to the enemy; who gave way as the battalions rushed forward, leaving several guns in the possession of the assailants, and about five hundred men killed and wounded.

Had the mounted cavalry not been detached with General Beresford, in all probability the whole of the artillery would at that moment have been captured.

The 57th and the 24th experienced some resistance, but drove all before them with almost uninterrupted progressive movement.

The enemy were no sooner routed than great anxiety was occasioned by want of water.   The heat of the sun and its reflection from a white sand, the depth of the sand, the exertion of the onset, and the very apprehension of the inability to slake thirst, occasioned great distress.   The soldiers dropped fast; and several sailors died at the guns they had been dragging through a soil, over which it was supposed by the enemy to be impossible that cannon could be brought by the mere exertion of men.

After some search a small pool was found, and the commander-in-chief himself superintended the distribution of its precious treasure.

The fainting troops being revived, the army moved on to Riet Valley where a partial disembarkation had been effected to alarm the rear of the enemy; and there an ample supply of water was obtained.

General Janssen retired with his broken force to gain the kloof of Hottentot Holland, after detaching the remains of the French marine battalion, whose conduct had been conspicuously gallant and loss great, to Hout's Bay, with orders to assist in the defence of the town; and after disbanding in the field the Waldeck battalion, with the exception of the light infantry company whose conduct had gained and merited his approbation.

That the Waldeckers did not act with great zeal may be true. And it was natural, considering that the greater part of the battalion was composed of Austrian and Hungarian prisoners sold to the Dutch. But there was no truth in the charge made against them, that there was a previous arrangement between them and the invaders which pledged their defection in the field.

They esteemed the Governor-general Janssen, but they felt no interest in the defence of the colony. On the contrary the Cape had appeared to them an intolerable place of banishment; and in one month thirty-nine individuals, including several officers, had put a period to their own lives. One of them, a young man of the greatest promise, had thus perished only three days before the arrival of the English.

Many of the Waldeckers indeed, it is true, enlisted afterwards in the British corps. But their frequent desertions proved that they were actuated by no other motive than a desire to relieve themselves from the inconveniences attending a confinement in the Amsterdam battery. And the commander-in-chief found himself obliged eventually to order the execution of three men, that a check might be opposed to a systematic desertion threatening the loss of every man who had enlisted: an execution that under all the circumstances was one of the most painful ever witnessed.

General Janssen has been condemned for hazarding a battle in an open country with a motley force of three thousand men, however well provided with artillery: but he thought that the honour of his country demanded the experiment, and he flattered himself that fortune might favour the counsel. He also entertained a hope that the British armament was composed of recruits for India and boy régiments, instead of battalions of mature, and in some instances veteran, composition.

Nor was the anticipation of a fortunate opportunity for the achievement of victory during the conflict, altogether chimerical. For if the three hundred burgher cavalry, and the one hundred and fifty regular Dutch cavalry moving with the guns, had seized the moment when the British line was charging, to wheel in upon its exposed flank, the issue of the day would probably at all events not have been so decisive; and any check to infantry in their state might have been very fatal.

Even after the infantry had retired the cavalry might have disputed some of the laurels of the victors.

General Janssen was also unfortunate in not having reached the heights of Blueberg in time to crown them as he intended. Surprised on his march by the sudden appearance of the English on the crest of the heights, he had not time to make a suitable disposition of his force.

There were indeed more favourable fields of battle than Blueberg; if the character of the ground alone was to be considered in the selection of position. But in Africa the tactician must regulate his art by the facilities which the locality affords for the supply of water: and this supply was to be obtained in the neighbourhood of Blueberg, or the British army would have perished.*

When General Janssen had retired to Hottentot Holland's kloof, the inhabitants of Cape Town, aware of the fruitlessness of resistance and apprehensive of an assault, determined to surrender; and General Ferguson arranged the terms of capitulation. The town was quietly occupied and the inhabitants crowded forward to see the entering army. Considerable public property was found in the stores, and a large sum of money in the treasury; notwithstanding that the government of the mother country had never been called upon to defray any of the expenses of the colony. But the captors felt considerable dissatisfaction on discovering that several merchant vessels, richly laden, had been sunk; after the retreat of General Janssen, and when the inhabitants had agreed to oppose no further resistance, but to trust to the clemency and liberality of the invaders.

The burning of the battery of seventy-four guns by order of General Janssen on his retreat, was an act of a different character, and therefore excited only regret.

* A melon field is supposed to have saved a great portion of the French army in Egypt, moving from Alexandria to Rosetta.—R. W.

The next morning the French detachment which had passed from Hout Bay round Table Land and entered the Cape Town during the night unperceived, (executing a march that had been presumed to be impracticable,) surrendered voluntarily at the British head-quarters.

General Ferguson, who had been detached with his brigade to Weinberg, took some prisoners at a neighbouring post: and General Beresford, with the 59th Regiment and another corps, marched on to Stellenbosch. A force was also despatched by sea to Algoa Bay to cut off the retreat of General Janssen from Caffre-land, on which he threatened to retire.

The cavalry was mounted by requisition on the best* horses of the country and sent to Stellenbosch.

Various marches and countermarches towards Roode Sand pass were afterwards made; but the final surrender of General Janssen prevented a campaign that promised to be most harassing and protracted.

General Janssen stated that the desertion of his troops and motives of humanity influenced him to relinquish his intention of withdrawing further into the interior, and carrying on a desultory and savage warfare with the aid of the Caffres.

Had the general persisted he might have gained some advantage by fatiguing his enemy and disturbing their arrangement. But he would have ruined a colony where he was universally esteemed: nor could his country have required desperate perseverance, entailing such calamity on the inoffensive population.

The remaining force of General Janssen under his own orders, and consisting of about twelve hundred men, descended the kloof; and under the escort of the British cavalry marched to a camp near Rondebosch, where their cannon, arms, and horses were delivered up to the English.

General Janssen returned to the government house where his family had resided during his absence, and remained some

---

* The inhabitants are particularly partial to long tails. The cavalry commanding officer having docked all the horses, the owners allowed the cavalry to retain them at a valuation: a proposal which otherwise would not have been complied with except on most exorbitant terms.—R. W.

time. The Dutch officers were quartered in the town till their embarkation, which took place in about a month: and no incident occurred to interrupt the cordiality, on the faith of which these arrangements were made.

The capture of the *Volontaire* frigate which, ignorant of the place being in possession of the British, had run into Table Bay, put the commander-in-chief and the commodore in possession of information, which inclined them to believe that an attack would be made by the squadron of Admiral Villaumez then at sea.

Preparations were made for defence: and the Dutch and French troops which had surrendered, were then embarked and sent to Europe.

In consideration of the handsome treatment of the English found on board two transports taken by the *Volontaire* on their passage from Gibraltar, by the officers of that frigate, they were not detained as prisoners: and a ship navigated by their own sailors was granted them for the voyage to France.

Admiral Villaumez, in whose squadron was a ship of the line commanded by Jerome Buonaparte, having obtained intelligence that the Cape was already in the hands of the British, and being in need of water, abandoned the projected enterprise: and in consequence, the supernumerary troops at the Cape which had been detained, were sent forward to India.

I have made no attempt to describe the country over the mountains; as Barrow has very accurately delineated the most interesting features and scenery.

In general it presents as far as Swellendam a sandy naked surface, on which a few farm-houses are seen at great intervening distances. At Plattenburg Bay there is a rich forest scenery; and at Algoa Bay a military post to command the coast and watch the Caffres, whose territory borders upon the Great Fish River.

The colony of the Cape occupies a space of 157,656 square miles. This tract is inhabited by thirty thousand whites: but as five thousand of these reside in Cape Town, each white individual may be said to have seven square miles allotted for his maintenance.

This immense dispersion of the white inhabitants is extremely prejudicial to the prosperity of the colony and the
supply of Cape Town; for the remote farmers can only reach
the capital with their produce once or twice a year. They
then come in waggons drawn by eight, ten, or more oxen, to
sell butter, wood, tallow, cheese, &c.: the whole of which,
however, does not exceed in value 6l. sterling. This they
spend in the purchase of European commodities.

The rains which fall in the winter render these journeys
very perilous, as the streams swell into formidable rivers;
and the impatience of the travellers to pass through them in
spite of the remonstrance of the drivers, is often the occasion
of many lives being lost.

The African farmer has been harshly described by some
writers. But although his habits may be indolent, and although
his mind may be uncultivated, he is always a hospitable, disin-
terested and cheerful landlord. And certainly he is a patron of
the eighth virtue, domestic cleanliness; for the same neatness
prevails in his house, whether the floor be brick, or only plas-
tered with the dry manure of cattle, as distinguishes the
houses of the Dutch families in Europe.

Few garrisons offer in time of peace a more agreeable
residence for those who do not concern themselves about the
European world. A handsome town, pleasing women,
hospitable society, good and cheap living, are indisputable
attractions: and here they are to be found. The sportsman
may also amuse himself all the year round by the chase of
every species of game; from the partridge, to the pelican and
the ostrich; from the hare, to the wolf, the tiger, the lion, the
hippopotamus, the rhinoceros, and the elephant.

The traveller may visit the Caffres, and see the finest-
grown people perhaps on the whole globe, and then contrast
the Bushmen.* If he has enterprise he may immortalize
his name in a new field, by an endeavour to penetrate from
Caffre-land to Morocco or Nubia; bearing in mind that the
giraffe, presumed to be a native of the district near the Cape,

---

* The Bushmen are in stature four feet six inches; the women, four
feet four inches: they live chiefly on bats, locusts, and roots.—R. W.

has preceded him in these tracts, to attend the triumphal march of a Roman conqueror through the streets of Rome.

The soldier, it is to be hoped, will have no opportunity to display his genius or practise the art of his profession in internal war. For the duty of a governor of this colony ought to be confined to the less ostentatious but more solid glory of promoting the welfare and happiness of the population of all colours, castes, and nations, under his authority or within the sphere of his influence.

Whether it is advantageous to England to maintain the colony is a question that has long divided public opinion. At the conclusion of the late war one party contended that the colony was too expensive to be kept; but on the other hand an ex-minister affirmed in the most emphatic terms, that the cession would be most injurious to the interests of the British empire in the East. The East India Company, which at one moment expressed indifference on the subject, seemed latterly to be persuaded of the importance of the Cape; and therefore aided with considerable means the late expedition, which has once more placed the Cape under the rule of the British government.

There can be no doubt that colonies are really valuable to the mother country when they augment the public revenue and assist the common security of her possessions. If maintained only as fiefs for dominion or patronage they are most prejudicial appendages: and the sooner they are relinquished the better for all parties.

The commerce of the Cape is at present confined to imports; and such is the interior condition of the colony that it can furnish for some years nothing, with the exception of a little wine, but a few hides for export. It would however but be just to extend the view over a quarter of a century, and consider whether any nucleus at present exists giving reasonable hope of a more profitable traffic at that period.

Corn, wine, brandy, tobacco, hides, wool, whalebone, and oil, are the articles on which a Cape patriot speculates as the source of future prosperity. These he insists will repay eventually the immediate fostering care of the mother

country. The Spanish sheep are said to have found a congenial climate and pasturage at the Cape. The specimens
sent to Europe are pronounced to be only in a third degree of
bastardy: and an annual improvement encourages the hope
and presumption that in a few years they will attain the perfection of the parent stock.

This branch of commerce is indisputably important; but it
is of less consequence since it has been found that the Spanish
sheep have been acclimatised, even with more success, in New
Holland. Moreover the experiment has yet to be tried
whether a cargo can pass the line and reach Europe, without
such injury to the article that the portion preserved will
become necessarily too costly for the British markets.

The article of corn is the next item for consideration. It
has already been stated that the colony comprehends 157,656
square miles, large portions of which are too mountainous for
cultivation. But the greater part consists of a level sandy soil;
covered with a strong pasture, and capable, after a couple of
years fallowing, of producing corn yielding from fifteen to
twenty fold, where water can be procured for the supply of
men and cattle.

At present the extreme produce of the colony is twenty
thousand mands of grain: a quantity so insufficient that, notwithstanding a restriction on consumption and the annual
importation of nearly a million pounds of rice, still since the
year 1801 there has been a continual alarming scarcity: and
since the last crop supplies have been required from every
quarter of the world.

It is possible that more corn may be grown: but it must
also be remembered that population is on the increase; for in
the year 1798 there were only 21,300 whites, 25,754 slaves,
and 14,883 Hottentots, whereas in the year 1804 there were
25,757 whites, 29,543 slaves, and 20,000 Hottentots; making
a difference between the years 1798 and 1804 of 13,361 souls.
Since that period the demand for corn has been increased by
European military and naval establishments; and there has
been a considerable augmentation of the number of horses for
the use of the cavalry and of private individuals.

Lands are not brought very rapidly into cultivation where

labour is very dear, where water is very scarce, where wood *
must be procured from great distances, where all the materials
for building are very expensive, where the implements of
husbandry are not readily obtained, where agricultural improvements are resisted by prejudice, where the purchase of
slaves requires considerable capital, and where slaves are
necessary so long as the odious slave system is tolerated by
the government.

Tobacco is grown in great quantities in some parts of the
colony near the Berg River; but the American tobacco has
the preference in the European markets.

The whale fishery has been commenced in Table Bay with
some promise of success to the adventurers; but not to an
extent that offers a probability of any very large advantage to
the colony.

Export of brandy has been trivial hitherto; and the quality
is not such as to ensure its being in much request.

The Cape wine (Constantia) in use in Europe, is a species
of liqueur of which the growth is very limited. The dry wines
are not likely to find a large sale there for reasons already
given; namely, that all of them have a sulphureous taste;
and that the common wines are very pernicious, as the sol-
diery here found even without accompanying inebriety.

The inhabitants are not rich enough to improve the
revenue of the mother country considerably by demand for
European produce. Coarse linens † are required for the slaves;
some broadcloth, cutlery and furniture may also be in request:
but exclusively of the wants of the garrison, the whole supply
needed would probably not exceed the consumption of one of
the smallest towns in England. In fact, unless the greatest
economy is exercised in the administration of the colony, the
Cape will probably become a serious drain upon the resources
of England; and the people of England must from their taxes,
and consequently from the produce of their own industry,
support their African establishment.

The financial calculations or speculations are certainly not

---

* One thousand slaves are employed daily at the Cape to obtain it.—
R. W.

† The slaves and children are chiefly clothed in leather.—R. W.

in favour of the Cape as a colony; and its value as a military and naval station has been much exaggerated.

Since navigation has improved so much, ships proceed at once to India without being under the necessity of touching at the Cape or any other port for refreshment; even though conveying troops: and there is reason to believe that a debarkation of troops there in order to prepare them for the climate of India is an unprofitable speculation, on account of the mortality occasioned by the quality and cheapness of the wine, from which they cannot refrain.

Again, Simon's Bay and Table Bay cannot be made defensible against a superior fleet: so that England might at any time, at least so long as she commands the dominion of the sea, which ascendancy will probably be maintained by her for many years, destroy all armaments fitted out at the Cape (supposing it to be occupied by a hostile power) without the intermediate expense of establishments in this colony. On the other hand, if she maintained the Cape and not the superiority at sea, she would derive no advantage from the settlement in the conduct of her intercourse with India.

To keep a great garrison at the Cape would be a superfluous expense. Cape Town cannot be defended against an invading superior force. The present line of fortifications requires four thousand men; and is still insecure, for it may be stormed or turned.

Instead of lines requiring such a garrison, it would be more advisable to destroy them and to erect several martello towers: with the left of the new line resting upon a work to be constructed near the Salt River, and with the right thrown forward to the point of the mountain which would terminate the semicircle; in the centre of which mountain line a fort is already built.

A second line might be formed from the castle, with the right flank thrown upon the mountain where York's Tower now stands.

Fourteen martello towers would sufficiently cover the whole space; and the garrison need not exceed eight hundred men, part of which might be formed of the burgher guard.

If moreover there were a corps in the field of one thousand Hottentots, five hundred British horse, and some artillery, an invading enemy would, when he had taken Cape Town, have to depend entirely on his shipping for subsistence; since such a flying corps would, if properly commanded and aided by the inhabitants of the colony, intercept all supplies, and be able for a long time, as it were to seal Cape Town hermetically on the land side.*

There is a question however whether the British can ever induce the Dutch descendants in the colony to adopt the English cause to the prejudice of Holland. Hitherto there is no symptom of abated affection for the mother country.

Some projects have been brought under discussion for the formation of new establishments on the shores of one of the eight rivers which flow into the sea on the southern coast: but they all have bars of sand at the entrance, which render navigation from the ocean impracticable. At the mouth of the Knysna alone it is said that at low tide two or three feet of water may always be relied on, and five or six at high tide: the opening too is about two hundred feet wide. But when it is considered at what great expense settlers must be brought from Europe, the financial advantage of an establishment there must be very problematical.

It was somewhere on this coast, about twenty years ago, that an Indiaman was wrecked. The surviving men were murdered by the natives, and the ladies who were passengers saved by them. Two of them were found to be living not long since. Communication was opened with them, and an offer made for their return to England; but they declined to accept it, stating that they had married, and that their return to Europe must be accompanied with sacrifices of affection and the painful idea of being subject to constant observation and remark. They only requested some European articles with which they might present their husbands as tokens of their attachment.

* A work might be erected with advantage in Gordon's Bay, as communication could be kept with it.—R. W.

END OF VOL. I.